Tom Holt was born in 1961, a sullen, podgy child, much given to brooding on the Infinite. He studied at Westminster School, Wadham College, Oxford and the College of Law. He produced his first book, *Poems by Tom Holt*, at the age of thirteen, and was immediately hailed as an infant prodigy, to his horror. At Oxford, Holt discovered bar billiards and at once changed from poetry to comic fiction, beginning with two sequels to E.F. Benson's *Lucia* series, and continuing with his own distinctive brand of comic fantasy in *Expecting Someone Taller*, *Who's Afraid of Beowulf?*, *Flying Dutch*, *Ye Gods!*, *Overtime* and *Grailblazers*. He has also written two historical novels set in the fifth century BC, the well-received *Goatsong* and *The Walled Orchard*, and has collaborated with Steve Nallon on *I, Margaret*, the (unauthorised) autobiography of Margaret Thatcher.

Somewhat thinner and more cheerful than in his youth, Tom Holt is now married, and lives in Somerset.

HERE COMES THE SUN
'A novel which contains many flashes of absolute genius.'

rst

Also by Tom Holt

GRAILBLAZERS
OVERTIME
YE GODS!
FLYING DUTCH
WHO'S AFRAID OF BEOWULF?
EXPECTING SOMEONE TALLER

I, MARGARET
THE WALLED ORCHARD
GOATSONG

LUCIA TRIUMPHANT
LUCIA IN WARTIME

HERE COMES THE SUN

Tom Holt

ORBIT

An *Orbit* Book

First published in Great Britain in 1993 by Orbit
This paperback edition published by Orbit in 1994

A CIP catalogue record for this book
is available from the British Library.

ISBN 1 85723 187 2

Printed in England by Clays Ltd, St Ives plc

Orbit
A Division of
Little, Brown and Company (UK) Limited
Brettenham House
Lancaster Place
London WC2 7EN

For
MY MOTHER
But for whose tireless encouragement
And selfless dedication to the furtherance
of my writing career
(To the neglect and detriment of her own prodigious talent
as a crime writer)
I would now be the son and heir of a bestselling authoress
Instead of just another
Penniless
Author

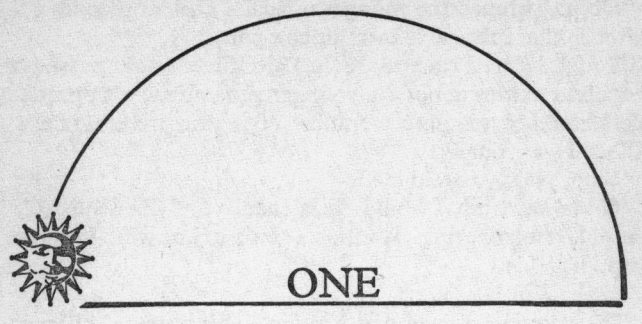

ONE

The sun rose.

It was dirty. It was late. It was thirty billion miles overdue on its next service. There was a thin film of oil on its surface, the result of a sprung gasket. But it was up and running, and that in itself was something of a miracle, all things considered.

'Over to you, son,' said the Principal Technical Officer, wiping his forehead with the back of his hand. 'Just don't drop it, all right?'

The Assistant Technical Officer scowled. 'You always say that,' he replied. 'And have I ever . . .?'

'Not yet.'

The older official looked down at the great fiery disc and smiled in spite of himself. True, he could hear the distinct grinding noise and smell the burning oil, but it was still an impressive sight. They'd built things to last in those days, which was just as well. Of course, they had the funding, then.

'Here,' said the younger official. 'The gyro's packed up again.'

'Gyro,' replied his colleague scornfully. 'Bloody modern tat. You'll just have to fly it on manual, that's all.'

1

'Oh *no*,' whined the younger official. 'That's no good. If I gotta do that I'll have to miss lunch again.'

'Tough.' The Principal Technical Officer's soul passed a few observations about the younger generation, with particular reference to those members of it who wore earrings. 'When I was your age . . .'

'Yeah, yeah, you told me.'

'Given anything, I would, for a chance to fly her solo.' He paused, remembering. 'We took a pride in our work in those days,' he added.

'Yeah. Well.'

The younger official had a point. Things were different now, the Principal Technical Officer admitted to himself as he packed up his knapsack and put on his bicycle clips. Not quite so run down for one thing. The Great Bear wasn't held in its place in the firmament by three hundred thousand miles of insulating tape and a bent nail.

'You should think yourself lucky,' he said without conviction, 'that you've got a job at all.'

His junior colleague didn't even bother to reply; he was leaning on the dead man's handle, eyes vacant, Walkman headphones on, staring down towards Betelgeuse. Something told the Principal Technical Officer that if humanity made it through to nightfall with nothing worse than a few hours of inexplicable darkness it should count itself lucky.

Still, he said to himself, as he hoisted himself on to his ancient bicycle and pedalled stiffly away across the sparkling freeway of the stars, if you're going to take a pride in your work, your work's got to be something you can take a pride in. And if the whole shooting-match is virtually derelict, what can you expect? No wonder the boy's demoralised. Where's the point in bothering when nobody else seems to give a damn?

His way home took him past the moon-sheds and, following this train of thought, he slowed to a halt, leaned on his handlebars and looked in through the great double doors.

Inside, the moon was being winched back into dry dock for the day. From a distance, it never failed to take his breath away. Seen up close, it wasn't a pretty sight.

'Strewth,' the old official muttered under his breath.

Admittedly, it was quite some time – centuries, probably – since he'd taken the time to stop and look at it this closely, but there was no denying the fact that the old girl was in pretty poor shape.

'What have they been *doing* to her?' he said aloud.

One of the maintenance engineers, an alarming-looking youth with a Mohican haircut and a ring through one nostril, looked round and stared at him. He didn't seem to notice.

'What's up with you, grandad?' the youth demanded.

'You're not going to use sandpaper on her, are you?' the old official said, horrified.

'You what?'

No wonder, the old official reflected. No wonder the poor old bus has got all those great big pits and craters all over her once-smooth surfaces. He sighed; he knew there was no point uttering the words that were trying to squeeze their way through the gap in his teeth, but he said them anyway.

'You shouldn't use that stuff on the outer skin,' he said. 'First thing you know, you'll get pitting.'

'So what?'

So what indeed? Nobody cared, obviously; and as he cycled away, the old official couldn't find it in his heart to blame them. Where was the point in trying to keep it going when it was patently clapped out? They were going to scrap it soon in any case, they said, commission a brand new one. They'd been saying it for a long time now.

As usual, he stopped off at the Social Club for a tea and a bacon sandwich before going home. He parked his bicycle, chained it to a lamppost, and walked into the room, which looked like one of the more run-down East German railway stations. Another example, he couldn't help reflecting, of the way this whole operation is going downhill.

3

'What's happened to the pool table, Nev?' he asked.

'Jammed,' replied the steward, washing glasses. 'They're sending someone later on.'

'Right.'

'Or at least,' the steward added, 'so they told me.'

'Right.'

The steward made an indeterminate noise and put the bacon sandwich in the microwave. Another bloody innovation.

'Looking forward to the darts match tomorrow, Nev?'

The steward sighed. 'Cancelled, George old son,' he said. 'Due to lack of interest. Hadn't you heard?'

Jane stopped what she was doing and looked out of the window at the sun.

This, she reflected, is what they call too much of a good thing. All very well looking fondly back on the long, hot summers of one's childhood, but when you're stuck in an office with a glass roof, windows that don't open and a heating system mysteriously jammed on, even in summer, you start thinking nostalgically about good, solid rain.

'I can remember rain,' she said aloud. 'Gosh, that dates me.'

Three weeks, give or take a day, and already the newsreaders were smugly saying gloomy things about standpipes and hosepipe bans. What's wrong with a country where three weeks of sun turns the reservoirs into dustbowls?

She turned away from the window and tried to concentrate on the VDU in front of her. It was staring back at her with a sort of blank look, as if it had been sniffing glue. She picked up the phone.

'Trish,' she said. 'What's wrong with the screens?'

'System's down at Reading,' Trish replied. 'Back on after lunch.'

'Great,' said Jane. 'Tell them we'd be better off with a card index and a notched stick.'

Never mind, there's plenty I can be getting on with till then, said Jane to herself. Staring out of the window, for instance.

Instead, she looked through her handbag, found her address book and dialled a number.

'Apollo Staff Bureau,' said a voice like a lady Dalek at the other end of the line. 'Can I help you?'

'Yes,' Jane said brightly, 'I want a new job, please.'

'We could advertise it,' said the Chief of Staff.

The rest of the committee looked at him.

'Well,' said Personnel eventually, 'it's an idea, certainly. Where would you suggest?'

'Um.'

'Tricky one to place, don't you think?' Personnel continued, with the air of someone getting ready to ram a point into the ground. 'I mean, it's not one for the *Exchange and Mart*, is it?'

'Let's try being positive for once,' Staff replied testily. 'That's the problem, really, we're all too keen to look at the disadvantages and not the . . .'

'Absolutely,' Branch interrupted. 'With you all the way there. But I think Personnel's got a point too, you know.'

All God's children gotta point, said Staff to himself, it's just that some of them are bloody silly ones. He drew a spaceship on the agenda and tried to calm himself down.

'I still think,' he said, putting the tips of his fingers together as a means of stopping his hands clenching, 'that we should advertise it. I mean, why not? It's what they do in the private sector. They don't keep staff vacancies a deadly secret, like they were something to be ashamed of. They go out and they ask people to apply.'

'Right on,' said Personnel, with all the enthusiasm of a corpse. 'So where do we look?'

There was a silence.

'All right,' said Staff, 'what do you suggest? We need someone and we need someone quickly. You're the Personnel

5

Officer. What's your considered opinion?'

'I think it needs thinking about.'

Another silence; during which Staff noticed that the burning thrones they sat on, as a mark of their superior executive status, didn't burn any more. They just glowed intermittently and hummed.

'Have you thought yet?' he enquired.

'Not yet, no.'

'Fine,' Staff replied. 'You take your time.' He crossed his legs and started to doodle ostentatiously.

'Why don't we use the usual procedure?' asked a voice from the other end of the table.

'Because . . .' Staff started to say, but checked himself. There were times when his paranoia slipped the lead and got mixed up with his angst, when he sincerely believed that Finance and General Purposes was a management plant, deliberately seeded on to this committee to make sure that nothing ever got done. Since it was very probably true he invariably dismissed the idea from his mind; it is not just mankind who cannot bear too much reality. 'Because,' he went on, 'there's three feet of moss growing in the usual channels and something's got to be done.'

'Oh, we're all agreed on *that*,' Branch said. 'No question about it, *something*'s got to be done. On the other hand, we don't want to rush into something without having worked it carefully through. I mean . . .' He made a slight but expressive gesture and went back to impersonating a doorstop. Staff took a grip on himself, straining something in his integrity, and tried to sound conciliatory.

'All right, then,' he said, 'what about an agency? I gather they're very good at this sort of thing. You know, head-hunting.'

'Which agency had you in mind?' said Personnel.

'Look,' said Staff, 'this is supposed to be an ideas session, right? We're supposed to be a think tank, bouncing ideas off each other. Has anybody got any ideas at all?'

There was a slightly embarrassed pause; and then Personnel, judging his timing to perfection, smiled and cleared his throat.

'I've got an idea,' he said. 'I've got an idea that this needs thinking through carefully.'

'Me too,' said Branch. 'Looking at it in the round, I mean.'

'I think,' said Finance and General Purposes, 'that we should go through the established procedure.'

Staff closed his eyes. 'Good God, Norman,' he said to the ceiling, 'what an absolute stroke of genius. Yes, let's all do that, shall we? Well, thank you very much for your time, gentlemen. I honestly believe we've all made very real progress today. Same time next week then?'

Instead of going back to the main building, Staff turned left down the corridor, walked briskly on past the post room, turned right by the file store and pressed the button for the lift. Two minutes later, he swore at the lift-shaft and started to climb the seventeen flights of stairs that led to the DA's office.

'I'll show the bastards,' he muttered, rather breathlessly. 'Just for once, I'll damn well *show* the . . .'

The further up he went the dustier it got. There was something about the decor, something very subtle which you couldn't put your finger on, that suggested that nobody had been this way in a very long time, and that there was probably a very good reason for that. Perhaps, Staff said to himself, it's the fact that all the treads on this staircase are rotted half through.

At last, breathless and sweating, he found himself at the top of the building. It was dark here (no light bulb), and cold, and ever so slightly spooky. It was *years* since he'd been up this far. It was a fair bet that there was nobody here any more.

In front of him there was a glass door so grimy that he had to wipe it with his sleeve before he could read the lettering on it. But there was a light behind it, implying the presence of sentient life. That, as far as Staff was concerned, would make a pleasant change. He screwed up his eyes and read the inscription on the window.

D. GANGER

it said, and in smaller letters underneath:

DEVIL'S ADVOCATE

'Oh well,' said Staff to himself, repressing a shudder, 'I'm here now.'

He knocked smartly on the door and turned the handle.

'Try a bit of silver paper and some gunk,' said the Technical Adviser into the receiver.

The voice at the other end crackled at him. 'Will that work?' it enquired.

'Dunno.' The Technical Adviser leaned back in his chair and put a peppermint in his mouth. 'Might do.'

'Look,' said the crackle. 'I've got a bloody great disc of helium broken down over East Africa. Things are starting to get burnt. Suggest something.'

'Not my fault,' replied the Technical Adviser automatically. 'I told 'em at Depot it needed a whole new gearbox, but would they listen? Nah.' He crunched the peppermint into the mouthpiece, sending a noise like the end of the world down the wire. 'Look,' he said, after he had cleared the shrapnel off the roof of his mouth, 'tell you what I'll do for you. I'll send out Maintenance with the van. They'll have you back on the road again, no worries.'

The crackle reminded him by way of reply that the Maintenance Unit had been disbanded two years ago as part of the cutbacks programme, and its staff reassigned to Oceans. 'What about the backup team?' it suggested.

'Nice idea,' replied the Technical Adviser, thumbing through a roster. 'Trouble is, they're down at the Social Club at Depot fixing a jammed pool table. You want them, you got to fill in a Yellow at least forty-eight hours in advance.'

'Then what do you suggest?'

'You could get out and push.'

The crackle considered this, gave the Technical Officer some advice of an intimate nature, and disconnected itself.

The fish in Lake Victoria were finding that the ceiling was rather nearer than usual.

'Come in.'

Rather to Staff's surprise, the door opened easily. He blinked.

It wasn't quite the way he'd expected it to be. For one thing, it was clean. Cleaner, in fact, than the rest of the building. It was newly decorated. In one corner there was a highly advanced fax machine, flickering quietly, bringing up its lunch, while in the other stood a computer terminal which looked like the sort of thing George Lucas would have dreamed up if possessed by devils. There was also, Staff noticed, a substantial potted plant. Real, not plastic.

'It's because we're separately funded,' said a voice behind him. 'The benefits of decentralisation and all that. You're Chief of Staff, aren't you?'

The figure standing behind him was almost as disconcerting as the environment. It looked young, vibrant, full of energy. More amazing still, it looked like it was capable of enjoying itself.

'You're . . .' Staff said. The figure grinned.

'My name's Ganger. We haven't actually met, but it's my job to know things.'

By way of a disorienting remark, said Staff's soul to any part of his brain that happened to be listening, that's got to be in the running with *Are you sure you're feeling all right?* and *Excuse me, there's a bomb inside this banana.* Throwing people off balance was probably part of the job, too. Staff forced himself to relax.

'Sorry to barge in like this,' he said, 'but have you got a moment?'

9

Ganger nodded. 'Sure,' he said. 'Carol, I'll be engaged in the back office. Anyone calls, take a message.'

Staff's head swivelled like a windmill and he caught sight of a blonde head between two earphones. Laid-back nonchalance is all very well but there are limits.

'You don't mean to say,' he whispered, 'you've actually got a *secretary*?'

'Two,' Ganger replied, and Staff gave up the struggle. This was the sort of man who had a My-other-car's-a-Porsche sticker in the back window of his Maserati. 'Come with me. Coffee?'

Staff made a little noise without opening his lips. 'I suppose your secretary will bring it through to us?'

Ganger raised an eyebrow. 'Well, yes,' he said.

'One of your two secretaries?'

'That's it. If that's all right with you, that is.'

'That's fine,' said Staff. 'I think I've come to the right place.'

It seemed like a very long walk through to the back office, until Staff realised that it was the effort of walking through the carpet. You could easily lose a Mayan city in the pile and never know it.

'So what can we do for you?' Ganger said, waving his arm at a chair. Staff looked at him carefully. Perhaps it was an invitation to sit on it, but it seemed unlikely. It had the appearance of the sort of thing you pay money just to look at.

'Sit down,' said Ganger, 'please. We don't stand on ceremony here.'

Maybe not, but you sure as hell sit on luxury. Staff sat back, panicked for a moment until he got his bearings again, and cleared his mind.

'Actually,' he began to say, 'all it was . . .'

His lips froze. Ganger followed his line of sight and raised an eyebrow.

'It's a photocopier,' he said. 'You know, you put pieces of paper in one end . . .'

10

'I'm sorry,' Staff muttered. 'Like I was saying, I'm in a bit of a quandary, and I thought, you know, a fresh angle on the problem . . .'

Ganger nodded. 'I know,' he said. 'Do you advertise or do you go to an agency? Good question.'

'Look . . .' Staff tried to sit up, but the chair wouldn't let him. He struggled. Self-esteem wasn't the most significant part of his personality, but he was damned if he was going to end his career by slipping down the back of a chair.

'How do I know all this?' Ganger said. 'Simple. It's my job.' He paused, then smiled gently. 'Try straightening your back,' he said. 'It'll push you forward out of the cushion.'

Staff did so, then he scowled. 'You're a . . .'

'No, I'm not, actually,' Ganger replied. 'It's possible to read mortal minds, of course, but not ours. Jamming devices, you know. Really, it's just intuition and psychology.'

'Oh.'

'And microphones too, of course.'

'Ah.'

The door opened, and a female person brought in a tray with two cups of coffee. With saucers. Saucers that matched. I'd honestly believe I'd died and gone to heaven, thought Staff . . .

'Only that's not possible in the circumstances,' Ganger said, and laughed politely. 'Thank you, I'm flattered. All it takes really is good taste and careful management.'

'And separate funding.'

'That helps, certainly.' Ganger looked at him over his cup. 'My money's on an agency.'

'Really?'

Ganger nodded. 'Every time,' he said. 'Saves time, and in the long run money. Neither of which, if I'm right, you've got a great deal of.'

Staff tried unsuccessfully to balance his saucer on his knee, but the chair seemed to be breathing. 'All right,' he said. 'And what do I tell the rest of the committee?'

Ganger looked surprised: probably a whole new experience ...

'Not at all,' he said abruptly. 'Things surprise me all the time. Who gives a toss what the committee thinks? Anyway,' he added, 'if you're at all bothered about it, don't tell them.'

'But I've got to tell ...'

'Why?'

Staff was shocked; it was like being asked to justify breathing. Then the penny dropped. Different rules ...

'You tell me,' he said.

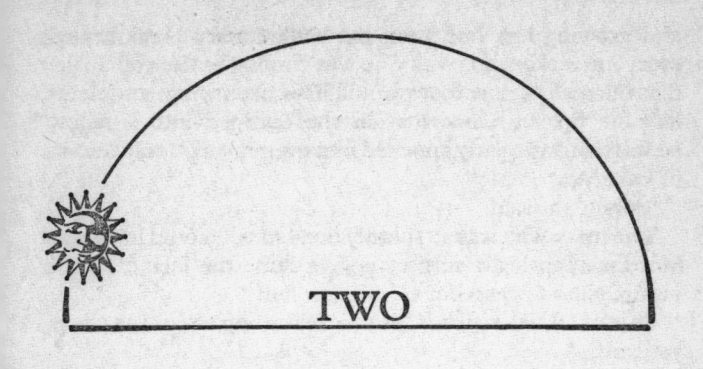

TWO

Jane was not a naturally discontented person; or at least, that was what she'd always led herself to believe. It was just that there were certain things that she found it hard to put up with. These things tended to change their shape depending on circumstances, just as clouds can sometimes be great fluffy dragons and sometimes wisps of low-quality cotton wool; sometimes it would be the plight of famine victims, sometimes it was the incredibly feckless way the stationery supplies were managed at work, and sometimes – quite often, and in point of fact, right now – it was the punctuality of the 42A bus that really managed to get to her. If there was a common factor, it was probably sloppiness.

The weather could do with sorting, too.

The British Nation, she said to herself, and its unique relationship with water: we either sail over it or stand under it. It took the Chinese, though, to invent the umbrella.

Since the 42A had patently been ambushed by the Hole in the Wall Gang, set on fire and abandoned somewhere further up the line, she decided to walk the mile from the office to the station. She splashed resolutely up the road, trying to avoid the larger puddles and speculating as to whether ditching fins and growing legs had been the evolutionary breakthrough everyone reckoned it was. She was coming to the conclusion that the really smart move would have been wings and floats, like the Spruce Goose, when she bumped into a fellow-pedestrian and nearly knocked him over into a puddle the size of Lake Van.

'Sorry,' she said.

The man, who was so sharply dressed you could have used him for open-heart surgery and, despite the lack of hat or umbrella, as dry as a bone, smiled at her.

'Not at all,' he replied. 'But you're wrong about the wings, you know.'

Jane's jaw flopped down like undercarriage. 'What?' she said.

'Wings,' the man replied, still smiling. 'If the ancestors of mankind had grown wings, they wouldn't have needed to develop manual dexterity and the use of tools. That way, their brains wouldn't have adapted and become what they eventually did become. Result, you wouldn't be a human, just a big pink bird, and the chimpanzees would be feeding you breadcrumbs in Trafalgar Square. Think about it.'

He nodded, side-stepped into the puddle (which divided on either side of his foot) and walked on, leaving Jane standing in exactly the right spot to receive the full force of the spray when a 42A bus went neatly through the puddle a few moments later.

Staff was reading a letter.

It wasn't easy going, because the script – and, indeed, the language – it was written in had died out centuries before; but he could understand that. The writer of the letter probably hadn't found the need to put pen to paper for a very long time.

Dear Sir, it said, translated:
I have to inform you that I resign. You probably don't remember

14

me though I saw you once at one of those receptions over the top of someone's head, you were shaking hands a lot and opening something. I've been raising the Sun for 777 years, 7 months and a week Thursday, but this is too much and I've had enough. It's a scandal, that's what it is, and they ought to do something about it. I have the honour to remain, etc.

Staff sighed, and put the letter face down on his desk.

They ought to do something about it.

Too right, he said to himself, and they will, just as soon as they find out who they are. And normal service will be resumed as soon as possible. And, naturally, we apologise for any inconvenience in the meantime.

'Hell,' he said aloud.

'Sorry, wrong floor,' said a voice from the other side of the desk. He looked up and saw Ganger, DA, sitting in the visitor's chair, smiling and looking far more comfortable than he would have imagined possible.

'It's a knack,' Ganger replied. 'You just have to wriggle about until you find a part of the seat that fits.'

That's what he does, Staff realised; he replies before you speak. Bloody irritating, of course, but certainly conducive to efficiency. Like a fax machine or something.

'And?' he said.

'Yes,' Ganger replied, and pulled a sad face. It looked hopelessly incongruous. Ganger's face was pretty exclusively smile-shaped. 'The problem is, how?'

'Exactly.'

'Well,' Ganger said, leaning back and folding his arms behind his head, 'there you have it. In a nutshell.'

Staff capitulated. 'All right,' he said. 'Can we go back over that and fill in the blanks, please?'

The sad face melted into the usual grin, like grilled cheese. 'You were thinking, Shit, there's another irreplaceable employee gone and handed in his notice, and what the hell are we going to do now? I replied, "Yes", because I'm buggered

15

if I can think of anything either. But the fact remains that he's got to be replaced, because otherwise it's going to be all jam for the electric torch manufacturers but no fun for everybody else, plus you'll have to pay the man in the moon double time and a half. The problem is, how do you fill a vacancy like that from the load of rubbish you've got available?'

'Exactly.'

'And there you have it,' Ganger said, smirking, 'in a nutshell.'

'It's very impressive, the way you do that.'

'Flashy,' Ganger replied. 'Telepathy is like television or tele-anything. Looks good, but doesn't actually help very much in the final analysis. Not,' he added quickly, 'that it really is telepathy; more a sort of partial insight. It comes in useful in our work.'

'Ah yes,' said Staff, leaning forward slightly. 'I meant to ask you about that.'

Ganger hitched up one corner of his mouth into yet another isotope of his perpetual smile. 'You're quite right,' he said. 'Up to a point.'

Staff growled at him. He laughed.

'It's all right,' he said, 'I'm on secondment. That means I have to play fair. That means you can trust me. Okay?'

'Perhaps.'

Ganger stood up and walked to the window. 'Good view you get from here,' he said.

'All the kingdoms of the earth,' replied Staff absently. 'Look, who exactly are your lot?'

Ganger continued to look out of the window. 'Simple,' he replied. 'We're them rather than us, but we're on your side really. Is that enough?'

'No.'

'Okay. We're a department, same as all the other departments, but we're pretty well autonomous within the quite strict confines of our brief. And the head of our department gets abjured a lot at christenings.'

Staff nodded. 'And all his works?'

'Right on,' Ganger replied. 'Also his pomps, not that he's got any really. Not in the last five years, at any rate.'

'Five years?' Staff raised an eyebrow. 'What's so special about . . .?'

'We got put out to tender,' Ganger replied. 'We were the guinea-pig, you see. Five years ago, we were the most hopelessly inefficient department in the whole set up . . .'

'Surely not?'

The back of Ganger's head nodded. 'Straight up. Hopelessly overstaffed, but undermanned at the same time. Work backing up, souls not getting processed, furnaces still powered by expensive, ozone-unfriendly sulphur, and worst of all, costing an absolute fortune. Really, the whole system was on the point of collapse. In fact, there were those who reckoned it had collapsed years before, only in the nature of things nobody had noticed.'

Staff picked up a pencil and started to fidget with it nervously. 'Nobody told me,' he said.

'Didn't they?' Ganger leaned on the window-sill and swayed slightly. 'I'm not in the least surprised. Not something they'd want you to find out about, really. Anyway, they reckoned that since nothing they could do could possibly make things worse, they'd try an experiment and put the whole operation in the hands of outside contractors. My lot got the contract, and since then . . . Well, you can judge for yourself.'

There was a silence, during which you could have counted up to seven comfortably, and ten if you gabbled a bit. 'Then you're not . . .?'

'Qualified?' Ganger laughed. 'Oh yes, we're all qualified. I'm not a mortal, if that's what you're thinking.'

'But if you're not a mortal, then you must be . . .' Staff's voice trickled away, like the last drops of water from a turned-off hose. The back of Ganger's head shook.

'Not necessarily,' he replied. 'Common misconception,

that. Most of us are left over from the previous systems, but . . .'

'Previous systems?'

'Ancestor worship,' Ganger explained. 'Classical mythology. Odin and Thor. There's one chap works in Accounts who used to be Osiris, or is it Anubis? Odd sort of bloke, but in his line of work it's actually an advantage to have the head of a jackal. Me, though, I'm from Philosophy.'

'Philosophy?'

'Absolutely,' replied Ganger, with a hint of pride in his voice. 'Personification of an abstract concept. I'm a child of late nineteenth-century German neo-nihilism. One of Nietzsche's gentlemen, you might almost say.' He laughed briefly at his own joke. 'Sorry, I'm drifting away from the point rather, aren't I? What I was going to say is that in our department, we do have a few members of staff who were originally mortals.'

Staff tried to find an appropriate word, or at least a noise, but there wasn't one. Instead, the room was filled with the noise of a jaw dropping.

'I have that effect on people sometimes,' Ganger agreed. 'I startled the wits out of a girl in the street earlier on. I want to talk to you about her later, actually.'

'You use *mortals*? On *official business*?'

'Ex-mortals,' Ganger replied gently. 'There are limits, naturally. But within those limits . . .'

'You can't,' said Staff, controlling his anger with difficulty. 'It's unheard of. It's against the rules. It's . . . it's . . .'

'Evil?' Ganger chuckled. 'Well, it would be, wouldn't it?'

'Will you kindly stop reading my mind?' Staff shouted. 'It's bad enough my having to live in it without strangers poking their dirty great snouts in there as well.' He pulled himself together. 'I'm sorry,' he said. 'But please, just for the time being, could you possibly?'

There was a pause. 'Could I possibly what?' Ganger said.

'Thank you,' said Staff. 'Could you possibly just wait for

me to say what I'm thinking, rather than going and looking for yourself? For one thing, it's bad form. You know, like reading the end of a book before you get to it. And it puts me at a disadvantage.'

'Not really,' Ganger replied. 'I can only read what's there, can't I? And anyway, it's not telepathy, it's just . . .'

'Insight, I know, you said.'

'Now you're at it.'

'Oh shut up.' Staff reached for the pencil again and started to chew it. 'These mortals,' he said tentatively.

'Ex-mortals.'

'Ex-mortals, then.' Staff felt his teeth meet around the graphite core. 'I suppose they're all, you know, in menial capacities. Hewers of wood, drawers of water, that sort of thing.'

Ganger shook his head. 'Not really,' he said. 'Upper executive, lower administrative grade, mostly. None in the upper grades of admin, but that's because they're relatively new and it all takes time. Dead men's shoes, you know, that sort of thing.'

For some reason, the phrase made Staff shudder a little, in context. 'But that's really . . .' He diluted the thought rapidly, just in case someone was peeking. 'Not really on, you know. I mean, mortals . . .'

'It's never been tried here, you mean.' Ganger turned away from the window, and Staff noticed, in the brief fraction of a second it took him before he could cauterise that part of his brain temporarily, that he looked a bit different. 'I know, it's hard to accept. But we're doing it, and it seems to be working. That's the joy of effectively running our own ship. If we do something outrageous, then who cares? It's just us, going to the devil in our own way. So to speak,' he added deliberately. 'And if it works . . .'

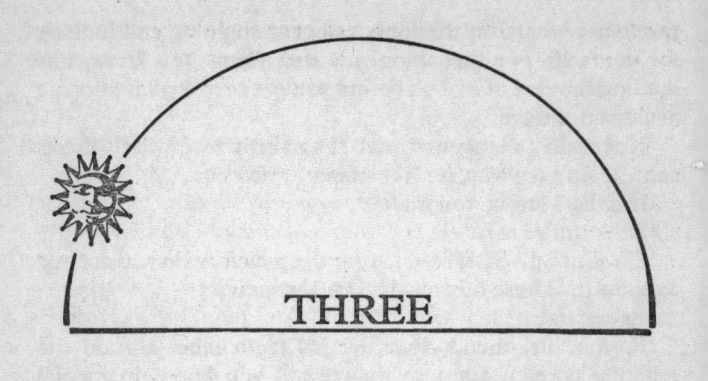

THREE

Between the acting of a dreadful thing and its first motion, all the interim is like a phantasma or a hideous dream. The genius and the mortal instruments are then in council, and the state of man suffers the nature of an insurrection.

'Oh hell, why not?' said Jane suddenly, aloud, and crossed the road into the shop.

'Two cream doughnuts, please,' she said to the girl. 'No, make that three. The fresh cream, not the artificial.'

Eyes like molybdenum steel augers bored into her soul as she fumbled in her purse for a pound coin, trying her inadequate best to look like someone who is buying cakes for three people, not just one.

'And a penny change,' said the girl. 'Thank you.'

Well, Jane thought, as she walked on down the street, it seemed like a good idea at the time. Eat a doughnut, girl, said the Father of Lies, you won't know yourself afterwards. Whereas in fact, her better part of reason told her, the only perceptible change will be round the back of her buttocks. Girls who eat three cream doughnuts have only themselves to blame if they end up looking like hovercraft.

'Never mind,' Jane said firmly. A man in a fawn overcoat

gave her a look and quickened his pace slightly. Never mind, she repeated *sotto voce*, at least it isn't chocolate. When you start mainlining chocolate in the middle of the day, it's time to give up and die.

She found a bench in the park, sat down and looked at the paper bag on her knee. Cream had saturated it in patches, making the paper transparent, and she shuddered slightly. Had a tramp been passing just then, he would most certainly have been the recipient of unexpected charity; but there was nobody, except a couple of glue-sniffers under a plane tree on the other side of the Oriental pond, and the distant prospect of a jogger. She was going to have to eat them herself.

The first one wasn't too bad, although she was painfully aware that the cream had got out and was roaming around her face like a Dark Age horde. The second one wasn't too bad until about halfway through; and she abhorred waste, and you look such a fool walking around with one and a half cream doughnuts in a paper bag. So she finished it, sent her tongue snowploughing through the sweet slush on her upper lip, and closed the bag firmly. She felt slightly sick.

'It's a symptom, you know,' said a voice beside her.

She jumped. It was bad enough being addressed by a strange man in a park; the fact that it was the same strange man who frightened her half to death the previous day by reading her mind and then walking away dry-foot through a huge puddle only served to add inches to her take-off.

'Eating,' the man went on, smiling. 'Atavism, pure and simple. The hunter-gatherer inside us all reckons that if you've got something to eat, then that's all that matters, and so at the first sign of trouble we reach for food. It's all stress related, of course; and the things we eat make the stress worse. For a purely instinctive reaction, it's pretty counter-productive, wouldn't you say?'

'Go away,' Jane replied.

'You've got cream on your nose.'

'I'll call a policeman.'

21

The man smiled. 'For all you know,' he said, 'I am a policeman.'

'Then I'll call another policeman. Go on, get lost.'

The man crossed his legs and folded his hands round the junction of his knees. 'Another slice of atavism,' he said, 'though marginally more sensible. What a mess humanity is.'

He vanished.

In the ensuing cloud of mental static, Jane became aware that she had somehow managed to sit on the third cream doughnut. It's odd, the way you notice things like that.

'Where have you gone?' she said.

'I haven't gone anywhere,' replied the voice. 'Did you realise you're sitting on . . .'

'Yes.'

'There you go,' said the voice. 'Telepathy. We can really get a move on now, don't you think?'

Jane stood up to walk away, turned and brushed ineffectually at the adherent doughnut. 'Don't you dare,' she said.

'I wasn't going to,' replied the voice. 'Being a spirit, I am not susceptible to mortal desires; and even if I was, I'm not sure removing flattened cream cakes from the back ends of people would be quite my thing. If you sit down again, nobody will see you've got a doughnut sticking to your . . .'

Jane sat down. She didn't like this one little bit; but of all the things she was, she wasn't afraid.

'Well?' she said.

The air hung around her, empty and quite blatantly transparent. She began to wonder whether . . .

'Sorry,' said the voice, 'I was forgetting. I'm still here.'

Jane stared straight in front of her. 'Are you a ghost?' she said.

'No,' said the air. 'The term ghost implies someone who is dead. Never having been alive, I cannot be dead. Next question.'

Jane turned her head and looked slowly around. There

wasn't a tree or a bush for ten yards around, so it wasn't some silly fool ventriloquising. The voice was quite soft, but distinctly external. She didn't know what voices inside your head sound like, but this was definitely an outside broadcast. She turned her head back and continued to stare forwards.

'Well?' she repeated.

'If you continue sitting on that doughnut,' the voice replied, 'it'll ruin your skirt. Compacted fresh dairy cream and gaberdine don't go, or so they tell me.'

'If you go away,' she said, 'I will remove the doughnut. While you stay here, visible or not, I have no intention of indulging your warped sense of humour.'

There was a long silence, and then the voice spoke again. This time, though, it was definitely *inside*.

'Happy now?' it said.

'Certainly not,' Jane replied. 'Go away.'

'I just did,' replied the voice. 'I went back to the office and I'm making myself a cup of tea. What the hell more do you want?'

'Don't you dare make a cup of tea inside my head,' Jane replied. 'I won't have it, understand?'

'What'll you do, then, blow your nose?'

Jane wriggled violently in her seat, trying to dislodge the doughnut. Inside her head, she could feel laughter.

'Stop that,' she said, 'you'll give me a headache.' The walls of her skull stopped vibrating. As far as she could tell, the doughnut was still there.

'Who are you?' she asked.

Her brain hummed, and the message, when it came through, was wordless and vague; repellent, but attractive too. What remained of her defence mechanisms prompted her not to understand it.

'Very well,' said the voice, audible inside her head once more. 'Here's three clues for you. Talk of me and I appear; the proverbial alternative to me is a lot of sea water; and, like your average cream bun, I have a tendency to take the hindmost. Or at least,' the voice corrected itself, 'those should help you identify our head of department. Actually, though, we're more of a team. The cult of personality, though . . .'

'I see,' said Jane, primly. 'I'm afraid I'm going to have to insist that you leave.'

'You can't insist unless you've got an or-else,' replied the voice. 'What'll you do to me if you don't?'

'I shall make the sign of the cross,' Jane replied awkwardly. 'So there.'

The voice smiled – it was that sort of voice. It would have had a radio producer standing on his hands with pure joy.

'Can if you like,' it replied. 'Won't do you the slightest bit of good, and I shall be bitterly offended. We have feelings, you know. All these spiritual stereotypes would be history in a truly enlightened society. But we're used to it. We make allowances.'

'Can I get rid of you?'

'Not really,' the voice replied. 'I suppose you could get one of those portable stereo things with earphones and try and blast me out, but I'm not sure that that wouldn't be counterproductive. I mean, I'm not vain, but which would you rather have banging about inside your head, me or Def Leppard?'

Jane considered this. 'Are you planning on staying long?' she asked. 'Because if you are, it might just be worth it. And there's other things beside heavy metal that you can play loud, you know. I was on a train the other day with a man who was listening to *Götterdämmerung* on his Walkman. You could hear it buzzing away from the buffet car.'

'Threats,' said the voice coldly, 'are the last resort of the inadequate negotiator. Were you thinking of the Solti recording, by the way, because I prefer it, on balance, to the Karajan.'

'Why can't I get rid of you?' Jane demanded. 'You'll make me late for work.'

'You let me in,' the voice replied. 'You listened to temptation.'

24

'Did I?'

'What you're sitting on proves it,' replied the voice, smugly. 'Go on, I said, be a devil. I didn't actually mean it like that, of course, but you seem to have got the message.'

'That makes sense,' Jane replied thoughtfully. 'As a rule, I don't even like cream cakes. What are you doing here, anyway? Do you want me to sell you my soul or something?'

The voice laughed, making her hair shake slightly. 'My dear girl,' said the voice, with genuine amusement, 'why on earth should I want to do that? I can get souls any time I want, trade. The public,' it continued, 'have this peculiar idea that all we care about is souls. Me, I can take them or leave them.'

'So what do you want?' Jane demanded.

'I want,' said the voice, 'to offer you a job.'

Jane caught her breath in amazement. Unfortunately, in doing so she inhaled the last of the cream, huffed for about a tenth of a second, and then sneezed mightily. When she'd recovered from the shock, the voice had gone.

Staff looked at his watch.

'Well?' he said.

There was a squelching noise, and Ganger materialised on the other side of the desk. Staff was amused and pleased that, for once, Ganger wasn't looking like a designer-shirt advertisement. He was wet and shaking slightly, and his stiffed-up haircut had been blasted down over his forehead.

'Sorry I'm late,' Ganger said. 'I got sneezed.'

'That's all right,' Staff replied equably. 'How did you get on?'

'I'd say,' Ganger replied, mopping himself with a handkerchief, 'that she's thinking about it. Either that, or she's booking in at one of those places where they don't mind if you think you're a tree just so long as you don't drop leaves on the stairs.'

Staff tapped his teeth with his pencil. 'But she didn't give you a decision?'

'Lord, no,' Ganger replied. 'Wouldn't have expected her to. In fact,' he admitted, 'I'd only just introduced the subject when I had to split. It's typical of the problems I have with women,' he added. 'I just get right up their noses, you know?'

Fine, said Staff to himself, I'd always wondered who writes the script for *Spitting Image*, and now I know. 'But you did tell her about the job?' he said. 'I mean . . .'

'Well, I mentioned it.' Ganger shrugged. 'You can't rush these things. It's one of the lessons we've learned in our own mortal recruitment programme. Anyone who wants the job really isn't going to be suitable.'

Staff nodded. 'So?' he said.

'So,' Ganger replied, reaching in his pocket for a comb. 'The next stage is, we scare the poor kid absolutely shitless. You can leave that bit to me if you like.'

Staff pursed his lips. 'Is that going to be, you know, absolutely essential?' he asked. 'I know you lot are allowed a certain latitude in the way you do things, but over here we've got to watch ourselves.'

Ganger nodded briskly. 'Absolutely essential,' he said. 'You've got to do that to induce the right ambience of mild paranoia. Like they say, nobody in their right mind would do this job anyway.'

'Well.' Staff opened the top left-hand drawer of his desk and found a peppermint. 'Let me know how you get on.'

'Will do.' The chair emptied itself. Staff sat for maybe thirty seconds, looking at it. Then, with one smooth easy movement, he reached into the open drawer, grabbed an inhaler and sniffed ferociously. There was a sort of peculiar popping noise, and Ganger was lying on his face on the floor beside him. Staff put the inhaler back in the drawer and closed it.

'Serves you right,' he said. 'I thought I'd made it quite clear that I didn't want any of this mind-hacking stuff, but I suppose you didn't listen. In one ear and out the other, that sort of thing.'

Ganger grinned ruefully and rubbed his knee. 'Force of habit,' he said. 'Won't happen again.' He got to his feet, dusted himself off and walked to the door.

'By the way,' he said, as he turned the handle and half-inserted himself into the gap. 'While I was in there, I couldn't help noticing. That stuff with the blue stockings and the polar bear. Very original.'

He closed the door just before the stapler hit it.

In the Blue Mountains, high above the encircling plain, a woodcutter paused from his work and leaned on his axe. The sun, chugging along on two cylinders and with a pair of tights doing service for a fan belt, glinted on his curly red hair and fearless blue eyes. Far away, a bird sang.

'Greetings, Cousin Bjorn,' said a voice behind him. 'Yet another really beautiful day, is it not? Pleasantly mild, yet neither too hot for work nor too cold for a moment merely standing and listening to the voice of the stream as it laughs its way down the hillside to our tranquil village.'

'Drop dead, Olaf,' Bjorn replied.

Olaf shrugged. 'It is a pity that one so young and so blessed by Nature should be as sour at heart as a green apple,' he observed tolerantly. 'Nevertheless, I am sure that sooner or later you will overcome your internal anguish and find true peace. In the meantime, there is wood to be cut.' He shouldered his axe and walked away down the hill, whistling a folk-tune.

Bjorn could take a hint. He lifted the axe, whirled it round his head, and brought it down on the base of the tree. The head flew off and landed in the crystal waters of the stream.

'How unfortunate,' observed a white-haired, rosy-cheeked woodcutter, who had been tying his shoe behind a venerable elm.

'Yes,' Bjorn agreed. 'Another eighteen inches to the left and it'd have taken your leg off.'

The elder, whose name was Karl, sighed, seated himself on

a tree trunk, and motioned the young man to join him.

'Hostility,' he said, offering Bjorn an apple, 'is like a rough-handled axe. It wounds those you use it against, and it blisters the hands of the user. Try and be a little more peaceful within yourself, Cousin Bjorn. Life is a wonderful thing.'

'Apples give me gut ache,' Bjorn replied. 'Specially bloody Cox's.' He threw the apple away over his shoulder. 'Now would you mind shifting yourself, because if you don't you're going to be right under this tree when I chop the bugger down.'

Karl shook his head and smiled. 'You'll have to find your axe head first, Cousin. Always remember that,' he added, as he got up and walked away. 'Always find your axe head before you start to cut down your tree.'

Bjorn made a rude noise and stumped across to the stream. It took him quite some time to find the axe head, during which his shoes got absolutely soaked.

'Good-morning, Uncle Bjorn,' said a voice above his head. He looked up to see a little girl, about ten years old, in a pretty blue dress. 'Mother thought you might be hungry, so she sent you some food. If you would like a refreshing draught of beer, I can run back to the house and get some for you.'

Bjorn lifted the napkin and made a face. 'Leave it over there,' he said. 'And tell the dozy cow I can't stand waffles, right? Waffles give me wind.'

The girl nodded. 'Uncle Bjorn,' she said, 'I was running blithely through the woods just now and I saw a beautiful flower, as blue as the heavens themselves. Look, I picked it to show you. It's such a lovely flower, I'm sure there must be a wonderful story about it and how it got its name.'

'It's called dungwort,' Bjorn replied. 'Use your imagination.'

'Oh.' The girl curtseyed prettily. 'Well,' she said, 'I'd better be getting back to the house, before Mother wonders where I've got to. Do be careful with that great sharp axe.'

'Scram.'

The girl curtseyed again and danced off down the hill, leaving Bjorn alone at last with the trees, the birds, the squirrels and his ingrowing toenail. For a while he stood and looked aimlessly about him, until his eye lit on one tree that he recognised. It was a tall, ancient oak and he remembered it well; he had climbed it as a boy, and his grandfather had often lifted him up into its branches, pointing out to him all the marvellous things he could see. How wonderful it is, his grandfather used to say, to sit in a high tree and look out over all the kingdoms of the world, as if one were God's own eyes!

Bjorn braced his feet, grinned, and set about cutting it down.

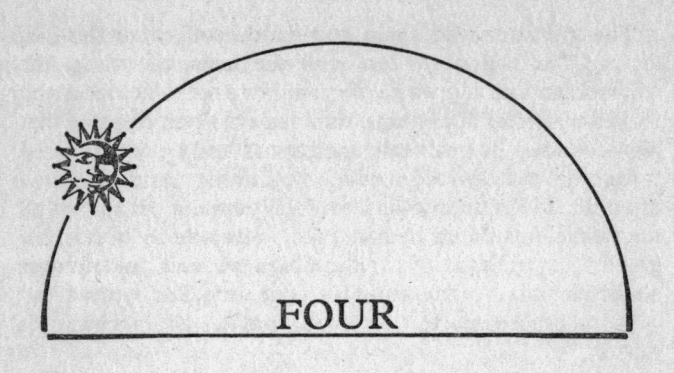

FOUR

It's a strange feeling, knowing that someone else has been inside your head; halfway between having a beetle down the back of your neck and being burgled.

Jane's first instinct, on getting home after an afternoon at work when she had got precisely nothing done, was to wash her hair; but it didn't really do the trick, somehow. She still felt that sensation – irritating more than anything else – of being bunged up with something, the way you feel after you've been underwater and got water trapped inside your ear. Holding her nose and trying to blow through it didn't really achieve anything either, however.

Silence made it worse, and so she switched on the television. At first the mixture of irritation and fascination inspired in her by the discovery of a brand new Australian soap opera distracted her, and she spent at least six minutes sitting in front of the screen trying to work out whether Terry was Gloria's sister or Tracy's boyfriend's son; and then she started to get the unpleasant feeling that all the voices were inside her head, and several generations of brown-skinned, bright-eyed Aussies were conducting their tangled personal relationships right between her ears. Hurriedly she flipped channels and watched three minutes of a cookery programme before switching off and trying the stereo instead.

That seemed to work. She remembered that, for all its apparent show of bravado, she'd got the distinct impression that the voice had sounded apprehensive when she'd threatened to flush it out with music. She selected *Fifty Favourite Marches By The Band Of The Coldstream Guards*, a present from an elderly uncle with a very odd notion of generosity, put on her headphones and sat down. After ten minutes ('Lilliburlero', 'Colonel Bogey', 'The Girl I Left Behind Me' and, incredibly, 'When I'm Sixty-Four') she came to the conclusion that demonaical possession was a damn sight better than premature deafness, and turned that off, too.

She made a cup of tea.

'All right,' she said, 'I know you're in there. Come out.'

Absolute silence, both internal and external. Perhaps, she said to herself, I'm going mad.

This possibility (oh hell, the milk's gone off, I'll have to use powdered) hadn't occurred to her before, but her innate sense of logic recommended it to her most strongly as an explanation consistent with the known facts. If it was the right explanation, it would require serious thought and quite possibly a major adjustment to her lifestyle. Girls who hear voices inside their heads have only two options: they can raise armies and drive the English out of Aquitaine, or they can seek professional help.

'I wouldn't do that,' said the voice. 'You're not like her at all.'

Jane relaxed. She wasn't going mad after all.

'Out,' she said firmly. 'Where I can see you.'

'Very well.'

The man materialised against the worktop, picked up her cup of tea, and sipped it. She switched the kettle back on and took another mug down from the rack.

'Not like who?' she said.

'Joan of Arc,' the man replied. 'Funny girl, our Joan. Not

mad, not by any stretch of the imagination, but definitely the sort that gives sanity a bad name.'

'That's my tea you're drinking. The milk's off, by the way.'

'In addition to which,' the man went on, 'because she spent so much time in a helmet she had *the* most appalling build-up of wax in her ears. It really puts you off, that sort of thing.'

'You've just made that up,' Jane said. The man grinned.

'Ten out of ten for intuition,' he replied. 'You're quite right. When Joan of Arc was around I wasn't more than a niggling little theory at the back of the European subconscious. I got all that stuff from one of the blokes in our department. Claims he invented the wax cotton jacket back in the fifteenth century just through having to crawl in and out of her ears all the time.'

'Fascinating,' Jane replied. 'Look, is there any point to this persecution, or is it just my bad luck? I must add at this point that I'm not the slightest bit frightened of you.'

'You're not?'

'No.'

'Oh shit. That's a nuisance. I have this theory about fear as an organic component of any fully integrated recruitment programme.' The man sipped his tea thoughtfully and Jane observed that the level in the cup hadn't changed at all. The little white flecks that signified needled milk, however, had vanished.

'Now that's odd,' she said. 'I thought your lot were supposed to turn fresh milk sour, not the other way round.'

'Static electricity,' the man replied, sipping again and pulling a face. 'Personally, I hate fresh milk. It sets my teeth off edge. Nine out of ten for observation, by the way.'

'Only nine?' Jane enquired, as the kettle boiled. 'Why's that?'

'Because,' the man replied, 'you should have recalled that the milk was fresh on the doorstep this morning, and it's been in the fridge all day. It's my presence that turned it bad, and now I'm doing the decent thing and turning it good again, by reversing the flow of ions temporarily.'

'You can do that, can you?'

'Oh yes,' the man replied, widening his grin as an archer draws his bow. 'I'm very versatile. You might say that I've got a lot of ions in the fire.'

'You might say that, yes.'

Jane dropped a teabag into her cup and poured water on to it from the kettle. It was stone cold.

'Childish,' she said.

The man lifted his left foot like a horse being shod and inspected the sole of his shoe. 'Not really,' he replied. 'Empty it out and have a look.'

Jane scowled at him and tipped the cup out into the sink. There was a clatter, and she saw four or five little lumps of what looked like glass.

'Diamonds,' the man remarked casually. 'Produced by electrolysis. They're not stable, mind,' he added, as Jane scrabbled frantically for them. 'They'll turn back into quick-dissolving sugar in a moment, just you see.'

So they did. Jane drew her breath in sharply.

'You haven't answered my question,' she said.

'Nor have I,' the man replied. He sat down on the kitchen stool, picked up a slice of Battenberg that Jane had been saving for a rainy day and bit into it. Its surface area remained undiminished, despite the crunching noises the man was making. 'Another proverb bites the dust,' he observed with his mouth full. 'You want to know why I'm haunting you?'

'I thought you said you weren't a ghost.'

'I'm not. I'm a . . .' He hesitated.

'You're a devil,' Jane said, calmly. 'I'd gathered that.'

But the man was frowning disapprovingly. '*Not* a devil,' he said. 'We don't use that word, it's got overtones. We consider that word pejorative and demeaning. We are a distinct meta-physical group with our own unique cultural and spiritual identity, and I'd be grateful if you'd respect that.'

Jane nodded. 'Okay,' she said, 'I can understand that, just about. What are you, then?'

The man's frown deepened slightly and he put the cake back, apparently untouched, on the plate he had taken it from. 'On the whole,' he said, 'we don't hold with generalising descriptive nouns. We firmly believe that each and every being in the cosmos is an individual, and . . .'

'Yes,' Jane said, folding her arms, 'that's fine. You're an individual. An individual what?'

'We don't like to . . .'

'Come on.'

'Well.' The man seemed distinctly embarrassed now. He picked up the salt cellar, shook a little out into the palm of his hand, and threw it over his right shoulder. 'If pressed, we prefer to describe ourselves as dæmons.'

'Demons.'

'Dæmons,' the man corrected her, hamming up the diphthong. 'From the Greek *daimon*, meaning a spirit, supernumerary god or præternatural entity. We feel . . .'

'But your leader is Satan, right?'

The man now looked distinctly offended. 'Wrong,' he said. 'Look, when you go out and buy takeaway chicken, you don't honestly believe that the business is still run by a seventy-year-old Texan colonel with a little white beard, do you? It's the same with us. We've kept the name, I suppose, or at least parts of the corporate identity, but we've moved on a long way from those days, I can tell you. We've diversified our interests into completely new areas.'

'Like the Mafia.'

'*Not* like the Mafia. Like Rupert Murdoch or Howard Hughes, even. We really aren't in the same business that we used to be in at all, even say two hundred years ago.'

'Don't tell me,' Jane said. 'You're moving into the area of communications and information technology. Or financial services, maybe. I could believe that,' she added thoughtfully.

'Let me make you a cup of tea.'

Jane shuddered involuntarily. 'No, thank you,' she said. 'I like my tea made with wet water and organic tea-leaves. I don't imagine there's much of either of those in any cup of tea you'd make.'

'You're being very hostile,' the man said.

'And you still haven't answered my question,' Jane replied sweetly. 'Why me?'

'Like I said,' the man replied. 'We want to offer you a job.'

'As a devil? No thanks.'

'Will you please not use that word.'

'You look rather silly when you're upset,' Jane observed, 'and not at all the way I'd expect a demon — sorry, dæmon, I hope I pronounced it right . . .'

'Perfectly. And how should I look?'

'Don't change the subject. I know the one about Jesus wanting me for a sunbeam, but I reckon your idea's a bit over the top, don't you?'

The man sighed, and Jane suddenly felt a pang of sympathy for someone else who'd had a long day. 'I'm sorry,' she said. 'Tell me about the job.'

The man looked suitably grateful. 'Thank you,' he said.

'And I'm sorry I sneezed you earlier,' Jane added. 'That was an accident, actually, honest. I get hay fever sometimes, in the summer.'

'How unpleasant for you. Basically, the job . . .'

'Yes?'

The man thought for a moment. 'Actually,' he said, 'it's a bit tricky to put into words, really. If I could just pop into your head for a moment . . .'

'I'd rather you didn't,' Jane said quickly, and then added, 'But thank you for asking, anyway.'

'Okay then,' the man said. 'I'll see what I can do just explaining it verbally, and we'll take it from there. Basically . . . Oh, *nuts!*'

Jane looked startled. 'What is it?'

The man looked sheepish. 'It's my bleeper,' he admitted. 'I'm on call, you see. Can I possibly borrow your phone a minute?'

Jane suppressed a giggle. 'You're the duty devil tonight, are you?'

'Will you *please* . . .?'

'Be my guest,' she said. 'It's in the other room. Not long distance, is it?'

The man made a sort of simpering noise. 'Not at all,' he said. 'It's about a mile and a half to my office, as the lift-shaft plummets.' He walked through, shutting the door behind him. Somehow, Jane managed to keep herself from listening at the keyhole.

The door opened, and the man's face appeared round it. 'Sorry about this,' he said. 'Something's cropped up, I've got to dash back to the office. Look, can you forget all about this for the time being and we'll talk later?'

Jane nodded. 'Though I can't promise to forget *all* about it.'

'Don't you worry about that,' the man said. 'And I'll take care of the phone bill, too. Thanks for the tea.'

He vanished.

Jane stood stock still for about twenty seconds. Then she blinked twice, shook herself, and realised that she was in the flat.

'Funny,' she said aloud. 'I can't remember taking my coat off.'

She considered the matter for a while, until something at the back of her subconscious assured her that it really wasn't worth worrying about. Instead, she decided, she'd have a nice cup of tea and a slice of cake, wash her hair and then watch the telly for an hour or so before going to bed.

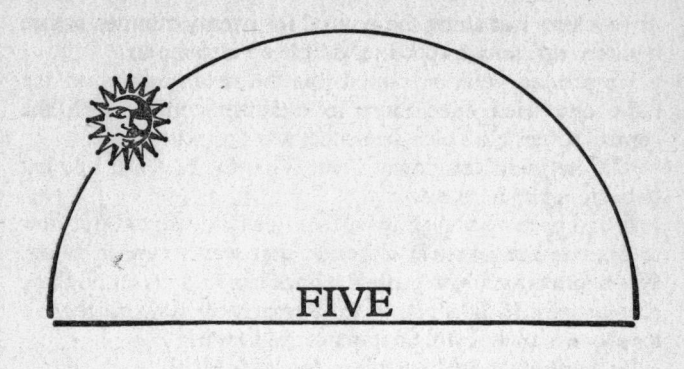

FIVE

Wayne, trainee technical assistant (second grade), looked down over the dashboard of the sun and wondered if something was wrong.

If it was, he told himself, then it wasn't his fault. He hadn't asked to be transferred at a moment's notice from Tides, where he had just mastered sweeping up the staff canteen floor, and to be given this bloody great big thing to fly. Nobody had told him how to fly it, probably because nobody seemed to know. The sum total of hands-on vocational training he had received comprised the words 'I think the ignition is that one there'.

Why was everyone down there looking at him?

He'd heard somewhere that mortals aren't supposed to look directly at the sun, because it damages their eyes or something equally feeble. Pretty well everything damaged mortals, as far as he could gather. If half of what he'd heard was true, it was a miracle there were any of them left.

It hadn't been easy getting the stupid thing off the ground in the first place, and the damage wasn't his fault either. After all, anybody with any sense would naturally assume that it took off vertically. Certainly nobody told him you had to drive it very fast along the ground for twenty minutes before it picked up enough speed to wobble off into the air.

He pressed what he hoped was the speak button on the radio and tried once more to establish contact with the control tower. His voice, he noted, was thin with panic.

'Oi,' he said, 'you down there. What the fuck am I meant to be doing up here, anyway?'

It had been very slightly easier once he'd worked out how to operate the joystick; although that was a case in point. You'd think that if you pushed it back it would make the thing go upwards. It didn't, though. Remarkable how quickly an ice-cap will melt if you do low swoops over it.

'Is there anybody down there, for shit's sake?'

He gave up. On the left-hand side of the console there were some buttons he hadn't pressed yet. He pressed them. They didn't seem to make any difference.

There had to be some way to make this thing fly steady. If he could get down lower, perhaps somebody on the ground would know what to do, and they could shout up at him and tell him. He noticed a lever with a red knob on it, and pulled. That certainly made a difference.

'Help!' he screamed.

About five minutes later, once he'd got used to flying along upside down, he managed to grab hold of the lever again and tried to pull it back. It wouldn't budge. It was stuck.

At least, he said to himself, I can't see what's going on on the ground. I don't think I'd want to know, somehow.

Instinct told him that since he couldn't see where he was going, the sensible thing would be to try and go higher, because the higher up you went, the fewer things there were that you could possibly bump into. The odd star, perhaps; maybe a comet or two. Not the ground. He wrestled with the joystick, but now that was jammed too. He had a notion that he was going into a spin, zooming downwards. If the great burning disc he was attempting to manipulate hit the ground, the chances were that it would probably perform a massive leg-break and whizz out into the back end of the universe for six byes.

Not my fault, he muttered, as he strained against the stick. Not my fault, not *my* fault, not my *fault* . . .

Jane woke up and sat bolt upright in bed. Something was wrong.

It was, she realised, the dawn. It was doing something it shouldn't be doing. It was flashing on and off.

With her head still full of damp, heavy sleep, she stumbled out of bed, clumped to the window and hauled on the curtains. Dear God, she thought, I'm right.

The sun, riding high – very high – in the morning heavens was flicking on and off like a huge, blazing indicator. Blinding flashes of light, then sudden darkness, twenty times a second. All the signs were that planet Earth was approaching a junction and preparing to turn left.

Perhaps, Jane said to herself as she struggled into a pullover, it's an eclipse. Lots of eclipses. Perhaps they're using up an enormous backlog of eclipses before they pass their best-before date.

She stopped and thought for a moment. There was, she realised, something else.

Very slowly, she turned round and looked for her watch. It was difficult going, because the stroboscopic effect of the flashing sun made it impossible to focus or judge distances. Eventually, though, she found it and peered at the dial. It was half-past eleven. At night. She'd only gone to bed an hour ago. What the hell were they doing having dawn?

Perhaps, she thought, there'll be an announcement in a moment. There is no cause for alarm, it's only a drill. We're having a dawn-practice and we forgot to tell you. Sorry about that.

Then she twigged. The sun was going the wrong way. Instead of East-West, it was going West-East. She could tell this because, in addition to flickering away like very old film footage, it was going at one hell of a lick.

Jane stood there, one small mortal trying to make sense of the Universe. All things considered, it was a pretty ambitious undertaking, and nobody could have blamed her if she'd not even tried. Aristotle had tried, after all, and Thomas Aquinas, and Descartes, and Einstein, and a lot of others too, all of them better qualified and probably far better paid than she was. The combined results of their researches, one had to admit, had not been impressive. Nobody could possibly have reproached Jane if she had failed. But she didn't; in fact, although she wasn't really conscious of it, she hit the nail on the head dead centre and with considerable force.

'Oh dear,' she said. 'Somebody's made a banjax.'

As if to congratulate her on the accuracy of her summary, the moon rose from behind a clump of very frightened-looking clouds, zoomed across the sky, stopped just underneath the sun and hovered there. On the perfectly blank silver sphere of its face, Jane was sure she could make out an expression, and it reminded her of her geography teacher at school. Jane frowned.

'Honestly!' she said.

Then she drew the curtains tightly and went back to bed.

Wayne, trainee technical assistant (second grade), opened his eyes and looked up.

Not that it was up, strictly speaking, because he was still flying along in a dead spin, upside down, straight towards the centre of the earth. As far as he was concerned, however, it was up. They call it relativity, and up to a point it works.

'Ger,' he said.

Directly above, or perhaps below, his head, he could see the moon. What was more, he could see the man in the moon. And the man in the moon wasn't pleased, apparently.

To be precise, he was standing up in his cockpit waving his fists in the air and shouting. He was too far away for Wayne to be able to hear him, let alone read his lips, but he had a pretty shrewd idea of the general gist of what was being said.

'Not my fault,' he yelled. 'Not my *fault*!'

What the hell, the man couldn't hear him anyway. Wayne shrugged, relaxed his shoulders, and leaned back in the seat. Any minute now, he reckoned, he'd collide with the earth and none of it would matter very much anyway.

As he slid back in the seat, it so happened that his elbow banged against the control panel, and something got switched on.

'. . . THE BUGGERY DO YOU THINK YOU'RE DOING, YOU DOZY YOUNG BUGGER, PULL THE BLOODY STICK BACK AND OPEN YOUR SODDING FLAPS!'

Ah, said Wayne to himself, that must have been the radio. Now perhaps we're getting somewhere.

'Here,' he shouted. 'Can you hear me?'

The voice from the radio, which he assumed was that of the man in the moon, didn't answer his question in so many words, but the impression he got was that yes, they had established radio contact. He took a deep breath.

'Here,' he said. 'How do you fly this poxy thing?'

There was a moment of stunned silence.

'You mean you don't *know*?'

Wayne scowled. 'Course I don't bloody know. You think if I knew I'd be flying it upside down straight at the bloody ground?'

The moon wobbled on its course. 'Didn't anyone, like, *tell* you before they let you take her up?'

'No,' Wayne replied. 'Look . . .'

'All right,' said the man in the moon, quickly, 'keep your head, there's nothing to it really. You see that stick thing in front of you?'

Wayne looked down. 'Yup,' he said. 'I tried that.'

'Shut up and listen. That's your joystick, right? Now to the left of the joystick there's some levers. That's your flaps. Now, ease the stick back with your right hand, lift the flaps with your left. Easy does it. I said easy! Gently!'

41

Amazingly, Wayne could feel the sun responding; levelling out, slowing down. He gripped the stick hard. The voice over the radio sounded quiet and reassuring with just a soupçon of blind terror.

'Now then,' said the voice, 'just by your left foot there's a pedal. That's the brake. You got that?'

'Yeah.'

'Gently mind, that's it. Not too hard, mind, or you'll stall her. Now then, ease forward on the stick, that's it, lovely job, and open the throttle just a crack . . .'

'Which one's the throttle?'

'Right foot. No, no, that's the clutch, *that*'s it. Just a crack, mind, or first thing you know you'll be up the back of the Crab Nebula. Come on now, son, just a little bit more, you've got it. Now hold it like that.'

'Like this?'

'NO!'

There was radio silence for a moment as sun and moon took evasive action. By rights, the violent jinking of the moon should have whipped up a tsunami that would have gone over North America like a carpet-sweeper and given Japan a spring-clean it would never have forgotten. As it happened, however, they were hopelessly under-manned at Tides, owing to the secondment of key personnel to other departments, and everything stayed exactly as it was.

'USE YOUR BLOODY STICK!'

'Like that?'

'Yes. More so. Put your back into it.'

'Like this?'

'Yes.'

The sun seemed to hover for a moment; then it seemed to drop like a stone, just for a fraction of a second; then it caught itself, wobbled heart-stoppingly, and pulled away, flying straight and level. The moon closed in and followed it cautiously.

'Nice work,' said the man in the moon, with a trace of

admiration cutting the fear and the relief. 'Just one more thing.'

'Yes?'

'Switch the bloody flasher off, will you? You're giving me a headache.'

Wayne crunched his eyebrows together. 'Flasher?' he said. 'What's that?'

'The flasher. The emergency warning lights. You've been flashing on and off, didn't you . . .? By your left hand, it's a little blue button with an arrow on it . . . That's it. You're doing just fine.'

In the cockpit of the moon, George let out a long sigh and wiped half a pint of sweat off the bald dome of his head with the back of his hand. Bloody short retirement it had turned out to be, after all. Still, he said to himself, the lad looks like he's got the hang of it, amazingly quickly as well; a natural, obviously. Just as well, too.

'Right,' he said. 'All we've got to do now is to turn it round.'

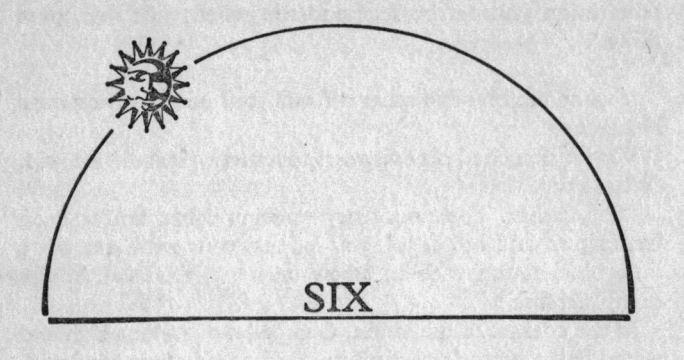

SIX

High above the peaks of the Blue Mountains, the sun, under escort, completed its banking manoeuvre, straightened out, and began to head East. On the ground, all the villagers except one threw their hats in the air and cheered.

'Well, well,' said old Ari, the blacksmith. 'It's not every day you see something like that.'

The other villagers were silent for a while. Even by their standards of simple-hearted straightforwardness, old Ari did come out with some pretty asinine comments from time to time. Still, he made a cracking good horseshoe, so nobody really minded.

'There's something to tell the grandchildren about, eh, Bjorn?' remarked Gustav, lowering the shard of smoked glass through which he had prudently watched the whole thing. 'Remarkable.'

Bjorn said nothing. He was fitting a new handle to his axe, having broken the old one when he lost his temper earlier on. Bjorn got through more axe handles than the rest of the community put together.

'I never cease to wonder,' Gustav went on, knocking out his simple corn-cob pipe on the sole of his boot and stuffing tobacco into the bowl, 'at the infinite variety of Providence and her astounding . . .'

'I don't,' said Bjorn. 'If you've got nothing better to do than stand there yakking, you could pass me that rasp. Poxy bloody cross-grained stuff, hickory.'

Gustav passed him the rasp. 'I mean,' he went on, 'sixty-seven years I've been alive, and I've never seen the like. Never in all my born . . .'

'I have.'

Gustav's merry, weather-beaten old face contracted into an unaccustomed frown. 'You have?' he asked.

'Oh yes. More times than you've had hot dinners. Give me the wedge. No, not that one, the small one.'

'That's very remarkable, neighbour Bjorn,' said Gustav, with a voice entirely devoid of disbelief. 'I haven't, and I'm much older than you.'

Bjorn stood up and banged the axe head three times on the ground to seat it in the handle. At the third blow, a long crack appeared in the handle. He swore, broke the handle over his knee, and reached for the auger.

'You should be more careful,' Gustav said. 'You could hurt your knee, doing something like that.' Bjorn laughed un-pleasantly.

'Fat chance.'

This was, Gustav couldn't help feeling, a typical sort of conversation with young Bjorn. Strange, he looked a pleasant enough sort of fellow. Perhaps he had had an unhappy life before he came to the village.

'Are you sure you've seen things like . . .?' Gustav pointed at the sun. Bjorn nodded.

'Yeah,' he said. 'I used to work for them, didn't I?'

Jane looked suddenly round, the toothbrush still in her mouth.

'Look . . .' she started to say. The man made an apologetic gesture.

45

'Sorry,' he said. 'I didn't realise. I can come back later if . . .'

Jane looked at him. Yes, there was something about him that told her that he was another one of Them. What was it, now?

'You're a different one, aren't you?' she said. 'I mean, you're not the same one who came before, are you? Or are you him with a different body on?'

'No,' the man replied, 'I'm a different one. My name is Staff.'

'Staff?'

The man shrugged slightly. 'It's not my actual name,' he said, 'but it's what everybody's called me for longer than I can remember. It's short for Chief of Staff.'

'Ah.' Jane extracted the toothbrush and laid it down on the soap-dish. 'I wish you lot wouldn't keep creeping up on me like this.'

'I didn't mean to creep,' Staff said. 'I just . . .'

But Jane wasn't going to be conciliated that easily. 'I mean,' she said, 'there I am, brushing my teeth, and suddenly there's this face over my shoulder. Did you ever work for a man called Hitchcock by any chance? Fat bloke, big nose.'

The man looked puzzled. 'Not that I can remember,' he said.

Jane smiled apologetically. 'Sorry,' she said. 'Human joke. I don't suppose you devils know much about the movies.'

The man looked hurt. 'Actually,' he said, 'I'm not a devil. Not at all.'

'Sorry,' Jane said, 'I meant to say dæmon, it just slipped out.'

'I'm not a dæmon, either,' the man replied. 'I'm a . . .' He paused, and blushed. 'Well, I'm not a dæmon. Different department.'

Jane thought for a moment, and then a slow grin spread over her toothpaste-flecked face. 'I've got it,' she said. 'You're an angel.'

'Please,' said the man, 'I really would prefer it if we didn't use that word. It's so . . .' He waved his arms helplessly.

'Well,' said Jane. 'What word should I use?'

'Public servant,' said the man, firmly. 'I think it's a much better word, really, don't you?'

Jane nodded, and looked at the man carefully. Tall, grey-haired, thinning a little on top and thickening out a bit round the middle, with a lot of hair on the backs of his hands and wearing a suit with rather shiny cuffs. Public servant did seem to fit the bill rather better than angel. 'Quite right,' she said. 'Look, can we get out of the bathroom, please?'

'Yes, of course.' The man moved awkwardly and opened the door for her. Jane tried not to mind.

'Coffee?' she said.

'Yes, er, thank you.' The man sat down on a straight-backed chair and folded his arms. He looked embarrassed.

'I've put the kettle on,' Jane said. 'Now, is all this connected with what happened to the sun just now?'

The man nodded. 'You're very observant,' he said.

'Not very,' Jane replied, wrinkling her nose. 'I mean, look at it sequentially. The sun goes haywire, supernatural beings start following me about, you don't have to be Aleister Crowley to get the idea that there may be a common factor . . . Sorry, did I say something wrong?'

'No,' said the man, 'or at least, you weren't to know. It's just that we don't mention that person in the Department.'

'Person? Oh!'

'Exactly,' said the man. 'You may remember Peter Wright; you know, *Spycatcher*? Well, think on, as we used to say when I was a boy.'

'Oh.' Jane bit her lip. 'Look, can we get to the point? What do you lot want with me? The other one – the, er, dæmon – said something about a *job*, but I . . .'

She tailed off. The man was nodding his head.

'A *job*?' she repeated. 'You can't be serious, surely.'

The man stood up and walked to the window. 'Well,' he

said, drawing the curtains slightly, 'you saw all that today, I take it? The sun and everything?'

'Yes indeed.'

The man cringed slightly. 'Wasn't very impressive, was it?'

Jane shrugged. 'I don't know,' she said. 'Was it supposed to be? I mean, I'm not really up on portents and things like that. I thought that sort of thing only happened when people like Julius Caesar got stabbed, and there isn't anybody like Julius Caesar about much these days. I mean, you've got to be realistic, haven't you? The whole lot of them aren't worth a light shower between them.'

'It wasn't a portent,' said the man quietly. 'You'd guessed, hadn't you?'

Jane nodded. 'Have you got my mind bugged, or something? Because if you have . . .'

The man shook his head firmly. 'Nothing of the sort, please believe me,' he said. 'But we at the Department . . . well, you had guessed, hadn't you?'

'Yes,' Jane said. 'If you mean that business with the sun was a cock-up, then yes.'

'It was,' said the man, and shuddered. 'Staff shortages.'

Jane raised an eyebrow. 'Staff shortages?'

The man nodded. 'It's a nightmare,' he said. 'An absolute bloody nightmare. Honestly, I haven't the faintest idea where it's all going to end.'

From the kitchen, Jane heard the click of the kettle switching itself off. She decided to ignore it.

'But how can you have staff shortages?' she asked, bewildered. 'I mean, I thought the whole point of you . . . you public servants was, you go on for ever. Immortal, you know.'

'Immortal,' said the man quietly, 'doesn't mean you go on working for ever, it just means that you have a very long retirement. Which means,' he added, 'that with each year that passes, paying the pensions takes up more and more of the available budget. At the moment, pensions account for ninety-nine-point-nine-seven-two of our available revenue. Think about it.'

Jane thought about it. 'I see,' she said.

'Exactly,' said the man. 'And that's only part of it. Put bluntly, we're running out of manpower. You see, every time a public servant retires, there's a vacancy, right?'

'I suppose so,' Jane said. 'I hadn't thought.'

'Take it from me,' said the man. 'There is. Now, the number of . . . I don't know how to put this.'

'You don't?'

'No,' said the man, shaking his head. 'It's delicate. Um. Where do you suppose angels – public servants – come from?'

Jane felt her tongue go dry with embarrassment. 'Er, mummy public servants and daddy public servants?'

The man scowled. 'Certainly not,' he said. 'It's a metaphysical impossibility. No, the stork brings them, of course. And do you know what's happened to the natural habitat of storks in the last fifty years?'

'Um.'

'Well,' said the man, 'I think you can see what I'm getting at. The storks are dying out, so we're . . . well, it makes recruitment a problem. A bloody great big problem. And that's where you come in,' he added.

Jane felt herself going red all over. 'Now look,' she said.

'No, no,' said the man quickly, 'not like that. I mean, we've decided, or at least Mr Ganger and I have decided . . .'

'Mr Ganger?'

'You've met him,' said the man.

'Oh.'

'We've decided,' the man continued, 'that the only way out is to start recruiting mortals – suitable mortals, obviously – and, well . . .'

'Well, what?' said Jane. Her voice, incidentally, would have frozen oxygen. The man swallowed hard, and then made a show of noticing his watch.

'Good lord,' he said, 'is that the time? Anyway, you'll think about it, won't you? I mean, you'll be, like, the guinea ... I mean, a pioneer. That's right, a pioneer. The whole success of the programme ...'

'No.'

'And if it works,' the man said quickly, standing up and knocking over a small pile of tapes on the floor, 'it'll mean that we can start replacing key staff, reorganising the whole running of the department, and ...'

'No.'

'So you'll think about it. Good. Well, I'll be saying ...'

'No.'

'We'll be in ...' The man suddenly became translucent, 'touch. Please give it very serious ...' Then transparent, 'thought.' Then invisible. 'Thank you.'

'No,' Jane said. 'Absolutely not. No way.'

She stopped. She suddenly had the feeling that she was talking to herself.

'Honestly!' she said.

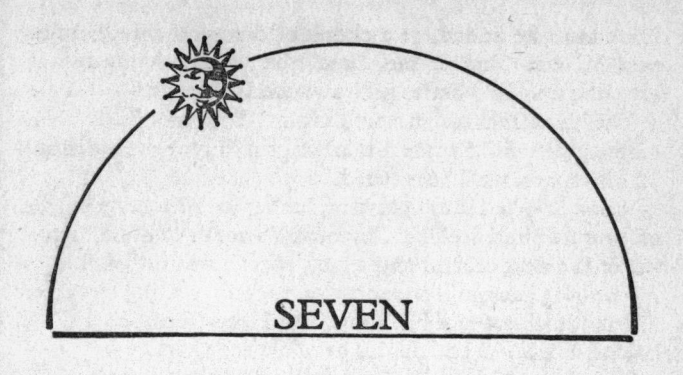

SEVEN

Look in Sir Isaac Newton's *Principia Mathematica* and you will learn all about gravity.

Gravity, according to Sir Isaac, is a natural phenomenon, as immutable as it is impersonal. Because of gravity, objects stay attached to the surface of the planet instead of flying off into the void. There's nothing mystical or even intentional about it; it just happens, because that's how the great machine works.

In all fundamentally important respects, Sir Isaac was right. Gravity is, as he observed, a physical force resulting from the interaction of bodies possessing mass upon each other. It is not dependent upon the whim of any deity or supernatural entity. It can, in other words, be relied on; provided, of course, that somebody remembers to grease the main drive-shaft once in a while.

'It's not my job,' complained the Head Technician loudly, above the ear-splitting scream of grinding diamonds. 'By rights, it's down to Maintenance to . . .'

The Technical Supervisor snarled at him. 'Well,' he observed superfluously, 'whoever was supposed to look after the sodding thing, it's seized. The gearbox's completely stuffed.

Look out!' he added, as a chunk of diamond shrapnel flew past his ear. 'Bugger me, Fred, the whole bloody thing's breaking up. We'd better get it switched off quick.'

The Head Technician stared at him. 'You can't do that, you lunatic,' he said. 'Switch this lot off, you'll get people drifting off into space, we'll be lynched.'

'Look,' replied the supervisor, 'either we switch the bugger off or it'll switch itself off. Something's got to be done, right?'

For the next second and a half, speech was impossible, as the bearing manifold suddenly shattered, spraying egg-sized diamonds about like birdshot. The Head Technician dived behind a flywheel and put his head between his knees.

'Come out of there, you coward!' yelled the supervisor.

'Not my problem,' the Head Technician shrieked back. 'You look in the files, chum, you'll see. I wrote a memo about it five years back. I warned you lot that if the whole gearbox wasn't renewed ...'

'Shut up,' the supervisor observed, 'and bring me a spanner. All we've got to do is slip the clutch and let it freewheel while we bodge up the transmission. Its own momentum'll keep it turning for hours.'

The Head Technician considered this for a moment. 'Bollocks,' he opined. 'It'll just grind to a halt, and then you'll have all the mortals floating upwards yelling at us. You may not give a toss about your pension, chum, but ...'

The ball race chose that moment to fuse, filling the air with a sparkling cloud of diamond dust. Planet Earth wobbled sharply on its axis.

'All right,' hissed the Head Technician, 'only if this goes wrong, you just remember it was your idea, right? Like, you gave me a direct order and ...'

'Shut up,' the supervisor reiterated, 'and find me that spanner.'

A few moments later, Planet Earth stopped shuddering and began to spin noiselessly, easily round its axis. It began to slow down ...

*

'Ouch!' said Jane, aloud.

It hadn't been her first choice as a flat; it wasn't really her kind of neighbourhood: it was a fair old hike to the station every morning, the bedroom wall needed papering badly, the doors stuck in winter and there was something of a condensation problem in the kitchen; but hitherto at least, she'd never had any problems with the ceiling being too low. Until now, apparently.

She looked down. Yes, there was the floor, just where she'd left it. There was her furniture. Same old furniture, mostly the unsuitable and heterogeneous offerings of relatives and friends, except that previously it hadn't shown any signs of wanting to jump off the ground and float about the place like a shoal of dazed tuna. And there was her breakfast – mug of coffee, slice of toast – swimming obligingly towards her through thin air.

She grabbed at the coffee-cup as it floated past, missed the cup but not the handle, and spilt the coffee. It fell upwards and splashed against the ceiling.

Gingerly, and conscious that there were rather more cobwebs up here than Mrs Beeton would have approved of, Jane raised her left hand above her head and pushed the ceiling away from her. She felt herself bob downwards for a few feet, and then the current, or whatever the hell it was, caught her up again and lifted her slowly upwards. She kicked violently with her feet, but it didn't help. She hit her head gently on the lampshade, pushed off again, and walked on her hands across to the door frame.

'Somebody,' she said to a passing telephone directory, 'is going to have some explaining to do.'

The directory fluttered its pages and continued to drift upwards, until it was splayed open against the plasterwork. Jane gripped the wooden frame of the door with both hands and tried to haul herself downwards.

'That's better,' she said, as her feet connected with the

carpet. She looked down. The fibres were trying their best to stand on end, giving the impression of one very frightened Axminster. Worse still, all the dust she hadn't got around to hoovering out of it was slowly rising. It got up her nose and she sneezed.

A flower vase drifted past her, upside-down and bobbing about erratically as air escaped out of its inside. This wouldn't do at all. She managed to propel herself on to the back of the kitchen table, which was passing by slowly and ponderously, a mere foot or so above the ground. As she had hoped, her weight helped to push it down, and she found herself a mere six inches above floor-level. What she needed now, she reckoned, was some sort of punt-pole.

A passing golf umbrella solved that problem, and soon she was punting cautiously across the floor, steering clear of drifting armchairs and trying not to hit the walls too hard, towards the window. She had an idea that things were going to be a bit surreal out there, and it was a pity that her camera was presently nuzzling against the ceiling-rose like a small black remora.

'Good lord,' she said.

In a way it was really rather beautiful. Peaceful, certainly. The drivers of the cars had mostly had the sense to switch off their engines and they were now simply drifting aimlessly, a few inches off the ground, while airborne pedestrians hung on to their door handles. A school of red buses sailed gently past the request stop opposite the corner shop, while the newsagent's stock in trade sailed gracefully, almost majestically, into the air, flapping their leaves like enormous, slow-motion herons. An open umbrella fluttered away past her window on its way to the stars.

'You see what I mean?' said a voice above her.

She looked upwards to see Staff flat on his back against the ceiling. She tried not to laugh, but there are limits.

'I'm sorry,' she said. 'But you look so . . .'

'I know,' he replied sadly. 'You think you're having problems. Just count yourself lucky you've got a corporeal body. You have no idea how difficult it was getting here.'

Jane pushed hard on her umbrella, and the table rose upwards. She was just able to grab hold of Staff's left foot before it fell floorwards again, and she towed her visitor down with her. As she had expected, he weighed nothing.

A little undignified scrambling enabled Staff to get on the table, and he secured himself to it by wrapping his arms round one of the legs. Even so, the lower half of his body pointed resolutely upwards, with the result that he looked like nothing so much as a large, respectable tadpole.

'Anyway,' he said. 'Surely now you can't deny that there's a problem.'

'Oh, there's a problem all right,' Jane agreed. 'Like how I'm going to get coffee stains off the ceiling. It's Artex, you know.'

'I gathered,' Staff replied. 'It's like sandpaper, that stuff. Oughtn't to be allowed.'

'Sorry.'

'Not your fault. Look,' he went on, 'unless we find some way of getting things sorted out, it's going to get worse. You must see that.'

'But,' Jane started to say; then she corrected herself. 'Are you sure I'd be able to help?' she said.

'Yes,' Staff replied, 'you and others like you, but you first. You see, if you make a go of it, we can recruit others. Management won't be able to stop us. We'll be able to fill all the vacant posts, get the plant and machinery properly serviced; that way, we won't have all our staff and resources tied down coping with emergencies.' He paused to fence away a teapot that seemed to want to get inside his jacket. 'Come on,' he said, 'what do you say? Anything's got to be better than this.'

Suddenly, the world started to move again. For a split second, Jane felt it distinctly; the violent shock of an incredibly rapid acceleration, rather like the awful feeling you get the first time you're in an aeroplane taking off. Then she was rather too preoccupied with the spectacle of all her possessions falling to the ground and smashing into tiny pieces to bother with detailed observations of that kind.

'Right,' she said and, using her thumb and forefinger, picked a razor-sharp shard of casserole out of her hair. Outside, the air was suddenly full of the sound of many motorists restored to normality and lamenting their lost no-claims bonuses with the help of their horns. The last glossy magazine twirled a few times in the air and flopped to earth like an exhausted pigeon.

'You're on,' she said.

'Tell me,' said Gustav tremulously, 'all about it.'

The fire burnt low, so that the interior of Gustav's small but cosy cottage became full of deep shadows, each one a curtained doorway into hostile infinity. Using his teeth only, Bjorn removed the crown cap off a bottle of Carlsberg and spat it accurately into the grate.

'Not a lot to tell, really,' he said. 'I applied for the job, got it, tried it, didn't like it, told them to stuff it, moved on. Simple as that.'

'Um,' said Gustav, 'yes, I suppose it is, really. But tell me,' he went on, overcoming his feelings of acute apprehension. 'What was it really like? Being an angel, I mean.'

There was a silence: a huge, heavy, abrasive silence you could have ground corn with. The firelight glinted red on Bjorn's eyes, making Gustav shrink back into the chimney corner.

'You ever call me that again,' Bjorn growled, 'I'll pull your lungs out through your nose and make you eat them, okay?'

'I'm very sorry,' Gustav squeaked. 'I'd got the impression . . .'

'Because,' Bjorn went on, 'we don't like that name, right? It's a poncey name. Makes you sound like a right fairy, being called that.' He paused to glower savagely into the fire. 'Makes you think of little lacy dolls with wings and Christmas trees shoved up their jacksies. Anybody tries that with me, they'll get what's coming to them, understood?'

'Understood.'

'Fine.' Bjorn took a long pull of beer and burped assertively. 'The lads and me, we used to call ourselves "the Boys from the Blue Stuff". Sounds better, you know, meaner. More macho. And we didn't fart around playing harps, either.'

'Absolutely not,' Gustav agreed, nodding furiously. 'Right on,' he added.

'Right on what?'

'Sorry.'

Bjorn drank some more beer and scratched his ear thoughtfully. 'I'm not saying we didn't have a few laughs, mind. I mean, it wasn't all answering prayers and polishing the sun. Bloody awful job, that was,' he parenthesised, 'took all the skin off your knuckles if you weren't careful. Bloke I worked with, he got his fingers caught in the works when he was trying to clean them out and nobody noticed. They launched the damn thing same as usual and he was left there, trapped, dangling by his fingers, yelling his head off, but nobody heard. You just imagine that,' he went on, after a deep shudder that started just below his neck and finally earthed itself out through the soles of his feet. 'Just imagine it, hanging by your fingers from that bloody great hot thing, miles above the ground, for a whole day. And when he tried to get compensation, what did they say? Should have observed the safety procedure, they said, all his own silly fault, served him right. He went a bit funny in the head after that so they put him on Earthquakes. Nobody notices if you're a bit funny in the head on Earthquakes.'

'I see,' said Gustav. 'Well . . .'

'We were always having them,' Bjorn ground on, staring straight in front of him into the fire. 'Industrial accidents they called them, only some of them weren't accidents if you ask me. You can't tell me a grown man suddenly falling off a perfectly wide, fenced-off catwalk into the works of the grass-growing plant was an accident, or a coincidence. Just so happened he'd found out about the foreman and the cocoa money, that's all. Of course, they hushed it up. Blamed it all on the frosts, they did.'

Gustav smiled and tried to seep away into the cracks between the stones, but there was too much of him for that. 'Gosh,' he said.

'Right bastards, some of those foremen were, mind,' Bjorn went on. 'There was one when I was on Miracles – some years ago, this is, because they've closed that department down now. Evil Neville, they used to call him. Short, round bloke, face like a road map. Whenever we were told to turn water into wine, he'd be in there with his mates and a couple of hundred jerrycans, and the poor bloody punters would have to make do with water turned into lager. Couldn't tell the difference half the time. No wonder the whole department got such a bad name with the high-ups. Talking of which, you got any more?'

He waved the empty bottle, and Gustav, simpering, fetched another. It had cobwebs on it.

'Cheers,' Bjorn said. He decapitated it, absent-mindedly swallowed the top, and slurped deeply.

'It sounds very unpleasant,' Gustav said.

'Unpleasant!' Bjorn sniggered noisily. 'You're telling me, sunshine. I could tell you some stories, no worries. What about that time we were working Nights and Norm the Headbanger got completely rat-arsed and left his brother's old van parked right in the middle of the Great Bear? Or there was that time Mad Trev and me were working on Rivers, and Trev got taken short just before the flooding of the Nile. Those Egyptians sure got a shock that year, I'm telling you.' He laughed brutally. Gustav closed his eyes and felt sick. He had a little picture of an angel over his bed: his mother had put it there years ago, telling him that it would watch over him while he was asleep. As soon as he was alone in the house again, he told himself, he'd get a shovel and bury it under the oak tree.

'Not that it was all bad, mind,' Bjorn was saying. 'There was guard duty, f'rinstance. I liked that. They gave you this flaming sword and you stood about in front of the gates of Eden, and anybody who was daft enough to try and get in there – shunk!' He made a sharp, graphically illustrative movement with the bottle, spilling the few remaining suds it contained over the back of his hand. 'Don't get up,' he said. 'In that cupboard, right?'

He lurched to his feet and went to the cupboard. Gustav shut his eyes.

'Here,' he heard Bjorn call out. 'There's no more beer left, that's a bummer. Hold on, though, this'll do. Cheers.' Oh wonderful, Gustav thought, he's found the paint thinners.

'Help yourself,' he said, in a small, tinny voice he barely recognised as his own.

'Anyway,' Bjorn said, sitting by the fire again and wiping the neck of the bottle. 'I stuck it as long as I could, but in the end I couldn't stick it any more.'

'Really?'

'Yeah.' Bjorn drew heavily on the bottle, winced and licked his lips. 'I reckoned it was, well, brutalising me, you know? Like, when I was young they said I was sort of sensitive, you know, feelings and all that. So I reckoned, if I stick this job any longer, what's going to happen to me? I could end up turning into a really nasty person if I wasn't careful. So I quit. Probably I was just imagining it,' he added, 'but you can't be too careful, right? I mean, there's integrity, for one thing.'

'Er, right.'

'So,' Bjorn said. Then he sat silently for a very long eight seconds, glaring viciously into the fire. Just as Gustav was beginning to feel a scream welling up inside the pit of his stomach, Bjorn got up, drained the bottle, and put it down on the table with a bang. 'You know what,' he said, 'it's done me good, you know, talking about it. I feel –' he burped savagely '– much better now. In fact, we must do this again sometime, right?'

Gustav closed his eyes. On the one hand, his mother had told him never to tell deliberate lies. On the other hand, his mother had told him a lot of stuff about angels that had turned out to be rather wide of the mark.

'Right,' he said. 'I'd like that.'

'Yeah.' Bjorn rose to his feet, groped for his axe, and staggered clumsily to the door.

'Strewth,' he said, poking his head out into the cool, sweet, night air and sniffing distastefully. 'Smells like armpits out here. Cheers, then.'

'Cheers.'

Gustav closed the door after his guest, bolted it, put the shutters up, and collapsed into his chair, trembling. From the distant village street he could hear the distinctive sound of a man with an axe playing Try-Your-Strength games with the village pump. He winced.

The picture of the angel disappeared from above Gustav's bed shortly afterwards, and was replaced by a Pirelli calendar.

'Oh,' said the charge-hand.

Far below, an enormous brown snake of muddy, foul-smelling water thrust its snout into the gaps between the skyscrapers. Apart from the occasional crash of falling masonry, the great city was quite astoundingly quiet.

'I thought you meant Memphis, *Tennessee*,' the charge-hand went on, slightly apprehensively. 'So there's another Memphis, is there? That's confusing.'

'Isn't it?' his superior replied, through tight lips. 'Sorry, perhaps I should have explained a bit better. I thought it'd be clear, even to a complete idiot, that when I said flood the Nile as far as Memphis, I meant Memphis, Egypt. Obviously, though, I was wrong.' He pushed his cap on to the back of his head and scratched his bald patch thoughtfully. 'You know what,' he added, after a moment. 'This is going to take a bit of sorting out, this is.'

'Ah.'

'I mean,' he went on, 'just to take the small details first, there's your crocodiles, right?'

'Crocodiles?'

'Crocodiles.' He pointed. 'Must've got swept along with the current or something. Look, there's one now, just crawling up the steps of the Fire Department building.'

'Oh yes, I can just make it out. Gosh, that's . . .'

'And in ten minutes,' his superior went on, 'when we whack all the pumps back into reverse and start draining the water away . . . Well, there's going to be a lot of them left behind, right?'

'Um.'

'But,' his superior went on, 'that's really a minor point, and probably nobody's going to notice, what with rebuilding the whole goddamn city, and flying in emergency aid, and what not. Still, I just thought I'd mention it. Let you have the fully-rounded picture, so to speak.'

'Right.' The charge-hand nodded. 'Got that.'

'There's also,' his superior went on, his face gradually tightening like an overstretched guitar-string, 'the fact that the Egyptians are now one river short. They're not going to be pleased, you know. I get the feeling they're, you know, attached to it.'

'Yes?'

His superior nodded. 'You been working in this department long?' he asked. The charge-hand did some mental arithmetic.

'Not *very* long,' he said.

'How long exactly?'

'Um, eight hours,' the charge-hand replied. 'Before that, I was on Truth.'

'Truth. I see.' His superior nodded a couple of times, and then a few times more simply out of momentum. 'Doing what, exactly?'

'Mumblemumblemumblemumble.'

'Sorry?'

'I made the tea,' the charge-hand replied. 'And sometimes I went out to the shop to get doughnuts and things. We used to do a lot of just sitting about in Truth, see.'

'That follows.'

'It's the Daughter of Time, you know, Truth,' the charge-hand added, nervously. 'Not many people know that, but it's . . .'

'Right.' His superior jammed his cap squarely on his head, lifted his sagging shoulders, and scribbled on his clipboard so hard that the point of his pencil snapped. The fragment of graphite flew wide, tumbled down through the firmament, hit the Earth just outside Petrograd, and ended up in the State Geological Museum marked *Fragile*. 'I guess we'd better make a start on getting it sorted, then. First, we'll need a Form KRB1, supported by a blue chit and a Requisition in Form 4.'

The charge-hand made a note in his pocketbook. 'Got that,' he said. 'Right.'

'After that,' his superior went on, 'we'll need a couple of buckets and some mops.'

'Two – buckets,' the charge-hand said slowly as he wrote, 'assorted – mops. Yes?'

'That'll do to be going on with,' said his superior. 'So I'll leave you to it, all right?'

'But . . .'

'After all,' said his superior, a rainbow plainly visible through his torso, 'you're the charge-hand. It says so on your badge. Good luck.'

He retreated rapidly, and soon was nothing more than a tiny speck, indistinguishable among the flock of ibises circling the helipad on the roof of the First Consolidated Bank.

The charge-hand stood for a while, looking in the direction he had taken, and then frowned and said something under his breath. It might have been 'bucket', or at least something quite similar.

'Excuse me.'

The charge-hand turned to find a smallish female mortal standing behind him. She was wearing, he noticed with mingled amazement and disgust, a bright blue lapel-badge with 'Inspector' written on it.

'Where did you get that from?' he demanded.

'The badge, you mean?' Jane said. 'Oh, a man gave it to me. A man by the name of Staff, if that means anything to you.'

The charge-hand blinked four times, said, 'Oh,' and then took off his cap. 'How can I help you, miss?' he added warily.

Jane looked down at the city below her. Out of irresistible force of habit, the mighty river was depositing its massive cargo of alluvial silt in through the windows of third-floor offices. She wasn't quite sure what the people in those offices did for a living, but she was prepared to bet money that it wasn't growing rice.

'It's more a case of how I can help you,' she said. 'You see, I've been assigned.'

'Assigned?'

'To help,' Jane explained. 'I'm new, you see. It's a . . .' She searched the back end of her mind for the right phrase. 'It's a management training programme. I'm here to learn the work of various departments, before I'm finally placed where they think I'll be most suitable.'

'I see,' said the charge-hand. 'You, er, know something about tidal rivers, then?'

'Not a great deal,' Jane replied. 'I had a sort of idea that they aren't supposed to flow slap bang through the middle of major urban thoroughfares, but maybe I'm a bit behind on the latest developments.'

The charge-hand sat down on a lump of scrap cloud, put his index finger in his ear and wiggled it about. 'If that's irony,' he said, 'then it's not allowed. There's strict rules about irony.'

'Really,' Jane said, looking at the city. 'You know, I think we ought to do something, don't you?'

The charge-hand sighed. 'Yeah,' he said. 'All right. I'll fetch the buckets.'

Jane looked at him for a moment and considered reminding him about the irony statutes. Then it occurred to her that he might be serious.

'No,' she said, as calmly as she could. 'Don't do that. I've got an idea.'

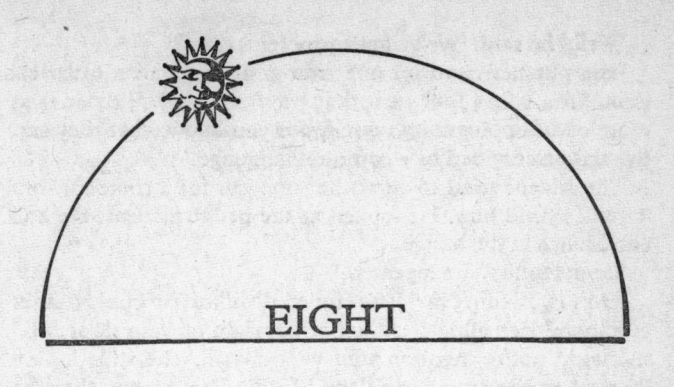

EIGHT

It was lucky that the Mayor's office was on the top floor of the City Hall building. Had it been anywhere else, it would have been flooded out, with grave consequences for the smooth and efficient administration of the City. As it was, the nerve-centre of the governmental system was intact and functioning, which made up to a certain extent for the fact that the rest of the system was under three feet of muddy water. The Mayor, a pragmatist whose electoral image was 'early laid-back pastoral', had decided to face the challenge posed by the inundation, borrowing a hat with some hooks stuck into it and hanging a sign on his door-handle which read *Gone Fishin'*.

'Come in,' he said, in answer to the knock on the door. Then he frowned.

'How did you get here?' he asked.

Jane came in, shooed out an inquisitive crocodile with her handbag, closed the door behind her, smiled, and sat down. 'Easy,' she said. 'I walked.'

The Mayor was about to argue when he caught sight of the bright blue badge. For some reason which his mind couldn't adequately process in the time available, it seemed to explain everything.

'Well,' he said. 'We've got a problem, right?'

Jane put her head on one side and gave him a quizzical look. 'You could look at it that way,' she said. 'I'd see it as more of an opportunity myself, but you know what they say, two nations divided by a common language.'

The Mayor tried to work that one out for a moment, but it was beyond him. He looked at the badge instead. He had confidence in the badge.

'Opportunity,' he repeated.

'Don't you think so?' Jane smiled. 'Millions of cubic tonnes of mineral-rich alluvial silt deposited right on your doorstep,' she said, 'not to mention your window-sill,' she added, 'at a time when the situation in the Middle East means that the price of phosphates on the world commodities exchange is pretty near an all-time high.' She winked. 'I think somebody up there loves you, don't you?'

'Um,' said the Mayor. He could feel a sort of prickly itch in the small of his back. 'Mineral-rich, you said?'

'Very much so,' Jane replied confidently. 'Pump out the water and carry it away and sell it, simple as that. I suggest you put it out to commercial tender.' She stood up and straightened her skirt. 'Then you use the proceeds to rebuild the city, you see. And, well, I don't have to tell a man of your obvious intelligence and sensitivity what a wonderful opportunity this'll be to get on with all those wonderful slum clearance and highway improvement projects you've been talking about all these years. You know, show the voters that you really are a man of your word, that sort of thing. But I expect,' she added sweetly, 'I can leave all the details to you.'

On her way out, her high heels pecking at the surface of the water as she went, she met the charge-hand. He had a full bucket of water in each hand, and was trudging slowly east.

'You needn't bother with all that now,' she said brightly. 'I've sorted it. We'd better be going.'

'How d'you mean, sorted it?' demanded the charge-hand. 'I mean, who's going to clear up the mess?'

A crocodile the size of a middling to large park bench waddled towards them, jaws agape. Jane tossed it a peppermint and it retreated, coughing. 'The mortals,' she replied. 'Coming?'

The charge-hand frowned. 'Will they want paying?' he said. 'Because there's not much left in petty cash after we bought a new handle for the mop, and you can't go using the cocoa money, the lads won't stand for it.'

'They'll do it for free,' Jane replied. 'Now hurry up and get rid of those buckets, and then we'd better nip over to Egypt.'

The charge-hand rubbed his chin. He didn't want to be caught out a second time.

'That's Egypt in Africa, right?' he said.

'More or less,' Jane replied. 'They don't know it yet, but they're just about to discover that this is a heaven-sent opportunity to build hydro-electric plants without the water getting in the way. All right?'

The charge-hand furrowed his eyebrows, and then he caught sight of the badge on Jane's lapel. It was very bright and singularly blue.

'Yeah,' he said, relieved, 'right. That's a pretty good idea, that is.'

'Ingenious,' Ganger said, leaning forward and switching off the monitor. 'Don't you think?'

'Novel, certainly,' Staff replied. He put the tips of his fingers together and frowned.

'Not all that novel,' Ganger replied. 'It's been done before. Basically, it's just persuading the mortals to turn our mistakes to their advantage. And you've got to admit, it's worked all right in the past. Think,' he added with an involuntary grin, 'of manna.'

In spite of himself, Staff grinned too. The manna story was an old chestnut in Departmental circles; the story of how a containerised shipment of manna had got spilt all over the Sinai desert once upon a time, just as a party of mortals came

67

wandering along and walked right into it. The fortunate part of it was that, although the Public Servants knew precisely what manna was (hence the Departmental expressions 'dropping someone right in the manna' and 'up manna creek without a paddle'), the mortals had never come across the stuff before and were quite remarkably taken with it.

'Maybe you're right,' Staff said. 'I'm not denying the girl has –' He paused while the librarians of his mind shuffled their card-indices furiously, '– talent, but that's not what I'm mainly concerned about. There's a lot of people out there with talent, some of them,' he admitted, 'mortals . . .'

'Most of them,' Ganger interrupted softly. Staff didn't contradict him.

'On the other hand,' he went on, 'talent's no use if using it is counterproductive. If it, well, rocks the boat.'

Ganger frowned. 'It strikes me,' he said, 'that nobody notices very much if you rock the boat when it's sinking rapidly anyway.'

'Don't you believe it,' Staff replied sharply. 'I read a book once,' he added, and Ganger noticed with surprise that his voice had dropped rather low, until it was scraping its hubcaps on furtiveness. '*Social Interaction In The Workplace*, it was called. There was a rule in it.'

'Get away.'

Staff scowled. 'Don't be so bloody funny,' he hissed. 'It's a prohibited book, I'll have you know.'

Ganger nodded. 'I'm sorry,' he said, 'I was forgetting where I was. Where I used to work, remember, all we're allowed is prohibited books. I remember the scandal once when someone smuggled in a copy of *The Swiss Family Robinson*. They were fighting like maniacs to get hold of it . . .'

Staff blinked and paused until he could remember where he had got to. 'Anyway,' he said, 'this rule said that in order to preserve the natural equilibrium within an enclosed workplace, the pressure of internal paranoia rises to counterbalance the level of external pressure from without. It's a well-known phenomenon, apparently.'

'I think I get you,' Ganger replied, stroking his chin. 'Sort of, if you can't stand the heat, knife the chef.'

Staff raised an eyebrow. 'You could say that,' he replied. 'What I'm getting at is, the worse things get, the more touchy and difficult the high-ups are going to be about anybody trying anything that isn't, well – you know, done.'

'Not a lot *is* done around here these days,' Ganger couldn't help replying. 'Specially maintenance. But I think I can see what you're getting at. This is one sinking ship where the rats are staying put and everyone else is leaving, yes?'

Staff fiddled with his propelling pencil, breaking the lead. 'Indeed,' he said.

'So we've got to be careful, in other words?'

'Yes.'

'Right.' Ganger stood up and put his hands in the side pockets of his jacket, his thumbs remaining outside. 'So we'll be careful. No problem. What'll we try her out on next?'

Rocco Consanguinetti was one of those people who do one thing at a time, and do it well. At the moment, he was making a pizza, and he was concentrating. The result was obvious; it was the sort of pizza that would get hung in the Metropolitan Museum of Art one of these days if some thoughtless idiot didn't eat it first.

'Rocco, for Christ's sake.' His sister Rosa's head snaked round the swing door and scowled at him. 'There's people chewing the tablecloths out there. How long does it take to make a pizza?'

'It takes as long as it takes,' Rocco replied without looking up. He had a feeling that he had used one olive too many, and Rocco felt about waste the way Nature feels about vacuums. 'Give them some more bread or something.'

Rosa scowled at him. 'Bread costs money, Rocco,' she replied. 'Also, if hungry people stuff themselves full of bread, they make do with *antipasti*, they don't want the main course as well. They certainly don't order ice-cream to follow. We owe the bank money, Rocco. Work faster.'

But her brother merely set his jaw and studied the pizza from another angle. He had been wrong. The tenth olive was indispensable.

'Finished?'

'No.'

'Oh, for . . .' Rosa retracted her head, and Rocco started to lay the pepperoni; slowly, one slice at a time. A Double Roman isn't built in a day.

The jaw he had set was rather a remarkable one. It projected. It had magnitude. You would feel comfortable about mooring a new and expensive yacht to it if you wanted to be sure it would still be there when you came back from the Casino. It was, in fact, the Hapsburg jaw, as worn by Charles V, in full and exuberant flower; and Rocco, completely unknown to himself or anyone else, was, and had been for some years now, the Holy Roman Emperor. His election had been perfectly valid, and he had even been properly and correctly crowned and anointed – under anaesthetic, admittedly, while he was under the impression that he was having his teeth capped.

As the saying goes: just because a river goes underground doesn't mean it stops flowing.

It is, after all, essential that there be an Emperor: without him, absolutely nothing at all could be done. As the very title suggests, the post represents the fusion of temporal and celestial authority, and the Emperor himself is the spark-plug who transmits the divine fire to the profane cylinder of humanity. His assent (albeit given in his name by his agents under the authority of an eleven-hundred-year-old power of attorney, mistakenly signed by Charlemagne, who thought he was giving someone his autograph) is a prerequisite for the ratification of any statute, human or superhuman. But centuries of experience have taught the College of Electors that if the Emperor ever gets to realise what he actually is, he tends to interfere, usually with tedious results. On a need-to-know basis, therefore, it is generally held that His Majesty doesn't.

Apart from his virtually undiluted Hapsburg blood, Rocco VI was chosen because of his wisdom, his tolerance, his broad grasp of current affairs and because the present College of Electors (who are also the Emperor's trusted advisers and agents) like to do business over working lunches. A really great Emperor, they argue, ought to know how to handle anchovies.

The agenda for today's cabinet was short, even shorter than usual.

'To start,' said the Lord High Cardinal, 'I'll have the minestrone. Phil, you're having the *insalata di mare Adriatica*, Tony's plumped for the fish soup, and Mario's going to try the artichokes. They are fresh today, aren't they, Rosa?'

'They're always fresh,' replied the Emperor's sister. 'How many years have you guys been coming in here, anyway? You ever know the artichokes not to be fresh?'

The Lord High Cardinal assured her that he was only kidding. 'To follow,' he went on, 'I'm having the Sardinian veal, plus two sole. Mario, do you want the Messina chicken or the veal?'

'I'll have the veal,' confirmed the County Palatine. 'Chicken I can get at home.'

When they had all finished eating and drunk their coffee and picked their teeth with the proper wooden toothpicks you got at Rocco's instead of those damned plastic ones they have everywhere these days, the cabinet turned to the last item on the agenda. It was Mario's turn.

'Any other business?' he asked.

The Lord High Cardinal looked at his watch. 'If there is,' he said, 'it'll have to be adjourned till next time, because the game starts in half an hour and I need to go to the drugstore first. Next Tuesday?'

The other Electors confirmed that Tuesday would be fine. Then, in accordance with ancestral tradition, the Imperial Treasurer took four toothpicks from the glass and broke one, and they drew lots to see which of them was going to sign the bill.

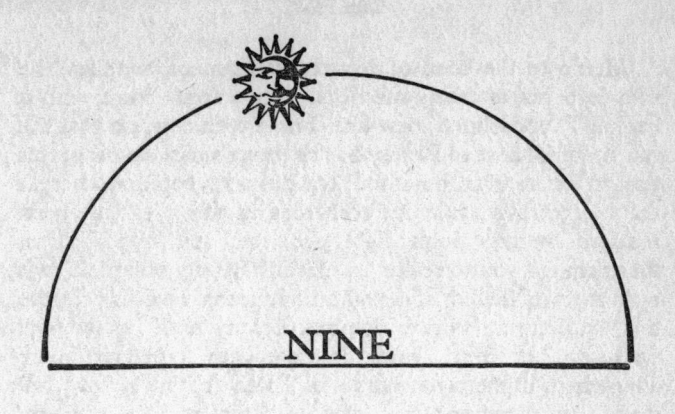

NINE

'Thank you,' said Staff, cautiously. 'That's very, um . . .'

Clerical gave him a slightly distant smile and returned to her desk, leaving him with rather mixed emotions. On the one hand, it was touching to think that she had remembered his birthday; on the other hand, it was profoundly tiresome that she had chosen a present more than usually unidentifiable. If he assumed it was an executive paperweight and left it lying on his desk, it would most probably turn out to be a labour-saving kitchen device and its continued presence in the office would cause immortal offence. If, however, he took it home and put it in the big box in the cupboard under the stairs, it would undoubtedly turn out to be an executive paperweight, and he'd end up having to make his own coffee every morning for the next two thousand years. Difficult.

'Many happy returns, Skip.' It was Denzil, from the post room, with a palpably bottle-like shape suffused in brown paper. Staff smiled warmly. He didn't drink, but at least he knew what the present was and could guess approximately how much it had cost. It was the sort of present the authors of *Social Interaction In The Workplace* heartily recommended. He could give it, he decided, to the window-cleaner for Solstice.

'Memo to the head of department, general supplies,' he said into his dictating-machine. 'Re, colon, Truth with a capital T, underlined, new line. I note with concern that the raw material cost of Beauty has risen yet again, comma, this time in excess of six point four two per cent, comma, whereas the budget allocation for resources in this area has been reduced by two point eight per cent, full stop. I must therefore ask you to revise the existing Beauty oblique Truth ratio as from the first of next month full stop. I would propose that until future notice, comma, Beauty shall be sixty-six point six per cent Truth, comma, with a proportionate adjustment in the inverse ratio for Truth oblique Beauty, full stop. New paragraph, row of dots. Chief of Staff etcetera. Thank you. Tape ends.'

He put the tape in the tray for Clerical to collect and sighed. Everyone was going to blame him, and it really wasn't his fault. Never mind, it couldn't be helped. Nothing can be helped, ever. He shuffled about in his in-tray, looking vainly for something he felt he could manage to cope with.

'Hi.'

He looked up, and saw Ganger, in his usual stance, half-in and half-out of the doorway.

'Happy birthday,' Ganger said. 'I got you something. Quite fun.'

He threw a small parcel through the air. Staff caught it and, feeling rather self-conscious, unwrapped it.

'Thank you,' he said, after a long pause for inspection. 'It's really, er.'

Ganger smiled. 'There's a leaflet inside the box,' he said, 'which explains what it is.'

'Ah.'

He found the little piece of paper and unfolded it. BLANK PAPAL BULL, it read. FOR YOU TO EXCOMMUNICATE THE PERSON OF YOUR CHOICE. There followed two columns of instructions in small print.

'The receipt's in there too,' Ganger said. 'If you don't like it, you can change it. What's the plan?'

'Ah yes,' said Staff, putting the box carefully away in his top desk drawer. 'I've been thinking about that.'

'Me too,' Ganger said.

'What I'd decided,' Staff went on, raising his voice slightly, 'is something a little bit less risky this time, something more straightforwardly administrative. I mean, we don't want to put her off by just giving her crises to sort out, do we?'

'All right,' Ganger said, sitting on the corner of the desk and picking up the Executive Present. 'What had you in mind? Hey, a mate of mine's got one of these. They're very good if you can get them properly tuned in.'

'Yes,' Staff replied firmly. 'I was thinking of Records.'

Ganger gave him a look. 'Oh come on,' was all he said. The rest could easily be implied from context.

'Yes, I know,' said Staff. 'But we don't want to give her the wrong impression, do we? I mean, seventy per cent of what we do is just plain, unexciting clerical work; sorting papers, answering queries, filing, ordering, that sort of thing . . .'

He stopped. There was something extremely inscrutable about Ganger's usually mobile face. 'Maybe you're right, though,' said Staff quickly. 'We can put her on that later. How about a tour of duty on Earthquakes?'

Ganger shook his head. 'No,' he said, *'you're* right. Absolutely. No, don't bother to get up, I'll deal with it. I'll let her know straight away.'

He stood up, pressed a switch on the side of the present that Staff had completely overlooked, and left the office. As he closed the door, a few wafer-thin rose-petals formed spontaneously in mid-air and drifted floorwards. When they touched the carpet, they melted like snowflakes.

'Records,' said Staff aloud. 'Records.'

A small red light suddenly appeared on the side of the present, then it went out again. Staff spent the next quarter of an hour staring at it and then covered it up with an office circular.

'Records,' he said a third time. '*Records*. Beats me.'

'It's very simple when you get used to it,' said Norman, the supervisor. 'Once you've been here a few months, you'll find the work is pretty straightforward.'

Jane nodded. First impressions, she knew, can be deceptive, but it looked to her as if straightforward was putting it mildly. As far as she could judge, it consisted of picking the envelopes out of the trolley, reading the number stamped on the side, taking the envelope to the appropriate shelf and leaving it there. She could, she decided, do it in her sleep; in fact, that would probably be the best way to approach it.

'If you need any help,' Norman was saying, 'just ask.'

Thanks, said Jane to herself under her breath; the sort of help I'm going to need here is not the sort you're likely to be able to supply. She smiled, and headed for the trolley.

On her seventeenth visit to the shelves, she collided gently with a bespectacled male person, who fell against a shelf, dislodging its contents.

'Sorry,' she said.

'Don't worry about it,' said the person. 'These things tend to happen in an infinite universe. By the way, you're standing on my foot.'

'Oh. Sorry.'

'Not at all. Thank you, that's *much* better. Do please continue with what you were doing while I laboriously put all this lot back.' He scowled at her, and stooped wearily down.

'Please,' said Jane through stiff lips. 'Let me help you.'

The person gave her a prickly smile. 'How excessively kind of you,' he said. 'Gosh, how original of you! For years now, I've been putting them in numerical order, but you're quite right. Think what an exciting challenge it'll be for the researchers if they're all jumbled up together like that.'

Jane drew in a half-lungful of breath and started again, while the person looked at her.

'You're mortal, aren't you?' he observed.

'Yes,' Jane replied. She stood on tiptoe to replace 26576768/766543765/2308J/3C.

'Do pardon my saying this,' the person said, 'but wouldn't you perhaps find it rather more – conducive, let's say – back on Earth with all the other, er, people? I understand,' he added, 'that there's plenty of room for everyone down there. Up here, on the other hand, it's a touch on the cramped side, if you're not used to looking where you're going.'

For a moment Jane stood with her mouth open; then it occurred to her that she should have prepared herself for this sort of thing. Since she hadn't, she determined to ignore it.

'Not really,' she replied, therefore. 'In fact, it's pretty much the same up here as down there I find. Would you be very sweet and put this one back up on the top shelf for me? I can't quite reach.'

The person glowered at her, and then complied. 'It's been a funny old day so far,' he observed, groaning as he stretched. 'I overslept, arrived here late, found that someone had moved my trolley, forgot my sandwiches, slipped on the polished floor and bruised my knee, and now I've been knocked to the ground and trampled underfoot by a mortal, and it's still only ten-thirty.'

Jane allowed herself a smile. 'That's unusual here, is it? Sounds like an ordinary day where I come from.'

The person raised a corner of his mouth. If hyaenas are dogs, it was a smile. 'So I'd gathered,' he replied. 'In fact, I understand you people have a special word for it. Life, or something like that.'

'Fancy you knowing,' Jane replied. 'Thank you so much for your help.'

At a quarter past eleven there was a coffee break. To her disgust, Jane found that Departmental coffee tasted very much like the coffee she was used to at home, except that it had even more chicory in it. Her back hurt and her mind had got pins and needles in it for want of activity. For the first time ever she began to wonder whether data inputting at Burridge's had been quite as horrible as she'd thought.

'My word,' said the person, suddenly appearing behind her shoulder as she drained her coffee down to the silt. 'What a lot you've managed to get done.'

In spite of herself, Jane felt pleased. She wanted to say, 'Of course I have; I'm a mortal, after all,' or something equally inflammatory, but she very sensibly didn't. Instead she made vague and quiet thanking noises.

'Beats me how you can do it so fast,' the person went on, 'ordering them, stacking them, *and* writing the numbers up in the Register.'

Inside Jane's heart, something small but not entirely trivial broke. 'What Register?' she asked.

The person smiled, properly this time. 'The Master File Register,' he replied. 'Didn't they tell you about it? You write down the number of the file, and what shelf it's on, and under which section of the shelf, and other things like that. Otherwise, you see, the researchers won't have the faintest idea . . .'

'Thank you,' said Jane. 'I see. Nobody did mention it, actually, but I suppose I should have worked it out for myself.' She put her cup down on its saucer. 'I suppose I'd better go back and do that, hadn't I?'

'That would be a splendid idea,' the person agreed. 'Oh, by the way. Aren't we forgetting something?'

Jane stopped still and turned her head slowly. 'Are we?' she said. 'Sorry, we didn't mean to.'

'Thirty zlotys for the coffee,' said the person sweetly. 'We always put the money in that tin on the shelf there. It helps,' he added, 'to avoid bad feeling and disruptive outbursts of temper.'

Jane sighed. 'That's a nuisance,' she said. 'You see, I've only got terrestrial money. I don't suppose they accept that here, do they?'

The person shook his head. 'Not really,' he said. 'I mean, yes, it's the thought that counts, but it doesn't actually buy a new catering-size tin when the present one runs out. Let me,' he added unpleasantly, 'lend you thirty zlotys until you get paid.'

'Thank you.'

'Don't mention it.'

The person, having watched carefully while she put the money in the tin, walked away, leaving her to scream silently in peace and quiet. Then she found Norman and asked him to explain properly about the Register.

There was a crash. The four intruders stopped dead in their tracks, or at least they tried to. Alcohol, however, tends to enhance momentum. They fell over each other. In the far distance a dog barked, then fell silent.

'Mind where you're putting your bloody feet next time,' Darren hissed. 'There's guard dogs about. I heard one.'

'Bollocks,' Jason hissed back. 'Haven't had dogs here for years. Cutbacks. Didn't you know?'

Darren shrugged and fumbled in his pocket for the key to the hangar which he'd lifted off the hook four hours earlier. He was still worrying about the possibility of dogs, but he wasn't going to let his mates see he was worried. He had his cloud credibility to think about.

The lock clicked and he pushed hard on the door. As it rolled back a single piercing ray of light speared out into the blackness. Jason hurriedly threw himself against the crack.

'You prat,' he snarled. 'All that bullshit about dogs and then you nearly let the light show. What a *wally*!'

The four adventurers squeezed through the crack and then drew the door to behind them.

Inside the hangar it was, of course, as bright as day; in fact, very considerably brighter. For a moment they all stood dumbfounded by the sight; even Darren, who worked in the shed during the day, had never been this close to the thing before. It was enough to fry your brains.

Dave was the first to break the silence, and he did it with a nervous giggle.

'Oh come off it,' he said. 'We're *never* going to be able to fly this thing.'

It was intended merely as an observation, but somehow it got badly mutated on its way out past the gate of Dave's teeth, and by the time it reached Jason's ears it was a challenge with a strong superficial likeness to a taunt.

'You reckon,' Jason said. 'Watch this, then.'

'I didn't mean . . .' Dave started to say, but his friend was already halfway up the ladder towards the cockpit. There was nothing for it but to follow.

'I'm beginning not to like this,' observed a voice from the foot of the ladder. 'Why don't we just forget about it and do something else? We could go and smash up a few phone boxes or something instead.'

'You've lost your bottle,' Jason sneered. 'You haven't got the nuts, have you?'

'No,' replied Adrian, with a remarkable note of sobriety in his voice. 'Not for this I haven't, anyway.'

Dave and Darren paused on the ladder because this was somewhat disturbing. It was commonplace in their social circle that Adrian played the complete head-case, afraid of nothing. His favourite way of letting off steam, it was widely rumoured, was spray-painting graffiti on the sides of moving asteroids. If Adrian didn't fancy it, the chances were that there was an element of risk.

'Stuff you, then.' Jason's voice drifted down from the top of the ladder, but it sounded far away and hollow. He had clearly found out how to get into the cockpit. 'Hey, those morons left it unlocked. What a load of pillocks, huh?'

'Nobody gives a toss,' Dave agreed, but his thoughts were elsewhere. Maybe this wasn't such a good idea, after all. It really was very big, very big indeed.

'Gotcha!' There was triumph in Jason's voice, and the other three exchanged glances. 'You coming, Ade, or not?'

Adrian paused for a moment; then he shrugged and shinned quickly up the ladder. He wasn't afraid any more –

it had gone past that stage – and he was very curious to find out what was going to happen. 'Coming,' he said.

'Only if you're not going to bottle out,' Jason shouted back. "Cos if you suddenly get scared, I'm not stopping, right?'

'Get stuffed,' Adrian replied, and from his tone of voice the others could tell that he was himself again: the same Adrian who thought nothing of playing Chicken on the edge of Time. 'We'll see who shits himself first, my son.'

Jason grinned. He was sitting in the pilot's seat, trying to guess which controls did which. He hadn't, he realised, the faintest idea.

'Here,' he said. 'How do you make this thing go?'

Adrian shrugged. 'I dunno,' he said, and leaned forward. 'Let's try this.' He sprawled his hand out into a pink fan and pressed as many buttons as he could.

'Don't do that, you luna . . .' Dave started to scream, then his mouth went dry and his tongue became inextricably welded to his palate. The hangar had suddenly become filled with the most agonising light, and all around them they could feel the pulsing of a planet-sized engine.

'Switch it off, for fuck's sake!' Dave yelled, but nobody moved. They were all paralysed with terror, and besides, it was painfully apparent that it was too late now. The thing was beginning to move.

Slowly at first; then, as it built up momentum slipping down the ramp, very fast, then faster and faster still. As if in a dream, Dave noticed that the hangar doors were firmly shut. But the chances were, he felt, that that wasn't going to make much difference. In fact, it was extremely doubtful whether anything was ever going to make any difference ever again.

The four joy-riders had just enough self-possession left to hurl themselves to the floor of the cockpit as the giant machine ploughed through the diamond-and-titanium doors of the hangar like a bullet through a bubble, left the ramp, hung for an everlasting fraction of a second in mid-air, and then began to drop like a very large stone. Then the engines fired.

It is at such moments that essential character, distilled and compressed, is most easily observed. Dave and Darren both howled 'Shiiiiiiiiiiiiit!' and tried to squash themselves into the same small space under the computer console. Jason sat flattened against the back of the pilot's chair, his face apparently splattered across the front of his head in an expression of sheer horror that would be worth millions to an ambitious film producer. Adrian grabbed wildly for the joystick, and pulled.

The sun checked itself, seemed to hesitate, and then lifted.

The sun rose.

'Where is it now?' Staff demanded.

There was silence at the other end of the wire.

'Well?'

'Well,' said the voice, and Staff could feel the effort of self-control running up through the wire. 'You know that sort of lacy constellation just under the armpit of Sagittarius? Like an ammonite with woodworm, I always think. It's out there.' A pause. 'Somewhere.'

Staff let the hand with the phone in it wilt. Disasters he could cope with – anyone whose days are spent in any form of high-level administration gets withdrawal symptoms without at least one disaster before breakfast – but there are limits. His lips went through the motions of repeating the word Somewhere, but his larynx wanted no part of it.

'You still there, Chief?' said the voice.

He put the phone back by his ear. 'Yes,' he said. 'Look, I know this is a damn silly question, but I owe it to myself to ask. Is there any chance whatsoever of getting it back?'

'None, Chief. Sorry.'

Staff winced like a salted slug. 'Right. Fine. Thanks for letting me know.'

The line crackled a bit. 'So what do we do now, Chief?' said the voice nervously.

Staff sighed. 'Heaven only knows,' he said, and put the phone down.

He was, of course, lying.

Jason was worried.

He had good reason to be. He was a long way from home, his companions had blacked out – for good, by the looks of it – the fuel gauge was deep into the red bit on the far left-hand side of the dial, and there was a funny rattling noise coming from under the bonnet. The only good thing about running out of fuel, as far as he could see, was that when it happened, then the bloody thing would slow down and perhaps even stop. He had been trying to make it do that for some time.

The monotony of the view from the cockpit window didn't improve matters. It had been as black as two feet up a chimney for the last forty million light years, and that sort of thing can get to you once the effects of the beer start to wear off. To put the tin lid on it, he found that he'd run out of cigarettes.

And then he saw the light; just a tiny little pinprick, far away in the distance, but definitely light. For a few seconds he was elated, until he remembered that (a) light didn't neces-sarily connote safety or help, and (b) even if it did, he couldn't steer the damned thing towards it anyway.

He needn't have been concerned. The engine chose that moment to drain the last drop of fuel in the back-up reserve emergency tank, and the sun decelerated and started to drift. A few minutes later, the gravitational field of whatever that bright thing over there was started to have effect, and the whole contraption slowly turned and started to travel towards the light. Jammy.

The light was a star. The star had a planet; you could see it from light years away. It was big and bright, and blue with the most incredible oceans Jason had ever seen. It was, he realised with a leap of the heart, inhabited. And he was headed straight for it, at a nice slow drift. He'd have called it Destiny if it wasn't for the fact that he'd worked there for six months and knew how it really worked; so he called it bloody good luck instead.

Soon, much sooner than he had imagined, he was close enough to see the two wide belts of golden asteroids that encircled the planet, and a few miniscule sparkles of flashing metal which could only be space stations. He was nearly there.

'Help!' he screamed. It was, he knew in his heart, a bit early to expect anyone to hear, but there was no harm in just warming up, so to speak. He also stood up in his seat and waved both his arms.

And then . . .

It was one of those moments when the soul dies: when all the lights go out and all that remains is the horrible feeling of having got it wrong. He shaded his eyes with his hand, hoping against all the probabilities that he was mistaken, but he wasn't.

They weren't space stations; they were parking meters, and he had no change of any sort whatsoever. Likewise, the things he had taken for a twofold belt of golden asteroids were something rather more prosaic but utterly unambiguous. They were double yellow lines. To ram the point home to the point of complete and utter superfluity, the planetary authorities had picked out the words

NO PARKING

in glowing red dwarves right across the azimuth.

'Fuck,' he said.

If it had been a smaller planet, of course, it would have had to orbit him rather than the other way round. As it was, there was nothing he could do except scream a lot and wave his fists about and, after a while, once the lack of food and the helium-rich atmosphere began to tell on him, he couldn't even do that.

When he had been there for a very long time, so long that

he could no longer quantify the time with any degree of accuracy whatsoever, he became aware of strange, immaterial figures wandering about the cockpit. They spoke in strange, distorted voices and had a disturbing tendency to walk right through him and out through the cockpit into the blackness outside. They ignored him completely, being apparently entirely engrossed in inexplicable conversations of their own which he was quite incapable of following beyond a few tantalising phrases.

There is no reason to believe that he isn't there to this day. Certainly, the inhabitants of the planet would have had no reason to disturb him, given that his timely arrival saved them the expense and trouble of launching a purpose-built satellite to bounce their afternoon soap-operas off. The fact that, by some strange quirk of optical distortion, Jason occasionally features in some of the episodes, probably adds to their overall enjoyment.

'Now then,' Staff said. 'Let's just pause there a moment, shall we, and recap for a minute. We have the following suggestions.'

It was an hour and seven minutes later, and the pale, taut faces round the boardroom table were uniformly blank. Nobody was in any hurry to say anything.

'First,' Staff continued, 'we have the proposal that we get the moon back down, spray it all over with luminous paint, bang it up there at sunrise, and hope nobody notices. Now, it strikes me that there are a number of potential difficulties with that idea.'

He proceeded to enumerate them. When he had finished, nobody spoke, and he took the silence as his cue to move on to the next suggestion.

'Next, we've got the proposal that we shove a big illuminated sign up in the sky saying *Normal Service Will Be Resumed As Soon As Possible*.' He breathed in, and then out again, with the air of someone making the most of it while he still could. 'Now I've got nothing against that, nothing at all, as far as it goes, but in the longer term . . .'

There was no need to go on. The heads nodded. Ways and Means, Staff noticed with a flicker of amusement, was already fast asleep; which, given the circumstances, must be a Pavlovian reaction to being in Committee.

'As for the idea,' he went on, 'that we run out an extension cable from the heart of the Great Cloud of Unknowing and try and rig up a set of floodlights as a temporary measure: I've got to admit that as far as I'm concerned it's the best one we've come across yet, but I still think we've got some way to go before we're actually there. I mean, logistically . . .'

There was a cough from the side of the table, and everyone looked round at a small but extremely – well, *normal*-looking figure standing there holding a large tray.

'Excuse me,' said Jane. 'You ordered coffee.'

She had been working late, trying to sort out the mess she'd made earlier on in the day, and when the Committee came stumbling in to use the boardroom, she had been told, as the only female life-form in sight, to get coffee for twelve. Being female, she had managed it.

Staff smiled bleakly. 'Thanks,' he said. 'Just put it down there, we'll help ourselves. Now then . . .'

'Excuse me,' said Jane again. Everyone looked at her.

'Sorry to butt in,' she went on, 'but I couldn't help overhearing, and I was just wondering if you'd considered . . .?'

Finance and General Purposes sat upright, looking like a stick of anthropormorphic dynamite, but Staff caught his eye and he subsided.

'Well?' he said.

'Only,' Jane said, in a small but clear voice, which re-minded Staff of something vaguely familiar, something he seemed to remember from a very long time ago. What was it? Ah yes, he suddenly remembered: it was the sound of somebody being sensible. 'Maybe you're approaching this from the wrong direction, if you see what I mean. I know it's really nothing to do with me,' she went on, 'but perhaps . . .'

There were signs of unrest from around the table. Either this person – this *mortal* – was going to offend their ears with a stream of idiotic and untimely nonsense, which would be bad enough; or else she was going to make an intelligent suggestion. For her part, Jane was aware of a squashed feeling, as if she was an over-boiled potato under a steamroller. As was her habit when she felt nervous, she smiled.

'It just occurred to me,' she said, 'and I hope you don't mind me saying this, but if you're trying to find some way of bodging up some sort of substitute thing so that nobody'll notice, I don't really think you're going to have much luck. No,' she said, shaking her head. 'What I reckon you need is a diversion: you know, something to take people's attention off the sun so that they wouldn't notice even if there was nothing there at all.'

There was quiet in the boardroom, compared to which the inside of the average tomb would sound like Rome in the rush hour. Just as the silence was about to solidify and start dripping down the walls, Finance and General Purposes shook off his air of stunned torpor, fitted a less than pleasant expression to his face and cleared his throat.

'Very good,' he said. 'And what would you suggest?'

'Well . . .' Jane said.

In the grey desolation of the small hours of the interstellar morning, the big abandoned lot, out round the back of the Great Cloud of Unknowing, hummed to the roar of an infinity of different kinds of power tools, variations on the scream of metal cutting into metal, instructions and swear words. The activity was indescribable; usually movement is perceptible because it is seen against a background of rest, but here there was no background.

Everyone – the whole supernatural host, everyone – was on overtime.

There were two main groups. The smaller group, comprising about a sixth of the whole, was cutting an enormous disc out of a galaxy-sized sheet of the first quality sixteen-gauge celestium carbonate, while an army of gantries stood by to install a million miles of electric flex and twelve billion lightbulbs. A sub-section of the group was fitting a huge black velvet bag over the moon and rigging it up with a tow-hook. In the distance, a fleet of astro-freighters were bringing home a hastily gathered harvest of small and relatively unimportant stars which were going to be used for fuel to run the generators.

The other group was five times larger and infinitely busier. They were loading the boots of 10^{23} cars with 10^{74} cardboard boxes.

Staff, watching the proceedings from a point of vantage on the roof of the Fate Office, glanced down at his watch and bit his lip. Three hours to go. Either this was going to work, or else he was going to look the biggest prawn in the entire universe of time and space.

'All right,' he muttered into his walkie-talkie. 'Tell Phase One to move out.'

The empty vacuum of the back lot was suddenly stiff with the tortured vibration of sound-waves as the buzz-saws jarred through the last few miles of celestium carbonate. The disc leaned horribly and fell free on to the supporting cat's cradle of titanium cable. There was a dazzling flash of welding gear as the electricians set to. The engines of the moon began to hum as her crew warmed her up for her unscheduled flight.

'Phase One,' said the walkie-talkie. 'Ready, and rolling.'

On a signal from the control tower all the 10^{23} cars started their engines at once. Trying to encapsulate the effect of so much noise in mere adjectives would be like trying to squidge the sea down into an egg-cup; suffice to say, it was *loud*. The column began to roll.

'This had better work,' Staff growled, as the structure of the cosmos braced itself to withstand the vibration of so many humming engines. 'Because otherwise . . .'

'Oh, I expect it'll be all right,' Jane replied, pouring boiling water from her thermos on to a teabag. 'I mean, everyone was always saying how the old one was clapped out and on its last rays anyway, and wouldn't it be a simply splendid idea to get a new one, except it would cost too much and take too long to build. I expect the idea was to save up Esso tokens for the next sixty thousand years and finance the refitting programme that way.' She sighed. 'It really only goes to prove that you can get things done around here, just so long as it's an absolute emergency, and they think you're doing whatever it is you're doing for a totally different reason. Funny, don't you think, the lengths you have to go to?'

The new model sun, its lights blazing, was lowered from its scaffolding on to an enormous trailer, while the tow-rope was lowered into position and made fast to the back bumper of the moon. Painfully slowly, complaining every step of the way at the unaccustomed weight, the moon began to taxi down the strip.

'Here goes,' said Jane. 'Fingers crossed.'

The details of the Great Diversion are so well known and form the basis of so many religions that it would be superfluous to recount them here. All that needs to be mentioned for our purposes is that when humanity awoke in the dim light of a weak, flickering 60-watt dawn, it didn't notice anything funny about the lighting. Everybody's attention was riveted to the towering letters of fire, pinned to the back of a rainbow that arched across the firmament and announced

BIGGEST EVER CAR BOOT SALE NOW ON!!

to all mortals, creatures of a day, buyers on impulse, across the face of the globe. No sooner had their brains digested the message than the encircling horizon glared yellow in the indeterminate grey light with the glow of innumerable courtesy lights as 10^{23} car boots opened as one car boot, and mankind, lifting its eyes heavenwards, saw that it was true. As one leading theologian is reported to have remarked, as a way of proclaiming a New Covenant, it beat rainbows into a cocked hat.

Those who comment on such things in the calm seclusion of history point out that, as diversionary tactics go, the Great Diversion was a pretty neat piece of thinking. Not only was mankind's attention distracted long enough for the workshops of heaven to cast, found, finish and launch a brand new, all-alloy sun with teflon bumpers and an ABS braking system; the proceeds of the sale were enough to pay for the thing with enough left over to repaint the outside of the hangar and fit a proper padlock on the door, and the warehouses of General Supply were purged of twenty thousand years' worth of accumulated junk; which in turn provided Norman and his staff in Records with the storage space they needed to put in place a new and vastly more efficient data storage and retrieval system. In fact, some commentators say, bearing in mind the circumstances of the event, and the person whose idea the whole thing was, there's a good case for saying that that was in fact the underlying point of the whole exercise.

'Well?' Bjorn repeated. Old Gustavus looked sheepish and evaded his eye. He muttered something about a once in a lifetime bargain.

Bjorn grinned. 'Yeah,' he said. 'Only you don't know what it is.'

'Um.'

'And it doesn't work.'

'Um.'

'And bits keep coming off in your hand every time you pick it up.'

'It was a *bargain*,' Gustav retorted, stung. 'Twenty-four ninety-nine. And I beat him down from thirty-five.'

'I know what it is.'

'And it was the last one he had left,' Gustav continued. 'In fact, he said he was saving it for someone, but ... You do?'

'Yes,' Bjorn replied, and yawned. 'You've been done,' he added.

Gustav scowled. Then he noticed a mark on the back of the casing, took out his handkerchief, spat neatly on a corner and rubbed the spot until it was clean again. 'Nonsense,' he said. 'It was reduced. Slight exterior damage, he told me, doesn't affect the working in the least ...'

'Right,' Bjorn said, and bit the top off another bottle. 'And I can see how, you being a woodcutter, it's really essential for you to have a temporal distortion refractor that you know is going to work. Yup,' he added, with a positive nod of his head, 'I guess you're right, at that.'

Gustav blinked. 'I'm sorry?' he said.

'Temporal distortion refractor,' Bjorn repeated carelessly. 'Used to use them a lot when I was on the Time gangs. They're really good for flattening out time warps. Of course,' he added as an afterthought, 'that's not a whole one, that's just the mainframe stabiliser unit. Still, if you can get it to work, maybe the next car boot sale you go to, you'll find the rest of the gear – you know, the rocker box, the induction manifold, all that stuff – and then you'll be in business. And you'll need the batteries too, of course.'

He grinned again and drank some beer while his neighbour sat and stared at his purchase for a while. In the distance could be heard the soothing coo of a woodpigeon, sleepy in the warmth of a late summer evening.

'I think,' said Gustav firmly, 'I'll put a tablecloth over it and stand it in the corner by the log-basket. It'd look nice there, and I could use it to display my bowls trophies.'

'Yeah,' Bjorn said. 'Or it'd make a great footstool.' He parked his boots on it, folded his arms behind his head and lay back.

'Did you go to the sale, neighbour?' Gustav enquired. Bjorn shook his head.

'Listen,' he said. 'Any old Departmental stuff I wanted, I

nicked before I packed the job in. It's all a load of crap anyway, most of it. All clapped out, and it was junk when it was new, as often as not. Buy it cheap and flog it to death, that's their motto. You take leap year, for instance.'

Gustav raised an eyebrow. 'Leap year?' he said.

'Yeah,' Bjorn replied. 'Leap year. Bloody typical, that is. I mean,' he went on, warming to his theme, 'suppose you were building a Seasons plant, you wouldn't cut corners and go around buying in second-hand tat from the breakers' yards, would you? No way. Stands to reason, you buy the real thing and then it's not going to break down and you don't have to go fixing it every five minutes when it gets out of sync. That's not the way they see it, of course, oh no. And that's why we've got leap year. You didn't think it was, like, deliberate, did you?'

'Um.'

Bjorn sniggered unkindly. 'No way,' he said. 'Main bearings completely shot, so a bloke I used to know on Maintenance told me once. Miracle the whole thing doesn't pack up on them. Serve them right if it did.'

He fell silent and lay on his back, scowling at his toes. A family of chipmunks scampered up and down the branch above his head, chirruping wildly. A dragonfly droned past, the sun flashing on its kaleidoscope wings.

'What a beautiful day,' Gustav remarked involuntarily. 'Really, neighbour Bjorn, it does my old heart good to see it. Can't you just –' He paused. He knew he was wasting his breath, but he couldn't help it. The infinite wonders of nature never failed to move him, even at his age. 'Can't you just *feel* the thirsty earth drinking in the life-giving warmth and the seeds bursting into life under the soil. Can't you just . . .'

'Yeah.' Bjorn was looking puzzled. 'Yeah,' he repeated, 'you've got a point there.' He frowned, sat up, absentmindedly swatted the dragonfly with the back of his hand, and stared thoughtfully at the sun for a very long time.

'Funny, that,' he said.

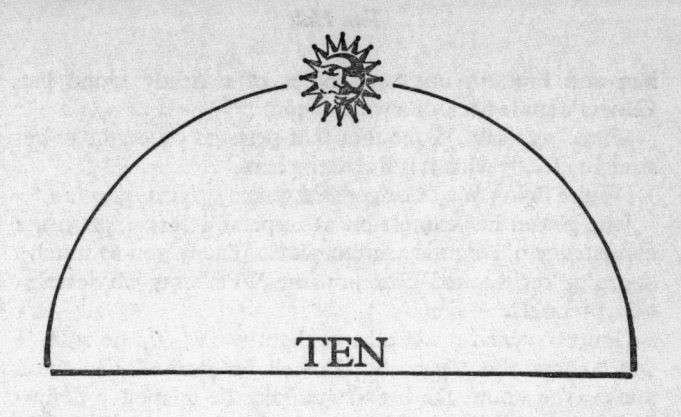

TEN

'Ah,' said Jane briskly, 'I was hoping I'd get a chance to have a word with you.'

Ganger's hand had been on the door handle. He froze; then he turned round and smiled.

'Sure,' he said. 'Look, just got to make a few quick calls, then . . .'

'It won't take a moment, I promise,' Jane replied grimly – you could have sharpened chisels on her tone of voice – so that Ganger subsided and seemed to lose about an inch in height.

'Fine,' he said. 'Come on in.'

Although she'd spent the last two hours waiting for Ganger outside his office, this was the first time she'd actually been inside it. She wasn't impressed. An office, her expression clearly said, so what? The fact that it has recording angels instead of dictaphones makes it different, not necessarily better. Ganger wilted a little more; if he'd had petals, some of them would have fallen off by now.

He perched, nevertheless, on the edge of the desk, and waved her to a chair. 'What's all this about then?' he asked.

'Just one or two things,' Jane replied. She dipped into her

bag and brought out two copies of a neatly typed list. Ganger's smile became a windscreen.

'First,' she said, 'I thought that perhaps we ought to get straight exactly what it is I'm doing here.'

'You're doing fine,' Ganger said quickly. 'Next question.'

Jane glazed her expression of respectful contempt to the consistency of ceramic armour plate. 'Thank you so much,' she said, 'but I asked *what*, not *how*. What's my job description, precisely?'

Ganger sucked his cheeks in slightly. 'We-ell,' he said, 'I don't know about you, but I'm all for flexibility in these things. You know, the broad outlook, the adaptable definition, the overall view . . .'

'Yes,' Jane said, 'I'm sure you are. It wouldn't do if we were all alike, would it?'

For a moment, Ganger's perennial smile had a lot of big sharp teeth in it which hadn't been there a moment ago; then he recovered himself. 'Fair enough,' he said. 'Well, I suppose we could say . . .'

'I thought Management Trainee,' Jane interrupted. 'Oh, by the way, you don't mind if I take a few notes, do you? It does so help when you're trying to remember what you said later on.'

Ganger's throat moved slightly, as if he were swallowing a small plum-stone. 'No,' he said, 'you go ahead, that's fine. Well, yes, I suppose Management Trainee covers it more or less, you know, in general terms, bearing in mind that . . .'

'Next,' Jane continued, 'I think it's time we had a little chat about salary, don't you?'

The upturned corners of Ganger's lips flickered briefly. 'Salary,' he repeated.

'That's right,' Jane said. 'I've been asking around, and . . .'

'I beg your pardon?'

'I've been asking around,' Jane said, with very slightly exaggerated clarity, 'and the general opinion seems to be . . .'

'You've been *asking* people what they *earn*?'

'That's right, and . . .'

'Just walking up to them and *asking*?'

'Exactly. Now . . .'

'And they've actually *told* you?'

'Yes,' said Jane. 'And the impression I get, and of course you'll correct me if I'm wrong, is that the going rate for junior management in this setup is twenty-five thousand kreuzers per annum. That seems reasonable enough, doesn't it?'

Ganger sat monolithically on the desk-top with his mouth open.

'Subject,' Jane went on quickly, 'to upwards review every six months, naturally. Now, the next thing I wanted to talk about . . .'

There was a noise from the back of Ganger's throat. 'Twen–' he croaked.

'I'm sorry?'

'Twenty-five thousand kreuzers,' Ganger said. 'My dear girl . . .'

It was unequivocally the wrong thing to say. To do him credit, Ganger realised this before the fatal words were more than a few inches out of his mouth, but by then it was too late. Before he could speak again, Jane's eyes filmed over with permafrost, and her lips set in an invisible line.

'Right,' Ganger said, in a very small voice. 'Yes, that's fine. I'll see to that straight away. Yes, absolutely. Now then, was there something else?'

'Yes,' Jane said. 'Please don't think I'm complaining, but it does seem a bit of a waste of my time to have to commute here from Wimbledon every morning. I have to change trains twice just to get to the stellaport, and then there's all that hanging about getting through Customs . . .'

'I'm sure we can do something about that,' Ganger said quickly. 'I could have a word with the guards, you know . . .'

'I was thinking,' Jane said, ignoring him completely, 'about a relocation allowance. Plus superterrestrial weighting, of course, because . . .'

She stopped speaking. Ganger had gone a very funny colour.

'Um,' he said. 'Look, I'm going to have to talk to some of my colleagues about that, because . . .'

'Alternatively,' Jane said, 'I gather there's going to be a staff flat falling vacant soon in the basement of the Weather building. I could have that, couldn't I?'

Ganger had agreed, enthusiastically, before he suddenly realised that he'd been outgambited. He opened his mouth to speak, and then subsided.

'Just a few more things,' Jane went on. 'Holidays, normal working hours, pension scheme, that sort of thing. We might as well clear them up now, while we're on the subject, don't you think?'

There was a long silence, and Jane could feel Ganger trying to prise a way into her mind, for all the world like a psychological double-glazing salesman. She put the chain firmly on the door of her subconscious and gave him a look.

'Yes,' he said quickly. 'Why not? I suppose,' he added, 'you had something in mind?'

'As it happens,' Jane replied pleasantly, 'yes. Now, then . . .'

'The work we do here,' said the director, 'is specialised. Very specialised.'

He pressed a button on the console, and the far wall of the enormous room flickered and became one huge screen. At first sight, while Jane's eyes were getting used to the brightness, it looked blank; then she realised that it was cross-hatched with millions of tiny fine lines, connecting hundreds of thousands of minute points of pink and blue light.

'Each little light,' the director went on, 'represents one of our clients – we like to call them clients, you know, because we feel that above all we strive to offer a personalised service.'

Jane thought of the name of the department – Office of the Director of Star-Crossed Lovers – and felt the urge to protest, but she didn't.

'Ah,' she said.

'The pink dots,' the director went on, 'are our lady clients, and the blue ones are of course the gentlemen. The lines connecting them are what we call the fate-lines. You'll see,' he went on, pointing at the screen with a lecturer's stick, 'that one tends to get a few patterns emerging on a fairly regular basis. Here,' he said, pointing, 'we've got a classic eternal triangle – lovely example, this; you'll notice that all three sides are precisely the same length. Quite rare, nowadays.'

'Really,' Jane said. 'Gosh.'

'Yes.' The director stood speechless for a moment, transported by the geometrical perfection of the thing. 'Remarkable specimen, all things considered. When they're that precise, you know, the links are quite extraordinarily strong. I'm writing a paper on them, as it happens,' he added diffidently. 'Just a little monograph, of course; but, I flatter myself, not without a certain intrinsic interest.'

'Absolutely,' Jane said.

The pointer moved to another sector of the screen. 'And this,' the director said, with a glow of pride, 'is a quite lovely example of an H/A Syndrome Major. Bless my soul, yes,' he added, leaning forward and squinting. 'Exquisite. Just look at those reciprocities!'

Jane coughed slightly. 'H/A?' she asked.

'It's short for Heloise/Abelard,' the director explained, 'although there's a tendency in some circles nowadays to call them R/J's.'

'Romeo/Juliets?' Jane hazarded.

'That's right,' said the director, with slight distaste. 'But really, that's a misnomer, because properly speaking the R/J Minor Syndrome is an entirely separate and self-contained sub-group, with its own characteristic matrix of tension. They're quite rare, unlike H/A's, which are quite common, in their natural state. Ah, now here's something I want you to see. Look.'

He directed Jane's attention to what looked to her like a small, perfectly symmetrical spider's web, with four or five separate points of pink and blue light flickering desolately in the meshes. Jane swallowed hard.

'Classic trifoliate misunderstanding,' the director said, 'with an impacted rebound just here, look. They're completely self-explanatory once you get the hang of them, of course.'

For a moment, Jane couldn't quite grasp what he meant; then, as she concentrated on the spider's web, it all became lucidly clear. The two brightest points of light were palpably the original lovers (sorry, *clients*), but the thread that had originally joined them was hanging loose, broken in two equilateral parts. Around each original client there was a separate web, into which another client had been drawn (the rebound, presumably), thereby creating another little separate vortex of misery for the jilted partner who should have been linked up to the reboundee. From a distance, the overall pattern was immediately apparent and infinitely depressing.

'The wonderful thing about this particular formation,' the director was saying, 'is that, where conditions are right, potentially the pattern is infinitely self-repeating. It just goes on and on and on, duplicating itself over and over again.' He uttered a small, weak academic laugh. 'We sometimes say it has a life of its own, but of course, that's not strictly true. Eventually, something happens to break the sequence and then the whole thing grinds to a halt.'

'Um.'

'Yes, it's a pity, in a way,' the director sighed. 'It's such an intellectually satisfying configuration, in my opinion. Not like this,' he added, pointing at another section of the screen. Jane looked across, and saw something which immediately put her in mind of what usually happened to expensive pairs of tights.

'This,' said the director, with a perceptible curl of the lip, 'is what we call an HBH Convergence.'

'Right,' Jane said. 'HBH standing for?'

'Heartbreak Hotel,' the director replied. 'It's not a very common phenomenon, although they're on the increase, I believe.'

Jane peered; and again, the thing became obvious. There was one big blue dot, she observed, and lots of little pink dots, which had torn away from their ordained pairings and followed the blue dot, like iron filings with a magnet. She frowned involuntarily; she knew the feeling. In fact, she had a shrewd notion she knew the blue dot concerned. Nigel something, used to work in Accounts . . .

'And over here,' the director said, 'we've got the mainframe computer, which we use to plot out the various conjunctions and configurations before we put them up on the screen. In the old days, of course, we used to have to do it all by hand. It made life terribly simple.'

'You mean,' Jane said, 'complicated, surely.'

'For the clients, I mean,' the director replied austerely. 'We just didn't have the capacity, you see; with the result that far and away the most common basic configuration, right up to about fifty years ago, was the absolutely basic BMG/BMG/HEA Simplex.'

'I'm sorry?'

'Boy Meets Girl/Boy Marries Girl/Happy Ever After,' the director translated. 'Millions of them, all dull and boring like that, simply because we didn't have the facilities. Now, of course, it's completely different, thanks to this little box of tricks here.' He patted the computer affectionately. 'This is only the third generation, of course. By the time we've got the sixth generation installed and operational, we're hoping to be able to extend our service to the entire mortal population.'

'Um.'

'And of course,' the director said, 'the marvellous thing is that the computer never sleeps. Which means that even now, when the Department has closed down for the night and everyone's gone home, the little black box is still awake, twitching a wire here, nudging a client into adultery there, on a twenty-four-hour, round-the-clock basis. Anyway,' he said, switching off the screen and putting the lid back on the console, 'that should give you an idea of the sort of work we do here. We're only a small department, but I think I can say we're a happy one.' He gazed self-containedly over Jane's head at a spot on the darkened wall. 'I always say,' he continued, 'that it's one of the few departments in the whole of the Service where you can point to an end result and lay your hand on your heart and say to yourself with pride, "I did that." Yes,' he added, 'I confidently expect that you're going to enjoy working here.'

'Yes,' said Jane grimly, 'I rather think I am.'

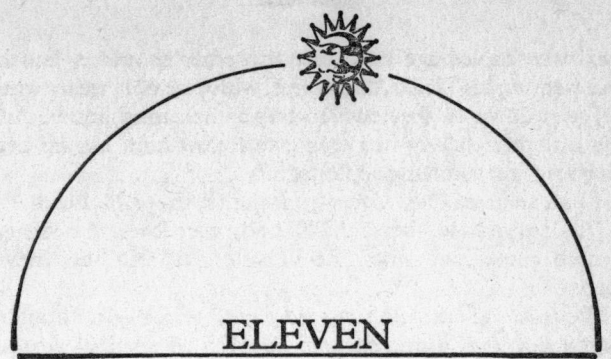

ELEVEN

The village cockerel woke up, glanced instinctively at the sky and did a double-take. Funny, said its genetic memory to its motor centres.

Little Helga (who was rapidly becoming Big Helga, but the inhabitants of the village affected not to notice) yawned, rubbed her eyes and set off to the dairy to do the early milking. She was just crossing the yard, pail on arm, when she stopped and stared. Then she dropped the pail and ran back to the house.

'Listen, everyone!' she called out. 'Neighbour Bjorn is leaving the village!'

There was, for the first time in the history of the family, complete silence in the kitchen. Well, not complete silence: Minoushka stepped back on the cat's tail, with highly vocal consequences, and there was a noisy clatter when Grandmama dropped the porridge spoon; but at least nobody spoke.

Little Helga, being young, misinterpreted the reaction as signifying disbelief.

'Honest,' she said. 'I saw him going up the path to the top of the hill, and he had his axe over his shoulder with a big red spotted handkerchief tied to the handle, and he

101

was carrying a huge sack over the other shoulder, and he was wearing his Hell's Angels vest, which he only wears when he goes down to the town to buy intoxicating liquor. And the little brown dog was trying to follow him, but he kept stopping and throwing apples at it.'

More silence. Then Great-grandfather shook his head.

'It's impossible,' he said. 'Nobody ever *leaves* the village. People come here from the outside, yes, but they never leave.'

'Because of it being idyllic here,' Great-grandmother explained, with a microscopic quantity of residual wistfulness in her voice. She had fallen in love with the village the moment she set eyes on it sixty-two years ago, but before that she had lived in Chicago, and she couldn't help remembering, sometimes, that in Chicago they were admittedly short on idylls but hot as mustard on sanitation and running water. 'The whole point of idyllic is, you stay.'

'Oh dear,' said Grandmother. 'If he's leaving, it can only mean he's been unhappy here. Oh, the poor man!'

'We must counsel him,' said Grandfather firmly, rising from the table and removing his bib. 'We would never forgive ourselves if he left and we didn't try to stop him.'

'We would have failed him,' Grandmother added, 'in his hour of need. It would mean we are bad neighbours.'

Helga lowered her head and peered out of the window. It wasn't easy to see through, because the unutterably picturesque leaded panes were so distorted with genuine age that light only squeezed through them after a severe struggle.

'Do hurry,' she said, anxiously. 'He's stopped to try and find more apples to throw at the little brown dog. If you hurry, you might just catch him.'

So Grandmother and Grandfather and Great-grandmother and Minoushka and Little Helga and Lazy Olaf and Little Torsten dashed out of the house and up the hill, to where Bjorn was taking careful aim with a suitably aerodynamic Granny Smith.

'Surely,' panted Grandfather, catching his breath. 'Surely, neighbour Bjorn, you don't propose to leave us without even saying goodbye.'

'Goodbye,' Bjorn replied. 'Satisfied?' He let fly, and the little brown dog finally took the hint and retired, hobbling, to the woodshed. Bjorn picked up his luggage.

'But why?' Little Torsten demanded. 'Have you not been happy here, dear neighbour Bjorn?'

'No.'

'Where will you go?' wailed Grandmother. 'What will you do?'

Bjorn considered for a while. 'First,' he said, 'I'm going to find the nearest town that's got a halfway decent bar and a cinema that shows dirty movies, and I'm going to . . .'

'Why does he want to see dirty movies, Grandmama?'

'Hush, Torsten.'

'Yes, but Grandmama, if the film's got all dirty, doesn't that mean the pictures will come out all blurry and . . .'

'*Hush!*'

'And after that,' Bjorn went on, 'I'm going to find out what's happened to the sun. All right?'

The villagers stared at him as if he was mad.

'What do you mean, neighbour Bjorn?' asked Lazy Olaf slowly. 'It's the sun, that's all. There's nothing wrong with it. Look.'

He turned and pointed at the sky. The sun, as it happened, was obscured by a blanket of cloud.

'See?' Bjorn said. 'It's what we call a cover-up where I come from. Somebody's made one hell of a cock-up, and they're keeping it under wraps.'

'Maybe,' replied Grandfather. 'Or maybe it just means it's going to rain soon. Rain is good, neighbour Bjorn. It makes the crops grow and nourishes the little seedlings and . . .'

'Yes, yes, I know,' Bjorn interrupted impatiently. 'I used to make the stuff, okay? And I could tell you things about how we used to do it that'd make your hair stand on end,' he added.

'Look, just take it from me, all right? That is not the real sun. Something has happened to the real sun, and whatever it is they've got up there is a substitute, okay? Okay.'

He turned definitively and started to walk away. Little Torsten wiped away a tear.

'Don't go,' he whimpered.

Bjorn hesitated slightly, and then quickened his stride. Little Torsten started to cry.

'*Please* don't go,' he wailed through his tears. 'Even though you're grumpy and bad-tempered sometimes, and you never have a kind word for anyone and never help anyone out and never say thank you when Aunt Gretchen gives you griddle-cakes and you get drunk on Wednesday nights and go around being sick in people's hanging baskets and you're cruel to animals and you tread on the flowers round the village pump and you never to go church and you haven't paid your contribution to the poor relief fund for three years and you park your cart in Uncle Gustav's parking space and you steal the food we leave out for the poor blind boy and you cheat at dominoes and you cut down Grandmama's cherry tree for no reason at all and when she complained you called her a rude word and you leave empty crisp-packets all over everyone's front gardens and you trod on my toy horse once and when I cried you laughed at me and Hilda says you've got the manners of a warthog and the weeds from your garden blow out all over Uncle Carl's potato patch and you put vodka in Big Peter's orange juice at his wedding and Uncle Christian swears blind you've moved your back fence three feet over into his garden and you drew a moustache on the picture of the Blessed Virgin in the little white chapel, we still love you.'

There was a thoughtful silence.

'Do we, though?' said a voice at the back.

'And he took my bicycle once without asking,' said Grandmama. 'And when I found it again, the forks were all bent.'

'And there's my lawnmower,' added Lazy Olaf. 'When am I going to get that back, I ask myself.'

'He still hasn't paid for that broken window.'

'Loud music all hours of the day and night.'

'Revving up his chainsaw when people are trying to sleep.'

Grandfather stooped to pick up an apple lying on the ground in front of him. 'Go on,' he shouted, 'get on out of it. We can do without your sort around here.' He threw the apple.

'And if he comes back again,' said Grandmama, savagely, 'we'll set the dogs on him.'

The little brown dog, which had come bounding out with its tail wagging, bared its teeth and snarled.

Halfway up the hill, Bjorn broke into a run.

'She's keen, certainly,' said the director. 'I have high hopes, you know. We need that sort of dedication and commitment in this department.'

The director's secretary sniffed. 'Look,' she said. 'Someone's left the lights on all weekend.'

'Oh dear,' the director replied, fumbling in his pocket for the key. 'Wait a moment, though. It's not locked. What on earth . . .?'

He pushed open the door carefully and walked in to the main office.

'Good-morning,' Jane called out from behind the console. 'I worked over the weekend, hope you don't mind. You're right, it's easy once you get the hang of it. Of course, the computer helps marvellously. It's just like the one we used to have where I worked before, except that the memory's bigger, of course. Do you like it?'

The director was staring at the screen. From time to time, he made little choking noises.

The screen was different. Instead of the intricate cobwebs of inextricably tangled patterns, it looked like nothing so much as a very finely woven net.

'What have you done?' the director croaked.

'I've sorted it,' Jane replied cheerfully. 'Looks so much

better like that, don't you think? Everybody living happily ever after, you see.'

'But . . .' The director struggled for words. 'But, you stupid girl, they're meant to be star-crossed lovers.'

'So,' Jane replied. 'I uncrossed them. Simple as that,' she added, and put the cover back over the console. 'It'll make life so much easier in the long run if people aren't having to cope with shattering emotional crises all over the place. Do you realise how many working days were lost in the Soviet Union last year because of emotional trauma? I looked it up. Four million. And as for Scandinavia . . .'

The director collapsed against a filing cabinet, breathing heavily. 'You – uncrossed them,' he gasped. 'My life's work, and you . . .' He made a noise like a horse whinnying and grabbed at the side of the cabinet for support. His secretary moved across to the desk and sharpened some pencils.

'And,' Jane went on, 'I've programmed the computer to make sure they stay like that. It's much easier that way, you know, and ever so much more efficient. In fact, all it'll take from now on is one full-time member of staff to make sure it's running smoothly, and a couple of part-timers to do the filing. I'm sure,' she went on relentlessly, 'they'll be ever so pleased to hear that in the Treasurer's Office.'

On the screen behind her, a galaxy of perfectly regulated blue and pink dots flashed in harmonious concord. All over the world, boy was meeting girl and falling in love, and they were immediately going out and choosing bathroom curtains together. The director's secretary shrugged.

'Well,' she observed, 'I'll say this much, it's a darned sight tidier than it used to be. I never could be doing with all those messy loops and squiggles.'

The director propped himself up against the filing cabinet and took off his spectacles. 'Miss Frobisher,' he roared in a voice like thunder. 'Be so kind as to get me the Chief of Staff on the telephone immediately.'

But Miss Frobisher wasn't listening. She was gazing, with an expression on her face like Stout Cortez finding a parking space in Piccadilly, at the electrician, who had come in to replace a light-bulb in the washroom. And he was gazing back.

'Bingo,' Jane commented. 'You see what I mean about efficient.'

With a cry of enraged anguish the director dragged himself to his feet, shook a fist in Jane's direction and staggered out of the door in the direction of the Main Office. For the record, he got no further than Accounts; where he happened to share a lift with a rather nice, motherly lady from Pensions. When, three months later, they got back from their honeymoon, he resigned from his old job and applied for the assistant librarianship in the reference section.

'This protégé of yours,' Ganger said. 'I'm beginning to get bad feelings about the whole idea.'

Staff checked himself between the second and third syllables of '*My* protégé?' and considered. He had, after all, been in the service for a very long time now, and one learned to expect this sort of thing. As the old Catalan proverb says: he who chooses to live among rats should not get aerated at the sight of paw marks in the butter.

'Why?' he said.

'Well.' Ganger took up his usual position on the edge of the desk. Obviously chairs were completely *passé* where he came from. 'Admittedly she's got talent. Talent, yes; also initiative, drive, authority, intelligence, all that stuff. But, you know, I can't help thinking she's getting above herself. I mean, first that thing with the sun, and now all this stuff with Star-Crossed Lovers. Like, wiping out a whole department overnight. You've got to draw the line somewhere, haven't you? She's making too many enemies too soon.'

Staff stroked his chin with the rubber on the end of his propelling pencil. 'And that means she's making enemies for us, you mean?'

'Naturally.' Ganger picked up a handful of paperclips and

started to weave them into a chain. 'Major aggravation, at this rate. You don't need me to tell you that.'

They considered the matter in silence for a while.

'Finance and General Purposes smiled at me in the corridor the day before yesterday,' Staff said at last. 'I spent the rest of the morning searching this office for hidden microphones.'

'Find any?'

'No,' Staff replied. Then he put his finger to his lips, picked up his empty coffee-cup, inverted it and put it over the buzzer on the edge of the desk. 'Yes,' he went on. 'Six. I left that one where it was to make them think they'd won.'

'I wouldn't worry about it,' Ganger said, smiling. 'Sure, they've got every office in the building bugged – oh, and by the way, if you only found six, there's three more about here somewhere, I was talking with that kid Vince from Supplies. But it's nothing to worry about.'

'Nothing to . . .' Staff lowered his voice to a whisper. 'Nothing to worry about,' he hissed. 'Have you the faintest idea . . .'

Ganger shrugged. 'It all comes back to staffing levels,' he said. 'Think about it. So they've got the room bugged. In order for that to mean anything, think of all the backup you'd need. You'd have to have a guy listening in on each office, and another two guys to transcribe it all, and another guy to sort through the transcripts and put yellow highlighter on all the treasonable bits. With an organisation this size, you're talking maybe a staff of twenty thousand people. You know how many people work in Internal Security? Four, and one of them's a trainee. All they do is go around putting the bugs in, maybe fixing them when they go wrong, putting in new ones when they get found, and even doing that, there's a waiting list of maybe six years. Nobody actually *listens*.'

'Um.' Staff thought for a moment, then rather shame-facedly removed his coffee-cup. 'Even so,' he said.

'Exactly,' Ganger replied, leaning forward. 'Even so. We

just can't afford to give those guys any more ammunition than we can help, and this crazy young kid of yours . . .'

'Not mine,' Staff couldn't help saying. 'You found her, remember.'

'Maybe, yes, but . . .'

'And you nagged her into joining.'

'Okay, yes, we're talking details here. It was your idea too. You didn't stop me.' There was a frown on Ganger's face; a very incongruous sight, like Genghis Khan in a dinner jacket. 'That doesn't alter the fact that we've got to be careful, both of us. It's a good idea, don't let's screw it up.'

'It was my idea to put her in Records,' Staff pointed out. 'And it was you who made sure she was on hand when the sun got stolen. In fact, I'm not so sure . . .' He stopped abruptly, aware that he'd been thinking aloud.

'Sure,' Ganger replied. 'I put those kids up to it. We needed a new sun. The old one was a goddamn liability.' He leaned closer forward still. 'Now you see what you're implicated in, huh?'

Staff half-rose; then he sat down again. 'You lunatic,' he said. 'What did you want to go and do something like that for?'

'Never you mind,' Ganger answered, infuriatingly. 'My department has a cross-departmental brief. I have to keep several things going at the same time.'

'Is that an explanation?'

'Yeah. Trust me.'

'Oh.' Staff bit the rubber on the end of his pencil in half and spat out the result. He was nervous when people from that particular department said 'Trust me'; he couldn't help but visualise the scene, many years ago now, when one of them had said, 'Go on, eat the bloody apple; trust me.' Of course, that sort of thing couldn't happen now, not with the New Covenant and mortals being so depressingly litigious, but old habits die hard. 'I think,' he said decisively, 'we ought to call the whole thing off. You're right,' he added quickly. 'You've convinced me.'

Ganger was taken beautifully by surprise. 'Hold on, now,' he said. 'I didn't say we should call it off. All I said was . . .'

Staff smeared a bewildered look on his face. 'You said she was becoming a liability,' he replied. 'I agree with you. By the way, what on earth possessed you to agree to all those demands of hers – pay and so forth? You realise that she's only down on the books as a trainee.'

'Wait a minute, now.' Ganger was distinctly flustered, and his smile was melting and dripping down the side of his mouth, like jam on the run from a doughnut. 'I couldn't help it,' he said. 'The kid's got personality, I guess. She just sort of came at me.'

'Right,' Staff replied, nodding. 'And now I think it's about time she came at somebody else around here.'

Another silence. In the corner of the room, unnoticed by anybody at all, one of the hidden microphones went wrong and began broadcasting the BBC World Service to its receiving station.

'Like who?' Ganger said cautiously. 'I think you're up to something.'

'Me?' Staff did a very creditable impression of startled innocence. 'I've never been up to anything in my entire life. I was just thinking that, if she's been attracting hostile criticism from certain quarters, then it's about time we turned her loose on her critics. What do you reckon?'

'I don't know.' Ganger stood up and walked across to the window, inadvertently treading on another hidden microphone and squashing it flat. The device in question had been installed by the trainee, and nobody had told him about putting them where they won't get trodden on. 'That could make things worse, you know? The last thing we want to do is precipitate a confrontation.'

'Don't we?'

'Well, not that sort of confrontation.' Ganger was starting to exhibit signs of great tension; that is to say, he appeared perfectly normal but his shoelaces were untying themselves and then weaving themselves back into fantastically intricate knots. 'What did you have in mind, anyway?'

Staff smiled; at least, he drew his lips across his face like the curtain of an old-fashioned proscenium-arch theatre. 'Nothing too dramatic,' he replied. 'I just think that the girl's proved herself perfectly capable in the field, so why not try her out in administration? After all,' he added carelessly, 'she can't get up to much mischief sat behind a desk all day, can she?'

'I don't know,' Ganger replied, and his face was a blank. 'Can she?'

Staff leaned back in his chair and put the tips of his fingers together. He was enjoying himself.

'Let's find out,' he said. 'Oh, and by the way.'

When one has worked in an office where mind-reading is the norm rather than the exception, one can't help noticing nuances of expression, just as a telephone can't get away from the fact that there are always people wanting to talk through it, regardless of whether it's in the mood. Ganger's face remained blank, but one of his shoelaces broke spontaneously. 'Yes?' he said.

'While we're on the subject of bugging.'

'Mm?'

'I saw a psychiatrist yesterday,' Staff said. He waited for some pleasantry or other from his interlocutor, and then went on: 'I told him – quite untruthfully, as it happens – that for the last few weeks I've had this extraordinary idea that someone's been listening to my thoughts. Inside my head, I told him. I didn't expect him to take me seriously, of course, but he did.'

'So I should think,' Ganger muttered.

'Well, he wasn't your run-of-the-mill shrink,' Staff admitted. 'In fact, he's the head departmental analyst, so he's used to that sort of thing, I should imagine. And do you know what he suggested I should do?'

Ganger beamed. 'Go on,' he said, 'you tell me.'

'He said,' Staff went on, 'that it's not a particularly uncommon condition in our line of work. He said – and this is just what he told me, mind – that the only odd thing about it was that I'd noticed. Funny he should say that, since I was making the whole thing up, wouldn't you say?'

'Hilarious.'

'Anyway,' Staff went on, 'the point he was making was that apparently, one of our own departments, or at least a department of what you might call an associated agency, has perfected a technique of mental bugging, just so's they can keep tabs on what the rest of us are thinking. A bit spooky, that, if it's true.'

'You've got my hair standing on end,' Ganger said. 'Do go on, please.'

'Oh, there's nothing to worry about,' Staff said reassuringly. 'Apparently, there's a very simple solution to the problem. The boys in the research lab tumbled to it almost immediately. All you've got to do is *this* and . . . I say, are you all right?'

Ganger, who was sitting bolt upright with a face as white as the proverbial sheet, nodded his head stiffly. His hair really was standing on end, Staff noticed.

'Sorry?' he said. 'I didn't catch what you said.'

'IIII sssaiiiid yyyyyessssss, IIIIyummm fffiynnn, thannnnnx,' Ganger hissed. His eyes were bloodshot and he was starting to vibrate. 'WWWWwoulddddd yyyy kkkkkindllleeeee sssstopppp ddddoinggg thatttttt nnnow, pppppl?'

'According to my friend the shrink,' Staff continued, looking away and affecting not to notice anything unusual, 'it's just a question of earthing the interloper into one's brainwaves. It's easy once you've got the knack, he says, though how you'd ever know you were doing it right beats me. Still, he says there's enough electricity inside the average person's head to fry an intruder like a sausage. I'm sure he's exaggerating. What do you think?'

'Ggggggggggggggg.'

'Anyway,' Staff said, making a very slight movement, after which Ganger stopped looking like a cross between a straight-backed chair and a pneumatic drill and slumped on to the floor in a heap, 'it's just as well nobody's been trying to monkey about with the inside of *my* head, because he'd know he'd been in a fight if he did. My dear chap, what are you doing on the floor?'

'Resting,' Ganger croaked. 'I've had, you know, sort of a hard day.' He reached out a trembling hand and picked up the lenses of his glasses, which were all that was left, apart from a few droplets of melted plastic in the worn pile of the carpet. 'I think I'll get back to my office and do something.'

'Capital idea,' Staff replied. 'Mind how you go.'

'I will.' Ganger lifted himself on to his knees with an effort and crawled to the side of the desk.

'Want to borrow a comb?'

'Thanks,' Ganger mumbled. 'Don't think I'd have the strength to lift one right now, but maybe I'll take you up on it later.'

'Please yourself,' Staff said, picking up a file and opening it. 'You know what? The one thing that really cheers me up about this whole business is knowing that, come what may, you and I are on the same side. You know, implicit mutual trust, that sort of thing. It's a great comfort to me, it really is.'

'Um.'

'Cheerio, then.'

'Ciao.'

'Profiteroles,' said the Lord High Cardinal. 'I should live so long.'

The Count of the Stables winked at him. 'Go on,' he said, 'be a devi . . .' He checked himself. 'Go on,' he said. 'To-morrow you can have a salad.'

The Lord High Cardinal shrugged. 'You convinced me,' he

said. 'Or there's the *zuppa inglesi*.'

'Nah. That's for thin people. C'mon, go for it.'

'Okay.'

'Right,' said the Count of the Stables. 'That's six profit-eroles. Hey, Rosa, six profiteroles over here.'

'I got it,' replied the Emperor's sister. 'Just give me a moment, will you? We got no help again today.'

The County Palatine clicked his teeth. 'You want to get shot of that kid,' he said, 'she's no good to you.'

Rosa gave him a withering look, the sort of look that scours roses of greenfly and lifts impacted grease off the inside of neglected ovens. 'You know how hard it is to get help – even crummy help – this time of the year? You don't. You let me run my business, okay?'

She scuttled off under a ziggurat of dirty plates. The Electors sighed.

'She works too hard,' opined the Lord Treasurer.

'It's a shame,' agreed the Count of the Stables. 'We should find her a reliable waitress.'

The Count of the Saxon Shore grunted. 'Anything that'd improve the service round here would be fine by me. You can get peptic ulcers waiting too long between courses.'

A match flared at the end of an eight-inch cigar. 'You've gotta look after your health in this life,' commented the Lord High Cardinal, 'because if you don't, nobody else will.' He burped smoke, like a dragon with carburettor trouble, while the other Electors exchanged surreptitious glances. They had an uneasy feeling that the Lord High Cardinal had just made a pronouncement *ex cathedra*; in which case, somebody really ought to write it down. 'Anyway,' he continued briskly, 'to business.'

The Electors stifled a selection of sighs and yawns. A working lunch, in their view, was a truly wonderful idea, but not nearly as truly wonderful as a plain ordinary lunch, hold the work. Still, they had a Duty.

'Well,' said the Lord Treasurer, 'I did the books last night, and they're looking pretty healthy. We got,' he reached in his coat pocket for his spectacles and yesterday night's wine list, 'we got income, seventeen point four four six four four million kreuzers, expenditure seventeen point four four six three nine million kreuzers, capital reserves nil, income transferred to capital account nil, fixed assets nil, short term liabilities nil, written down balance fifty kreuzers, transferred to cash account fifty kreuzers. Okay?'

The County Palatine frowned. 'What does that mean, Tony?' he asked.

'It means,' replied the Treasurer with a grin, 'today we can afford to leave a tip.'

The Electors nodded their approval, and the Lord High Cardinal cleared his throat.

'Policy review time next, folks,' he said. 'Anybody got anything to say about our policy?'

'I think our policy is just great, Rocky. What do you say, Tony?'

'Yeah, it's a great policy, Rocky. Where's that damn broad with the goddamn sweet?'

'Okay.' The Lord High Cardinal pencilled a little tick on the back of the menu. 'Now then, what's next? Oh, nuts, I forgot the minutes of the last meeting. Anybody take any minutes last meeting?'

'Nah.'

'Okay then, approved as drawn.' The Lord High Cardinal raised his eyebrows and scratched them with the end of his pencil. 'That just leaves Any Other Business, guys,' he said. 'Hold on, though,' he added, as Rosa approached with a tray, 'here it comes now.'

When they had finished Any Other Business, and the Count of the Saxon Shore had had Extra Any Other Business with a side order of whipped cream, they sat for a while thinking and breathing heavily, until the arrival of the coffee recalled them to the next item on the agenda.

'Date of next meeting,' said the Lord High Cardinal.

'Thursday all right with you guys?' The Electors nodded. 'Okay, Thursday at twelve fifteen. Meeting closed. Hey, Rosa, where's the toothpicks? I got a big fat lump of veal gristle lodged behind my bridgework. You want me to choke to death here?'

Coffee was traditionally taken in silence, or at least without articulate speech, to give the Electors an opportunity to ruminate on the decisions they had just taken and if necessary review them or supplement them with a brandy or a small shot of grappa. It was, above all, a moment of tranquillity, essential in the headlong life of a monumentally important officer of state. Sometimes, however, something happened to spoil it; for example, the proprietor's sister tripping over her feet and depositing a plateful of tagliatelli verdi in the lap of the Count of the Saxon Shore.

'Yow,' howled the Count. 'You damn crazy bitch, that's hot!'

'Sorry,' said Rosa, perfunctorily. She leaned over and scooped the tagliatelli back out of the Count's lap on to the plate with a fork. 'You should count yourself lucky it was only a melted butter and cheese sauce. Bechamel sauce on a nice light suit like that, you'd be in real trouble.'

The Lord High Cardinal raised a caterpillar-like eyebrow. 'That's not like you, Rosa,' he said. 'You got something worrying you?'

Rosa sighed. 'That waitress,' she said. 'That so-called waitress. She only calls and says she's handing in her notice. On account of she's getting married and moving to Seattle. Some people just don't care.'

She bustled away to get a hot cloth. The Electors looked at each other.

'I move,' said the County Palatine, 'we find Rosa a new waitress. Seconded?'

'Seconded,' replied the Count of the Saxon Shore, grimly. 'As soon as possible. Wearing food isn't me, you know?'

'Right.' The County Palatine frowned. 'Anybody know of

anybody?' he enquired. 'Gotta be somebody good, mind. You know, reliable, honest, intelligent, hard-working, efficient. Sure-footed,' he added. 'Good sense of balance, all that kind of thing.'

There was silence, during which the sun broke through the thick mantle of cloud that had masked it for a week or so now, flashed momentarily and then ducked away out of sight once again. A brief flare of dazzle on the outside of the window seemed to inspire the Lord High Cardinal, for he suddenly clapped his hands together and rubbed them warmly.

'Boys,' he said, 'I know just the person.'

George sat down at the controls, fastened the safety harness and switched on the intercom. There was the usual crackle.

'Helios One to Control Centre, come in please, over,' he said, but without conviction. Old dog, screamed every fibre of his being, new tricks.

'Control Centre to Helios One, you are cleared, repeat cleared for commencement of preliminary take-off procedure in fifteen, one-five, minutes, over.'

George growled. He didn't like talking to a computer; it made you feel odd, it was like talking to yourself. Makes you go blind, talking to yourself, so his mother had told him. He blinked.

Not, he had to admit, that a lot of it was not an improvement. It worked, for a start. When you wanted it to turn left, you just wiggled the stick; you didn't have to lean right over and lean your back against the side of the cockpit. In fact, you didn't even have to wiggle the stick; something called an autopilot would do it for you. I wonder, George muttered resentfully to himself, how much he's getting a week. Probably non-union, too.

'Helios One to Control Centre,' he intoned. 'Commencing pre-take-off checklist programme, over.' He said it with roughly the same degree of expression and involvement as a forcibly converted Aztec saying the Mass in Latin, and without very much more idea what it was supposed to mean. It was all very well, sure; instead of having some brainless erk of a trainee standing out on the tarmac hauling on the propellor to get the thing fired up, all you needed to do was press a button. Provided, of course, you could remember which button. There were rather a lot of them, and they were all exactly the same shade of red.

Ah well. If things got tricky he could always ask the autopilot.

Instinctively he felt behind his seat for his thermos, and then remembered that in the shiny new design there were no convenient little ledges and nooks for secreting personal belongings in. Instead, there was a beverage control monitoring system, which unerringly threw a cup of warm, brown water all over him as he was coming into the bumpy stretch above 10.45 a.m. Time I retired, he said to himself. If only they'd let me, he added.

'*Control Centre to Helios One, scheduled take-off time minus fourteen, one-four, minutes, over.*'

If only, George continued to muse, the Boy hadn't gone off like that. He had talent for this job, the Boy had. Wonder where he was now? There'd been a rumour going about the Social Club that he'd packed in the Service altogether and gone off doing some job or other among the mortals. Still, they tended to say that about anybody who went missing for more than a week these days. Perhaps the Boy was going to be seconded back, now that they'd gone and bought this new model. A natural, that lad; fly anything, given time and provided nobody minded what he collided with while he was practising.

As take-off approached (what was wrong with calling it Dawn, by the way? Dawn had class; but you'd feel a bit of a Charlie talking about rosy-fingered take-off or the take-off coming up like thunder) something small but hard, like the ball in a pinball machine, started to roll about inside George's head; and maybe it was the faint jolt as the giant machine

118

lifted smoothly into the air that finally gave it the impetus to roll into place. Anyway, roll it did. Clunk.

There was something very wrong with this machine, and nobody had realised. What the hell was it?

George flipped the intercom back to transmit.

'Helios One to Control Centre. Am cruising at five hundred thousand, five-oh-oh-thousand metres and climbing, all systems functional, over.'

He replaced the microphone thing, looked around to make sure nobody could see him, and switched off the autopilot.

'No hard feelings, chum,' he explained. 'You're doing a lovely job, but you know how it is. Always was a rotten passenger, me.'

He took hold of the stick and instinctively moved it to the right position. At once he became aware of a minute difference in the feel of the thing. The pinball rolled round in its hole and settled again, and in the back of George's mind, some coloured lights lit up and shouted 'Replay!'

Slower. Ever since he'd switched it on to manual, it'd slowed down.

George glanced out of the side of the cockpit at the ground. Centuries of practice flying the old sun on manual had enabled him to gauge the airspeed simply by watching the ground, while his brain made a series of subconscious, lightning-quick calculations. He *knew* he was flying at the right speed, just by the way the shadows of the trees below him shortened and lengthened again as he passed over. And yet just now he'd slowed down. It's impossible to confuse deceleration with any other experience in the world; like mashed swede, there's absolutely nothing you can mistake it for. Which meant . . .

'Bugger me,' George said; and, in spite of himself, he chuckled. It only went to show, you do no good by fiddling with things just for the sake of it.

It explained everything; the wilting crops, the freakish behaviour of the tides, the fact that the Pole Star was halfway up the back of Cassiopeia's Chair, the friction burns down the left-hand side of the Kalahari Desert, the way his wife always seemed surprised when he got in from work these days.

The daft sods had made the damn thing go too fast.

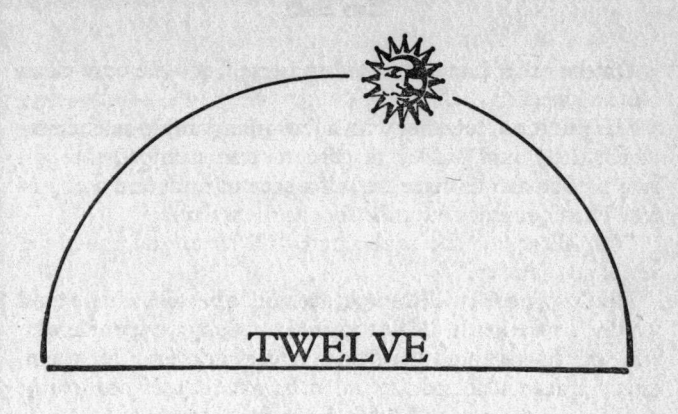

TWELVE

The alarm-clock buzzed. Jane made a squeaking noise, rubbed her eyes and extended an arm with the general idea of getting hold of whatever was making that horrible noise and throttling it. Then her memory fired up, and she groaned.

It was morning, and she had to get up and go to work. Oh *damn* ...

She brushed her teeth like a well-brought-up robot, combed her hair and looked at herself in the mirror.

'Hi,' she said. 'I'm Jane. I help run the Universe.'

It didn't sound any better this morning than it had yesterday. She shrugged, blew her nose and went to see whether the ironing-fairy had broken in during the night and made a start on the blouse dump.

It hadn't. Bother.

Hanging at the back of the wardrobe and looking as if it had been dead for some considerable time, she found the old blue blouse with the Princess Diana collar that her mother had given her for Christmas, back in the days when you could buy a whole roast ox, watch the bear-baiting and still have change out of a half-groat.

121

On the other hand, she said to herself, it's the only clean blouse I've got.

She put it on, together with a few other jumble-sale rejects which she found hidden in corners, and stumped through into the kitchen to make herself a slice of toast and a cup of tea. The floor crackled underfoot as she walked.

'Yes, all right,' she said aloud, 'I'll clean you tonight if you'll just shut up.'

Don't suppose I will, though, she said to herself, as she stood waiting for the kettle. I'll be too tired. And anyway, people who run universes should have their housework done for them, surely. I mean, it doesn't say *and on the eighth day, He changed the bed, cleaned the oven and did the hoovering*, does it?

That's probably because He was a He.

Smoke curled out from under the grill and she sighed. Speciality of the house, she muttered to herself, Toast à la Pucelle. She grabbed a knife and started to scrape, until she was left with a large pile of black dust and about four square inches of toast.

Job satisfaction, she said to herself, that's what I've got. You know, the lovely feeling that I'm making the world a better place. *Really* making the world a better place. Or will be.

Staff had explained all that to her. Yes, she'd ironed out all the problems of human personal relationships at a stroke, but of course it wasn't as simple as that. A built-in fail-safe in the programme slowed the process down so that the customers wouldn't notice anything different. Wouldn't do for the customers to notice anything, they'd get restive, start believing in things, bad for morale. This way, she reflected bitterly, they'll be happy ever after without realising it, and so they'll go on being miserable, the same as before.

'Yes,' she said to the kettle, 'but I did manage to get them to replace the sun, remember. I mean . . .'

The kettle looked at her without saying anything. It didn't need to. She looked away and tried to crush rock-hard butter on to the porcelain-fragile toast without smashing it in the process.

There was nothing to show for it. The less there was to show for it the better, and so far she had a hundred per cent success rate.

'The hell with this,' she snarled at the kitchen clock. 'If I had any brains, I'd go back to working at Burridge's. At least I was sure of getting away at five-thirty.'

The clock ticked. A fat lot of help you are, she thought. Still, I have to talk to you, because if I start talking to myself, it'll mean I'm going mad.

She dumped the last few shards of toast in the bin and made a mental note to try and buy a sandwich at the station. The station . . . Well, it was a different sort of commuting; bus to Waterloo, train to Salisbury, change for Amesbury, bus to Stonehenge, bodily translation from there direct to the office. Unless there was a go-slow or track repairs, of course, in which case she'd be diverted to the Cloud of Unknowing and have to try and find a taxi.

'And you can shut up as well,' she snapped at the egg-timer.

At the back of her mind, in among the almost-forgotten birthdays and rotting scraps of Maths O-level, a small and badly underpaid member of staff coughed nervously and suggested that something was probably fundamentally wrong with the whole set-up. Either you work on earth, it said, and you get all this hassle, but at least you stay a human being doing sort of human things, plus the ironing; or you work in the Empyrean and don't have to be bothered with matters corporeal. And while we're on the subject, it added, looking nervously over its shoulder, I don't know about you but I think there's something extremely fishy about this whole work thing, and it really doesn't add up at all, because . . .

It would have enlarged on this theme if something large, panther-shaped and blatantly alien hadn't jumped out of the shadows on the edge of the subconscious and bitten its head off. The small knot of thoughts which had gathered to listen to it quickly melted away. A few fractions of a second later, strange shapes in black overalls came and cleared away the mess.

Leave the washing-up till I get home, said Jane to herself. Gosh, must rush. Don't want to be late for work.

'You'll like the work here,' Staff had said. 'Relaxing. No pressure or hassle or anything like that, just straightforward clerical and administration. You probably need a rest after all that, um, recently.'

The phone rang again. Jane stuck her tongue out at it, and then picked up the receiver.

'This is Phil from Audit,' it said nastily. 'Look, aren't those 1998 projections down yet? You promised we'd have them a fortnight ago and we're completely stuffed without them.'

Jane sighed and went into Ansafone mode. 'My name's Jane,' she said, 'I've only been in this office a week and I haven't the faintest idea what I'm supposed to be doing or what's going on. If you would care to explain exactly what it is that you want me to do, I'll get on to it as soon as I possibly can. Thank you.' Then, out of what could be described as sheer devilment were it not for the risk of causing confusion in the present context, she made a *beep* noise, and waited.

There was, as usual, a disconcerted pause of about three-quarters of a second. 'Look,' said the voice, 'it's just not good enough. Unless I get those breakdowns on my desk by half past four this afternoon, there's going to be ructions, okay?'

The line went dead. Jane shrugged, replaced the receiver and turned her attention back to the bulging tray of papers in front of her. They were all sorts of different colours, and they were covered in print, typewriting and office-person's handwriting (which is cursive, semi-legible and entirely uniform in every office in the whole of Creation) in a wide assortment of scripts and alphabets; all of which, curiously enough, Jane found that she could read without difficulty. The only problem was that none of them carried any sort of clue on the face of them as to what they were or what had to be done with them; apart, of course, from the ones with URGENT (or even occasionally *URGENT!!!*) stamped on them in red. Clearly, she was meant to worry like hell about those.

The phone rang.

'This is Sylvia from Mainframe Base, as if you didn't know,' it said. 'We're still waiting. However much longer is it going to take you?'

'My name's Jane. I've only been in this . . .'

'And another thing,' the voice continued. 'You promised faithfully you'd let me have the Directory back when you'd finished with it, and that was three weeks ago. Now I suppose you've gone and lost it. Again.'

'. . . In this office a week and I haven't the faintest . . .'

'Don't give me that, dear. Unless it's here, *on* my desk, *with* the reports filed to date, in the next forty-five minutes, I'm going to have to file a Blue. I'm sorry if that seems aggressive of me, but you don't really leave me any choice.'

Line dead. Shrug. Now then, what on earth is this big green thing meant to be? Which way up, for a start?

'Excuse me.'

Jane looked round, startled. Apart from the lost, violent souls on the other end of the telephone line, nobody except the tea lady had spoken to her since she'd started there. Most of the time the other people in the long, echoing hall yelled into their telephones and slammed them down again. For all she knew, they were the people who kept phoning her up.

'Sorry to bother you, but do you think you could possibly explain something? You see, I'm new here.'

The person, once located, turned out to be a small, wispy female who looked as if she'd last eaten back when mammoth steak meant just that. Odds on there was a face somewhere behind those spectacles, but probably not a face of particular relevance to anything. Jane felt a brief pang of sympathy.

'I'll try,' she said, 'but I doubt it, really. You see, I'm new here myself, and nobody's told me . . .'

'Oh, but you must know more than me,' replied the girl. 'You see, I've only been here two years, so . . .'

She tailed off. Obviously she didn't like the look of the way Jane was goggling at her, like an amateur sword-swallower faced with a chainsaw.

'Two *years*?' Jane said. 'And you still . . .?'

'Haven't got the foggiest idea about anything, I'm afraid,' the girl replied, clearly deeply ashamed of herself. You could tell that from the fact that her fingernails were the least pink bit of her. 'Not a clue, honestly,' she added.

'But . . .' Jane pulled herself together. 'But what do you do all day, for pity's sake? I mean, you must do something.'

The girl nodded. 'Mostly,' she said, 'I answer the phone. I'm not terribly good at it, though, because I never know the answer to anything anybody ever asks me. I'm a bit worried about that. There's someone called Darren in something called Forward Budgeting who's been calling me every day for the last eighteen months, and . . .'

'I know him,' Jane interrupted. 'Wants it on his desk by two-fifteen or there'll be trouble.'

The girl smiled apprehensively. 'Yes,' she said, 'that's him.'

'And then he rings off without telling you what.'

'Yes, um.'

'Fine.' Jane breathed in slowly and deeply. 'And nobody else you've asked can help you?'

The girl frowned. 'Oh, I haven't asked anyone *else*,' she replied. 'I mean, they all look so busy, I was afraid to bother them. I only asked you because you look, well . . .' The girl trailed off; her fingernails now looked positively anaemic.

Jane looked around the room. It was true that, apart from herself and the girl, everyone else did look extremely busy. Mostly they were shouting into telephones and then banging them down; and when they weren't doing that, they were frantically rummaging through the coloured bits of paper on their desks, looking for something.

'Just out of curiosity,' Jane asked, 'what did they take you on as?'

'Computer operator,' replied the girl. 'Only the computer doesn't seem to work, does it?'

She nodded her head at the VDU on the top of Jane's desk. After the third day, when she still hadn't been able to get the bloody-minded thing to do anything more constructive than flash its lights at her and display the words *Hi! All rights protected!*, she'd followed what appeared to be the general practice of the office and converted the thing into a plastic cup stand. Some VDU's, she had observed, had several months' deposit of cups on top of them, which made the office look like a stalagmite farm.

'What is this office, anyway?' Jane asked. 'Someone told me when I first came here, but I've forgotten what they called it. It didn't seem to mean anything much.'

'Oh, we're Processing,' the girl replied, with a hint of crazy pride in her voice. 'I think we're terribly important, or else why do people from other offices keep ringing us up all the time? Oh, do excuse me.' She looked away and answered the telephone on her desk. Jane didn't need a vast amount of imagination to reconstruct the conversation from the side of it she could hear.

'Let me guess,' she said, as the girl lowered the receiver. 'That was Dave from Throughput, and unless it's in his tray by three o'clock, the world's going to end.'

The girl stared at her. 'So you *do* know what's going on,' she gasped.

Jane shook her head. 'I'm just a good guesser,' she replied. 'Look, instead of just sitting here like a couple of decoy pigeons, why don't we go and find someone and ask them? Someone who *does* know, I mean.'

The girl looked at her as if she'd just suggested tarring and feathering the Pope. 'What, leave our desks?' she said. 'I don't think we're allowed.'

'Oh, I think we are,' said Jane firmly.

'But . . .' The girl shot her a look of pure terror; the sort of look one unborn twin might give to the other if it suggested going *up* the passageway instead of down. 'What if the phone were to ring while we're away?' she quavered. 'I mean, there'd be nobody to answer it.'

Jane shook her head. 'Highly unlikely,' she said. 'And even if it did ring, how would anyone ever know? You see, there'd be nobody to hear it.'

'The person at the other end would know,' replied the girl, her lower lip quivering. 'Wouldn't they?'

'Their word against ours,' Jane said fiercely – indeed, Henry V couldn't have said it better. In this mood, not only would Jane have had them into the breach once more, she'd have made them wipe their feet first. 'Come on.'

Without looking at her colleague, she grabbed her handbag, stood up, and began to walk in the direction she believed was most likely to be north.

'Wait for me!' the girl gasped behind her. 'If you leave me behind I might get lost.'

'Keep up, then,' Jane said. 'And follow me.'

Although she was only dimly aware of it herself, one of Jane's greatest strengths was her ear for the right choice of words to suit any given situation. Thus, when at last they came upon a man sitting at a desk who wasn't talking on the phone, some internal word selection system put the magic phrase into her mouth without her having to think at all.

'All right,' she said, 'where is he? I want to talk to him *now*.'

The man looked up at her, terrified. 'You can't,' he replied. 'He's in with Them.'

Jane tightened the focus of her ferocious expression. 'How long's he been in there?'

'Twenty minutes,' the man replied. 'Half an hour. Forty minutes. At least.'

Jane breathed out; and if her breath didn't consist of blue-hot flame, it was only because of the No Smoking sign.

'Which room's he in? Come on, I haven't got all night.'

'Number Five.' The man pointed. As Jane turned her head to follow the line he was indicating, his phone rang, and he dived for it like a drowning man after a lifebelt. Two-thirds of a second later, he was shouting at someone.

'Right,' Jane said, and she beckoned to her acolyte. 'Now we're getting somewhere. Come on.'

The girl stood rooted to the spot. 'But we *can't*,' she said. 'He's in with Them, the man just said.'

Jane turned her head and smiled. 'Do you have any idea who he is?'

The girl shook her head.

'Me neither,' said Jane smugly. 'And what about Them? You know who They are?'

'No.'

'Well then,' Jane replied briskly. 'What you don't know about can't hurt you. Well-known fact. Coming?'

She marched up to the door, which had a big, slightly grubby '5' on it, knocked twice, and pushed open the door.

Then she stopped.

She was standing in a restaurant.

Furthermore, she was wearing a black skirt, shiny with age and the condensation of greasy food and sweat, topped by a white blouse and a pinny whose origins at least were decorative. She was holding a tray with three heaped plates of pasta on it. The door behind her closed.

'C'mon, for Chrissakes,' shouted a fat man, one of six fat men sitting round a table with a red and white checked tablecloth on it. 'There's people starving to death.'

'I know,' said a voice which Jane recognised as her own. 'Half the population of the Sudan, for a start. This lot'd keep most of them fed for a week, though it wouldn't do their arteries any good.'

Twelve round piggy eyes stared at her. 'Right,' she said. 'Who's having what?'

For six weeks, a long time ago now, Jane had been a waitress, in a Little Chef on a ring-road south of Nottingham. Six weeks was all she'd been able to take, because she'd come to the conclusion that feeding fattening food to fat people is basically immoral; but while she'd been there, she'd learned. How to balance seven plates at once while clearing up after a small child who's been sick after three consecutive knicker-bocker glories; how to serve a fried breakfast to three lorry-drivers who were trying to look down the front of her blouse, without hitting them with the ketchup bottle; how to watch thirty-seven eggs being fried simultaneously in dirty fat without becoming a vegan. She knew the ropes.

'Um,' said the fattest fat man, and pointed vaguely. Jane deposited the plates, turned on her heel and walked away as quickly as she could. Before she could make it to the door she'd come through, however, she nearly collided with a four-foot-high black-haired woman with her hands on her hips, who stood blocking her way.

'Listen,' the woman hissed, '''cos I'm only saying this once. Don't sass the customers, right? Now, there's two lasagnes over by the window.'

As if in a dream, Jane allowed herself to be diverted into what had to be the kitchen, where she found two plates of lasagne waiting for her. She picked them up and carried them to their recipients, who thanked her.

'Next,' the fattest man was saying, 'policy. Anybody got anything to say about policy, guys?'

'It's a great policy we got there, Rocky.'

'Yeah, don't let's fool around with it, it's working just fine.'

Jane's feet, meanwhile, had walked her back into the kitchen, where she took delivery of three portions of veal. There was a lot of cream on the veal, she noticed; in fact, if the proprietor of this restaurant took to buying his dairy products from Europe in future, there was a fair chance that the Common Agricultural Policy might make it after all. Jane frowned.

'Table for six,' hissed the short woman in her ear, 'and don't get fresh.'

'I thought you were only going to tell me once,' Jane replied, and darted through the door before a reply could be mustered.

'Stocktake,' the fattest man was saying. 'Anybody know if we got any stock, fellas?'

'Sure, Rocky, we got all the stock we can handle.'

'Don't you worry about a thing, Rocky. It'll be just fine.'

As Jane approached, the six men fell silent and she could feel their eyes on her again, like overfed leeches. She put the plates down and turned to withdraw.'

'Did I hear you right, lady?' said a fat voice.

Slowly, Jane turned round. She was smiling.

'I beg your pardon?' she said.

'I said,' repeated the fat voice, 'did I hear you right just now?'

Jane identified the man speaking and looked him in the eye. It was rather like falling into something sticky, but she persevered. 'That depends,' she said, 'on what you thought you heard me say.'

The man jutted some chins at her. 'I thought you said,' he replied, 'something about my food.'

Jane looked down, to confirm that he'd had the pasta. 'I did indeed,' she said. Gosh, observed a part of her consciousness cheerfully, this is just like old times, isn't it? The rest of her consciousness pretended it hadn't heard.

'You *criticising* my food?' the man said.

'No,' Jane answered, as sweetly as she could. 'I'm sure it's lovely food. It's the company it keeps that I have my doubts about.'

There was a silence round the table, as the twelve eyes grew round with amazement. Finally, one of the fat men turned to another.

'Hey, Rocky,' it said, 'I thought you said this broad was okay.'

Rocky shrugged. 'So did I,' he replied. 'Hey, you,' he said, addressing Jane. She raised an enquiring eyebrow.

'Me?'

'You.'

'Well?'

The man seemed to be having difficulty with his powers of belief. 'Who do you think you are, lady?' he said quietly. Something struck Jane as odd about the way he said it, until she realised that, whether the man knew it or not, he actually did intend it as a question.

'My name is Jane,' Jane replied. 'I've only been in this office a week and I haven't the faintest idea what I'm supposed to be doing or what's going on. If you would care to explain exactly what it is that you want me to do, I'll get on to it as soon as I possibly can. Thank you.'

Ten little piggy eyes stared at her in complete bewilderment. The other two narrowed slightly.

'You're new to this work, aren't you?' said their owner quietly.

'No,' Jane said, 'I've done something similar before.'

'Is that so?' The man maintained his expression, giving Jane the feeling of being under a powerful X-ray that could see what she'd eaten for the last six days. Then one of the ends of his mouth flicked up a little. 'You like this sort of work?'

'No,' Jane replied.

'Not good enough for you, huh?' Again, Jane felt she was in the presence of a genuine enquiry.

'Let's say it doesn't tax me to the limits of my capacity,' she said. 'In fact,' she added carefully, 'it wasn't my idea in the first place.'

'No,' the man said. 'I guess not.' He widened the smile a micron or so. 'I'll say this for you, kid, you've got guts.'

'So have you,' Jane replied involuntarily. 'Lots and lots of them.'

The man didn't seem to mind; and Jane slowly became

aware of a feeling she didn't like. Either the man was getting bigger, or she was getting smaller, or both. She broke off eye contact, and looked at the one piece of bread remaining in the basket.

'So what kind of work are you looking for?' the man said. 'Not office work, I guess.'

'I've done that,' Jane said quietly. 'Not really me, some-how.'

'I guess not.' Suddenly he chuckled. It was rather an attractive sound. 'Maybe you should try your hand at a few things, you know, look around a bit till you find something that suits you.'

'Thanks,' Jane said. 'I'll remember that.'

'Like I said,' the man repeated, 'you've got guts. Just don't make a pain of yourself in anybody else's if you can help it, okay?'

Jane mumbled something. Just now, she was thinking how nice it would be to get back to her desk and talk to somebody on the telephone. More her sort of level, somehow.

'Now,' the man said, 'let me tell you something.'

He half stood up, and began whispering in Jane's ear. It was rather like having your ears syringed by a blind octopus, but the words that she was hearing took her mind off that aspect of it.

'Thank you,' she said. 'You've been most helpful.'

The man smiled, widely this time. 'You're welcome,' he said. 'Oh, and kid—'

'Yes?'

'Before you go, tell Rosa this veal needs warming through,' the man said. 'Now get outa here.'

Jane pushed the door of Number Six. This time, she didn't bother to knock first.

The occupant of Number Six was not a human being, nor even vaguely anthropomorphous. What Jane found sitting in the expensive-looking leather swivel chair was a chipmunk.

'Excuse me,' Jane said.

The chipmunk looked up from the pile of papers in front of it and wiggled its nose. 'Well?' it said.

For a split second, something shorted in Jane's mind, and she couldn't think of anything to say. Anything, that is, apart from 'You're a chipmunk', which probably didn't need saying right now.

'Correct,' said the chipmunk. 'Did you come in here to tell me that?'

The short cleared. 'Not you as well,' Jane replied testily. 'Can everybody in this place read minds?'

The chipmunk's whiskers quivered slightly. 'I can't,' he said. 'It's just a ninety-nine per cent certainty I know what you're thinking. And before you waste your effort wondering, I can take any shape I like. I use this one for people who come barging in here without an appointment,' he added, 'because it disconcerts them.'

'Fine,' Jane replied. 'I want to talk to you about how this department is run.'

'I know you do,' replied the chipmunk. 'Now get out.'

By way of a reply, Jane sat down and folded her arms. The chipmunk sighed and nibbled a small area of veneer off the edge of its desk.

'I can give you five minutes,' it said.

'Thank you.' Jane smiled, opened her handbag and produced a notebook. 'I'll come straight to the point, then, shall I? This entire department is superfluous.'

The chipmunk stood up in its chair and waggled its forepaws briskly; then it sat down again, turned round three times, and crouched with its ears back. 'Rubbish,' it said.

'Fact,' Jane replied. 'The alleged purpose of this department is general administration for the whole operation. It's superfluous because it doesn't administer anything. And the reason for that is that the system broke down 107 years ago.'

The chipmunk disappeared. In its place, there appeared a

long, green snake with diamond markings. 'Really,' it observed.

'Really,' Jane replied. 'Take it from me. Ever since then, the input's been continuing to flow in, but the output's ground to a complete halt. Such administration as actually takes place is entirely spontaneous and *ad hoc*. I think that's the expression I want,' Jane added.

'It'll do,' the snake said. 'Where does your information come from, by the way?'

'A man in a restaurant told me,' Jane replied. 'For instance, this department is supposed to channel funds from the Treasurer's office to the Destiny department, via a system of requisitions and pink chits. In practice, Destiny keeps its money in a cocoa tin behind the clock in the machine shed. When there's nothing left in the tin, the duty supervisor sneaks into the social club while the barman's having his lunch, using the duplicate key belonging to the captain of the bowling team, and takes the change from the till. The barman in turn writes it off against breakages. Correct?'

The snake darted a fine tongue at her and hissed. Jane nodded and went on.

'This department,' she said, 'is also nominally responsible for the allocation of staff to, among others, the Perjury department, the main job of which is to strike perjurers with lightning. Perjury has a staff of seventy operatives and six supervisors, all on full pay, but nobody gets hit by lightning because the post of departmental head has been vacant for over 300 years. The net result is that, although perjury among mortals is regularly detected and noted in the Records, perjurers aren't being zapped at because thunderbolts can't be drawn from the stores without a green chit signed by the departmental head. All that the operatives can do, therefore, is stick their tongues out at the perjurers and shout rude words at them; and since all Perjury staff are required by the rules to be invisible and imperceptible to mankind . . .'

There was a soft rustling noise as the snake wound itself

round the arm of its chair. 'Go on,' it said.

'Need I?' Jane replied. 'If you want me to, I will. I can tell you about how the staff pension fund never reaches the pensioners, not because the money isn't there, but because Gary in Pensions is waiting for the 1897 returns and can't issue a mauve chit without them; so everybody puts five kreuzers a week into the Solstice Club at the newsagents' round the corner from the Earthquakes building, which does the job perfectly well. Or there's stationery; shall I tell you about how the unissued stock of paperclips recently broke away under the force of its own mass and is now the centre of a whole new planetary system out the other side of Orion's Belt?' Jane paused for breath, and because she had run out of examples. The snake looked at her.

'So,' it said at last. 'There are hiccups here and there. Big deal.'

Jane bit her lip; was it her imagination, or could she hear the faint clunk of a called bluff? 'Hiccups,' she repeated. 'The sort of hiccup they had in San Francisco in 1906.'

The snake lifted its head, wondered what to do with it, and threaded it through the handle of its briefcase. 'We'll give what you say very serious thought,' it replied. 'In the meantime, perhaps you feel you ought to be seconded to some other department.'

Anger is a curious thing, with a behaviour pattern rather like that of a Honda CX550 motorcycle. Sometimes you can give the throttle just the slightest of tweaks, and the next thing you're aware of is the ambulancemen picking bits of hedge out of your lower abdomen. Sometimes you stamp the gear lever down into fourth and twist the throttle right round, and the beast just looks up at you out of its cow-like instrument panel and slows down to a gentle stroll. The only thing you can rely on is its habit of running out of petrol exactly halfway between filling stations.

Jane's anger, to continue the simile, had just boiled dry; and, as she looked the snake in the eyes and tried to think what to say next, something told her that it was going to be a long, hard push home.

'Perhaps that'd be best,' she said softly. 'Thank you for your time.' She got up, collected her handbag, and left the office.

As she was clearing her desk, the phone rang.

'You shouldn't have done that,' said Ganger's voice. It sounded cheerful. 'Not at all wise.'

'I expect you're right,' Jane replied. 'Who was that man in the restaurant?'

The line seemed to go numb. 'That was Rocky,' said Ganger, and his voice sounded as if he was speaking through two pillow-cases and a sock. 'You weren't supposed to meet him, either.'

'He seemed to be expecting to meet me,' Jane said.

'I know. Anyway, there we are. Come and see me at half nine tomorrow, and we'll talk. Oh, and by the way.'

'Yes?'

'You're doing just fine. Trust me.' Ganger smiled into Jane's ear, and hung up.

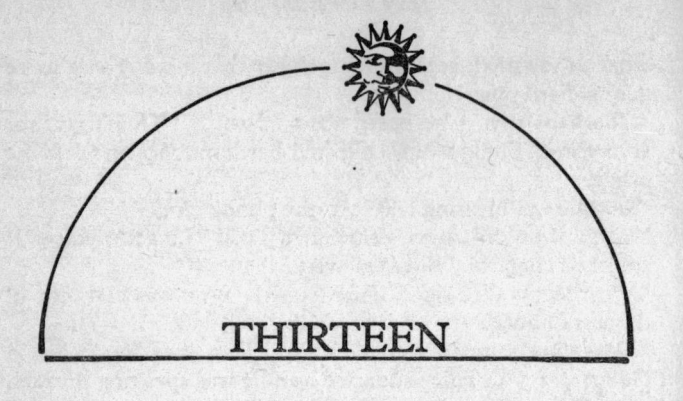

THIRTEEN

The sky is very high here.

In most places, the sky is just, well, high; a sort of blue tent that keeps the stars out and the air in. Here, it's different. Here, it's so high above sea-level that the existence of the ground is little more than an unsubstantiated rumour. There is also a castle.

A big, frilly, no-expense-spared, Ludwig of Bavaria special. And it's bobbing and floating about, like a balloon that's been at the sherry on an empty stomach, with nothing holding it up apart from the thought of the quite appalling effect it would have on the ground if it ever stopped floating.

When it comes to a bare-knuckle fight between gravity and social conscience, gravity loses.

As you approach, picking your way cautiously through the thermals and taking care not to tread on the heads of any high-flying birds, you can hear snatches of a strange and bewildering noise, wafted at you by the semi-feral winds that hide out in the major altitudes. From this distance, and bearing in mind the uncanny distortions of wind and the Doppler effect, you could almost believe that you were listening to several thousand people whistling – flat, off-key –

the disjointed scraps of a half-familiar tune.

Welcome to the Castle in the Air, headquarters of the Department of Omens and Auspices. The men standing in inch-perfect rows in the courtyard are trainee Messengers. Once they graduate, they will spend their working lives delivering dreams, uncanny flashbacks, moments of déjà vu, and other similar communications. At the moment, they are being taught the extremely tricky art of making the unique noise known as the postman's whistle.

Now, supposing you look very carefully, you'll notice one small figure in the Departmental blue-and-gold uniform, whose hair is rather longer than the rest. If you can somehow force your ears to blot out the general cacophony, you'll notice that this one individual is defiantly whistling, in tune and without sudden disconcerting pauses, a tune which is unmistakably 'Sergeant Pepper's Lonely Hearts Club Band'.

Guess who.

'You mustn't think of it in those terms,' Ganger had said, as they trudged up the Castle's drive. 'That's negative.'

'Really,' Jane replied. She would have expressed herself more fully, but the gradient was steep, and her knees were beginning to feel as if some joker had whipped the sinews out of them while she wasn't looking.

'Believe me,' Ganger said. 'Even if we were trying to keep you out of the way for a while, which we aren't, we wouldn't do it by putting you in the Messenger service. It's far too high profile for that.'

'High,' said Jane, breathlessly sardonic (try it for yourself), 'profile. Running errands. Delivering messages.'

'Yeah.' Ganger stopped for a moment, ran his finger round the inside of the button-down collar of his Abercrombie and Fitch pink shirt, and breathed in. 'Hardly hidden away in some out-of-the-way back office, is it?'

Jane wiped sweat out of her eyes with her thumb and forefinger. 'Not exactly challenging, though. Not precisely demanding the highest levels of executive performance. I thought you said I was a high-flyer.'

Ganger started to look down, then checked himself quickly. 'You want to go any higher than this, you can find your own way.'

Jane kept her face straight, just. 'You're not afraid of heights, are you?' she said.

'I'm bloody terrified of heights,' Ganger replied. 'Think about it, will you? My natural environment isn't high up on top of things; in fact, it's the exact opposite. I get vertigo standing on thick pile carpet sometimes. And,' he added, 'if you think that's so terribly amusing, we'll pay a visit to my departmental HQ one of these days, and we'll see how you like that.'

Jane made a contrite sort of breathless gasping noise, and they continued their climb in silence, or at least without words, for a while. Eventually, Jane bit her lip.

'Sorry,' she said. 'And I do appreciate you coming along to introduce me. Thanks.'

Ganger smiled. 'Think nothing of it,' he said. 'That's fine.'

'I'm sorry?'

'I said that's fine.'

'I'm sorry,' Jane shouted back, 'I can't hear you for the blood pumping in my ears.'

'It's not important.'

'Sorry?'

'I said it's ... Nothing.'

'Are we there yet?'

Ganger opened his mouth, thought better of it, and nodded. In front of them, its drawbridge lowered over nothing at all and resting on even less, was the gatehouse of the Castle in the Air.

Over the keystone of the arch there was a board of wood. Wind at barometric pressure had long since scoured it of varnish, but still faintly visible were the words:

The Laurels

painted in faded white. Jane raised an eyebrow.

'We tried calling it that for a while,' Ganger explained, 'but it never seemed to catch on somehow. You wait there while I knock.'

He advanced up to the massive gate and lifted the knocker, using both hands and putting his back into it. He managed to raise it a full inch before he had to let go.

'It's not a real knocker, you see,' he said, rubbing his arms gingerly. 'Or at least it's real, but it's an ideal knocker. You know, the way knockers should be in an ideal universe. And in an ideal universe, people take a lot more exercise than we do.'

'Um.'

'So,' Ganger went on, 'I guess we'll have to do the next best thing.'

He stooped slightly and walked down under the gate. Jane followed, her belief not so much suspended as dangling by a thread.

'Mind how you go from now on,' Ganger called out to her as they emerged into the outer yard. 'The whole of this place is an Excluded Liability Zone.'

Jane blinked. 'Excuse me?' she said.

'Excluded Liability Zone,' Ganger repeated. 'Absolutely necessary, in view of the sort of work they do here. You see, if we could be held accountable for any of the information that we pass on from here – in perfectly good faith, you understand – we'd be in court so fast our feet wouldn't touch. Talking of which, look out for tripwires.'

'Tripwires.'

Ganger nodded. 'And dogs, of course. It's part of the training programme, you see.'

'Dogs I can understand,' Jane said, thinking of postmen again. 'But why tripwires?'

'We deliver supernatural promptings to some of the best-

defended people in the cosmos,' Ganger replied with a hint
of pride. 'You know the sort of thing. Merchant princes who
won't clinch a deal unless they get an okay from their
astrologer. Lunatic third-world dictators who take their
policy guidelines from the spirits of their ancestors. Identical
twin brothers of Latin American drug barons. When you're
on a job like that, tripwires come as light relief. And the worst
part of it is,' Ganger continued, grinning, 'you have to keep
whistling. It's the Code, you see.'

'Um.'

'Whistling, scattering rubber bands everywhere and never
turning up with a Recorded Delivery unless you're sure the
recipient is out. It's a point of honour. They're very strict
about it.'

Directly under their feet the sun chugged past, twenty
minutes ahead of schedule. Was it Jane's imagination, or did
the pilot wave? Ganger stopped and straightened his tie.

'Right,' he said, 'we're here. Now then, I have a strange
feeling you're going to do all right here.'

'Funny you should mention that,' Jane replied. 'So have I.'

'Naturally,' Ganger said. 'Think about it.'

Bjorn hesitated.

Some hard things have been said about him recently, so the
record should be set straight. He had his failings, true, but
when it came to balls, he had more of them than Dunlop and
Slazenger put together. Equipped with an axe, a home-made
grappling hook and Great-grandmama's washing-line, he
was getting ready to burgle the Portals of the Sunset.

He reminded himself to stay cool, but it wasn't really
necessary. Slowly and methodically, he checked his equipment, pulled his mask (one of Old Gretchen's black leg-
warmers with two eye-holes cut in it) over his face and crept
forwards.

About here, somewhere, there should be an invisible
electric fence.

He knew all about the fence. A long time ago, when he was working on Security, he and Thick Mick and Kevin the Pisser had had the job of installing it, one wet Friday afternoon. As he had anticipated, it did not detain him long.

The searchlights mounted on Number Three and Number Four observation towers would have been a serious hazard, if it wasn't for the fact that keeping the bearings oiled and in good repair had been the responsibility of Old Nobby from Maintenance ever since the Fall of Man. Nobby had long since worked out what axle grease was for. He ate it.

So far, so good. There were three machine-gun nests in Number Five observation tower; but what with the cutbacks and everything, the gunners were never issued with more than five rounds of ammunition each per year, and they were under strict orders to save those for the twenty-one-gun salute for the Commandant's birthday. Given this limitation, the gunners (probably still Daft Terry and Gormless Dave, even after all these years) tended to spend their watch in the guardhouse playing endless games of dominoes, which somehow or other neither of them ever seemed to win.

Having penetrated as far as the outer perimeter fence, Bjorn stopped and assessed the task now facing him. This was where the fun started.

For reasons which need not concern us here, nobody in the village had ever seen the need to spend good money on a pair of wirecutters. Bjorn, who had spent his meagre savings playing the Speak Your Weight machines at the Wolfhound bus depot on his way out, was therefore going to have to improvise. Over it, or through it.

He decided against over it. If memory served him correctly, the posts holding it up were put in by some friends of his from the Department of Works, and so the chances of it bearing his weight were not high. Through it, however, meant cutting a hole through the wire mesh without waking the entire guard. He frowned, and checked through his rucksack for inspiration.

Having rejected the spare pair of underpants, the roll of extra strong mints, the broken watch and the July 1985 edition of *StreetBike*, he was left with a tin opener, a leaky felt-tip pen and a Zambian Army Knife. The latter item had one overwhelming advantage over its Swiss rival which outweighed its various drawbacks in Bjorn's estimation. It was given away free with litre cans of lawnmower gearbox oil. He took it out of the rucksack and fumbled for the sawblade attachment.

It says something about the quality of Departmental fencing wire that Bjorn was through and out the other side in three minutes flat. (For the record, when the Zambian Army wants a fence cut, they don't hang around breaking their fingernails trying to get the sawblade out; they get on the radio for a squadron of MiGs.)

According to the periphery defences design specification, there are seventeen acres of minefield between the inner and outer perimeter fences. According to the latest Security Department stock audit, the Department possesses five mines, at least three of which were in working order when last inspected. Bjorn gritted his teeth and ran for it. There are times in a man's life when he just has to ride his luck.

Which brought him, breathless but unscathed, to the foot of the inner perimeter fence. This was rather more of a challenge, since it hadn't been installed by the Department but taken over without substantial modification from the chicken farm which had been on the site before the Department requisitioned it. Here Bjorn suffered his first major setback. He tore the right leg of his trousers, about an inch below the knee.

'The thing to remember in this job,' said the Dream-Master General, 'is never to turn your back on small dogs.'

Jane nodded. 'Right,' she said. 'I think I can remember that. And all the rest of it,' she added, 'such as finding the recipient, climbing in through locked and barred windows, all that sort of stuff; I suppose that just comes by light of nature.'

The Dream-Master gave her a disapproving look. 'All right, Miss Clever,' he said, 'we'll come on to the various procedures in due course. We can't run before we can walk, you know. I was just telling you, for your own good, you look out for small dogs.'

'I always have,' Jane replied, with feeling. 'Especially when sitting down in a strange house. Look, I didn't mean to sound cocky, it's just that I want to get on with it. The practical side, I mean.'

The Dream-Master nodded. 'All in good time,' he said. 'Now, first you'll do your basic training. That's effecting entry, recipient identification drill, and elementary brain infiltration. That's the easy part.'

'Um.'

'The tricky part,' the Dream-Master went on, 'is getting out again afterwards.'

Behind the rail of Number Nine observation tower, Trooper 2314 Starspear identified his target and took careful aim. He sighted along the broad barrel, checked that his feet were braced and his arm was high and rigid, breathed deeply in and smoothly out, and . . .

'Unlucky,' observed Trooper 8345 Moonblade. He walked over to the board, pulled out the darts, and placed his feet on the chalk line.

'Double six for game,' he remarked confidently.

At the bottom of the tower, Bjorn paused and unwound ten feet of washing-line from inside his anorak. It was a long time since he'd done anything like this – in fact, the most recent occasion he could remember was when it was his turn to raid the Canteen at Destiny for digestive biscuits – but there are some things you just don't forget. He flexed his fingers and deftly attached the grappling-hook to the line with three superimposed granny-knots.

Far above his head – and below his feet too, for that matter, but let's not confuse the issue – the stars twinkled. A stray photon or so glanced harmlessly off the tines of the hook as he whirled it three times round his head and let fly.

There are, of course, other things that you *do* forget, and the art of throwing grappling-hooks is one of them. After a few minutes of serious thought, Bjorn picked himself up, rubbed the back of his head vigorously, and set about rewinding the rope round his forearm in long, slack loops.

'Double two for game,' said Trooper 8345 Moonblade grimly. He steadied himself, threw his weight forward on to the front foot in the approved manner, and . . .

. . . And watched incredulously as a big black hook appeared over the rail of the tower, buried one of its talons in the dartboard, and whisked it off the wall and away into the darkness.

Far below, he could just hear a soft thud, followed by a faint cry.

'I think we'll have to call that a draw, Dave,' said Trooper 2314 Starspear, just managing to force the words out of his mouth before the whoop of triumphant relief beat them to it. Seven kreuzers had been riding on the outcome, and he had been on double one for the last six throws.

'Some bastard nicked our dartboard,' replied Trooper 8345 Moonblade furiously. 'Did you see that, Nev? Some bastard just . . .'

There was a whooshing sound, and the hook reappeared, hovered in the air for, say, a two-fiftieth of a second, and fell on to the rail. As it retreated, one of the tines caught and held firm.

'I think there's something in the rules about it,' persevered Trooper 2314 Starspear. 'I think what it actually says is if the dartboard gets eaten by a passing column of soldier ants, but it's the same thing really . . .'

'Nev,' whispered his colleague urgently, 'there's someone climbing up the tower.'

They looked at each other.

'We're being invaded, Dave,' said Trooper 2314 Starspear. 'Look, don't we have to do something, or . . .?'

Trooper 8345 Moonblade gave him a long stare. 'Yeah,' he said, 'sure we do. We report it.'

Below them they could hear grunts and soft oaths, such as might be made by (for example) a large man climbing painfully up a thin nylon rope without wearing gloves.

'Report it?' repeated Trooper 2314 Starspear. 'You sure? I mean, don't we just, like . . .?' He pointed to his rifle, which was leaning against the corner of the far rail. His colleague shook his head vigorously, dislodging various items.

'Don't talk bloody soft, Nev, for crying out loud,' whispered Trooper 8345 Moonblade urgently. 'For all we know, if we . . . start anything, it could be a thing. You know, diplomatic implement. We could really be in trouble. Just hold your water, wait till they've gone and report it, right?'

'But.' Inside Trooper 2314 Starspear's head, everyday civilian logic battled with military logic. 'But what if they, like, attack us, Dave?'

Trooper 8345 Moonblade stared past him to the rail, where a large hand was reaching up and scrabbling for a hold. He swallowed hard.

'Use your brain, son,' he hissed. 'We hide, right?'

Breathing hard, Bjorn hauled himself up to chin level, swung a leg over the rail, and flopped on to the floor of the tower. He lay for a few moments where he had fallen, catching his breath and swearing. Then he raised himself on his elbows and looked about him.

Nobody here. Well, he'd guessed that from the fact that he'd got this far without being shot. The odd thing was, though, that the only thing that gave you the impression of the place being deserted was the actual absence of people. Everything else pointed to active occupation; the still-warm mugs of tea, the glowing single-bar electric fire, the two rifles leaning against the rail, the forage caps hung on the radio aerial, the two pairs of shoes visible under the blackout curtain . . .

Bjorn froze for a moment. Then he grinned.

With an easy movement, he removed the grappling hook, transferred it to the opposite rail, and cast the line over the side. Then, with a slight wince and a muffled cry of pain, he hoisted himself over the side, slid down the line, and disappeared. A few moments later, the grappling hook wobbled, came loose and disappeared after him. Then silence.

'Oh look,' said a voice behind the blackout curtain. 'Here's the spare dartboard.'

'Dave . . .'

'That's lucky, isn't it, Nev? You know, thinking about it, I believe you're right. Drawn game.'

'Dave . . .'

'Mugs away, right?' The curtain parted, and Trooper 8345 Moonblade emerged purposefully and hung the dartboard on the hook.

'Dave,' said Trooper 2314 Starspear, 'we'd better notify HQ, like you said, before he has a chance to get too . . .'

'I said,' repeated Trooper 8345 Moonblade meaningfully, 'mugs away.' He thrust the darts into his colleague's hands.

'But Dave, there's only one of him and if they start looking now, they'll find him and . . .'

'He'll tell them that two of the Department's crack special forces hid behind a curtain while he legged it over the side and got away.' Trooper 8345 gathered an ample handful of the front of his comrade's battledress lapels and held it for a few significant seconds. 'Look,' he said, letting go. 'You don't want to go around sending off daft messages like that. For a start, nobody'd believe you.'

'They wouldn't?'

Trooper 8345 Moonblade shook his head. 'Nah,' he replied. 'They'd just think you were making things up. Or imagining things, as a result of the nasty blow to your head.'

'But I haven't had a nasty blow to my head, Dave.'

'These things can be arranged, Nev.'

The two men exchanged non-verbal communication for two, maybe three seconds. You can say a lot in three seconds if you don't have to bother with words.

'Right,' said Trooper 2314 Starspear, placing his left foot carefully alongside the chalk line and taking the first dart in his right hand. 'Doubles for in.'

There was, Jane decided, nothing to it.

She turned and frowned at the window, which obligingly slid down and closed itself noiselessly. A sign with her left hand filled the room with a soft green light, imperceptible except through a Messenger's specially treated contact lenses, but more than adequately bright to illuminate the simple operation of dream delivery.

Jane pulled on her rubber gloves; then, with the tip of her extended index finger, she gave the sleeper the very gentlest of prods, just on the point of his shoulder. He made a piggy noise and rolled on to his side, right ear uppermost.

Piece of cake, muttered Jane under her breath. Too easy, surely.

From the black canvas holster slung from her belt she took the long black syringe, broke it open and felt in her hip pocket for the sealed foil capsule which contained the dream. Using her teeth as she'd been taught, she tore the capsule open and tipped its contents into the chamber of the syringe. As they fell through the air into the chamber the green light flashed momentarily on them. Jane nearly dropped the syringe.

For training, naturally, they'd used blanks. This was the first time she'd seen a live dream, and she didn't like the look of it one bit. It lay in the chamber, flashing and squirming. She shuddered.

In the green glow it resembled a transparent sausage, crammed full of little wriggling people and things, coloured lights, explosions and lightning changes of scene. Since the

149

sausage was a mere three inches long, and apparently contained a cast of thousands, the individual items were all rather too small to make out, but the impression they gave in the round, so to speak, wasn't pleasant at all. She wondered for a moment who the recipient was, and what precisely was going to happen to him.

None of her business, she decided firmly. With an easy motion she clicked the syringe shut, flicked off the safety and poised it carefully over the sleeper's ear. Now then, she could feel her lips miming, this isn't going to hurt . . .

Quickly and firmly she shot the plunger home and pulled the syringe smoothly away. The sleeper jerked slightly, moaned and turned over on to his other side. Mission accomplished. Goody.

The sleeper sat bolt upright.

He was, Jane noticed for the first time, wearing a pair of dark purple satin pyjamas with a monogram on the pocket. Any nascent sympathy she might have had for the sleeper soaked quietly away between the floorboards of her mind. A quick glance reassured her that he was still fast asleep, eyes tightly shut, breathing regular.

'*Hey!*' he said.

Jane blinked. She hadn't been told about anything like this.

'*What the hell do you mean, the ides of March? It's the middle of September, and what are ides, anyway?*'

'Um,' Jane replied. The sleeper slept on.

'*That's not an answer,*' he said. '*Look, are you sure you've delivered the right message to the right person here?*'

'I think so,' Jane said. 'I mean, this is 47 Newport Drive, Cardiff, isn't it?'

The sleeper nodded. '*Yes, it is, but this doesn't make sense. I'm expecting a highly important dream about Marshfield Consolidated $9\frac{1}{2}\%$ Convertible Unsecured Loan Stock, and you come shoving my ears full of something about bewaring the ides of March. Are you sure you haven't got your wires crossed somewhere?*'

'Hold on,' Jane said. She was beginning to feel distinctly uncomfortable. 'Let me just check what it says on the wrapper. Here we are,' she went on, smoothing out the foil and peering at the script. 'Jeremy Lloyd-Perkins, 47 Newport Drive, Cardiff. That's you, isn't it?'

The sleeper nodded slowly, like a puppet with rusty hinges in its neck. '*Sure that's me,*' he said. '*But that's not my message. They must have got them muddled up at the depot.*'

Jane wrinkled her nose. 'You seem to know a lot about this,' she said. 'For a human being, I mean.'

'*I've been a subscriber for five years,*' the sleeper replied, and Jane noticed how little his lips moved when he spoke. '*I suppose I should be used to it by now. Still, it's a bit poor, if you ask me. Only last month I was expecting a hot tip on the Beaconsfield International rights issue, and all I got was some load of old tosh about cancelling my passage on the* Lusitania. *I don't want to be difficult, but it does make it hard to plan your long-term investment strategy when you can't rely on your supernatural advisers.*'

'Um.'

'*Look at it from the other guy's point of view,*' continued the sleeper, swaying slightly backwards and forwards. '*I mean, there's some poor sod somewhere who's going to have to face these ides of March things armed with nothing more relevant than an insight into the FT 100 Share Index for 18th September. He might get into serious trouble, you know?*'

'I'm sorry,' Jane said dispiritedly. 'It's not my . . .'

Without moving a millimetre, the sleeper managed to give a remarkably good impression of an impatient gesture. '*That's all very well,*' he said, '*but it's not helping me any, and I don't suppose the unfortunate bastard who sailed on the* Lusitania's *going to be feeling much more cheerful about it either. Even though,*' he added, '*he has the satisfaction of knowing that if only he hadn't drowned he could have cleaned up something rotten in early trading.*'

Jane shrugged. 'I'll mention it to them back at headquarters,' she said. 'But that's all I can do, I'm afraid.'

'*Oh no you don't,*' the sleeper said, and his arm shot out and closed around Jane's wrist. '*You're not going anywhere until I get my dream. And don't try struggling, or I'll wake up.*'

Jane felt her jaw drop, but she couldn't see any point in doing anything about it. When you're stuffed, you're stuffed.

'You're hurting my wrist,' she pointed out.

The sleeper sneered. '*Tell me all about it when I'm awake,*' he replied.

'Be fair,' she pleaded. 'How am I supposed to get you your dream if you won't let me go?'

The sleeper laughed, through nis nose. '*Not my problem,*' he said. '*I'm asleep, remember, I'm not in a position to do your thinking for you. Just get it sorted, or there'll be trouble.*'

'I see,' Jane replied, and there was an edge to her voice you could have shaved with. 'In that case, I'll see what I can do.'

With her free hand, she fished out another foil packet, chosen at random, tore it open and held the capsule in her teeth while she drew the syringe. She loaded it, noting with a certain grim satisfaction the nature of the contents. 'You want another dream, Mr Lloyd-Perkins,' she said. 'Here you go.'

Quick as a flash running for a bus, she drove the plunger home, and the transparent sausage sparkled briefly as it travelled through three centimetres of air. The sleeper jerked violently and let go his grip, and Jane dived for the window, remembering just in time to scowl at it. It opened briskly, apologised as she sailed through it, and snapped shut after her. As she landed lightly on the balls of her feet, she could hear Mr Lloyd-Perkins screaming in his sleep. His own silly fault, she told herself as she switched on the ignition of her starcycle, for trying to take it out on an innocent messenger.

When she was safely clear of Newport Avenue, she pulled up under a street lamp and examined the empty foil packet.

Nostradamus, it read, *Concerning the End of the World*, and below that, in smaller type:

BEST BEFORE: 17th FEBRUARY, 2706

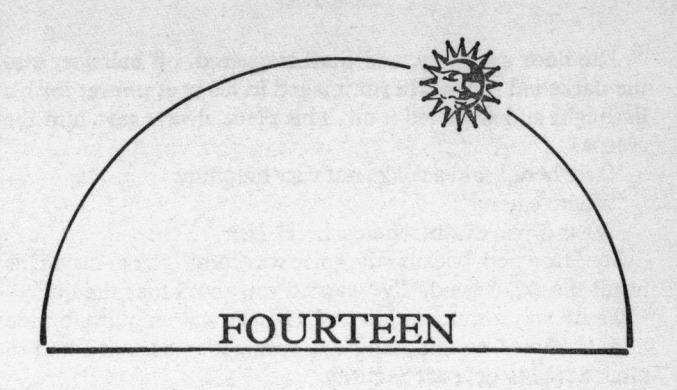

FOURTEEN

Part of Staff's duties was the inspection, on a more or less regular basis, of some of the outlying departments which had no internal review system of their own. He didn't enjoy doing it at the best of times, and Complaints was perhaps his least favourite.

Access to Complaints is, naturally, open to everybody and everything in the universe, regardless of species, metaphysical status or temporal orientation; however, for the sake of internal administrative efficiency, the Department reserves the right only to consider complaints which are submitted in the prescribed form.

The prescribed form is Form C301, a fifteen-page booklet printed on pages of beaten gold, twelve miles long by five miles wide. Once completed, the form must be submitted in triplicate, and the top copy must be countersigned by an apostle, saint (minor Celtic saints excepted), archangel, Bodhisattva, Taoist patriarch, dæmon of Grade 5 or higher, Elector of the Holy Roman Empire or other person of similar standing in the community.

'Hello,' Staff called, pushing against the door with all his weight and heaving. 'Anybody here?'

The door gave way, and Staff staggered, off balance, into the darkened office. He rummaged in his coat pocket for his flashlight and switched it on. This place always gave him the creeps.

'Over here,' said a voice, not very helpfully.

'Where's here?'

'What d'you mean, where's here? *Here*.'

Staff frowned, because the voice was coming from inside his head. 'Look,' he said, 'I've warned you about that already.'

There was a muted plop and Ganger was standing beside him. 'I know,' he said, 'and I'm sorry. It's just that I had to hitch a ride to get past Security.'

Staff nodded. 'Fair enough,' he said. 'So what was so important that it couldn't wait till . . .' The words evaporated on his lips like rain on a blast-furnace as the beam of his torch licked something huge and shiny in the far corner of the room. A part of his brain – the part where most of his thoughts refused to go, except in pairs in broad daylight – said *I know what that is*. The rest of his brain pretended it hadn't heard.

'I know,' Ganger said. 'A bit of a turn-up, really. Still, there's a first time for everything.'

Staff stopped dead, turned and looked at him.

'You don't mean to say,' he said slowly, 'that somebody has actually . . .'

'Complained, yes.' Ganger nodded. 'Fortunately,' he said, 'it isn't valid.'

The torch-beam flashed on what seemed to be an infinity of gold space, and the photons bounced, and bounced, and bounced. 'It isn't?'

'Nope.'

'Why not?'

'I don't know about you,' replied Ganger, 'but I don't think Colonel Gadaffi falls within the permitted class of countersignatories. Apart from that, though, it's all in order and according to Hoyle.'

Staff scratched his chin. 'It's a moot point, actually,' he said. 'Anyway, we can leave that to the boys in Legal. Who's it from?'

'That's the puzzling thing,' Ganger replied, fiddling aimlessly with his key-ring. 'Nobody seems to have heard of him. Let's go see if the name rings any bells with you.'

With the help of a turbo-charged golf-buggy which they found in an outhouse, they made the journey across Form C301. Eventually, after taking a wrong turning just after paragraph 658(c)(iv) and running out of petrol on the slopes of the embossed seal, they came to the right place. Ganger put on the handbrake and replaced his sextant in the glove compartment.

'Here we are,' he said. 'Look.'

Staff moved his feet, and saw directly under them the words *Jeremy Lloyd-Perkins*, shallowly engraved in the soft metal.

'Who?'

'Search me,' Ganger replied. 'I tried looking him up on the computer, but of course the blasted thing was down again. I've got my secretary going through the card-index right now.'

Staff knelt down and ran a finger over the scored marks. 'So what's he complaining about?' he said.

'That's what I thought you ought to see,' Ganger replied. 'Come on.'

The draftsman who designed Form C301 had so many questions of an apparently irrelevant but of course strictly necessary nature to ask that the space left on the form for the actual complaint measured eighty millimetres by twenty. Mr Lloyd-Perkins, however, was gifted with small handwriting. Ganger produced a magnifying glass and held the torch while Staff examined the tiny words.

'Um,' he said.

'Exactly,' Ganger replied. 'It's not looking good, is it?'

Staff got up and brushed gold dust from his knees. 'I don't

suppose it was her fault, though,' he said. 'You know as well as I do that the sorting office up there is a mess. That's one of the reasons why we sent her there.'

'Sure,' Ganger replied. 'That's not the point, really, is it?'

'It isn't?'

Ganger shook his head, produced a collapsible shooting-stick from his coat pocket, drive its point through the thin gold membrane, and sat down. 'Of course not,' he replied. 'Think about it, will you? Here's a mortal nobody's ever heard of, right? From what he says here, I gather that he's a subscriber to Oracle, for the financial news. In other words, he's got a soul equipped with Teletext, but otherwise he's probably just a small-timer. Okay so far?'

Staff nodded.

'So,' Ganger continued, offering his colleague a peppermint, 'you don't suppose for one minute that he's in a position to know about the complaints procedure. Even if he does, nobody's going to tell me that somebody who lives in a four-bedroom house in the suburbs of Cardiff can afford this much gold just to complain about a garbled message. No, somebody's put him up to it.'

Staff looked up. 'One of us, you mean?'

'Someone in the Service, certainly,' Ganger replied.

'With a view to implicating you and me, you reckon?'

Ganger nodded. 'Smart move,' he said. 'Whoever it was knew there'd have to be an inquiry, and even if she's cleared, it'll still bring the fact that she's a mortal, hired without the authority of a resolution, out into the open. Clever, no?'

Staff nodded, his jaws working slowly and methodically on the peppermint. 'I'm not very happy about that,' he said.

'Me neither.'

'I think,' Staff continued, his brows lowering, 'that counts as playing silly-buggers, and I don't reckon we should put up with it.' He shook his head. 'No,' he went on, 'that won't do at all. Have you got any idea who . . .?'

''Fraid not,' Ganger replied, standing up and folding the

stick away. 'I'm making discreet enquiries, of course, but that's going to take time. I guess all we can do is be on our guard, and wait and see.'

Staff nodded. 'I suppose,' he said, 'sooner or later whoever it is will want to know why nothing's been done about the complaint. I don't suppose he knows it isn't valid.'

'Maybe not,' Ganger said. 'It could be that this is just intended as a warning, but I don't think so. It's a bit, well, monumental for that.'

'I've seen subtler hints,' Staff agreed, as the light from the torch played over the golden prairie all around them. 'Oh well, thanks for letting me know.'

'My pleasure,' Ganger said, and grinned. 'In the meantime,' he said, 'I suppose I'd better just get this cleared up. You know, put on microfiche.'

Staff nodded. 'Right,' he said. 'And, um, what happens to the original? The hard copy, so to speak?'

Ganger shrugged. 'Oh, I don't know,' he said with slightly exaggerated carelessness. 'Bin it, I suppose, or file it away somewhere. Mustn't let the place get cluttered up with piles of redundant old forms, must we?'

On their way out they were passed by a three-mile-long column of container lorries with an escort of soldiers equipped with axes, shovels and heavy-duty gear. As the lead jeep went by the driver raised his arm and gave Ganger a cheery wave.

'Friend of yours?' Staff asked.

'Never seen him before in my life,' Ganger replied. 'Keep in touch.'

'Hey!'
 'What?'
 'Over here.'
 'Ouch!'

Bjorn stood up, stepped over the recumbent guard and ran swiftly across the short patch of open ground between the guardhouse and the hangar door.

It was a long time since he'd been here last, but he was still taken aback by all this security. The laws of departmental entropy dictated that there should be less security, not more, and that what security there still was shouldn't work. Even in his day, the hangar had been protected from the attentions of intruders by a wooden gate kept shut by a bit of wire looped round the gatepost, and a lifesize cardboard cut-out of an Airedale silhouetted against the sky. Actual guards with rifles and steel helmets (he rubbed the side of his hand vigorously until the circulation started to move again) would have been out of the question. It all went to confirm his earlier impression that something was going on around here. He leaned back into the shadow of the door-frame and, having checked to make sure the coast was clear, he fished in his pocket for his penknife.

Nailfile; no. Corkscrew; no. Tweezers; no. Thing for taking stones out of impalas' hooves; no. Ah, here it was; jemmy.

He extracted the blade, inserted it between the door and the hasp of the padlock, and jerked hard. The blade broke.

Astonished, Bjorn picked himself up off the ground and stared at the lock. Admittedly, you wouldn't normally rely on the metallurgical expertise of the Zambian State Arsenals for anything much more strenuous than opening a letter – an airmail letter, at that – but even so. This padlock was Departmental property. In his experience, a gnat sneezing a mile away should leave it hanging from its shank like a hung-over bat.

His train of thought was derailed by a sound like the Milan rush hour played at full volume on Dolby stereo, and he instinctively ducked. This is serious, he said to himself, covering his ears with his hands. A burglar alarm. A burglar alarm that works.

Something was *definitely* going on around here.

Bjorn burped disgustedly, unslung his axe from behind his back, took two steps backwards and let the padlock have it.

'Ugh,' said a voice behind him; followed by the sound of a man falling over. Bjorn looked over his shoulder, to see a heavily armed trooper lying at his feet, with a dent in his steel helmet you could store linen in, and the head of Bjorn's axe lying on the ground beside him. The padlock, however, was still there. Bjorn frowned, until his forehead resembled the knee of a pair of unfashionably wide cord trousers. This wasn't the usual sort of Department padlock, the sort that you get free at petrol stations if you stop off to ask the way to the M34 and don't buy anything; this was a *padlock*.

'Okay, chummy.' Bjorn could feel something cold and hard in the small of his back. 'Spread 'em, and no funny business.'

He sighed, turned round, picked the trooper up by his lapels, put him in a handily situated dustbin and rammed the lid down hard. Some things, he was relieved to see, didn't change. They may have snazzy new molybdenum steel padlocks; but the sort of men who end up working in Security are still the ones who get chucked out of Earthquakes because they can't quite make the grade, intellectually speaking.

'Next time,' he said, not entirely unkindly, 'you could try holding the rifle with the bit with the hole in it pointing *away* from you.'

He gave the hangar door a final kick, yelped involuntarily, and trudged off into the darkness.

'Down there,' Jane shouted above the roar of the engine, and pointed. The pilot nodded uneasily.

'I still think . . .' he shouted back.

'Sorry?'

'I said, I still . . .'

'What?'

The pilot scowled. He knew she could hear him, and he was pretty sure she knew he knew. But for the life of him he couldn't think of a way of *proving* she knew he knew she knew. He gave up and decided he'd just fly the plane instead.

'There,' Jane was yelling in his ear, 'just by the big lake, can you see? That's it. Go down lower.'

It's not right, the pilot said to himself. We'll get into trouble. I'll get into trouble. I really shouldn't be doing this.

'Hold her steady,' Jane shouted. 'I'm going to release the rockets *now*.'

It's really down to what's allowed and what isn't, continued the pilot's train of thought – and as trains of thought go, this one's the Sundays only 06.34 service from Llanelli, stopping at all stations to Neath; because if the pilot had enough brain to half-fill the cap of the average biro, he'd still be cruising at sixty thousand feet, with the intercom switched firmly off – and this has got to be something that isn't. He tried to communicate his anxiety to his passenger.

'Are you *sure* you want me to . . .?'

'Sorry?'

The pilot swore under his breath and pushed the joystick down. He was going to regret this.

Crown Prince Konstantin of Anhalt-Bernberg-Schwerin, enjoying a pleasant drink beside the pool, saw something rather odd reflected in the plush blue water. He sat up and looked skywards over the rim of his Porsche sunglasses.

'Karl,' he said.

'Highness?' The footman, impeccable as always in the full dress uniform of an Equerry, Second Class, with crossed mulberry leaves and bar, materialised behind him. The prince noticed that he was trying, very hard but in vain, not to giggle.

'Karl,' he went on, running a finger lightly over the sabre scar on his left cheek, 'there is in the sky something not in the ordinary. Are you seeing it also?'

'*Jawohl*, Highness,' relied the footman. 'I am seeing it also.'

'*Sehr gut*,' the Prince replied. You can't be a Prince of the Blood and descended through fifty-nine unbroken generations from Charlemagne without having enough sang-froid to keep champagne chilled in a firestorm. 'For a moment I thought my eyes on me tricks were playing.' He pushed the sunglasses back to the bridge of his nose, said, 'That will be all,' and returned to his ski catalogue.

The footman clicked his heels, retreated soundlessly behind a row of mulberry bushes and collapsed into imperfectly muffled laughter, while overhead high-level winds started the long job of breaking up and dispersing an intricate pattern of vapour trails, which read:

KONSTANTIN VON ROSSFLEISCH YOU'VE HAD YOUR CHIPS

The heavens themselves blaze forth the death of princes; also their births and marriages, their official engagements, the dates of their more important garden parties, and all the rest of the mind-numbingly interesting information that one finds under such bylines as *Court Circular* in the newspapers with the awkwardly big pages.

Royalty are different from you and me. They don't panic. They don't run to and fro like headless chickens just because they get a warning from heaven telling them they're about to die. For example; the last thought that crossed the Prince's mind, about a seventy-fifth of a second before the bomb concealed in the four-foot-high inflatable rubber swan bobbing on the surface of the pool went off, was: How on earth did they manage to do the apostrophe in YOU'VE?

'In fact,' Jane continued, 'I don't see why we can't do the same thing right across the board.'

The Dream-Master General chewed a lump out of his moustache and swallowed it. 'You don't,' he said.

'No.' Jane sat down, uninvited, on the edge of the desk and reached in her bag for her notebook. 'I've been giving it some thought, doing a few outline costings, that sort of thing, and really . . .'

Very few people can say three dots and *really* mean them,

but Jane could. The Dream-Master General picked up a heavy rubber stamp reading FRAGILE (for use on the dreams of idealists, naturally) and started to peel the rubber bit off the wooden backing.

'For a start,' Jane continued, 'this personal hand-delivering of everything. That's out. I mean, it's so inefficient it's positively prehistoric. I gather you've got one guy who has to dress up in a red bathrobe once every year and deliver presents to every child in the known world. Have you any idea what that costs you in overtime?'

'You don't feel,' said the Dream-Master, in the tone of voice you'd expect from a volcano with indigestion, 'that it's an essential part of a truly personal service?'

'No. Another thing that's got to be sorted is the sorting. You've got to face up to the fact that what we're dealing with here is messages, not premium bonds. Fair enough?'

'So what,' croaked the Dream-Master, 'do you have in mind?'

'Computerisation,' Jane replied promptly, 'and bar codes. It's very easy once you get the hang of it.'

'I see. In future, everybody's dreams are going to have little patterns of wiggly lines in the bottom right-hand corner, are they?'

'You can disguise them as railings,' Jane said. 'Or stationary zebras, or something like that. All you need is a little imagination.'

'You forgot to tell me,' the Dream-Master observed, 'how we're going to deliver the dreams without roundsmen.'

'Did I?' Jane smiled. 'By fax, of course. Direct instantaneous transmission, brainwave to brainwave. And all during off-peak hours, too. It'll be cheaper, as well as quicker and more confidential.'

'I see.' The Dream-Master leaned forward, with the air of someone playing an ace. 'And what about prodigies?' he demanded sharply.

'Sorry?'

'Prodigies,' the Dream-Master repeated. 'The skies raining blood. Spectral armies fighting in the clouds. Plagues of frogs.'

Jane shook her head. 'They'll just have to go,' she said. 'I mean, as information technology, frogs have had their day. So have plagues of anything.' She paused to examine a cracked fingernail, and then continued: 'You've got to meet the changing needs of the consumer. These days, if you get a plague of anything, people aren't going to go running to the nearest soothsayer. They'll be too busy organising emergency relief rock concerts.' She made an expressive gesture with her hands. 'It all comes down,' she said, 'to cost-effectiveness. Time and motion, if you like. Time, as in not wasting; motion, as in not just going through.'

'Really.'

'Anyway,' Jane said, standing up. 'It'll all be in my report. I expect you'll get your copy in due course.'

The Dream-Master stood up too, and suddenly banged the desk in front of him. 'And just who do you think you are?' he said.

'Easy.' Jane gave him a long, hard look. 'I'm a mortal. Or, if you like to look at it another way, I'm one of the poor bloody customers. The end users. The unfortunate souls who have to use the services all your blasted Departments actually provide. The punters, in other words.'

The Dream-Master grinned. 'Exactly,' he said.

Jane sat down again, put her head slightly on one side and raised an inquisitive eyebrow. 'Please go on,' she said.

'Think about it,' replied the Dream-Master. 'You've got mortals–' He picked up the stapler from his desk-top, moved it six inches to the left and put it down again firmly. 'And on the other hand, you've got us.' He lifted his coffee mug and placed it carefully on top of a pile of petty cash vouchers. 'Understand?'

'No.'

'Then I'll explain. Mortals have it easy. They're born, they lounge about for a few years, whingeing, they die. We have to work here. Mortals–' He pushed the stapler off the desk into the wastepaper basket. 'But we're different. We're for keeps.' He picked up the coffee mug, which a sheet of paper had fastened itself to the bottom of, and then put it down again. 'You want to grasp the fact if you're going to work here.'

'Another thing that's wrong with this Department,' Jane observed after a long pause, 'is the disgraceful waste of perfectly serviceable office equipment.' She picked the stapler out of the bin, dusted it off and put it back on the desk. 'I take it you're not really sympathetic to my proposals?'

'You could say that.'

Jane sighed. 'And you don't think that anybody else will be, either?'

The Dream-Master nodded. 'Let me give you a word of advice,' he said. 'Try and get it into your head that improvements are not necessarily good. In fact,' he added forcefully, 'usually quite the reverse. Remember that and you won't go far wrong.'

'Thank you.'

'I haven't finished yet,' the Dream-Master continued. 'Once upon a time, long ago, there was another bright spark, just like you. Originally worked in this Department, oddly enough. Thought everything around here needed a good shake-up, reckoned we were all far too set in our ways and a thorough pruning would do us all the world of good. Clear out the vested interests and the restrictive practices, start from scratch. That sort of thing.' He sighed. 'It all sounded so good that we tried it, just for a while. Biggest mistake we ever made.'

'Really.'

'Oh yes.' the Dream-Master lolled back in his chair and put his hands behind his head. 'The idea was to create a whole new level of staff to take over the running of the world, look after it, repair it, make sure everything was kept clean and tidy and in good running order. And that's what we did. We recruited them, trained them, and handed over the whole shooting-match. They were called,' the Dream-Master added, almost as an afterthought, 'the human race.'

'Um.'

'Yes,' snapped the Dream-Master, 'um. Bloody silly idea, wasn't it? And you know what happened to the bright spark who suggested it?'

Feeling like the poor fool who's lent her watch to the conjuror, Jane shook her head. 'No,' she said. 'Do tell me.'

A grin like a septic dawn spread over the Dream-Master's face. 'He got posted,' he said.

'Posted?'

The Dream-Master picked up the Fragile stamp, pressed it on an ink-pad and brought it down on the desk-top so hard that it snapped in two.

'Yeah,' he said. 'Posted.'

Jane considered this for a moment. 'Wasn't that rather difficult?' she enquired.

'Nah,' replied the Dream-Master. 'Once we'd got his head through the flap, the rest just sort of followed.'

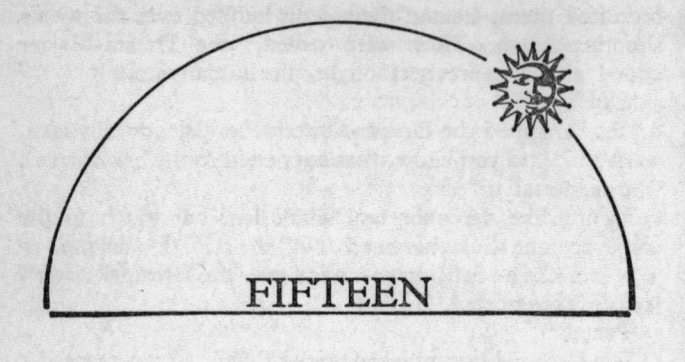

FIFTEEN

'Sod,' said Bjorn. He twisted uncomfortably round, and tried to see what had grabbed hold of his leg. The part of him that still occasionally harboured optimism hoped that it would turn out to be a smiling blonde air hostess.

It was, in fact, a man-trap. Close, but no cigar.

A fairly humane man-trap, it has to be said. The jaws weren't lined with inch-long steel spikes; in fact, they were padded with foam rubber and covered with chamois leather. There was also a notice, probably insisted upon by the Administration's hyper-paranoid legal advisers, engraved in tiny letters on the trap's upper mandible. It read:

CAUTION: THIS TRAP MAY BE DANGEROUS TO ELDERLY OR DISABLED PERSONS. MEMBERS OF THE PUBLIC ARE ADVISED THAT THEY GET CAUGHT IN IT ENTIRELY AT THEIR OWN RISK.

Bjorn grunted and tried prising the jaws apart with what was left of his axe. There was, of course, a man-trap-opening attachment on his Zambian Army Knife, but he'd broken that a day or so ago trying to cut into a pat of hot butter.

Overhead, the beams of many searchlights were producing a complex and geometrically satisfying display which, combined with the blaring of sirens and the thundering noise of many speakers playing back tapes of barking Rottweilers, added up to one of the most original *son et lumière* performances in cosmic history. You had to be there, of course.

Bjorn was, and wished he wasn't. The axe handle, seasoned hickory, groaned accusingly and splintered without shifting the jaws of the trap at all. The torches waving about in the distance wouldn't be in the distance for very much longer. What to do?

'Gotcha!'

A light shined straight into Bjorn's eyes, and he automatically shied away from it, raising his hands to shield his eyes. He had enough problems as it was, he felt, without having great big blobs of yellow custard cluttering up his retina for the next five minutes.

'All right, chummy,' said a voice from behind the light source. 'Throw down the gun. Easy, now.'

Bjorn sighed. It was going to be one of those nights, he could tell.

'How?' he said. 'I haven't got one.'

The torch-beam didn't blink exactly; but there was a sort of sympathetic modulation in the flow of photons as its owner registered surprise.

'But you're a dangerous intruder,' he said.

'Yeah,' Bjorn replied sourly. 'Looks like it, doesn't it?'

The torch came closer. 'So what are you armed with, then?' the trooper enquired curiously. 'Bombs? Gas grenades? Flamethrower?'

'No.'

The torch-beam wavered again. 'Don't believe you,' said the voice behind it. 'Come on, you've got to be armed with *something*. Nobody breaks into a high-security compound without something.'

Bjorn considered. 'I've got a bust penknife, a broken axe-

167

handle and a pair of socks,' he said. 'Now, could you see your
way to getting this fucking thing off my leg before it stops my
circulation completely, please?'

The trooper hosed Bjorn down with the torch from head to
foot, shrugged, and came closer. When he was within arm's
length, Bjorn reached out, pulled his feet out from under
him, and knocked him silly with the rim of his own steel
helmet. Then he grabbed the man's rifle, and used its barrel
to force apart the jaws of the trap. It wasn't easy even then;
by the time he'd finished, he was holding the only rifle in the
cosmos capable of shooting directly behind the person firing
it. Essential equipment for self-defence in the corporate
jungle.

Pausing only to stuff the socks in the recumbent trooper's
mouth and steal his packed lunch, Bjorn jumped to his feet,
winced, and ran off into the darkness. Behind him, very close
now, he could hear the blood-curdling baying of quadro-
phonic Dolby hounds, with the occasional crackle.

Something materialised in front of his face and he ran
straight into it. If the way he rebounded like a tennis ball and
sat down with sparks coming out of his ears was anything to
go by, it was quite possibly an electric fence. He forced
himself to stop vibrating, picked a handful of spent volts out
of his eyebrows and blinked four times. This was heavy stuff.
Whatever it was they'd got in that shed, they didn't want
anybody else to know about it. Which was odd, considering
that it was hoisted up into the sky every morning where
everybody on earth could see it.

'Psst.'

Bjorn lifted his head, spat out an amp and peered into the
darkness.

'Over here.'

'Why?' Bjorn enquired.

The darkness hesitated. 'Look,' it hissed, 'do you want to
be rescued or not?'

'Depends,' Bjorn replied. 'Who are you?'

'Dop sent me.'

'Oh.' Suddenly, a great light dawned in Bjorn's mind; figuratively speaking, of course. Otherwise, light would have seeped out through his ears and given the troopers something to shoot at. 'Oh,' right. Coming.'

'This way,' hissed the voice. From the way it expressed itself exclusively in whispers and hisses, it was either the tutelary spirit of a cracked gas-main or a chatty snake. But if it was a friend of Dop's, that didn't really matter much.

Dop was the sort of bloke you could really trust.

From where Jane was sitting, wearing the great halo of noise and vibration like a hair-dryer, it looked like a giant millipede in dayglo socks. The more you looked at it, the less you actually made out. Everything just seemed to melt into a continuum of twinkling red and white light.

She switched on the intercom. 'It's very pretty,' she said. 'What is it?'

The pilot's laugh bounced around inside her headphones. 'It's the main stretch of the Renaissance bypass, between junctions 16 and 17,' he replied. 'Want to take a closer look?'

'Okay,' Jane replied, and the helicopter slowly lost height. As they closed in, the continuum became marginally less continuous. It looked less like a fibre-optic cable with indigestion and more like the pattern of millions of tiny dots of light, each close behind the other, each moving so slowly that you had to stare quite hard to perceive any motion at all.

'Fine,' Jane said. 'It's a traffic jam.'

'Almost,' the pilot replied, 'but not quite. Going in closer.'

Lower still, and the millions of tiny dots broke up into vague but distinct shapes, like a newspaper photograph under an extremely powerful magnifying glass. They reminded Jane of something – cars, to be precise, and lorries and motor-cycles and vans – but it was only a similarity. They were palpably vehicles, but there the resemblance ended.

'What are those things?' Jane asked.

169

'Lives,' the pilot replied. 'No, that's not strictly true. If we're going to be all technical and correct, they're presents.'

'Presents?'

'That's right. And before you ask where's the wrapping paper and cards, I mean presents as opposed to pasts and futures. Okay?'

Jane frowned. 'I don't think I . . .'

'Well you wouldn't, would you?' the pilot replied. 'I mean, you're down there somewhere. Part of you is, anyway.'

'Um.'

So low now that each individual thing was plainly distinguishable from the mass, even if it didn't look at all like anything Jane had ever seen before. Try and imagine one of those old Heinkel bubble-cars that's suddenly come to life, and you may be able to creep into the corner of the same frame of reference.

'See the sign up ahead?' said the pilot. 'There's a clue for you.'

Jane peered forward. Despite the pitch darkness above her, she could see reasonably well at ground level, thanks to the lights of the things. There was indeed a sign; very much like a road-sign.

'I can't quite . . .'

And then she could. It was an awkward moment. It read:

DEPARTMENT OF TIME
T49 CREATION-DOOMSDAY EXPRESSWAY;
RENAISSANCE BY- PASS NOW OPEN
ANOTHER CENTURY COMPLETED: AHEAD OF SCHEDULE
BY ELEY TIMESTONE PLC

At Jane's request, the helicopter climbed higher, until the continuum reappeared and the individual lights merged once more with the general flow.

'That's one of the good bits,' the pilot was saying. 'It's the bit they show in the reports. Further on, where the whole bloody thing's falling to pieces, it's not so pretty.'

'Um.'

'It's supposed,' the pilot continued, 'to be, like, continuous. Time, like an ever-rolling stream, and so forth. That's the theory.'

Jane swallowed hard, and tried to fool herself into believing that the heaving in her stomach was something to do with the way the helicopter was rocking about in the thermals. 'I see,' she lied.

'Doesn't work like that, of course,' the pilot went on remorselessly. 'I mean, it's becoming a joke. If it's not a whole carriageway coned off because they're repairing the membrane of the space-time continuum, then it's resurfacing; which means contraflows, of course.'

'Contraflows,' Jane repeated.

'Bloody horrible things,' the pilot said, nodding. 'Just up there, between junctions 19 and 20, they've rerouted all five lanes of the Pastbound carriageway on to the hard shoulder of the Futurebound, and they expect it to work.' The pilot took one hand off the joystick, felt in his pocket, and found a stick of chewing gum. 'No wonder you get hold-ups,' he said.

'Hold-ups,' Jane said. 'In Time.'

'It can be a real bummer,' the pilot agreed. 'Not to mention the confusion. I mean, there you are, quietly edging your way through the first few decades of the sixteenth century, and you look over your shoulder and see all these blokes in bomber jackets and flared jeans and Status Quo T-shirts zipping along past you on the inside. I'm not at all surprised some of them freak out and try and cut across the lanes.' A red light flicked on just below the fuel gauge and started to flash alarmingly. The pilot put his fingers in his mouth, and then reached out and put a blob of chewing gum over it. 'I haven't the foggiest what that light's for,' he commented. 'In the manual it just says "Emergency".'

Jane opened her eyes – somehow or other they had come to

be shut – and nerved herself to look down. It was like . . . Hell; there was no point her trying to fool herself with similes. Now that she actually knew what it was, there didn't really seem much to be gained from trying to compare it with something it wasn't.

'But the hold-ups,' she repeated doggedly. 'In *Time.*'

The pilot chuckled. 'I bet you thought Time always travelled at the same speed,' he said. 'Well, now you know.'

Jane felt her jaw sag, as if someone had cunningly managed to whip all the bone out of it without her feeling a thing. 'It doesn't?' she said.

'Course not,' the pilot replied. 'I mean, it's supposed to, sure; that's what the speed limits are for. But does anybody take any notice? Do they hell as like. And they call that progress!'

Jane tried thinking about that one, but her brain wouldn't bite on it. 'Do you mean it used to be different before?' she hazarded.

'No,' the pilot said. 'They call it progress. That's the word tney use for it. Or sometimes they call it innovation, or the relentless force of socio-political development. What they mean by that is, some flash bugger in a souped-up cafe racer doing a ton down the outside lane. It doesn't half screw things up when that happens, I can tell you.'

'Er.'

'That's if he's on the Pastbound carriageway,' the pilot added conversationally, 'because then he's going from the future into the past. If he's on the other side of the road, of course, he's a rabid reactionary trying to turn the clock back. Either way, if he gets done he loses his licence automatically, and a bloody good thing too.'

The calm, unflappable part of Jane's mind sorted out the words necessary for her to ask the pilot to confirm that it was possible for people to travel from the future into the past. The rest of her mind switched off the lights, locked up and went for a coffee. She closed her eyes, but it didn't seem to help.

'Can we get this straight?' Jane asked. 'There's people going from the past to the future, yes. I can handle that, I think. But people going from the future to the . . .'

The pilot turned his head and gave her a funny look. 'Yes?' he said.

'I'm sorry,' Jane replied, feeling rather as if she had a wet sock in her mouth. 'Is that possible?'

'It's more than possible,' the pilot said. 'It's absolutely essential. Can you imagine the mess you'd have up the top end if they didn't?'

Jane said nothing. The wet sock had become the last sock of all, the one you find wedged in a crevice in the back of the drum of the washing-machine three days after you did the actual wash. The pilot seemed to sense the difficulty she was having, for he changed his tone of voice down a gear and spoke a little more slowly.

'Look,' he said, 'you're a mortal, right, you've got all that blood stuff sloshing about inside you. Think what would happen if all the blood only went in one direction. You'd get a sodding great build-up in your feet, and the rest of you would . . . Well, anyway, think of it like that, if you can. Presents circulate in the same way. If they didn't, the past would go to sleep. You'd have pins and needles right up your racial collective subconscious. See what I mean?'

'You mean,' Jane replied, with extreme caution, 'that people keep going round and round in circles? For ever and ever?'

The pilot scratched his nose with the heel of his hand. 'Well,' he said, 'I suppose you could put it like that. It's more your classic river analogy, really, but I didn't want to explain it that way because it's such an awful cliche. You've got your river, right?'

'Which river?'

'Oh, any river. Rain falls in the mountains, it collects and runs across the plain in a river to the sea, the sea evaporates and falls as rain on the mountains. Now do you see?'

'No.'

'Fair enough.' The pilot's voice seemed very far away, somehow; or perhaps it was very long ago rather than very far away. 'Anyway,' he said, 'I gather that you're going to help us sort it all out. I bloody well hope so,' he added. 'It needs it.'

It's impossible to explain the operation of Time simply, especially if you're trying to fly a helicopter as well. Attempting to understand the way it works purely from a verbal description is like learning to play Mah Jong without a Mah Jong set. It can't be done.

Instead, look back down the carriageway to a point where the two streams of light eventually merge into one, then zoom in close and stare. This is Time, coming into operation . . .

. . . On a day when it's really slashing down, with the mud bubbling up around the ankles of the extremely self-conscious party of worthies in sodden grey suits and yellow plastic hard hats, standing around a length of damp pink ribbon stretched half-heartedly across the shining tarmac.

'. . . Gives me very great pleasure,' Staff is saying, as the rain drips off the peak of his hat on to his tie, 'to declare this astro-temporal expressway well and truly open.'

He reaches for the pair of scissors on the velvet cushion; and as his fingers make contact, he's making a very quick assessment of the whole idea, and thinking: Yes, but . . .

He's thinking: Okay, the old system worked, but that's not to say it's going to go on working, what with the vast increase in Time use expected in the next five million years. It's got to make sense to do it this way. Join it at the Big Bang, and then straight through to the other end without having to stop for anything. Absolutely no risk of anybody getting lost in the Industrial Revolution, or taking the wrong turning at the Fall of Constantinople.

And so he cuts the tape. And in that fraction of a second between the two blades of the scissors meeting, and the severed ends of the tape falling away, he thinks: Well, we all make mistakes.

Because, before they built the expressway, it worked. It shouldn't have, of course. It should have been absolute *chaos*.

Instead of a straight line joining the two ends of the universe, there was a maze of single carriageways and winding little lanes, creeping on its tortuous way from one crucial event to the next, completely haphazard, uncoordinated and unplanned; rather like history itself. The traveller had to get off the ferry, thread his way through the back alleys of prehistory to get on to the Neolithic ring-road, pootle round that to the big roundabout on the outskirts of the Bronze Age, take the second turning on the left (otherwise he'd find himself evolving back into an ape) for the long drag across a thousand years of flat, boring timeways with no chance of overtaking until he got on to the downhill straight into the Roman Empire. Then he'd be faced with the sheer hell of cutting across the city traffic (you know what the traffic's like in Rome these days; well, it's actually improved out of all recognition) before taking the last exit for the gearbox-numbing journey through the Middle Ages – uphill all the way, stuck behind a succession of slow-moving ecclesiastical Long Vehicles – only to find himself confronted with the brain-twisting complexity of the sixteenth-century flyover network . . .

Anything's got to be better than that.

Wrong.

So wrong, in fact, that after the first of the disastrous multiple pile-ups on the Futurebound carriageway of the T7 there was a full inter-departmental inquiry. Needless to say, it never actually published any findings; but it leaked like a six-month-old torch battery, and the unauthorised disclosures made alarming reading.

For a start, because the route was now so straight, everyone was travelling far too fast. Apart from the drastically increased risk of collisions, this meant that travellers were getting from one end of the universe to the other in at least half the time, often less; with the result that at the other end (where they have this really *amazing* set of traffic lights) the size and mass of the tailback was threatening to destabilise the equilibrium of eternity, quite apart from there only being three operational toilets in the cafe in the last lay-by. Unless something was done, there was going to be trouble.

So, very reluctantly, the Administration decided that there was nothing for it but to send the whole lot of them back the way they'd come ...

The idea wasn't intrinsically bad. Instead of everyone trying to squash through the exit gates at once, there would be a filter system; any travellers who couldn't get through would be sent back round in a gigantic loop down the Pastbound carriageway to the start, and then they'd return back up the Futurebound side and have another shot at getting through the gates. It was a sort of holding-pattern, with presents circling in the system until they got clearance to leave.

What with the panic of getting the Pastbound carriageways built before the fabric of space and time got seriously bent, nobody had the leisure to think the project through; with the result that the awful consequences of having the same traveller driving along the same route two or three times *at the same time* – in two or three different instalments, if you like – weren't appreciated until it was too late. Reports of travellers on their second circuit driving too fast on the outside lane and running into the back of themselves still on their first circuit came as a complete and horribly unwelcome surprise. The difficulties over the insurance claims alone were enough to put a permanent kink in causality.

Each attempted solution led to further and worse problems. The idea of a speed limit was one of the least inspired; the sort of travellers who obeyed the speed limit were the sort who were already causing havoc by dawdling along on the inside – still faffing about in the Reformation when they should have been the other side of Napoleon, for example –

while the tearaway element who were causing the problems simply ignored it. Putting sleeping policemen across the carriageway at notorious temporal blackspots did no good at all, particularly when the policemen started waking up.

Meanwhile, what with everyone driving round the system two, three or even four times more than originally intended, the carriageways themselves began to crack up. The tarmac simply couldn't stand it. Extensive frost damage along the entire length of the Ice Age didn't exactly help, and it wasn't long before, at any one time, up to a third of the entire system was coned off for repair, causing the worst problems yet. Discontented travellers began making their own unofficial exits off the expressway back on to the old, disused network of lanes and byways, with the result that they got to the Exit long before anybody else, themselves included. As a panic measure, the Administration introduced a number of diversions to get the traffic moving again, which meant that any number of crucial moments in history turned out not to have happened at all. The Trojan War, the reign of King Arthur, the golden age of English cricket all suddenly ceased ever to have existed, with side-effects that defied calculation.

One rather sad knock-on effect of all this was that Staff foresaw the whole ghastly mess just as he cut through the ceremonial ribbon. It would perhaps have been some consolation for him to know that the problem had already been solved, if it wasn't for the fact that the solution was destined to be held up in a contraflow on the T93 on the outskirts of Agincourt, finally arriving too late to be of any relevance, and being swept back into the stream of traffic.

The only person who derived any benefit at all from the whole fiasco was the Flying Dutchman; who sold his ship, bought a set of spanners and a small yellow van, and is now doing a roaring trade as a breakdown service.

Staff closed the door and threw his raincoat over the back of a chair. It had been a long day.

Senior members of the Administration are expected to live close to the central office complex. Unless they're extremely lucky (like Ganger, for example, who was able to wangle a long lease of a houseboat moored on the left bank of the Styx) this means a tiny little flat in one of the five labyrinthine complexes that were built on the site of the old dockyards. For your premium of a billion kreuzers and your fifty thousand kreuzers a year ground rent and service charge, you get windows that don't open, lifts that don't work and condensation you could swim in. There are no roof-gardens or window-boxes, but if you have a horticultural streak there's always the mould on the curtains.

On the doormat there were three envelopes. Staff picked them up, poured himself a stiff shot of distilled water, and sat down in the one chair that space permitted in his living-room.

The first letter was junk mail from the United Perpetual Bank, offering him a discount on eternal life insurance and a credit card supposedly accepted by five million religions cosmos-wide. For an extra sixty thousand kreuzers a month, the United Perpetual people would be delighted to allow him to participate in their Special Select Reserve pension fund, which was guaranteed tax free owing to its registered office being situated in the Eye of the Beholder. If his application form was received within seven days, they'd even give him a free radio alarm clock.

The second letter was from the compilers of a publication called *Truly Important People of Yesterday*, and he was warmly invited to complete the enclosed personal biographical questionnaire in order that his biography could be included in the next edition, along with 190 million other truly important people who the publishers reckoned were good for the two thousand kreuzers they were charging per copy. He binned that one, too.

The third one he had saved until last, because it looked important. For a start, the address was hand-written, and his name was spelt right. He slipped his finger under the flap and pulled, and a moment later Ganger jumped out, landed heavily on all fours on the carpet and sat up, massaging his neck.

'Before you say anything,' he said, 'no, I don't think I'm getting paranoid about making sure we aren't seen together. Maybe I'm a touch overcautious, but there's no point in taking silly risks.'

Staff frowned. Entrusting oneself to the local postal system, which had the tendency to send all letters to a distant galaxy on principle, seemed to him to be the silliest risk going.

'Now you're here,' he said, 'can we get on with it? Only I've got a lot of ironing to catch up on, and . . .'

Ganger stared at him incredulously. 'Ironing?'

Staff flushed. 'Yes,' he snapped, 'ironing. And there's the kitchen floor to wash.'

From where he was sitting, Ganger could see the kitchen, and it struck him that it was so small that you could clean it very quickly just by spilling your drink. He confined himself to raising an eyebrow.

'Okay,' he said. 'I'll cut away to the main frame, shall I? It's vitally important to the entire future of the cosmos that we go for a pizza.'

Staff blinked. 'I see,' he said. 'Vitally important.'

'Vitally.'

'Who's paying?'

'I am.'

A smile like – well, in the circumstances, *not* like the sun emerging from behind a cloud; like something equally life-enhancing but without the overtones – flicked across Staff's face and earthed itself in his collar.

'Done with you,' he said.

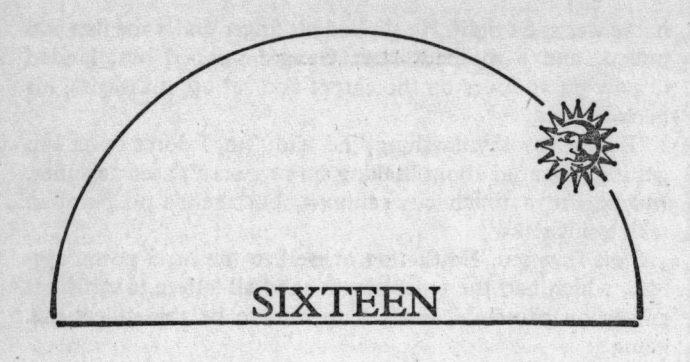

SIXTEEN

'Look,' said Bjorn, stopping suddenly and placing a shovel-sized arm on his guide's sleeve, 'where is this?' There was a faint crackle and Bjorn hastily removed his hand. It was tingling painfully.

The guide pointed down the tunnel. 'Look,' he replied.

For the record, the guide was a small, hunched entity entirely wrapped up in what looked like an oversized monk's habit. In fact the costume was so voluminous that Bjorn had to take his own word for it that there was anyone in there at all.

'Where?' he said.

'There,' the guide replied. 'My name's Tzzx, by the way.'

'Sorry?'

'Tzzx.'

'I thought that's what you said.'

Bjorn's eye followed the line of the pointing sleeve and lit upon a sign nailed to the wall. By the dim ambient light – it gave Bjorn a really nasty shock when he realised that it was coming from inside Tzzx's cowl – he could just about read what it said.

It said:

PICCADILLY CIRCUS

It also said:

TIMES SQUARE

and

PLACE DE LA CONCORDE

and something else in cyrillic lettering, and something else in Chinese, neither of which Bjorn could read. To make matters worse, it said them all at the same time.

'Um,' Bjorn said. Tzzx chuckled, and a few blue sparks floated out from under his robe.

'I know,' he replied, and Bjorn noticed that he didn't so much speak as crackle. 'Confusing, isn't it? And now we'd better be getting on, or we won't miss the train.'

'Do we want to miss the train?' Bjorn enquired.

'Well,' Tzzx replied, 'since it'll be coming down this tunnel at approximately fifty-five miles an hour, I think it'd be sensible.'

Tzzx scuttled away up the tunnel, moving amazingly quickly, and Bjorn followed him. For someone who was completely swathed in ill-fitting brown sackcloth and had no perceptible legs, Tzzx had a fair turn of speed; and the way he managed to avoid treading on his own hem was little short of miraculous.

'We're in the subway,' Tzzx was saying. 'I thought it'd be quicker than walking.'

'We are walking,' Bjorn pointed out. 'Running, even.'

'Yes,' replied Tzzx, and Bjorn noticed that the gap between them was widening, even though he had broken into a jog, 'but we're walking in the subway. Makes a difference, you see.'

'Does it?'

'Naturally. Ah, here we are.'

The ceiling lifted and the walls became wider apart. On the left-hand side, Bjorn could see a platform, about two feet higher than the floor of the tunnel. It looked remarkably like a platform in a station on the Paris Metro.

'If you like,' Tzzx called out, 'we can take a train the rest of the way.'

Bjorn clambered up on to the platform and sat down beside the cowled figure on a bench. It took him several minutes to catch his breath.

'I bet you don't know how the subway works,' Tzzx said.

'You like betting on certainties, I can tell.'

Tzzx laughed again. Funny sound, Bjorn thought; like the noise you get when you accidentally put something metal in a microwave and switch on.

'The subway,' Tzzx said, 'is an urban short-haul passenger transport network, designed to take the load off congested surface routes in peak time.'

'Really,' Bjorn replied. 'You amaze me.'

A fat green spark floated out from under the cowl, drifted in the air for a few seconds, and vanished. 'All right,' said Tzzx, 'if you don't want to know . . .'

'Sorry,' Bjorn said. 'But I knew all that bit already. I've been on subways hundreds of times. But not this one.'

'There's only one,' Tzzx replied. 'Ah, here's the train.'

Sure enough, a tube train pulled into the station and opened its doors. Bjorn frowned. It was unmistakably a tube train. In fact, that was what was getting to him: it was the most quintessential tube train he'd ever seen.

'Come on,' Tzzx said. They climbed in and sat down. The compartment was empty, apart from a half-empty carton of pasteurised milk, which got up in a marked manner and moved right down to the other end.

'Milk doesn't like me,' sighed Tzzx. 'It thinks I turn it sour.'

'How do you mean, there's only one?' Bjorn said. As he spoke, he realised what his subconscious had been driving at.

The compartment they were sitting in was every underground railway carriage he'd ever been in: in New York, Paris,
Moscow, London, anywhere. All at the same time.

'Exactly that,' Tzzx replied. 'There is only one network.
They just call it different things in different places.'

'Um.'

The train rattled away out of the station and into a dark
tunnel. Bjorn surreptitiously fingered his penknife in his
trouser pocket and tried to locate the two-handed claymore
attachment by touch.

'It's a whole different dimension down here,' Tzzx went
on. 'It really amazes me how few people notice. You'd have
thought it'd have been obvious.'

'Should it?' No, that was the little plastic magnifying glass
you couldn't actually see through. That's the scissors which
will just about cut sellotape three times out of seven. And –
ouch – that's the nail file.

'Think about it,' Tzzx replied. 'Name me a subway
station.'

Bjorn considered. 'Oxford Circus.'

The cowl nodded. 'A classic example,' Tzzx said, shooing
away a small steel bolt which had unscrewed itself from
somewhere and was now buzzing round his head like a
lovesick moth. 'Has it ever occurred to you that by the time
you've gone down the escalator and trudged along all those
miles of corridor to get on to the right platform for the
Central Line, you've really walked a damn sight further than
the actual distance between Oxford Circus and Bond Street.
And it still takes three minutes to get from Oxford Circus
station to Bond Street station in the train once you get on it.
True or false?'

Bjorn thought hard. 'Um,' he said.

'It's because of the dimensional shift, you see,' Tzzx
explained. 'In this dimension, all the destinations are exactly
the same distance from each other, and you travel–' He
hesitated, crackled like a car radio under a power cable, and

Tom Holt

continued: 'Well, it's like at right angles to sideways, I guess. Or, more accurately, at an angle of 450 degrees to the vertical.'

Bjorn relaxed. When you are trapped in a strange dimension with a weird shapeless stranger in a cowl who gibbers to you about mathematics, there's nothing like finding a ten-inch length of copper piping filled with lead at the bottom of your knapsack. Bjorn wasn't a hundred per cent certain where it had come from, but he was very glad it was there. He wrapped a hand round it gratefully.

'Okay,' he said. 'Suppose you're right, how come you don't get on the train at Les Invalides and find the next stop's Tottenham Court Road?'

Under the cowl, a blue light glowed smugly. 'Easy,' said Tzzx. 'Nothing ever exists in just one dimension. When you get on the train, usually you're also in the dimension of Time, and a whole lot of other ones which we needn't bother with right now. They restrain you from getting outside the matrix. It's like a sort of seat-belt or something.'

In the sorting-office of his mind, Bjorn picked out the word in Tzzx's last statement that had triggered off the alarm system in his pineal gland. It was 'usually'.

'Right now, though,' Tzzx went on, 'we're sort of free-floating outside all the regular dimensions. If you're interested, the three we're in are Metro, Fear and Bureaucracy. And if you hit me with that copper pipe, it'll be the worse for you.'

Bjorn tightened his knuckles around the pipe. There are times when it's appropriate to believe what you're told, and times when you hit people.

'You sure Dop sent you?' he asked.

'Ah.' Tzzx threw back his cowl and – this is a very approximate and inaccurate description of a profoundly complex operation – rolled up his sleeves. There was nothing to be seen but a fountain of blue and red sparks. 'I was having you on there, I'm afraid.'

184

Bjorn nodded, raised the pipe above his head and lashed out at the centre of the cloud of sparks with all his strength. There was a loud bang; then it started to rain molten copper.

'I was telling the truth about trying to hit me, though,' said a voice in the centre of Bjorn's brain. Then there was nothing except the rush of a few million particles being dragged apart and sucked away into an infinite vacuum.

Of the many results of this, the least significant was that an old lady living in a converted railway carriage somewhere in Nebraska received an electricity bill for eight million, three hundred thousand and thirty-six dollars, fifteen cents; which puzzled her. As she explained to her nephew, it wasn't the size of the bill so much as the fact that she'd only just paid the last one.

The forecourt of the offices of the Department of Time is about the only place in the entire Administration complex where you can ever have a hope of parking, and even then, you have to know the ropes.

What you do is this. Before you leave to go there, you phone Gerald, the doorman, and ask him to preserve a place for you. It's vitally important that you get the verb right. If in doubt, spell it for him; because if he just *re*serves you a place, then by the time you get to park, your vehicle will long since have fallen apart under the normal pressures of entropy. *Pre*serving is different; it involves using the Department's special relationship with time to backdate your reservation a couple of centuries or so. One final word of advice; it's well worth slipping Gerald a minimum of fifteen kreuzers once you've parked, unless you want to come back from your meeting to find that your vehicle has been valet-parked a couple of centuries away, probably in a stable and boxed in by ox-carts.

'Thanks, Gerald,' Ganger therefore said, and there was a clink of money changing hands. 'And do you think you could get us a taxi?'

'No sweat, boss,' Gerald replied, and winked. 'When were you wanting it for?'

(Please note Gerald's extremely careful choice of verb tense; it doesn't do to be grammatically imprecise around Gerald. The senior executive officer who once told him 'Call me any time you're ready' was forced to retire early with critical tinnitus, because Gerald is ready pretty well all of the time, and has been most of his life . . .)

'In about half an hour's time,' Ganger replied. 'In the future,' he added quickly. 'Okay?'

In fact, there are a great many things about the Department of Time which require extreme caution until you're used to how they work. You need a postgraduate degree in temporal theory just to walk through the revolving door if you want to come out in the same century you entered. This explains why Ganger and Staff went in via the coal shute.

They found Jane sitting on her own in a large office, behind a desk you could have played football on, hunched over a thick pile of papers, a calculator and a six-handed clock. She looked up as they walked in and frowned.

'Hello,' she said. 'You're late.'

Staff did a quick but violent double-take; Ganger merely smiled.

'I forgot,' he said. 'We should have known that you'd have seen today's rushes yesterday. Were we held up in traffic?'

Jane nodded. 'It's the one good thing about the old system,' she said. 'You can always take an advance look at what unforseen things are going to happen in the next few days. Gives you a chance to know what not to expect. Encourages sloppy planning, though.'

Ganger took his usual seat on the edge of the desk, noticing as he did so that the papers which covered the rest of it to a depth of six inches had been specially cleared away for him. Nice touch. 'Any progress so far?' he asked.

Jane shrugged. 'Depends,' she said. 'That's the tiresome thing about the whole set-up, really.' She sighed. 'For instance,' she went on, 'I finally managed to persuade the personnel people to try out some new staff rosters. Nobody liked the sound of them at first, but we negotiated a bit, and finally everyone agreed to give them a month's trial, starting on the twentieth.'

Staff nodded. 'Well done you,' he said. 'So where's the problem?'

'The problem,' Jane replied wryly, 'is that out there on the shop floor, it's been the nineteenth for the last three days. The same twenty-four hours, over and over again. I think it's called working to rule.'

Ganger clicked his tongue sympathetically. 'Never mind,' he said, 'it was a nice try. Come on, let's go and have some lunch. I thought we might try . . .'

'I know,' Jane interrupted. 'I booked us a table.'

'I recommend the veal,' Ganger said judicially, his finger traversing the menu. 'They do a very . . .'

'No thanks,' Jane replied. 'I didn't like it. There was too much tarragon, or something like that. I think I'll just have spaghetti.'

Staff looked up, with an artificially neutral expression on his face. 'What did I have?' he said.

'Scampi,' Jane replied, without looking up. 'It was cold, but you didn't want to make a fuss and send it back.'

'Thanks,' Staff said quietly. 'In that case, I'll try the osso bucco.'

'In fact.' Ganger leaned forward and pushed the menu aside from in front of Jane's face. 'In fact,' he said, 'there's not much point in us having this meeting, since you already know everything we said.'

Jane shrugged. 'Well,' she replied, 'I may, but you don't. I can tell you, though, it was a complete waste of . . . a complete wash-out,' she corrected herself. 'We didn't achieve any-thing.'

Ganger exchanged glances with Staff, and grinned. 'I

know,' he said. 'Smart move, huh?'

Jane looked at him blankly. 'I beg your pardon?' she said.

'Think.' Ganger leaned back and snapped a breadstick. 'This meeting's already taken place, right? Nothing can change that, sure, but that doesn't mean to say you've still got to go through with having the veal. You can have something nice instead. True?'

'Well . . .'

'Likewise,' he continued, after he'd cleared his throat of bread shrapnel, 'we don't *have* to reach the same depressing conclusions I gather we're going to reach in what I would call the Authorised Version. Do you follow me?'

Jane bit her lip thoughtfully. 'Well,' she said, 'I certainly don't remember you saying that. You mean . . .'

'Exactly.' Ganger smiled. 'The first version is strictly for the cameras. You realise that we were all under surveillance, of course.'

'Were we?' Jane asked. 'Or rather, are we?'

'Definitely.' Ganger unfolded his napkin and tucked a corner of it behind the knot of his tie. 'But the version the cameras will see is the Authorised Version. This one's one hundred per cent off the record.'

'It'll never have taken place, you see,' Staff broke in. 'So we can say what we like without fear of being overheard. It was his idea,' he added generously. 'This fellow here's got a brain like a pinball machine, but it does come in handy when the going gets devious.'

'I see,' Jane said, and in doing so told the truth. In exactly the same way, she could see a whole page of Chinese without understanding a word of it. 'So, what do we talk about?'

Staff poured himself a glass of mineral water, examined it carefully to make sure it was still there, and drank it. 'We felt it was time we sort of took stock,' he said gravely. 'See where we've reached, and so forth.'

'In other words,' Ganger went on, smoothly catching the narrative relay baton from his colleague, 'it's work-in-progress time. Mid-term report, if you like. Okay?'

Jane nodded. 'Fine,' she said. 'And before you start, if you want to call it a day, that's fine by me.'

The two senior officials looked at each other in surprise.

'Whatever makes you say that?' Staff demanded. 'Don't tell me you don't find the work challenging enough.'

Jane laughed sourly. 'Oh, it's challenging all right,' she said. After a moment's pause, she folded her arms and set her face in a grim, nobody-leaves-until-the-culprit-owns-up expression. 'I must say,' she said, 'I do think you two might have warned me before I started.'

'Didn't we?' Ganger said innocently. 'I thought we . . .'

'Did you hell as like,' Jane interrupted angrily. 'You told me you wanted someone with a fresh perspective and no vested interests to sort out the way this Administration of yours works. That's fine. Maybe I might be able to help you with that, a little bit. What you didn't tell me was that you want me just as part of some horrible office-politics thing of your own. Well, I'm sorry, but no.'

Ganger, for once, looked confused. At least, he wasn't smiling, and without a smile to hold them together his features tended to sag like an unpropped clothes-line. 'Hold on,' he said. 'That's not . . .'

Jane ignored him. 'Let me just give you an example,' she said. 'Take this Time thing. You wanted me to sort it out. Everybody seems to acknowledge it needs sorting out. Fine. I thought about it, and I think I've come up with an answer that works.'

Staff's eyebrows shot up like the price of gold in an oil crisis. 'You have?' he said. 'How?'

Jane frowned. 'It's really very simple,' she said. 'Instead of having it all just lying about and slopping around, all like-an-ever-rolling-stream-bears-all-its-sons-away sort of thing, you should put the whole thing on rails. Then everyone'd know exactly where it was meant to be going and we wouldn't have any more of those dreadful flashbacks.'

'What flashbacks?'

'Then everyone'd know exactly where it was meant to be going and we wouldn't have any more of those dreadful flashbacks.'

'What flashbacks?'

'Then everyone'd know exactly where it was meant to be going and we wouldn't have any more of those dreadful flashbacks.'

'What flashbacks? All right,' Staff admitted, 'point taken. But just think of the . . .'

'And don't say it was because of the cost,' Jane interrupted. 'Again, it's as plain as the nose on your face that you finance it by bringing in private capital. The shareholders put up the cost of building the track, and in return they get a slice of the tolls and fares in perpetuity.' She thought for a moment, and smiled. 'And boy, do I mean perpetuity. But nobody's done it, have they? And nobody's going to do it either. I checked the files.'

'You did what?'

'I checked the files.'

'You did what?'

'Hang on,' Jane said, and she banged the side of the table with the flat of her hand. 'Loose connection somewhere, probably. Sorry, yes, I checked the files. It's a funny feeling, you know, reading about what you're going to do in a dusty old file you find at the back of a pile of old boxes in the cleaning cupboard. Anyway, there it all was, and guess what? The idea was completely ignored, and I left the Department after fourteen days with absolutely nothing to show for it. Now then.' She leaned her elbows on the table and gave Staff the sort of look that would have made a mammoth in an ice-floe in Siberia start wondering where the sudden nip in the air was coming from. 'What's it all in aid of?' she asked. 'I mean . . .'

Before anyone could speak, they became aware of someone standing over them, radiating disapproval. Staff was the first

190

one to remember how his voice worked.

'Right,' he said. 'To start with, I think we're all having the melon . . .'

'You maybe,' said the waitress, her notebook closing like a carnivorous plant. 'Her, no. She's barred, OK?'

Ganger and Staff looked at each other. 'I beg your pardon?'

The waitress tutted like a distant machine-gun. 'Your lady friend,' she replied. 'Calls herself a waitress. Insults my best customers, leaves without saying nothing, then thinks she can waltz in here ordering melon. No way. Out. There's a Burger King two blocks down the street,' she added venomously. 'Say Rosa sent you.'

Idyllic. It was the only word to describe it.

In the far distance, a soft mist hung lightly over the blue hills. The long grass, still littered with pearly drops of dew, smelt fresh and clean. The slightest of breezes arched the long, stiff necks of the flowers that grew beside the gently murmuring stream. Here and there, a few sheep with pink bows tied round their necks lay under the shade of attractively gnarled oak trees, chewing slowly and counting humans. In the porch of the little loaf-shaped cottage, a young mother with a baby on her knee rocked slowly backwards and forwards crooning an ancient lullaby:

'*O abeth cynan sianon*
Cor-ara llana reanon
Y-tal ny rhian myanon . . .'*

Bjorn materialised, fell about five feet out of nothingness, landed heavily on all fours, recovered and looked about him. His senses took in all the available information and made a correct assessment.

'Oh *shit*,' he said. 'Not again.'

Lit: 'Listen, snotnose, go to sleep or I feed you to the dog, kapisch?'

*

'Have a nice day, now.'

'Yes, thanks,' Staff replied absent-mindedly, and lifted the tray. He steered it back towards the corner table, hampered in doing so by the fact that he could only just see over the top of the chips.

'Oh,' said Jane. 'I thought I asked for the Double Chilli Nutburger with regular onions.'

'Did you?' Staff gave her a long look, combining threats with entreaties.

'However,' Jane added quickly, 'this looks simply delicious, whatever it . . .'

'Right,' Ganger interrupted. 'Here we all are. To business.'

He twitched his handkerchief out of his top pocket and tucked it into his collar. The other two gave him hard, cold looks which he entirely failed to notice.

'Agenda time,' he went on. 'If we start off generally considering (a) our overall aim and objectives, (b) our achievements to date, (c) . . .'

'Your tie's just gone in the barbeque sauce,' said Jane.

'(c),' Ganger continued, moving his tie slightly, 'obstacles to be overcome, (d) . . .'

Staff coughed meaningfully. 'Yes,' he said, 'all right, we get the point. There's no need to be so damned ceremonious about it all.'

Ganger frowned at him; that is to say, he smiled at him with added eyebrows.

'(d) . . .' he said firmly.

Jane shook her head. 'Sorry to butt in,' she said, 'but can we start now? Only, I do have work I ought to be getting on with.' She stopped, and a sound like a laugh heard through a bacon-slicer came out of her mouth. 'Mind you,' she added, 'for the life of me I can't see the point. Can you?'

Ganger lowered his head and stirred his coffee with a pencil. Staff turned a chunk of crisp, golden something or other round in his fingers and stared into the salt-cellar.

'Can you?' Jane repeated.

There was a moment of complete silence, except for the sound of 163 people eating and talking loudly in the background. Ganger removed his pencil from the coffee, wiped it carefully on the paper napkin and put it back in his inside pocket.

'Perhaps,' he said slowly, 'we ought to explain.'

Jane blinked, said 'Oh,' and instinctively reached for a chip. Ganger's elbow was in the way. Ah, but Man's reach must exceed Man's grasp, or what's a Heaven for?

'Go on,' she said, her mouth full.

Staff put down his crisp, golden whatever, which was moulting a sticky red and yellow sauce down the back of his hand, making him look like a wounded Martian. Then he looked Jane in the eye.

'It's like this,' he said. 'What we told you about the Administration being right up a tree and needing an outside view and a new broom and that sort of thing is absolutely kosher and on the level. You know that, you've seen for yourself. But there's more to it than that.'

'Yes?'

'Absolutely.' Ganger, leaning forward to emphasise the importance of his words, froze; then he slowly lifted his arm, inspected his elbow and shuddered. 'But really, it's all part of the same thing. I mean yes, the Administration is in a real mess. But how do you think it got that way?'

Jane thought for a moment. 'Things do,' she said.

'Of their own accord, you mean?' Staff said. 'Entropy theory and its application to practical office management. It's true enough, as far as it goes . . .'

'Too right,' Jane interrupted. 'Ask anyone who's ever been responsible for paperclip distribution. I never believed in black holes and time warps until they put me in charge of the stationery cupboard one week.'

'But,' Staff went on, 'it's not the whole story. You see, things in their natural state don't naturally gravitate into a mess. For instance, if you pour sand out of a bucket on to the ground, it forms a nice neat cone. If you spill water, you get a lovely pool with the sides all nicely level and a precisely flat top. It's only work that flops about all over the place if you drop it.'

'That's because work isn't natural, you see,' Ganger interjected through a jawful of bap. 'That's your basic thermodynamics.'

'Is it?'

Ganger nodded, and wiped his lips neatly with the corner of his napkin. 'Work,' he said, 'is defined as the result of applying energy to a stationary mass . . .'

'That's filing, surely,' Jane murmured. Ganger ignored her.

'. . . Which in turn results in the mass acquiring momentum,' he went on, 'which leads on to movement, which creates friction . . .'

'Depends what you move. I once moved someone else's pot plant because it gave me hay fever, and there was friction for weeks after that.'

'. . . Which dissipates energy, resulting in entropy.' He picked up a lemon-scented paper towel and began absentmindedly folding it in ever-diminishing squares. 'Because of entropy,' he continued, 'work sort of frays at the edges. Bits come loose and fall off. These in turn become random particles of disorientated matter, possessing momentum but not direction . . .'

'Ah,' Jane said. 'You mean auditors.'

'These particles wander about, collide with other bodies, and thereby create other little chips and splinters of disorientated matter. And eventually . . .'

'Eventually,' Jane interrupted, 'they end up in some poor devil's in-tray at a quarter past five on a Friday afternoon. I know, I've been there.'

Ganger looked down at his fingers. The paper towel had by now become so infinitesimally small that for all practical purposes it had ceased to exist. 'It's these little bits of stray work that cause all the hassle,' he said. 'But it's not in-trays they end up in. It's people.'

'So,' Staff said, 'in order to solve the problems, you first have to solve the people. Agreed?'

Jane shrugged. As an original discovery, she felt the statement was on a par with trying to patent the wheel in 1986. 'Of course,' she said. 'But what's this got to do with . . .?'

'Tell her,' Staff said. Ganger opened his mouth and left it open. If a medieval cook had been passing, he'd instinctively have stuck an apple in it.

'Well,' Ganger said at last, 'what do you do if you've got a blocked drain? Get a drain-rod and give it a good sharp poke. And that's what we're trying to do. Trouble is,' he said, looking away, 'it's not as straightforward as that, quite.'

'Oh?' Jane said. 'Why not?'

'Because,' Staff replied.

'Ah,' Jane said, nodding. 'Now I get you.' She frowned. 'But where do I come in?' she said.

'Simple,' Ganger answered. 'You're the drain-rod, as per the original brief. Except that we didn't tell you about the people, only about the problems.'

'Exactly,' said Jane. 'Why was that?'

Staff shifted uncomfortably in his seat. 'Well,' he said, 'the thing is, you coming to work for the Administration was strictly our idea, Ganger's and mine. We were supposed to clear it with all sorts of people: committees, departmental managers, sub-committees, all that sort of thing. But we didn't.'

'Why not?'

'Because they wouldn't have agreed,' Ganger said. 'Plus, they'd have guessed what we were up to.'

'They're the wet leaves we were talking about just now, I take it?'

'Some of them,' replied Staff, nodding. 'So what we were

doing, being absolutely frank and open about the whole thing, was sending you in without any backup or support whatsoever, with the express purpose of getting up the noses of some of the most important people in the whole Administration. We knew they wouldn't let you do anything really useful; in fact, we're absolutely amazed how much you have managed to get done. No, the whole point of the exercise was to get them well and truly annoyed and angry; and then, with any luck, they'll make mistakes, and we'll have 'em.'

Jane sat for a moment. 'I see,' she said.'But why didn't you tell me all that in the first place?'

'Because you'd have refused,' Ganger replied. 'Wouldn't you?'

'I suppose so,' said Jane thoughtfully. 'Probably not, actually. But I wouldn't have done it so well. I'd have been all furtive and apologetic about it, I expect, because I'd have known I was up to something sneaky.'

'Sneaky?'

Jane nodded her head. 'Sneaky in a good cause,' she said, 'but definitely sneaky. As it is, I've charged along thinking I had right on my side and it's them who're being difficult and obstructive. Yes, I get the idea now.'

'Good,' Ganger said, cheerfully. 'This coffee, by the way, tastes as if it's spent the last year in a gearbox.'

'It certainly explains,' Jane continued, 'why you two have been taking such a keen interest in everything I've been doing.'

'You noticed that, then?' Staff enquired.

'Yes,' Jane said. 'I thought it was odd at the time, two high-ranking officials personally supervising just one trainee. You said it was because I was a guinea-pig . . .'

'Not so much a guinea-pig,' Ganger said, half to himself, 'more one of those white rabbits you get in research . . .' Staff kicked him under the table.

'Anyway,' Staff said, 'we've come clean, so what about it? Are you still going to carry on?'

Jane scratched the tip of her nose with her plastic straw. 'Oh, I don't see why not,' she said. 'It's not as if I've got anything better to do.' Suddenly she stood up. 'Of course not,' she said. 'I think this whole thing is probably a bad dream I've been having, and unless I wake up pretty soon I'm going to miss my bus. What the hell do you two think you've been playing at, anyway?'

Staff was about to say something, but Ganger shushed him. Other diners turned their heads and looked at them.

'First of all,' Jane continued, gathering momentum but not appearing to dissipate any energy in the process. 'This weirdo here comes and tells me he's a . . .'

'Not that word, please,' Ganger said softly.

'. . . And that he wants me to come and work for him, and until I agree he's going to camp out permanently in my ear. Then,' she said, turning to Staff, who instinctively moved a little further behind his coffee-cup, 'you turn up and tell me that unless I pack in my job with Burridge's and come and work for you instead, the world's going to end. And somehow,' she added, with feeling, 'you convince me – probably because of a couple of conveniently timed natural disasters – and so that's what I do. And first I rescue a major city from a flood, and then I help you cover up the fact that you're so damned laid back that anybody can just walk in to your premises and help themselves to the major star of their choice, and I somehow start believing, Yes, maybe this is for real after all. And then . . .' She paused, scrabbling around for words in the same way a motorist at a toll booth searches for an elusive coin. 'And then, just when I'm beginning to be able to look at myself in the mirror every morning without wanting to burst out laughing, you tell me that what I'm really doing is helping you two with some weird boardroom coup or other. Well,' she said, 'you can take your job and you can stuff it, because . . .' She stopped dead. 'My God,' she whispered, 'I've been wanting to say that to somebody all my life, and now I actually have. Whee!' She pulled herself together, straightened her back and

picked up her handbag. 'Sorry,' she said, 'but I'm through. I'd
give you a month's notice, but after a week in the Department
of Time I shudder to think what you'd do with it. Goodbye.'

She turned her head towards the door and started to walk
towards it.

Bearing in mind the way the cosmos is run, and who runs
it, credit has to be given for the fact that she got over halfway
before the ground suddenly opened and swallowed her up.

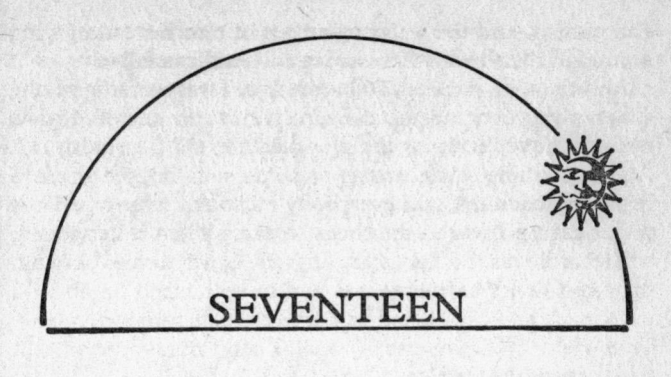

SEVENTEEN

Bjorn carefully took the basin off the fire and tested the water with his finger. Then he took off his boots and put his feet in it.

He'd been a long way: up as far as the first range of picturesque blue hills to the east and halfway to the shadowy forest-clad slopes in the west, and still without finding so much as a kebab house, let alone the Kentucky Fried Chicken of his dreams. Shadowy forests and verdant meadows, yes; food, no. He poked his little fire with a stick and cast a furtive glance over his shoulder at a shyly grazing fawn.

This place, he said to himself, is the absolute *pits*.

Above him the sun shone, casting long, sharp-edged shadows on the bowling-green grass of the river valley. He lay on his back and stuck his tongue out at it.

Years ago, he remembered, I worked for those bastards. Best years of my eternal bloody life I gave them, lugging great heavy boxes about mostly. It wasn't fun, exactly, but at least a bloke could go down the Social Club with his mates, play a few frames of pool, have a couple of pints and a bag of chips afterwards, throw up over a parked car or two and trip over a dustbin before going home. At least there were pavements, and gutters, and the water came out of taps instead of lying around in river-beds where leaves and stuff can fall in it.

And then, he recalled, still years ago, I was working on the sun; nothing exciting, just cleaning it off at the end of the day, hosing it down, scraping the squashed flies off the windshield. And something went wrong or some daft bugger made a really big cock-up, and everybody reckoned I knew what it was, because I was in the sheds working when it happened, whatever it was. So they said, anyway. News to me, but still, they said that whatever it was had to be hushed up and I'd have to go, and I could either start a new life somewhere else, somewhere *idyllic*, or else . . . well, I can't remember what, I think it was just Or Else.

Bastards . . .

The fawn was looking up at him out of great round black eyes. He relaxed and smiled.

'Here, baby,' he chirrupped. 'Whooza preddy liddle deer, den?' With some of those wild leeks from under the trees over there and maybe some watercress, he whispered to himself, you could do worse.

And then the fawn pricked up its ears, swivelled its head, and darted away. A forlorn attempt to hit it with a rock at twenty yards failed. Bjorn sat down again and started to massage the soles of his feet.

And then looked up. There was a girl standing over him: a tall girl, with long, straight hair, a sort of chestnut brown, and light blue eyes and a kind of mischievous-angel half-smile on her slightly parted lips. And, more to the point, knockers like footballs. Bjorn opened his eyes wide and let his jaw drop.

'Um,' he said, but it came out as a real thoroughbred mumble. 'Sorry, was that your, um, deer?'

The girl brushed a strand of hair out of her eyes and knelt down beside him on the grass. She was wearing a simple peasant blouse, the sort that they don't even bother putting the price on in Printemps, and in her right hand she held a basket of strawberries.

'*Na searan thu chulain-bach ma?*'† she said. Bjorn had a couple of goes at swallowing his Adam's apple and grinned stupidly.

'Er, yeah,' he said. 'Right. Um.'

The girl laughed; and her laughter was like the soft splashing of a mountain tarn; or alternatively, ice-cold lager hitting the bottom of the glass. Bjorn blinked and instinctively started to pull on his boots.

'*Be curailin suine pel-riath mo,*'‡ said the girl, and it occurred to Bjorn, apropos of nothing much, that her eyes were like . . . well, they were like . . . well, they were pretty neat eyes, you know?

'Hi,' he croaked. 'I'm Bjorn. Yup. Right.'

The girl laughed again, and this time, hell, you could almost taste the hops. Then she took a strawberry from the basket and popped it into his mouth before he could close it.

'Er, right,' he said. 'Thanks. Thanks a lot.'

The girl leaned forward and kissed the top of his head, and it seemed to Bjorn that the smell of her hair was like the first cigarette after a twelve-hour night shift in the explosives store. Then she giggled, stood up and walked away.

About five minutes later, Bjorn stopped staring at where she'd been, and spat out the strawberry. His left leg had gone to sleep and something small and hairy was running about inside his boot. In the shade of a thicket of wild laurels, two shy, velvet-antlered fawns were laughing themselves sick.

Jane opened her eyes.

And a fat lot of good it did, too. In order for your eyes to be of any use, it helps if you're not in a windowless cavern hundreds of feet below ground, with the lights off.

'Hello,' said a voice above her.

---

†*Lit:* 'Yeah. Your other brain cell burnt out or something?'
‡*Lit:* 'You could do your flies up too, while you're at it.'

She tried to move, but that was a wash-out too. Somebody or something had done a pretty neat job of tying her to what her intuition told her was a railway sleeper. A long way over her head, more or less where her instincts suggested the voice was coming from, she became aware of a low crunching noise, like a steamroller creeping slowly up a gravel path.

'Hello?' she whispered.

'Oh good, you're awake,' replied the darkness. The voice was masculine, probably, but beyond that it was monumentally nondescript. It had no accent, gave no indication of age; and if it happened to be speaking in English, Jane felt, that was probably due to some fiendishly advanced simultaneous-translation system. 'My name is,' and it said something Jane didn't grasp, but which sounded very like Eyesee. Couldn't be that, of course. Stood to reason.

'What am I doing here?' Jane enquired.

'I don't know,' Eyesee replied, 'I can't see in this light. Don't you think it's terribly dark in here?'

'Yes,' Jane replied, trying to ignore the creeping sensation she was experiencing, which felt rather the way she imagined it would feel if you had someone cleaning the marrow out of your bones with a pipe cleaner.

'Shall we have the lights on, then?'

'Yes, please.'

Well, we all say silly things sometimes, and she wasn't to know. So, when the lights suddenly came on and she started to scream uncontrollably, there was a small part of her brain that was able to say, 'Wasn't my fault,' and mean it.

'Gosh,' said Eyesee, 'is there anything the matter?'

By way of reply, Jane screamed some more; a lot more, in fact. Even when the lights went out again, she carried on whimpering and gibbering for nearly two minutes, which is a long time.

'Better now?'

'Nnnnnn.'

'Sorry?'

'Mmmmmmmm.'

'I hope I didn't startle you,' said Eyesee. 'Perhaps I should have mentioned that some people find my appearance distressing. Me for one,' he added.

Jane subsided into a series of short, mucous gasps. The voice waited for a while, and then cleared its throat softly.

'It scares the living daylights out of me sometimes,' Eyesee said. 'Depending on what frame of mind I'm in. By the way,' he went on, 'my name. Actually my full name is Executive Officer i/c Reprogramming and Mental Aberration Adjustment. My friends call me Eyesee for short. Or rather, they would if I had any.' He paused. 'I don't, though,' he added. 'I think my appearance is against me, you see.'

'Mmmmmm.'

There was a sigh. 'Before that,' Eyesee went on, 'I was called Retribution, and I didn't mind that, because then I could be Rhett for short, like Rhett Butler. But the chaps Upstairs thought Retribution was a bit downbeat, so they changed it. These days they like to stress the *positive* aspects of the work we do here. Uphill job, mind.'

Jane sat frozen. She was aware of the inordinate length of time it was taking the big blob of sweat to reach the end of her nose, and it dawned on her, or at least upon a part of her mind that was playing roughly the same role in this episode that the orchestra played in the sinking of the *Titanic*, that Fear is another dimension.

'Anyway,' Eyesee went on, 'I don't mind what I'm called these days, now that I've had a chance to get used to it. It's pretty apt, really, because people see retribution the way they want to see it, so I look different to everyone. Horrible, of course, but different. So I think Eyesee is a pretty good name, don't you think?' The voice paused. 'Because it's up to your *eye* to *see* me the way you think I ought to be, okay? How did I come across to you, by the way?'

Jane swallowed hard, and discovered that someone had laid a thick concrete path right down her throat. 'You were very big,' she said. 'Huge. And slimy. And you had little strips of flesh still stuck to your bones. And there were these maggots . . .'

'Ah.' There was, far away in the darkness, a faint sniff. 'Seems like you didn't catch me at my best.'

'Um.'

'Maggots, did you say?'

'Mm.'

'What a perfectly horrid idea,' said the voice. 'I must say, you've got a rather nasty imagination there. Perhaps you ought to see somebody about it.'

There was a long silence.

'Well,' said Eyesee, 'this is all very well but it's not getting us very far. Look, would you mind awfully if I just had a little light? I promise to keep out of your field of vision. Only, well, the truth is I get sort of nervous in the dark. It's probably because I'm afraid that I'm out there somewhere. Maggots,' he repeated with distaste. 'Whatever next!'

'Go ahead,' Jane quavered. 'I'll shut my eyes.'

There was a click, and then a faint glow began to permeate the darkness, like ink soaking into blotting-paper. 'People find that closing your eyes doesn't actually help,' Eyesee remarked. 'Tell you what, I'll hide behind the flywheel. You won't be able to see me then.'

Slowly and deliberately, Jane counted up to ten. 'Ready?' she called out.

'Ready.'

She opened her eyes. To her overwhelming relief all she could see was an enormous machine. It wasn't anything identifiable like a printing press or a hydraulic ram; imagine a top film designer had been told to design a machine for a horror-film set – that's what it was like. A really *top* designer.

'Where am I?' she whispered.

'Do you know,' said Eyesee's voice from behind the machine, 'it's amazing how many people say that. And before I started working here I thought it was only in books. You're in Justice.'

Jane's eyes widened, until her memory told her to pack it in. 'Department of Justice?' she said.

'Got it in one. This is the engine room, as you'll probably have gathered already. What you're looking at right now are the actual Mills of the Gods.'

'That grind slow but exceeding small, you mean?'

'That's them,' Eyesee replied. 'Actually,' he added, 'they don't, not just at the moment. Right now, they grind large and exceeding lumpy. In fact, ninety-five per cent of the time they don't grind at all.'

'Um,' Jane replied. 'What am I doing . . .?'

'Partly,' Eyesee went on, 'because the nut on the drive shaft connecting the flywheel to the cams has stripped its thread, and would you believe, you can't get them in that size any more because these days they're all metric. Partly because even if they were in full working order they can't afford to run them for more than an hour a day because of the price of coal. Partly . . . well, mainly actually, because there's really no call for them these days.'

'Right,' said Jane. 'Look, why am I tied to this lump of wood, and what am I doing . . .?'

'In theory,' Eyesee went on, and Jane began to wonder whether the maggots were really the least bearable thing about him, 'they don't need them any more because of me. De-automation, they call it. All the rage. Who needs machines when you can have people, they say. They don't give a damn for the effect it's going to have on the lives of hundreds of thousands of ordinary . . .'

Jane coughed sharply. 'Excuse me,' she said. The sound of her words faded away.

'What they say is,' Eyesee droned on, 'who needs Justice anyway? Outmoded concept, superhumanity has moved on since those dark and far-off days, that sort of thing. The idea is that they're phasing Justice out and replacing it with Retribution. Sorry, with Reprogramming and Mental Aberration Adjustment. That's me,' he added bitterly. 'And

Rehabilitation, of course. He's about here somewhere.'

Jane swallowed. 'He is?'

'Unfortunately,' Eyesee sighed. 'Nasty piece of work. He makes me look like Tyrone Power, by the way.'

'Ah.'

'The idea being,' said Eyesee unpleasantly, 'that Retribution may be nasty but at least it's likely to be pretty exciting, whereas Rehabilitation is just incredibly pointless and boring. They're right about that, at any rate.'

Jane digested that statement for a moment. 'Are there any more of you?' she asked tentatively.

'Not full-time, no,' Eyesee replied. 'There's Government, of course, but she only comes in two mornings a week. Which is just as well if you ask me, because there's only two cups in the kitchen and if there's one thing I can't stand, it's having my morning coffee out of a mug.'

'Government?'

'It's got Snoopy on it, as well,' Eyesee went on. 'I'll swear it curdles the milk. Oh, yes, Government. You know, in a democracy people usually get the kind of government they deserve.'

'Oh. Right. Look, what *am* I doing here?'

There was a long, long silence, during which Embarrassment joined the host of other unpleasant things floating about in the stale air.

'Yes,' said Eyesee eventually. 'Look, it wasn't my idea. Not my idea at all.'

'Please . . .'

'I mean,' Eyesee said, gathering a bit of his customary momentum, 'it's bad enough being stuck down here in the dark and the damp with only Rehabilitation for company – the only card game he knows is snap, by the way, because of course he disapproves of gambling. He cheats.'

'Why . . .?'

'Are you down here, yes, I was just coming to that.' There was another pause. 'And as for his charming habit of drying his socks over the radiator . . .'

'Please,' Jane said sharply. 'Why am I here?'

'You really want to know?'

'Yes.'

'You're sure? I mean, a moment ago you really wanted the light on, and . . .'

'I'm really sure, yes.'

'Well,' said Eyesee; and Jane would have sworn he was taking a deep breath if she didn't know for a fact that he'd have nowhere to put it, 'the truth is, you've been promoted.'

You could have heard a pin drop. It would have had to have been a largish pin, because of the background noise. A crowbar, say. But at least nobody spoke.

'Promoted.'

'I thought you didn't really want me to . . .'

'Promoted to being tied up in a dark cellar with a thing with eighteen-inch maggots crawling in and out of its . . .'

'Please!' Eyesee exclaimed. 'Oh God, you'll have to excuse me a minute.'

The light went out, and Jane heard the sound of footsteps, followed by retching noises. A few seconds later, the lights came back on.

'Sorry,' said Eyesee hoarsely. 'But I've got a weak stomach, actually, and the thought of . . .'

'That's perfectly all right,' said Jane, with feeling. 'It was thoughtless of me. But are you sure you mean promoted?'

'As opposed to what?'

'Well, found guilty, for starters. This really doesn't fit in with my definition of upwardly mobile, you know.'

There was a long sigh, and Jane tried not to visualise what the breath was coming out of. 'It's a bloody awful job,' said Eyesee at last. 'Still, someone's got to do it.'

'Oh,' Jane said. 'I think I see what you're getting at.'

'Do you?'

'Yes. I've been got rid of, haven't I?'

'That's right,' Eyesee replied, avoiding Jane's eye. 'I'm very sorry,' he added, 'truly I am.'

'Can they do that?' Jane asked, after a moment. 'I mean, is it, well, legal, just tying an inconvenient member of staff to a plank of wood and abandoning them in a cellar for ever and ever?'

'Oh, absolutely,' Eyesee confirmed, and a hideous squeaking sound suggested that he was nodding his head, or what had remained of it, vigorously. 'Their legal department's thought it all through very carefully. You see, the Code states quite clearly that the employer is obliged to pay the employee the correct salary – depending on grade and experience, of course – and contribute to the pension scheme and let the employee have the agreed number of days' holiday each year. There's nothing in there about what the employee shall or shall not be tied to.'

Jane giggled. There was a faint metallic ring to her voice which suggested that although she wasn't yet hysterical, this was only because she was saving hysteria for later. 'But I'm not really an employee,' she said. 'I mean, I'm mortal. If I stay here, then sooner or later I'm going to die. Doesn't that sort of put a different complexion on it?'

There was a long pause. 'Are we talking about statutory sick pay here?' Eyesee enquired cautiously. 'Because I don't know if death entitles you to that. Maybe it comes under the heading of early retirement. I think I'd have to look that one up.'

'Would you mind going away, please?'

'Sorry,' Eyesee said. 'I've offended you, I can tell.'

'It's not that,' Jane assured him, 'really. It's just that you might get embarrassed when I start screaming, and . . .'

'Got you,' said Eyesee, hurriedly. 'Yes, you've got a point there. Very considerate of you. I think I might . . .'

He stopped in mid-sentence, because a wall fell on him.

The way Bjorn had worked it out was like this.

There is no such thing as an idyll. Real life is nasty, sordid and boring, all about going to work and having to shave and the dustbin bags getting ripped open during the night by next door's cat. Even in an infinite universe, there is nowhere you can get a plastic fork that won't break.

Therefore, the idyll I've found myself in is artificial, and somebody's put me here to stop me wandering about. Clever, really; if you want someone to stay locked up, put him in a prison he won't *want* to break out from. Or at least one where he only finds out it's a prison when it's too late.

He thought of Ilona's father, washing the ox-cart, not being allowed to walk on the floor, having to go out into the toolshed to smoke his pipe, and wondered what that poor bastard had done to offend the authorities. Something horrible, probably.

Having reached this conclusion, he set his mind to planning his escape. He reasoned:

This idyll is artificial, right?

That means somebody made it. It's a thing.

Things break when you hit them.

The trick was to find the right spot. Ten years of splitting logs in the other bloody idyll had taught him that it's no use going mad and slashing out wildly with the big axe, because all that happens if you do that is broken axe-handles. You have to find the seam, the flaw, the crack, the split, the lie of the grain, and you can be through it like ice cream through the bottom of the cone on a sunny day.

A hundred and seventy years in the Clerk of the Works' Department had taught him how to look at the sky and the horizon and find the join.

He waited till nightfall, hiding out in the hayloft behind the smithy. Just after midnight, he opened the skylight and looked up. It was a clear night, and the stars shone out of a black velvet sky like rhinestones. Good. That made it easy.

The sky, with its million twinkling points of light, is only wallpaper, after all, put there to cover over the cracks in the vault of heaven caused by the use of cheap, bulk-bought plaster. Like all patterned wallpaper, it's a real cow getting the edges lined up properly. If you look long enough, and know what you're looking for, sooner or later you'll find the point where the paper-hanger cocked it up; where the constellation whose real name is the Toothbrush of Adonis is duplicated on both sides of a millimetre-thick invisible line, and where the cosmos bulges out over an unsmoothed air-bubble. Follow the invisible line down to ground level, and you'll find a tree whose branches are a little bit higher on one side than the other. That's the join. Bjorn knew this because he too had served his time, up on a high stepladder with a bucket of paste and a long brush. He even knew what was underneath the stars . . .

(. . . A rather tasteless red textured flock, very frayed, with patches of mould in places and a few snags and nicotine stains here and there. Many people have wondered what was there before the Big Bang; well, where due north is now is where the dartboard used to be.)

If you're not in a hurry, it's possible just to peel the corner of the paper back, slip through and draw the paper back after you. If you couldn't give a toss, however, you simply pack dynamite round the roots of the tree, retire and light a cigarette, the butt of which you carelessly discard.

Eyesee brushed brick dust out of what for the sake of convenience we shall describe as his eyes and looked blearily upwards, to find himself staring at a distinctly unfriendly sight. It wasn't as bad as looking in a mirror, but it wasn't far behind.

'On your feet,' Bjorn said. 'Come on, I haven't got all sodding day.'

Eyesee blinked. 'Excuse me?' he said.

'On your feet,' Bjorn replied. 'Jump to it, or you'll get my boot up your . . .' He broke off, and frowned. 'Well, doesn't look like you've got one, but we can always improvise.'

Eyesee jumped up quickly. 'No,' he said quickly, 'I really wouldn't want you to go to any trouble on my account. What was it you wanted to know?'

'The way out.'

'Ah.' Eyesee cowered a little and backed away. He'd always wondered what it would feel like, being really frightened; well, he hadn't been missing much. 'That's going to be rather tricky, really, because there isn't one. At least, not in this dimension. I mean, not as such. Strictly speaking,' he added.

'Balls,' Bjorn replied. 'Talking of which . . .'

'This way.'

At this point, Jane woke up. She'd been hit, oddly enough, by a falling star, and a fraction of a second later by a hand-sized lump of plaster. She groaned.

Thirty seconds is plenty long enough for quite a complicated dream, and Jane had dreamed that she was lying, tied to a railway sleeper, in the vaults of some vague but sinister building, while a monster who somehow managed to look exactly like her worst nightmare hid behind a thing like a giant beam engine and explained that henceforth, everything in the world was now officially her fault. That's the trouble with the dreams you tend to get in the basement of the Department of Justice; no imagination.

'Oh,' she said. 'Oh *shit*!'

This is a complicated moment to describe, so we'll get Eyesee out of the way first. When Bjorn looked round, saw Jane and began staring, Eyesee ducked behind a lump of wall, tiptoed quickly away and found himself in the middle of a grassy meadow. Realising he'd come the wrong way, he turned to go back, only to find that the hole he'd just come out of had mysteriously vanished and been replaced by a slightly asymmetrical tree. He spent the rest of the night wandering about dejectedly, trying to avoid polished surfaces and pools of standing water, and at dawn came across a beautiful young shepherdess, who immediately took him home to meet her family. They were married three weeks later, and Eyesee now divides his time between washing up, exercising a small, vicious dog and painting the windows in the spare bedroom. Because he is simply Ilona's husband, nobody even notices what he looks like any more.

'Who're you?' Bjorn eventually asked.

'Queen Victoria,' Jane replied. 'Look, will you please get this log off me?'

Bjorn felt cheated. He'd wanted to make a good impression. He'd wanted to stroll over and say, 'Hey, lady, is that railway sleeper bothering you?' He'd wanted to cut through the ropes with one clean sweep of his Zambian Army Knife, but the big blade was stuck fast and the attachment for taking stones out of impala hooves was as blunt as an armchair. In the end he managed to saw through the rope with the tin-opener, but not before he'd trodden on Jane's foot and cut his fingers to the bone on the lanyard ring.

'There you go,' he said. 'No trouble.'

Jane sat up and massaged her foot. 'That's a matter of opinion,' she said. 'Look, you've broken my heel. Why don't you look where you're going?'

'Er.'

'Er, what?'

'Er. Sorry.' Bjorn stood on one foot and chewed his lower lip. Even thus might Perseus have looked, had he swooped down from the vaults of heaven on his winged sandals, decapitated the sea-dragon and then rounded it off by stepping backwards on to the tail of Andromeda's pet cat. 'Sorry,' he repeated helplessly.

'That's all right,' Jane sighed. 'Now, do you know the way out of here?'

'Um, no,' Bjorn replied, and blushed.

'You don't?'

'Sorry.'

'Never mind.' Jane stood up, took off her other shoe and neatly knocked the heel off against the side of the sleeper. 'They were new on,' she added ruefully. 'Oh well, can't be helped. Do you have such a thing as a torch on you, by any chance?'

Bjorn shook his head, unable to speak. To get a line on his

state of mind, imagine you've just kissed the sleeping princess in the enchanted castle, and she stirs, and opens her eyes, and turns her head, and then you notice the book beside her bed is called *1001 Cures for Chronic Insomnia*.

'Well, well,' Jane tutted. 'We'll just have to try and find the light switch, won't we? Come on, try and make yourself useful.'

When eventually Bjorn did find it (by walking into it and switching it on forcefully with his nose) he was extremely grateful. 'Right,' he said. 'Hey ...'

Jane gave him a look, and it wasn't friendly. Of course, it wasn't his fault that the switch that operated the huge machine was right next to the light switch, and that he had a fairly broad nose; but she really wasn't in the mood to make allowances.

'Don't just stand there,' she snapped. 'Switch the bloody thing off, quick.'

Bjorn reached out an arm, but too late. A force like a water cannon hit him in the chest and sent him bouncing off the walls like a squash ball, until he came to rest up in a corner of the ceiling. He had the unpleasant feeling that that was only temporary; basically, just so long as the ceiling could take the pressure.

'You *idiot*,' came Jane's voice from somewhere he couldn't see. 'What *have* you done?'

'Where are you?' he panted back. It wasn't easy; it was as if someone was trying to fold his shirt without removing him from it first. 'I can't ...'

'If you must know, I'm in the fireplace.'

Bjorn looked around, and noticed the tips of two shoes poking out of the chimney breast. Face facts, his soul whispered to his brain, even by your standards there have been more auspicious starts to a relationship.

'What's doing it?' he tried to shout; but his voice came out ironed and pressed.

'It's that stupid machine,' boomed the voice from the

213

chimney. 'It's pumping air into this room faster than it can escape. Any minute now and I'll be off up this chimney like a bullet up a gun. Satisfied?'

'Hold.' Bjorn struggled, pitting his pectoral muscles against the force of the machine. 'On.' That's embarrassment for you; real, ear-tingling, bowel-churning embarrassment. Adrenaline is positively inert in comparison. 'I'm.' He kicked frantically against the wall, but all he achieved was a short rain of crumbling plaster. 'Coming.' His hand found the penknife in his trouser pocket.

'Great,' Jane replied. 'That's really cheered me up, you know?'

Until recently, Bjorn had always prided himself that he'd kept in pretty good shape – until very recently, in fact; right up until a few seconds ago, when Life had suddenly decided that he'd look better in just two dimensions – and there was the little matter of his self-esteem being at stake here as well. With an effort that a mere scientist would have dismissed as physically impossible, he pulled the knife out of his pocket, opened the big blade first go, and let the pressure do the rest. It drove the knife into the wall, which went pop.

Then there was a long, loud, extremely vulgar sound, followed by a thump as Bjorn fell off the wall on to his head.

'It's all right,' he gasped, a few moments later. 'I've switched it off now.'

'About time too,' came the reply from a long way off. 'Now will you please get me out of this chimney?'

That proved to be the hardest one yet; and Bjorn was on the point of cutting his losses and tiptoeing quietly away when he noticed that the machine had a gear lever. And the gear lever had two positions; one marked *Forward* and one marked *Reverse*.

'When you've *quite* finished,' said Jane, as she crawled out of the fireplace, 'maybe we can get back to looking for the door.'

Bjorn nodded. There were little bright dots and flashes in

214

front of his eyes, and the rest of him felt roughly the way you'd expect a tree to feel after someone has just turned it into a newspaper. 'The door,' he whispered. 'Right. Um, I don't think there is one, you know?'

Jane breathed in deeply. 'We came in through the wall, you mean? Or did someone wash the Universe and it shrank?'

Bjorn nodded. 'I think I know this place,' he said doggedly. 'Used to work in this department once. This is one room where they don't need a door.'

The sardonic comment withered on Jane's lips. Instead: 'They don't?' she asked.

'No need,' Bjorn replied. 'The reason being, this place is basically, you know, inside your head. We're in Justice.'

'Justice?' Jane blinked twice. 'Look, where I come from, they have this thing called logic, and . . .'

'Yeah,' Bjorn replied. 'And Justice, like, it works by being what you think should actually happen to you. You know, conscience and all that stuff. So they don't have to bring you here, because you're already here to begin with. That's what they reckon, anyway,' he added. 'I never thought I had that much imagination, you know?'

Jane nodded. 'Nor me,' she said. 'I think they brought me here. If this was my conscience I reckon I'd have recognised it by now, it'd be full of unwashed cups and dirty kitchen floors.'

Bjorn raised an eyebrow. 'Since when did they need washing?' he asked.

'Later,' Jane replied. 'I think I've worked it out.'

. . . Very simple, though not very pleasant.

Where do you put inconvenient people so that nobody can ever find them? Inside your head, of course.

And suppose that you're not actually allowed to do it. You'd feel guilty, wouldn't you? Or at the very least, extremely worried about being found out. So, you put them in your conscience. Probably it just happens that way without you making a conscious decision, but it's a very suitable place, because, in the very nature of things, your conscience is the one part of your brain that's always kept sealed off from the rest.

'So where are we?' Bjorn asked.

Jane frowned. 'That's a good question,' she replied. 'First, I thought maybe I'd died and gone to Hell; but then I thought, Hang on, if this was Hell I'd be able to see the people who dreamed up the idea of putting fruit juice in little cardboard cartons with individual straws.' She sighed. 'So I guess it's option number two.'

Bjorn didn't actually click his tongue impatiently, because you don't do that sort of thing around visions of sublime loveliness. There was, however, a slight spasm in the muscles of his jaw. 'Go on,' he said.

'Which means,' Jane continued, 'we're inside somebody's head.'

There was a pause while Bjorn, for the want of a better word, thought about it.

'Nah,' he replied. 'We wouldn't fit, for one thing. You'd have legs sticking out through ears and all sorts.'

Jane sat down on a lump of masonry and inspected the damage to her footwear. 'It's all a matter of dimensions,' she replied warily. 'I could be wrong, but I've got an idea that you lot are rather more flexible when it comes to that sort of thing than we are. I mean,' she added with a slight shudder, 'all that business with Time . . .'

Bjorn frowned. 'What's that got to do with it?' he asked.

'I don't know,' Jane confessed. 'During physics lessons at school, I was always the one at the back of the class drawing sea-serpents in the margins. I just feel that anyone capable of coning off two lanes of the later Roman Empire isn't going to have too much difficulty in tucking us two away between their ears.'

Bjorn digested this for a moment. 'Okay,' he said, 'so we're inside some guy's head. No problem.'

He stood up, grabbed hold of a large lump of rock and started banging it against a wall. Plaster fell from the ceiling in little clouds.

'What exactly are you doing?' Jane enquired.

'Well,' Bjorn replied, between gasps for breath, 'if you're right, pretty soon a big hole's going to appear and a couple of aspirin are going to come flying in here. That's when we make our . . .'

Jane sighed. 'Maybe I was over-simplifying,' she said. 'I mean, yes, we're inside this person's head, but we're also in a different dimension. These things are very complicated, you know.'

'Oh.' Bjorn sagged, and let the rock fall. 'So what've you got in mind, then?'

'Nothing, really,' Jane replied sadly. 'I think we're trapped, if you really want to know. I think we're stuck in here for ever and ever. Brilliant, isn't it?'

Bjorn shook his head. 'You're wrong,' he said. 'Look, everything that exists is a thing, right? And everything that's a thing can be broken, or smashed up, or knackered, right? All we've got to do is find where to kick it, and we're away.' He stood up straight, put his shoulders back and started to walk purposefully round the room, stopping occasionally to bang the walls hard with his head.

For her part, Jane put her arms round her knees and curled up. It was bad enough being stuck, she thought; she could really have done without the company. Her ideal companion for the rest of Eternity was . . . well, it wasn't a subject she'd given a great deal of thought to, what with one thing and another – A-levels first, and then briefly the rain forests and the threat of nuclear weapons, and latterly mostly the quantum mass of accrued back ironing – but it certainly wasn't a six-foot blond Nordic idiot whose reading probably stopped short at *Alcohol 4.5% by Volume. Please Dispose Of Can Tidily*. If someone was out to get her, so far they were doing a pretty neat job.

'Hey,' Bjorn called out. 'Sounds pretty hollow over here.'

'What does?'

'The wall.'

'Oh.' Probably an inter-dimensional partition of some

kind. Gosh, thought Jane, I'm *hungry*.

'Definitely hollow,' Bjorn continued. 'Perhaps if I gave it a really good thumping with something hard and solid . . .'

'I thought you'd just tried that.'

'Well, it's better than just sitting there,' Bjorn replied coldly. He looked around, and then set about trying to lift a larger than average lump of masonry. He failed.

'Or there's the chimney,' he added. 'That looks like it goes somewhere.'

Jane sniffed. 'Quite probably,' she replied. 'Given that the Universe is curved, it probably goes backwards. Up itself. Eventually, I mean.'

'Yeah,' said Bjorn uncertainly, 'right. You know, what I could really use right now is a bloody big hammer.'

'Look,' Jane snapped, 'you're just wasting your time. We aren't inside a room, we aren't inside anything. We're just inside.' She waved her arms irritably. 'So will you please stop banging around, because you're starting to get on my nerves.'

Reluctantly Bjorn put down the promising-looking slab of breeze block he'd been trying for weight and balance, and paced up and down a few steps, humming. Then he got down on his hands and knees and tried staring up the chimney.

'Maybe,' he said, 'if we're inside this guy's head like you said, this chimney is actually a nostril or something. Yeah,' he added brightly, 'and that pump thing, you know, the one we had on just now, maybe that's something to do with the breathing gear.'

'Please,' Jane mumbled, as she lay on her back with her eyes closed, 'would you mind terribly much just shutting up for a while, because I'd like to try and get some sleep.'

Bjorn glowered at her. 'All right,' he growled. 'Just let me have one more go, okay?'

'Please yourself,' Jane replied irritably, and turned over on her side.

Bjorn nodded purposefully. He was in love, he was trapped

inside somebody's head, something he couldn't understand had tried to spread him all over the walls like butter, and what he wanted most of all in the whole wide world was fifty centilitres of ice-cold Budweiser. He spat on his hands, hefted the chunk of breeze block, and gave the corner of the mantelpiece a bone-jarring wallop.

Various things happened.

Several pieces of shrapnel broke off the mantelpiece; the lights flickered, Ganger materialised in mid-air, fell heavily and rolled on the ground, clutching his ankle and groaning; a hole appeared in one of the walls and the floor suddenly flooded with a sea of soluble aspirin.

The final event was Bjorn splashing across the floor, grabbing Ganger by the lapels and shaking him as if he contained a mixture of gin and vermouth.

'Dop, you bastard,' he snapped. 'What the hell kept you?'

Staff tightened his half-nelson on Finance and General Purposes' right arm and grinned like a maniac.

The trick was, apparently, to keep the bastard's mind occupied until Ganger could get out of it. This was getting increasingly harder.

'Another thing I bet you don't know about fifteenth-century Florentine religious painting . . .' he said.

'Dop?' said Jane. It wouldn't have taken much imagination to see wisps of smoke drifting out of her ears. '*Dop?*'

Ganger grinned sheepishly. 'D. Ganger,' he replied. 'What did you think the D stood for, anyway? Norman?'

There are times when you can feel the situation drifting away from you. 'But why?' she heard herself ask. 'Does that mean there's two of you, or what?'

Ganger shook his head. 'Coincidence,' he said. 'It just so happens that where I come from, Doppel is a very traditional Chri . . . very traditional name.' He paused. 'It's part,' he added, 'of our rich and ancient cultural heritage.'

219

'Where you come from,' Jane repeated. 'I thought you were a . . .'

'Yes,' Ganger interrupted, 'well, anyway. This isn't getting us anywhere, is it? Talking of which, I'll bet you don't know where you are. I mean, I could give you three guesses and you'd never . . .'

'Inside the head of the chairman of the Finance and General Purposes Committee,' Jane replied flatly. 'To be precise, locked inside his conscience.' She sniffed histrionically. 'Give me credit for a little common sense, please.'

Ganger sagged. 'Right,' he said. 'Now . . .'

'And I think I've seen everything I want to,' Jane went on brutally, 'so if you'll just see your way to getting me out of here, then I'll be very much obliged to you.'

'Right. Um.'

'And,' Jane added, 'you can accept my resignation. I've had enough of all this. I want to go back to being a terminally bored and frustrated human being stuck in the same old mindless rut, if that's all the same to you. In fact,' she added savagely, 'if ever I get out of this . . . this *head* in one piece, I'm going straight to the nearest poly. to enrol for accountancy classes. Got that?'

Ganger nodded. And then vanished.

He re-materialised in complete darkness, but that was all right. Something soft broke his fall. Something soft and strangely comfortable. He reached in his top pocket for his slimline flashlight. Then he grinned.

He was completely surrounded by ironing.

Further inspection revealed that it was ironing strewn untidily across an unwashed kitchen floor, while on the edge of the penumbra cast by his small torch he could make out the silhouette of a sink piled high with saucepans and baking trays. He nodded. He'd come to the right place.

Look, said the walls and the floor, this is ridiculous.

'Maybe,' Ganger replied, lying back on a heap of creased

and wrinkly cotton blouses and putting his hands behind his head. 'Quite possibly. But you can't blame me for trying.'

It's *absurd*, replied the walls and the floor. I'm inside his head, you're inside mine. It's going to end up like that trick where you have two mirrors facing each other, and the reflections go on and on for ever. For all I know, we could end up disappearing or something.

'Nah,' Ganger yawned. 'Trust me, I know about these things. I've been inside more heads than you've had hot dinners.' He paused and peered across at the sink. 'And that's saying something, apparently. Hey, Le Creuset. I've got a set of them.'

Leave my kitchenware out of this, replied the floor. And while you're in there, you can see for yourself. If you can find one scrap of remorse for me handing in my notice . . .

Ganger grinned. Then, slowly, he took a large, flat packet from under his coat and started to unwrap it.

Hey, shrieked the ceiling, that's not *fair*. You can't do that.

'Who's going to stop me?' Ganger said simply. Then he bit through a strand of sellotape.

But it's against the rules, howled the far wall. You can't bring things of your own into my head, it's brainwashing.

Ganger studied the floor pointedly. 'Looks like it could do with it,' he said. 'If your mother were to see this floor, she'd have a . . .'

You leave my mother out of this.

'I can do,' Ganger replied. He walked across to the sink, picked up a cheese-encrusted kitchen knife, and set to work with it on the wrappings of the parcel. 'Depends on how reasonable you can be.'

What've you got in there, anyway?

'Guilt,' Ganger chuckled. 'Highly refined, industrial-strength concentrated remorse. So don't sneeze or make any sudden movements, for both our sakes, or you'll spend the rest of your life with people hiding sharp objects whenever you come into a room.'

You bastard.

Ganger said nothing. He wasn't looking sheepish any more.

I think you're bluffing. You wouldn't dare.

'Bet?'

If you let go one drop of that stuff, as soon as you come out I'll kill you.

'Oh no you won't,' Ganger replied grimly. 'You'll be so sorry for everything else you've done, you'll positively beg me to let you carry on working for us. It's amazing stuff, this,' he added nonchalantly. 'In the plant where they process it, they have to stop every five minutes and confess.'

The walls seemed to shrink a little. The floor quivered.

'In fact,' Ganger went on, 'you wouldn't believe some of the things they confess to. We had an assistant production manager phone up the newspapers and claim responsibility for the San Andreas Fault the other day. Said San Andreas was framed. We had our work cut out hushing that one up, I can tell you . . .'

All right. You win. Put it away.

'I have a five-year contract in my left inside pocket,' Ganger said slowly. 'Also a pen. And something to rest on.'

All *right*. Just put it away before you drop it or something.

'Thank you,' Ganger said. 'You won't be sorry. Or at least, not half as sorry as you would have been if I'd . . .'

All *right*.

There was a blur.

It hardly lasted any time at all, which was just as well. Imagine a Cinemascope projection of the Rockies pulled through a two-inch hole, backwards.

'Here we are, then,' Ganger said cheerfully. 'All safe and . . .'

Staff looked up and let go of his prisoner. 'What the hell do you think you've been doing?' he demanded. The prisoner made a little moaning noise, sagged forwards and collapsed. Ganger looked at him.

'There wasn't any call to get heavy,' he said reproachfully. 'Besides, we need him.'

Staff growled. 'I didn't get heavy,' he said. 'Not unless you could call explaining the plot of *Tristan and Isolde* three times consecutively, *and* trying to make it sound interesting, getting heavy,' he added bitterly.

'Sounds pretty heavy to me,' Ganger replied. 'Never mind, though, here we all are.' He looked down and prodded the slumped body with his toe. 'Somebody throw a bucket of water over him or something.'

'Excuse me.'

Ganger and Staff looked round.

'Excuse me,' said Jane, 'but the deal's off. It was under duress, and absolutely unfair, and I'm not signing anything.'

She folded her arms, and Bjorn simultaneously took a step forward. There was an awful lot of him, and although it was undeniably true that mere physical violence wouldn't have any effect whatsoever on the likes of Ganger and Staff, they both shrank back a few inches. After all, there was no way of telling that *he* knew that.

'Who's this?' Staff asked.

'Ah yes,' Ganger replied, trying to smear a thin coat of self-confidence over his voice. 'Friend of mine I'd like you both to meet.'

Staff considered this for a moment. 'If he's a friend of yours,' he observed, 'then why's he holding you two feet off the ground by your lapels? Does that mean he's really glad to see you or something?'

'You bastard,' said Bjorn. 'You slimy, toffee-nosed little git. You went off and left me in that . . .' Bjorn paused and made a thorough search of his vocabulary for the right word; given the size of Bjorn's vocabulary, it was a bit like looking for a combine harvester in a haystack. 'In that *dump*,' he said decisively. Which only goes to show that you don't need to lug a dictionary round between your ears to be able to come up with the *mot juste*.

223

'Oh, come on,' Ganger replied. 'It wasn't that bad, surely.'

It was the wrong thing to say. Ganger suddenly found himself an inch away from the angriest pair of eyes he'd ever come across.

'Right, sunshine,' said Bjorn quietly. 'You can read minds, right?'

'Up to a point.'

'Maybe you'd fancy having a quick look round what I've got in mind for you.'

Ganger swallowed hard. 'I'd rather not,' he replied. 'You do realise, of course, that physical discomfort has no effect on me whatsoever.'

'Sure?'

Jane made a tutting noise. 'Put him down,' she said briskly. 'If you frighten him he'll probably go and hide in my subconscious, and I've had enough trouble with it over the years as it is. Who are you, anyway?'

Bjorn swung his head round, and blushed. 'Um,' he stammered. 'Like, well, my name's sort of Bjorn. That is . . .'

'Hello, Bjorn. Aren't you forgetting something, by the way?'

Bjorn's eyes filled with panic, as he struggled to identify the social error he'd just committed. Should he have shaken her hand, he wondered, or offered to give up his seat or carry her bag for her? Were you actually supposed to say your name on a first date? He looked around wildly for a door to open.

'I think she means about putting me down,' Ganger whispered.

Without moving his head, Bjorn relaxed his fingers slightly. There was a thump, and something down by his feet said 'Thank you so much.'

'How do you come into this anyway?' Jane was asking. 'You don't look like a . . .'

'He's not,' Ganger broke in. 'Or at least, he used to be. But he's not any more. Now he's a supergrass.'

Jane was just about to say 'A *what*?' and Staff was on the point of asking, 'Look, just what *is* going on here?' and Bjorn was poised to hit somebody, when the heap on the floor groaned and moved slightly.

And looked up. And saw Bjorn. And screamed.

Or at least one of him did.

One of the risks inherent in high managerial office, with all the accompanying stress and nervous tension of departmental politics, is that of developing a dual personality. Usually it's regarded as something to be avoided, but it can have its advantages.

To take a good example: it meant that whereas half of Finance and General Purposes' personality was making small squeaking noises and trying to hide itself in the pile of the carpet, the other half was striding angrily down the corridors of the Security barracks, yelling furiously and banging on doors with a riding crop. Where Finance and General Purposes had an advantage over the run-of-the-mill psychotic was being able to provide separate corporeal incarnations for each of his separate personas; or, to put it another way, two bodies to go with his two faces.

The one that went with his half-crazed-Dictator face was very big, dressed in the sort of black leather greatcoat the SS would have gone in for if they'd had access to top-quality dragon hide, and draped liberally with interesting-looking weapons. You'd need an active, not to say warped, imagination to work out what they were designed to do to you, but any fool could see they were weapons. Fiendish ones, probably.

'Come on, you goddamn sons of bitches,' he was shouting. 'Move it!'

He moved the stub of a cigar round in his jaw as he shouted. Somewhere just north of his hip pocket, a particularly abstruse weapon shrugged and metamorphosed smoothly into a pearl-handled revolver.

As his footsteps echoed away down the corridor, two
bleary-eyed spectral warriors opened their doors and looked
out at each other.

'Now what?' yawned one of them.

'You know what?' replied the other. 'I have this feeling we
aren't going to enjoy this.'

His comrade in arms suddenly became aware that he was
still wearing his Snoopy T-shirt. He turned hurriedly away
and reached for his regulation issue shapeless black cowl, and
so failed to notice that his colleague had come to the door still
holding the copy of *The Ballet-Goers' Companion* he'd been
reading, under the blankets, with a torch.

'Better get ready,' said the closet balletomane. They both
withdrew into their cells.

A few minutes later, they fell in for parade. Something
about their leader's manner as he paced up and down
inspecting them didn't do much to cheer them up. In this
persona, Finance and General Purposes was sometimes
known as the Grand Old Man, or Old Ironsides, or simply
The General. And a lot of other things, too.

He stopped and pointed with his riding crop, his hand
quivering with rage.

'Oh, shit,' whispered the Snoopy fan to his neighbour.
They surreptitiously swivelled their eyes to the left, saw what
the matter was, then quietly and sincerely thanked Providence that it wasn't them.

8765B had forgotten to take his face-mask off.

Accordingly, the row consisted of forty-nine billowing
black cowls, empty except for a pair of indescribably horrible
points of red light, and one pale pink face with spectacles and
razor-rash. Forty-nine pairs of indescribably horrible points
of red light closed, and the cowls surrounding them winced.
A spectral warrior who turns out on parade improperly
dressed doesn't get away with just whitewashing stones or
cutting the grass with nail-scissors.

'You,' hissed the General. 'Fall out.'

The pink face sagged like a deflating balloon and fell down inside the cowl. 'But . . .' said a tiny voice, from a long way down.

'I said fall out, soldier. You deaf?'

'Sir.' There was a sigh of pity and terror – the proportions were approximately those of an extremely dry Martini – as first the cowl and then the rest of the habit slowly crumpled to the ground and lay there in a heap, like a pair of drunken trousers. For spectral warriors, the words of command tend to mean what they say.

The General looked round, and bit into his cigar-butt.

'Whassa matter?' he snapped. 'You never seen an immortal soul busted before?'

Complete silence. When, eventually, the late 8765B's collar-pin hit the ground, it sounded like a small explosion.

'All *right*,' growled the General. 'Move it.'

There was a crash of boots on the tarmac.

With a grunt of satisfaction, the General gave the signal, and the column moved forwards at a terrified quick march towards the waiting trucks. Perhaps it would have comforted the spectral warriors to know that, about a quarter of an hour's drive away, exactly the same person as the hundred-per-cent bastard who was staring at them and willing one of them to have forgotten to blanco his bayonet frog was cowering under a chair and making noises like a petrified kitten.

Maybe not.

There was a hushed silence. You could almost hear the thought, feel the tension. If there had been a barometer nearby, it would have screamed.

Eventually: 'Yeah,' said the Count of the Saxon Shore, 'I'll have the veal as well. So that's three veal, one chicken, one osso bucco, and three bottles of the red.'

The Emperor's sister shook her head. 'Veal's off, sorry,' she said. 'I forgot to mention. Goddamn butcher didn't deliver again today.'

The Electors looked at each other for a long time. It was the County Palatine who eventually put it into words.

'Hey,' he said, 'what's going on around here?'

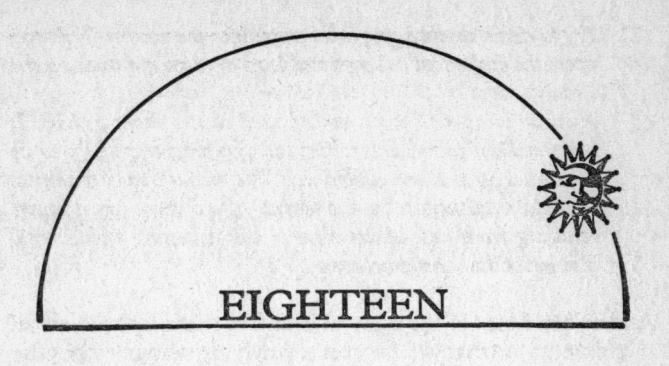

EIGHTEEN

Meanwhile, in the interests of clarity and a comprehensible narrative, take the next exit on the left, over the flyover, and back down the Pastbound lane almost as far as you can go . . .

To a time when there was virtually no Time at all, when the world was young and fresh, and still thinking, *Stuff it, it's years yet before I have to start thinking about pension schemes.*

A vibrant new administration has just moved into spanking new purpose-built offices, with state-of-the-art information technology, a highly trained and motivated young staff and an instruction manual. Which reads like this:

Congratulations! You are now the owner of a new Terra 57636. If properly looked after, it will give you many years of reliable and pleasurable service.

Although the Terra 57636 has been hand crafted using only the finest quality materials, in order to get the very best in performance and reliability from your machine, you should observe the following basic rules:

(1) Ensure that all surfaces are clean and free from excess oil. Do not remove the trees, as this interferes with the supply of oxygen to the intake manifolds.

(2) *Try to avoid discharging toxic waste into the oceans. This can upset the ecological balance and lead to excessive wear on the icecaps.*

(3) *Nuclear weapons should not be used in the Terra 57636. It has not been proofed to withstand the pressures likely to be generated by nuclear explosions. The manufacturers cannot be held responsible in the event of accident or damage resulting from non-observance of this warning, which will also invalidate the guarantee*

And so on. Most of the manual is in fact taken up with awful warnings as to what will happen to anybody who infringes the manufacturer's patent or makes unauthorised copies of the software; and a garbled version of this has survived to this day in the form of the Revelation of St John the Divine. The rest of the text was lost many centuries ago.

A minor but ambitious young official has just been appointed deputy head of the Sun Department, a relatively unimportant post, but even high-flyers have to start somewhere. It's his job to ensure that the sun is flown on exactly the right trajectory to ensure that it delivers just the right amount of light and heat to the world busily evolving below. Too little, and Life will be stillborn. Too much, and there's a risk that it'll turn out the wrong way. Strange, warped mutants with malfunctioning components and entirely unsuitable evolutionary matrices will emerge from the bubbling green soup that covers the surface, instead of the superbly constructed designer lifeforms that the manufacturers intended.

Look very closely, and in the corner of the hangar you'll see a scruffy individual in the first ever pair of worn-out jeans and the primal Def Leppard sweatshirt, loafing aimlessly around with a broom in one hand and a pair of headphones over his ears. It will be many millenia before the Sony Walkman is invented, but he's getting in some early practice. His chances of promotion are slim.

And on the sixth day, the minor but ambitious young

official woke up, put on his shiny black leather flying jacket and his goggles, and strolled confidently down towards the hangar. So far, he told himself, he'd done a pretty good job. The Boss himself had said so, and he ought to know. Pretty good job you're doing there, young 'un, he'd said, and you couldn't put it more clearly than that if you tried.

He climbed into the cockpit, checked the rear-view mirror and the oil gauge, and fastened the safety harness. Pretty good job, young 'un. Well, absolutely. Credit where credit's due, and all that.

'Flaps?' he shouted.

'You what?'

The official sighed. 'I said,' he yelled back, 'flaps.'

'What about them?'

'Are they engaged or aren't they? Come on, man, I haven't got all day.'

'Flaps engaged.'

'Switches?'

'Yeah.'

The young official made a despairing gesture. 'Oh, for crying out loud, are the switches on or off?' he cried. 'Or do I have to come and check them for myself?'

'Switches on.'

'Hoo-bloody-ray. Right then, contact.'

Pause.

'I said,' growled the young official, 'contact. But of course nobody is listening. I am talking to myself. Which is just as well, because it's the only way I'm going to get an intelligent conversation around here. CONTACT!'

'Yeah, right. Sorry.'

There was a thud; then a roar; then the hangar started to shake, as the huge machine's four enormous compression chambers slowly filled with cold, blue fire. The young official pulled his goggles down over his eyes, put the choke halfway in, and called out, 'Chocks away!'

And then he was flying. For a few seconds the world

seemed far too small to contain such a wild extravagance of movement; then the airbrakes caught and the giant projectile burst through the thin haze of water-vapour that hung over the sparkling new oceans, levelled out and started to fly straight and level.

A pretty good take-off, young 'un, said the minor but ambitious official to himself. Neat work. Nothing to it, really; all you have to do is hang on to this handle thing and it'll fly itself.

He leaned forward in his seat and peered over the side. Far away, he could glimpse through loopholes in the clouds a shining blue horizon, textured by the breeze into a million regular waves. In there somewhere, at this very moment, the atoms were rubbing together in a miraculously improbable way. Life was just around the corner.

Smiling, the minor but ambitious young official relaxed back into his seat, looked up at the endless blue ceiling above him and began to dream.

All right, *right now* he was doing a job that was little better than Executive Grade 2 status, but that wasn't going to last for ever. It wasn't as if they could just take a trainee, however talented, and plonk him straight down in a fifth-floor office; there were motions to be gone through, knees to be browned. Just as soon as you proved to them that you could do all this noddy stuff with one hand tied behind your back, they'd have you out of it and sitting behind a desk in no time flat. That would mean Clerical status; and once you'd got that, you were halfway there. Anyone with an ounce of go in him could whizz up the Clerical ladder like a rat up a drain with the bailiffs on its tail; and then you'd be in Admin. No more dealing with actual things, no more flying suns or grading snowflakes or lugging about tectonic plates. In Admin, they only dealt with the really important, totally nebulous things – five-year plans, forecasts, projections, economic models, cost-effectiveness ratios, overall strategies. There would be committees, sub-committees, quasi-autonomous review panels, watchdog commissions, one-man working parties. You would have absolute control, and maybe even a chair that swivels.

And then would come the real quantum leap; first to departmental status, before soaring upwards to the Empyrean heights of supervisory management; to permanent chairmanship of a committee so vast and so indefinable that the whole curved universe itself would be only part of its jurisdiction. As yet, nothing so mind-bendingly huge existed anywhere in the cosmos, apart from in the minor but ambitious official's imagination; but if it ever came to pass, it would have to have a name that was abstract to the point of stretching the parameters of applied metaphysics.

Finance and something. Finance and Ultimate Purposes. Something like that.

The minor but ambitious official smiled. He and the world were young, talented and going places together. He and the world were like *that*.

Oh.

Oh shit!

Actually, that too was way ahead in the future, but as we've already seen, the minor but ambitious official is way ahead of his time.

A long way below, but still rather closer than it ought to be, the surface of the sea boiled. Huge banks of water-vapour drifted up into the sky, bumped jarringly into temperature shifts, liquefied and fell back. Out of the water, jagged points of rock poked nervous and embarrassed fingertips, like guests who have turned up far too early for the birthday party of somebody they scarcely know. And deep down, in the very dregs of the ocean, something that had no business moving moved.

It wasn't quite the way it's depicted on the ceiling of the Sistine chapel. There's no inter-digital fireworks, no snap and crackle of white fire. There should have been, of course; and speeches, and a tape to cut, and a special presentation pair of silver shears, and a band. But there wasn't.

This is the way the world begins; not with a zap but a cock-up.

With a frenzied jerk on the joystick, the minor but ambitious official hauled the Sun back up to its proper place in the sky, and sagged forward against the straps of the safety harness. In his mind's eye, he saw two visions:

... The first, of the world as it should have been – the calm, dignified procession of perfectly formed organic pioneers rising serenely from the depths of the ocean to colonise the purpose-built land-masses, to evolve in a purposeful way into demi-gods, to begin the long but completely orthodox march towards reunion with their Creator, to the moment when they turn their smug faces to the sun and see only their own reflection ...

The second, of the world as it was going to be – nasty green slimy things slopping up on to premature beaches, twitching apologies for mandibles in the germ-ridden air; slowly squeezing themselves into all manner of outlandish shapes – ammonites, dinosaurs, mammoths, monkeys, things even more obscenely ludicrous than monkeys; things that would slip out of control and start smashing the place up, building motorways, exterminating whales, waging wars, wearing fluorescent green beachwear ...

Very carefully, the minor but ambitious official looked all around him, and then down at the seas below.

Maybe nobody would notice.

Not yet, anyway. And by the time they did, who could possibly tell whose fault it had been? He fixed his eyes on the western horizon, steadied his grip on the joystick, and began to whistle aggressively.

Some time later, he made a faultless landing back at the hangar, cut the motors, and climbed rather unsteadily out of the cockpit. As he walked the long, long way across the hangar to the big double doors, nobody came running up, nobody called his name; there were no thick-set men in raincoats, no soldiers, nothing – just the erk with the broom and his headphones, prodding half-heartedly at the first few molecules of dust as they drifted through the still-pure air. He closed his mind to the problem, and gradually the problem began to disintegrate. Fragment of the imagination, trick of the light, nothing moved at all. Pretty good job, young 'un. Thanks, sir, glad you liked it.

'Bit low there, weren't you?'

The minor but ambitious official spun on his heel and stared. For his part, the erk with the broom made a more than usually half-hearted stab at an atom of grime, and scratched his ear where the headphones chafed the lobe.

'Sorry?'

'I said, bit low there this morning. Could've been an accident, going as low as that. You know, could've set something off before its time.' The erk raised his head and grinned. 'You want to be more careful,' he added.

'I don't know what you mean,' replied the official, apparently through a mouthful of cotton wool. 'I kept at exactly the right height all the way.'

'That's all right, then,' replied the erk, widening his grin. 'Must've been imagining things.'

'Well, don't do it again,' the official snapped. 'And get on with your work. This place is an absolute tip.'

But the grin only became wider, and the official turned away and nearly ran for the doors. As he retreated, he may or may not have heard somebody muttering something like, Calls himself a *high*-flyer, big joke. *Low*-flyer'd be nearer the mark ... He grabbed the door, hauled it open, and slammed it.

And it came to pass exactly as the minor but ambitious young official had foreseen. He got his promotion, the world got mankind, and nobody said anything. True, there were a few heads shaken at hyper-departmental level, and there was a full internal inquiry. And then nothing.

Nothing, except a face burned deep in the official's mental

retina, a grin, the memory of a tiny movement in the depths of the sea. Meanwhile, two careers developed: one dizzily ascending, one sort of slithering along the bottom. Maybe, said the official to himself a hundred times a day, he's forgotten all about it. A brain like that needs all its capacity just to make sure the beer ends up in the mouth and not down the front of the shirt. If he was going to say something, he'd have said it by now. And then the grin would float by like a stray patch of anti-matter, and whisper, *Don't kid yourself. He hasn't forgotten*.

As an interesting footnote to all this, it's worth recording that the evolutionary development of the human waste disposal system was the result of the young official's subconscious desire to have something appropriate to mutter under his breath every time he thought of it.

'Oh,' Bjorn said.

'Exactly,' Ganger interrupted. 'That's why, as soon as he was appointed chairman of the Finance and General Purposes committee, the first thing he did was have you spirited away to an idyll and kitted out with a brand-new identity. It was a good try, but doomed to failure from the start.'

'Oh,' Bjorn repeated. He was thinking, Stuff me, what a lot of long words this jerk knows. 'Come to think of it, I remember something like what you just said. But I never thought . . .'

From the floor there was a howl that set all the atoms in the cosmos on edge. Ganger stared.

'You mean you hadn't . . . I mean, it didn't occur to you . . .'

'Nah,' Bjorn replied. 'Course, now you tell me, it all sort of makes sense. Yeah, you've got a point there.' He leaned down and put his lips close to Finance and General Purposes' ear. '*Bastard!*' he shouted.

'Well,' said Ganger quickly, 'anyway, that's beside the point. Now we all know, and that's what really matters, isn't it? In case you're wondering how I found out . . .'

'You read his mind, didn't you?' said Staff quietly.

'So?'

Staff was white as a sheet and trembling. 'That's not *fair*,' he said. 'You shouldn't do things like that.'

Ganger looked as if he'd just been kicked in the nuts by an angel. 'Oh come off it,' he said. 'You've just heard me say that this jerk is responsible for *everything*. He's a goddamn evolution criminal, that's what he is. You do understand that, don't you?'

'Of course I do,' Staff shouted. 'That still doesn't make it right. You can't just go about peering in through people's ears like that.' He turned away. Ganger shook his head in disbelief and turned to Jane.

'You don't think it was wrong, do you?' he said.

Jane thought about it for a moment. On the one hand, she didn't hold with bugging. On the other hand . . . She thought for a moment about Homo sapiens, and many things crossed her mind: toothache, the division of the species into two genders, acne, comfort eating, split ends, clogged pores, catarrh, armpits. You could forgive most things, given time, but you've got to draw the line somewhere. And feet. If this guy was responsible for feet . . .

'He had it coming,' she said; then she, too, leaned forward. 'Why five toes, you scumbag? Go on, answer me. Why five, for God's sake? Four not good enough for you or something?'

Ganger nodded. 'Motion carried, I think,' he said. 'Now then, all we've got to do is . . .'

The room suddenly filled with white light. From the street below, a tannoy invited them to reflect on the fact that the building was surrounded. If they had weapons, it might be a shrewd move at this stage to throw them out of the window.

Jane cleared her throat.

'Excuse me,' she said, 'but who's that, exactly?'

Ganger looked round at her. 'Out there, you mean? The

ones with the searchlights and the PA system?'

'That's right.'

'I have an idea it's my colleagues from Security,' Staff interrupted. 'This is just a wild guess, but I think they want to arrest us.'

'I see,' said Jane. 'Why?'

'It's what they're best at, I suppose,' Ganger said. 'I mean, why do painters paint? Why do potters make pots? The question we should be addressing is, will they succeed?'

For his part, Bjorn gave them the kind of stare that large, stupid people reserve for their intellectual betters when they're indulging in verbal fireworks instead of getting on with the job. That's great, it said, and you won't mind if I leave you to it and just look around for a gun or something. He started to search the drawers of the desk, and soon he'd found what he'd been looking for. The bad guys always have small, pearl-handled guns in their desk drawers.

'Right,' he said.

He crossed to the window and hurled a chair through it. Then he flattened his back against the wall, extended his arm through the shattered glass, and pulled the trigger.

Down below, a spectral warrior felt something land on top of his head. Gingerly he reached up and felt the crown of his cowl. It was damp.

Meanwhile, Bjorn was staring at the prisoner with contemptuous disbelief.

'A water-pistol,' he croaked. 'What sort of chicken-shit wimp keeps a pearl-handled *water-pistol* in the top drawer of his desk?'

'A pacifist?' Ganger suggested. Staff sighed and pointed at the three tall potted ferns on top of the filing cabinet, just before they disintegrated in a hail of automatic fire from the street below.

'Not so much a pistol,' he mumbled (inevitable, since he was now hiding under the desk, with his head wedged sideways into the carpet) 'as a novelty plant-mister. I seem to remember the lucky dip at the office party a few years back . . .'

'They seem to be shooting at us,' Jane remarked, enunciating the words with bell-like clarity. 'Should they be doing that, I wonder?'

Staff raised his head painfully and glowered at Bjorn. 'I think we seem to have started it,' he growled. 'They're just defending themselves.'

'Fine,' Jane replied. 'I can quite see their point. I mean, a water-pistol at this range, you could get absolutely *soaked*. You could get pneumonia.'

There was a hollow thump down below them somewhere, followed about half a second later by an explosion in the office. The room was suddenly full of charred and shredded paper.

'Somebody would have appeared to have taken out the filing cabinet with a wire-guided missile,' Staff announced. He sounded for all the world like a BBC Radio Royal Wedding's compère commentating on Armageddon. 'I can only assume they have their reasons, because . . .'

There was a faint *whoosh*, and something whirred past Staff's hiding place and vanished into the hole in the far wall where the filing cabinet had once been. It was Bjorn, jumping up, grabbing Jane in one hand and the hostage in the other, and running for it.

Staff realised that he was on his own. It crossed his mind that he shouldn't be.

Something else crossed his mind. On tiptoe.

'It won't do you any good, you know,' he sighed wearily. 'I mean, if I go, you go too, so you're just fooling yourself.'

Maybe, replied a voice somewhere in his memory, but it's all as broad as it's long. Besides, there's some amazingly good places to hide in here.

'Where?'

Well, said the voice, can you remember that time you went on that fact-finding visit to those caves, right down in the heart of that mountain somewhere?

'Vividly.'

Thanks. Yes, this'll do nicely. You can't remember a light, can you? It's as dark as a bag down here.

'No, I can't.'

Or a sandwich, maybe? Come on, you must be able to remember something to eat. I could be down here for a very long time.

Staff didn't bother to reply. Instead, he crawled out from under the desk, ducked as a lump of ceiling smashed down a few inches away from him, and then picked up his feet and ran.

He made it to the hole in the wall just a fraction of a second before it closed up.

'... me *down*!' Jane yelled, and then landed with a bump. 'Ouch,' she commented.

'Sorry,' Bjorn replied. 'I thought you said "put me down", so I did.'

Jane sat up and rubbed her shin vigorously, sending small and entirely unintentional electric signals running the length and breadth of Bjorn's spinal column. 'Where are we, anyway?' she growled.

'Dunno,' Bjorn said. 'Wherever this is, though, I don't reckon we should stay here. Those guys out there weren't just ordinary Security, you know. More like spectral warriors.'

Jane nodded, and then grabbed hold of the hostage by his nose.

'You,' she said. 'What's happening?'

The hostage, still tucked under Bjorn's arm like a quivering football, made a tiny mewing noise of pure terror. Jane sighed.

'Can you do anything to make him talk?' she asked Bjorn. He nodded.

'Mind you,' he added, 'all he'll probably say is "oh shiiiit", and "ouch, you're breaking my arm", and stuff like that, but ...'

There was a nervous cough from under Bjorn's armpit. *'You're in the vaults of the Central Administrative Section, directly under the closed file store,'* it twittered, *'and if you hurt so much as a hair of my head, then so help me I'll rip your lungs out and make Chinese lanterns out of them.'*

Bjorn stared down. 'You what?' he demanded.

'Don't blame me,' whimpered the tiny voice. *'That's not me talking. I'm absolutely terrified of you. It's him who's making the threats.'*

'Him?'

'Well, me. Other me. Him. Mercy!'

Bjorn frowned. 'You mean there's two of you?'

'Sort of. Well, no. There's just the one of me, but in two halves. One mind, two bodies, each body containing an undivided half-section of the same integral whole.' The voice hesitated. *'I'm the meek, cowardly one.* AND I'M THE COMPLETE BASTARD. *It's all to do with making schizophrenia work for you rather than being a handicap.'*

'All right,' said Jane, 'that'll do. At least we know where we are now.' She paused. 'Where are we?'

Bjorn furrowed his brow. 'We're under the closed file store in the vaults of . . .'

'Quite,' Jane interrupted. 'I meant, where are we in relation to the way out. The sort of answer I'm looking for,' she added helpfully, 'is either "This way" or "Follow me".'

Bjorn nodded. 'Follow me,' he said.

It was turning out to be a bad day.

The sun was refusing to start. A crew of seven muscular mechanics had given it their best shot and all they'd managed to do was flood the engine and bend the starting handle. The bright spark who'd suggested putting a set of jump leads on the battery of the moon was now in hiding, helped considerably by the fact that there was now no light of any description.

As a result of a freak short-out on the mainframe at

Weather, it was now slashing *up* with rain over two continents. The same fault was having drastic effects in Perjury, where the thunderbolt cannons had jammed themselves on automatic override and were giving insurance salesmen, Presidential spokesmen and the organisers of awards ceremonies a very hard time indeed. Fortunately, the manifold cam rocker on the Liefinder unit had sheared its locking stud, which meant that each shot landed precisely eighteen inches to the left.

Gremlins in the signal-box at Chronology processing meant that the Western hemisphere had just had sixteen consecutive bank holidays in the space of fifteen minutes.

The random selector needle at Requisitions, the central prayer-answering agency, had stuck solid on *God save the Queen*, with the result that Her Majesty had had a truly unpleasant morning being repeatedly snatched from the jaws of sudden and unexpected death by supernatural forces. A gang of maintenance men were crawling towards the stylus across the main resonator disc with big hammers and extremely mixed feelings; because if they got the bloody thing free and then it went and stuck on *Give us this day our daily bread*, they were definitely not going to be held responsible.

All dreams delivered within the last forty-eight hours had been returned marked *Not Known At This Address*. Some of them were ticking.

And finally, as if that wasn't enough to be going on with, the music of the spheres was suddenly distinctly audible throughout the length and breadth of the cosmos, and had turned out to be *That's Entertainment*, played with one finger on a Yamaha organ.

This is what happens when no-one's in charge.

'CHARGE!'
  'Er, chief . . .'
  'ARE YOU QUESTIONING A DIRECT ORDER, TROOPER?'
  'Not as such, chief, certainly not, no, perish the thought.

It's just, me and the lads, we were wondering . . .'

'WHAT?'

'Like, like, sort of, charge *where*, chief, because I mean, charge, yes, behind you every step of the way there, absolutely one-hundred-and-ten per cent commitment on all sides, no sweat, *guaranteed*, only it's just that as orders go, sort of like, ninety-nine-point-nine-*nine* per cent absolutely brilliant, but directionally speaking, I wouldn't say it was vague exactly, really *not* vague at all, vague's quite the wrong word for this situation, more sort of general, in fact, more *flexible* really, yes, that's it, flexible, but maybe just this once, you know, in the circumstances, perhaps if we were to play down the flexibility angle just *somewhat* in the interests of greater, well, er, precision, if you sort of catch my general drift, perhaps, well, it was just a thought, you know, maybe, er.'

'FOLLOW ME!'

'Thanks, chief. Got that. Right on. Right.'

'You're lost, aren't you?'

Bjorn stopped dead in his tracks and frowned. Having a vocabulary marginally smaller than that of the average phrase-book compiler has its drawbacks. What Bjorn wanted to do was to explain that the sort of place where they were now, you were always, by definition, lost; the crucial thing was to be lost in the right way; because then, once all your directional preconceptions had been stripped away and you were floating free, like a magnetic needle in a saucer of water, the chances were that (because, in a truly random environment, objects take the line of least resistance) the barometric pressure of convenience would draw you on in the right direction, much more swiftly and surely than if there was a bloody great yellow line drawn on the floor with THIS WAY painted in fluorescent letters every five yards.

What he actually said was 'Yuh.'

'Thought so,' Jane sighed. She sat down on something – it was too dark to see exactly what – slipped off her shoe and massaged the sole of her foot. 'I had this horrible feeling, you know?'

Bjorn braced himself and took one final slash at the cliff-face of language. 'We're, like, meant to be lost, right? 'Cos this isn't a place you can sort of find on purpose. It more sort of finds you.'

To his great surprise, Jane nodded. 'I see what you mean,' she said. 'Like the public lavatories in Italy. Yes, I can relate to that.'

There was a thoughtful silence, broken only by a faint, muffled, rather wet noise as the hostage surreptitiously tried to gnaw through the length of clothes-line by which he was tethered to Bjorn's wrist. Since the hostage had small, uneven teeth and the washing-line was the same hawser-like article Bjorn had helped himself to before leaving the Idyll, they were content to leave him to it until there was a risk of him choking on his own displaced fillings.

'Only,' Jane mused, 'you still haven't said where it is we're supposed to be going. I take it you do actually know? Or is that cheating?'

Bjorn made perhaps the greatest effort of his life. Well, not the very greatest; that had been when he'd passed by a pool of drying cement in the street and not left footprints in it. 'Well,' he said, hand-turning the words with exquisite care, 'yuh, I do sort of know where we're going, it's just I don't sort of *know*, you know? It's more like the place knows, and I don't.'

Jane tested the statement carefully and decided that it had the logical equivalent of a bent axle. 'You mean we're lost,' she said.

'Yuh.'

Jane stood up. 'That's fine,' she said. 'Follow me.'

She didn't know how she knew, she just *knew*. So she walked directly into the wall.

'Ouch!' she said, a moment later.

And in her mind, along with a tasteful display of coloured lights and a dull throbbing sound, like the sea, a voice said,

'Nice try, but you were a foot to the left. Try again.'

She tried again. And vanished.

Bjorn stared. There was the wall, and Jane had just walked through it. No dynamite, no careful feeling for the seams, not even a zip fastener or a yard or so of velcro. That was *cool*.

There was a soft clink. The hostage had broken a tooth.

Wearily, as if noticing his presence for the first time and deciding he didn't really hold with it, Bjorn grabbed the hostage in one hand and his knapsack in the other, then he emptied out the sack and stuffed the hostage into it.

The hostage was small, but not that small; there was no way he was going to fit in there, at least not without the sort of pruning and editing usually reserved for a young reporter's first major story. The head would have to go for a start . . .

He fitted. The sack could have been made to measure for him. How this came to be possible nobody knows, although it may have had something to do with the fact that the hostage sensed that if he didn't, he was going to end up reduced to his bare essentials, like a Jerusalem artichoke. Bjorn buckled down the flap, adjusted the weight on his shoulders, and took a long, shrewd look at the wall.

Some people are cool by nature. The rest of us have to try just that little bit harder.

He lowered his head and charged.

Jane sat up.

'I 'ink I 'oke y 'ose,' she said.

A party of nuns shifted their hand luggage from hand to hand and stared at her. A young couple sitting under the departure board giggled. Nobody moved to help her up, or anything like that.

A few seconds later, Bjorn stumbled heavily forwards, fell over her and landed in the lap of a sleeping Japanese businessman, who woke up and stared at him for a long half-second before ostentatiously taking out his handkerchief and wiping blood from his collar. The blood was coming from a nasty but superficial gash on Bjorn's scalp; nothing serious. Bjorn's head, it should be apparent by now, had the density of a collapsed star. In a head-butting contest, he could have taken on the whole of Mount Rushmore and won.

'Bloody hell,' he said. 'For a minute there, I thought we were in an airport.'

There was a pause, just long enough for Jane to satisfy herself that her nose was indeed still at unity with itself.

'You were right,' she said. 'I suppose it had to happen eventually.'

There was a voice, and it wasn't inside anybody's head, and what it said was:

Leydis and Gennelmein, thiz iz the lazzt corl for Bee Dubbyu Ay fly nummer Six Six Sebben to Blyblollolob. Passgers for Bee Dubbyu Ay fly nummer Six Six Sebben to Blyblollolob procee to gate nummer zerch where borin izz in progrez.

— just like flight departure announcers the world over.

(It's worth putting on record the fact that they don't deliberately mislead or misinform; it really gets to them after a while, and a lot of them end up with serious psychological trauma. It's just that they have this awful superstitious hang-up about not saying the names of places or the numbers of departure gates, which makes them subconsciously slur the words, or at best say them through three layers of compacted paper tissue.)

'Jeez,' Bjorn gasped, 'we *are* in an airport. Hey ...' He froze, then his hand flicked behind his back where he could feel a spreading, soul-chilling dampness making its way slowly down from between his shoulder-blades to the base of his spine. In his experience, only one thing seeped quite so thoroughly, and that was blood. He brought his hand back, placed it under his nose, and sniffed the tips of the fingers.

Actually, *two* things. True, one of them is indeed blood. This was the other one.

'Just out of interest,' Jane remarked, 'why have you got a baby strapped to your back?'

'That's not a baby, that's the hostage,' Bjorn said. Once he'd said it, of course, it occurred to him that you don't say words like *hostage* in airports, even airports that probably only exist in the vague and unfrequented dimensions under the stairs of the human brain. By then, of course, it was too late.

'I see,' Jane said, and nodded. 'He's turned into a baby.' She continued looking at Bjorn – just over his shoulders, to be precise – but her next words were addressed vertically. 'Well,' she said, 'that's fine. Don't mind me; after all, it's your continuum, you do whatever you like.' She shuddered. 'Anyway,' she went on, 'you agreed that we seem to be in an airport?'

'Looks like it,' Bjorn confirmed. He was trying to stuff a very, very disreputable handkerchief up the back of his shirt.

'Well, why not?' Jane replied, smiling brightly. 'Where better than an airport, if we want to go somewhere? I mean, we don't have any passports or tickets or anything like that, let alone any money, and . . .' She stopped herself, and then started again. 'That's not going to be a problem, though, is it?' she said. 'Now then, where was it we wanted to go?'

'Um,' said Bjorn.

'It's very logical,' Jane went on, sorting through her pockets with a sort of manic confidence. 'We wanted to go somewhere. Therefore we are in an airport. I think we can put that down to good old-fashioned cause and effect, somehow.' She paused, and considered briefly. 'In the old days,' she added, 'I think there was a lot of tedious mucking about with genies and lamps and three wishes, but I suppose they rationalised all that. Ah, here we are.'

She held out two passports, and two tickets.

Although she wasn't in the least surprised at the way they'd materialised, she was intrigued to notice that they were return tickets. One was marked THERE, the other BACK.

'Oh come *on*,' she exclaimed testily. 'Either the whole free will thing was a gag or it wasn't. You can't have it both ways.'

A nun looked at her.

'You keep out of it,' she snapped.

Jane and Bjorn Blyblollolob, passgers on Bee Dubbyu Ay fly nummer Squirch Frow Squirch to Somewhere Else, pliz proceed immidyatly to gate nummer miaow, passgers Jane and Bjorn Blyblollolop, fankyow.

Jane winced. Then she looked directly upwards once more.

'Thank you,' she said. 'And about time, too.'

'THIS WAY!'

'Actually, chief, that way's a . . .'

Splash.

Staff stopped running and collapsed against a door. It swung open, and he fell through.

It is important to remember that all offices are one office, all corridors are one corridor, and all fire extinguishers, wherever consciously situated, end up directly on a level with the kneecaps of stumbling people. Staff swore.

He was in his own office,

'Now hold on,' he panted to nobody in particular. 'If we're going to play silly beggars with each other, we might as well do it properly.'

The light switched on, apparently of its own accord. There was suddenly a cup of tea on the desk. Staff knew without tasting it that there were two sugars.

He realised that he hadn't had the faintest idea who he was talking to, but whoever it was had listened. It was terrifying.

'Ganger,' he whispered. 'Can you hear me?'

There was silence, internal as well as external. He shook his head frantically, but nothing rattled about in it. He even tried blowing his nose, but no dice.

'Um, can you hear me?' he said. 'How about one . . .' He looked about frantically, and saw the cup of tea. 'One digestive biscuit for yes, two for no.' Two digestive biscuits slid out of the air and into the saucer. They seemed to be grinning.

'I see,' Staff muttered, his teeth set. 'It's going to be one of those days, isn't it?'

(. . . And outside, in the world, a split pin in the gravity induction drive mysteriously floated out and fell on the floor with an unheeded tinkle. It caused a very localised problem; the world was unaffected except for a square mile of Amazonian rain forest, where the trees were suddenly sucked down into the ground.)

Staff walked deliberately round to his chair, sat down and put his feet up in one of the drawers. He reached out for the tea and biscuits. They moved, gently but firmly, six inches to the right.

'I suppose telling me who you are would be out of the question,' he said.

Two digestive biscuits, travelling like the razor-sharp throwing-discs of the Japanese Ninja, scythed through the hair on the top of his head and embedded themselves in the wall. He glowered at them.

'Fair enough,' he said firmly. 'I can wait.'

The universe – or at least the part of it filling Staff's office; the *relevant* part – held its breath. There was a puzzled silence. Staff folded his arms, leaned his head back and gazed at the ceiling.

Time, of course, is tricky stuff, and it would be fatuous to say 'half an hour passed,' or 'an hour ticked by,' under the circumstances. Better to say, 'some time passed,' and leave it at that.

Staff sat still, saying nothing, surrounded by nebulous bafflement. After a while, the ceiling began to flicker, and suddenly was covered with a profoundly weird version of Michelangelo's vision of creation. But Staff just closed his eyes.

Some time passed . . .

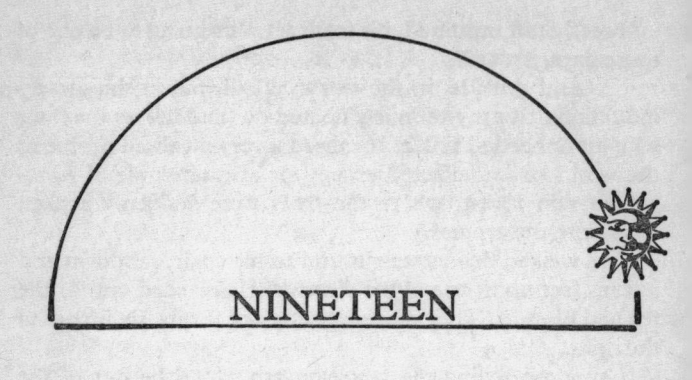

NINETEEN

A brief note on the culture, lifestyle and overall world view of spectral warriors.

Spectral warriors only know one joke. It goes like this:

Q: How many spectral warriors does it take to change a light-bulb?

A: One, and a stepladder. At a pinch, of course, he could stand on a chair.

Like all crack military units, they have marching-songs, the best-loved of which goes:

Underneath the lamp-light, by the barrack gate.

Darling, I remember the way you'd always gone by the time I got there.

Spectral warriors come into being when freeze-dried dragons' teeth are sown on the ground, and cease to exist when an enemy kills them, or (more usually) when they transgress their own Byzantine disciplinary regulations. Being composed entirely of spirit and ether, they do not require food and drink, or at least, they never get any. Very few of them survive long enough to find out whether or not it actually matters.

It would be wrong to say that spectral warriors are afraid of nothing: they're afraid of an enormous variety of things, and their anxiety is usually thoroughly justified. The only thing they aren't scared of is the enemy, because anything their opponents can do to them is going to be playtime compared to what's waiting for them when they get back to camp. This is, of course, intentional.

Platoon 384657J, Blue Company (known in the service as the Whimpering Eagles) burst through the plate-glass windows at a fast trot, fanned out and assumed the legendary Reverse Tortoise formation, a manoeuvre designed to enable the front-line troops simultaneously to envelop the enemy and get as far away from the commanding officer as possible. Then they took cover, deploying in the specially developed triplex enfilade pattern unique to the unit. Then they stood up and looked sheepish.

The lance-corporal turned to face the crowd of staring holidaymakers, and cleared his throat self-consciously.

'Wrong airport,' he said. 'Sorry.'

The entire section then withdrew, putting into practice the time-honoured embarrassed slouch.

The general drew a deep breath, as if to shout, but the words came out at an unexpectedly gentle muzzle velocity. It was like being cooed at by a man-eating dove.

'Right,' he said. 'This way, I think.'

'We haven't got *time*,' Jane hissed. 'Come on.'

Bjorn looked round, stupefied. He'd never seen so many cans of lager in his entire life. It was, he decided, either a vision of paradise or a challenge. He wanted it to be a challenge.

'Um, yuh,' he said. 'Just let me, uh, choose a six-pack, and I'll be right with you.'

He turned back, and gawped.

It wasn't the first time he'd been in a Duty Free, of course, but it was the first time he'd ever been in a *perfect* one. The thing which made it different from all the rest was the way it had nothing but beer. Lots of beer. There were cans as far as the eye could see; in fact, if he'd thought about it, he'd have realised that so much specific gravity in one place at one time was a direct contravention of the laws of physics.

'Stone me,' he whispered. 'They've even got Rottweiler Nine-X.' His hand reached out instinctively, like a seedling reaching for the sun – and with about as much chance of making contact, because Jane had caught hold of his ear and was pulling.

'For pity's sake,' she was saying, 'you may be a moron, but I'd have thought even you could recognise an obvious trap when you saw...' She stopped dead, her mouth hanging open, and her fingers slowly relaxed their grip.

Odd, Bjorn thought, I didn't notice there was a perfume counter. In fact, there wasn't one when I came in, just sixty thousand cans of Budweiser. He tried to interest Jane in this fact, but he was wasting his time.

'Please yourself, then,' he said. 'I'll just go back and have another look at the ...'

The beer had gone. It had been replaced by a million bottles of scent. Either the shelf-stackers had access to some fairly advanced technology, or something peculiar was going on.

Behind his back, the hostage started to cry.

'Hey!' Bjorn protested. 'That's not fair. I was just going to ...' He hesitated, while the world flickered. 'Oh,' he said. 'Right, that's more like it. Thanks.'

For her part, Jane was standing looking at the bottle of Chanel she'd just decided to buy and was trying to figure out why the label now read Jackal Extra Lite, Original Gravity 1034°–1038°.

Bjorn scratched his head. 'You know what,' he said slowly. 'I bet if you opened one of these cans there wouldn't be any beer in there anyway.'

Jane looked at him absently. 'Sorry?' she said.

'I think,' Bjorn replied, 'that all this is a thing. You know.

Illustration. Illusion. Figment of the whatsisname, imagination.'

'I know,' Jane said. 'And it was so *cheap*, too.'

They looked at each other.

'I don't like this,' Jane said. 'I wish we knew where we were.'

Bjorn shrugged. 'Doesn't matter,' he said. 'It's where we're going that matters.'

That sounded terribly impressive, and Jane nodded. 'Well said,' she answered. 'And where's that?'

Bjorn looked around. The Duty Free had vanished, and had been replaced by one of those little stalls that sell impractical pink socks. An electric trolley lumbered past and vanished into a gap between two delaminating dimensions.

'Dunno,' he said.

'Excuse me.'

The security officer looked round, and then looked up. About a foot above his head he could make out two tiny points of red light, like . . . Well, if he was a rabbit standing in the middle of a five-lane freeway, and if articulated lorries had red headlights, that's what they'd have looked like, only less, well, cosy.

'Sorry to bother you,' said a voice from a long way away, 'but could you possibly tell me the name of this delightfully appointed airport?'

The security guard licked his tongue round the inside of his parched mouth, and told him. The lights flickered for a moment as the black column they were attached to nodded. 'Thank you,' it said. 'Very much obliged to you.' Then it turned, inserted what would have been fingers if it had had hands into the black hole where its mouth would have been had it been fitted with one, and whistled.

The front of the entrance hall blew out in a confetti-storm of shattered glass, and the floor shook with the almost subterranean thumps of exploding stun-grenades. Disconcerting shapes, like clouds of black nothing, swung in on ropes, tried unsuccessfully to stop, and crashed into electronic departure boards with pyrotechnic results. There was a really revolting sort of burning smell – not exactly indescribable, because language is capable of an infinity of subtle modulations, but describing it with any accuracy would be a pretty antisocial thing to do. An abandoned luggage trolley quietly folded its wheels inwards and tried to crawl backwards into the wall.

Last of all, the general strode in. He stepped over the dazed body of the security guard, marched over to one slumped heap of smouldering black cloth, and prodded it with the toe of his jackboot.

'Idiots,' he said.

The remaining black shapes – still plenty of them – gathered reluctantly around him, as he studied the check-in area thoughtfully.

After a long time, the general turned due east, wiped melted soldier off the sole of his boot, and pointed.

'They went thataway,' he said.

Bjorn shuddered. The damp patch was expanding with all the speed of the First Mongol Empire, and was threatening to annex his sleeves.

'Er,' he said, before the embarrassment caught up with him and clogged up his vocal cords. He blushed.

'What?' Jane said, without turning her head. She was trying to follow the arrows that pointed the way to passport control, and was wondering whether it was the third or the fourth time they'd passed that photograph booth in the corner there.

'Um,' Bjorn mumbled, 'I think the, er, hostage needs changing. You know, like *now*, maybe. Sort of thing.'

'Changing?' Jane raised an eyebrow. 'You mean back into an adult? I don't think it's as easy as that. I'm coming to the conclusion that this whole thing is somehow linked up with the interpretation of empiric sense-evidence through a number of different logical systems, which means that . . .'

'No,' Bjorn insisted, 'I mean change like in, you know, nappies.'

Jane's face relaxed. 'Oh, I see,' she said. 'Right, you carry on, and I'll see if I can find out where these signs are supposed to be leading.'

Bjorn shook his head vigorously, like a dog drying itself. 'No,' he repeated. 'Like, I don't know how. Where all the bits and ends and pins are meant to go.'

Jane shrugged. 'Me neither,' she replied.

'But . . .' Bjorn managed to say, despite the fact that his lower jaw was doing its best to fall off his face. 'But you're a, um, female. You know about these things.'

'Uh-uh,' Jane replied firmly. 'Sorry, can't help you there, I'm afraid. All I know about babies is that you're not supposed to put them in washing machines. Makes the colours run, presumably.' She turned away pointedly and stared at the signs on the wall, until Bjorn gave up trying to outstare her and slowly unslung the knapsack from his back. His face was the colour of bolognese sauce as he grabbed hold of a pin at random and pulled. To judge by his expression, he was expecting an explosion on the count of five.

'And anyway,' Jane added, 'it's not a baby, it's a hostage, and traditionally it's the man's job to stay home and look after the hostages.' She looked round and then quickly looked away again. Bjorn gritted his teeth and tried to tell himself that what he was holding was in fact a crankshaft case, and what was running down inside his sleeve was in fact gearbox oil. It helped, slightly.

The bang they then heard was the front of the building being demolished.

Jane and Bjorn looked at each other.

'I think I know where it is we're going,' Jane said.

'Yeah?'

'Away,' said Jane firmly. 'Come on.'

In a belated attempt to appear inconspicuous they walked quickly rather than ran towards the nearest exit. A man in uniform tried to stop them, and then recoiled like a salted slug when Bjorn put a wet nappy in his outstretched hand. He made no further attempt to impede their progress.

They were in the baggage hall.

'Wrong way,' Bjorn muttered. 'We should have gone left back there by the . . .'

Jane shook her head. 'This'll do,' she said. 'If there's someone chasing us, we'd better hide until they've gone. If we just mingle in with the crowd here, maybe they won't see us. Anyway, they'll have assumed we've made a run for the planes.'

Trying to look tired and bored, they wandered down towards the carousel, Jane making little cooing noises to the hostage as they went. The hostage started yelling.

'That's fine,' Jane whispered. 'People naturally tend to avoid yelling children in airports, I've always found. It's good cover.'

'Great,' Bjorn snarled. There was about a mile of wet cloth wrapped soggily around his wrist, and a safety-pin had worked its way inside the sleeve of his shirt.

They made their way down through the crowd – and there was something odd about the people comprised in the crowd, but it doesn't do to stare – towards the baggage carousels, where they mingled.

'Here,' Bjorn whispered. 'There's something odd about . . .'

'Yes,' Jane hissed. 'I know. What do you expect me to do about it?'

Bjorn shrugged. Although he wasn't usually given to ruminating on the nature of the universe, he had long ago come up with a reason why female logic is different from male logic. It was complicated, internally coherent and had a lot to do with the fact that women, being on average the shorter sex, spend a lot of their time nearer the ground and are thus likelier to have their brains interfered with by geothermic radiation. He considered explaining it to Jane but decided not to.

'Excuse me,' Jane said, elbowing a bystander out of the way. 'Thank you.'

The funny thing about the other passengers was – well, it was hard to explain it exactly, but . . . no, the hell with it, there's no point lying when the only person you're going to deceive is yourself. Bjorn grasped the mental nettle, and then his dazed mind looked round frantically for a mental dock leaf.

They were transparent.

No, not quite; you could see through them, but only at certain angles. It was as if someone had cut out life-size pictures of people and then pasted them to life-size tailors' dummies made of ice. Or glass. You couldn't get paste to stick to ice, because it would melt or slide off or . . . Bjorn caught his train of thought by the scruff of its neck and whisked it back to the matter in hand. If you looked at these people at certain angles, they weren't there.

Fine, Bjorn thought. So what? I'm no bigot. I can handle black, white, brown or yellow, so I can handle transparent as well. No problem.

Not surprisingly, Jane had been working on the same problem, and the answer she'd come up with wasn't a million miles away from the truth.

(. . . The truth being that the other people in the baggage hall were there all right, but not one hundred per cent. One of the disadvantages of long-distance travel which has never properly been sorted out is the unfortunate truth that whenever a living creature goes an appreciable distance from home and is parted from his possessions, a portion of his soul stays with them until the eventual reunion. And when part of a man's soul is being hauled around on fork-lift trucks on to a conveyer belt after several hours crammed into the hold of an aircraft, it's only to be expected that there will be physical side-effects. Normally, of course, nobody ever notices, because everyone in a baggage hall is in the same situation, except for the porters, who are used to it. Since Jane and Bjorn had no luggage, they were able to see things as they really were, usually through the ribcages of the people standing next to them.)

'These people aren't all here,' she whispered. 'Don't worry about it.'

'I wasn't,' Bjorn replied. And then he stared.

Sailing up towards him was a large cardboard suitcase, a scuffed imitation leather hold-all and a canvas kitbag, none of which he'd seen for well over a thousand years, since the baggage handlers aboard the *Argo* had sent them to the Garden of the Hesperides by mistake.

'Um,' he said. 'Excuse me.' He leaned forward and grabbed the handles, which crumbled into dust in his hands. A thousand years is a long time to go round and round in circles.

'What are you . . .?' Jane screeched, as Bjorn leaped up on to the carousel and kicked the cases to the floor. He staggered, righted himself, and then collapsed backwards on to the toes of a small, elderly-looking man who was sitting on a very ancient suitcase indeed.

'Sorry, mate,' he mumbled.

'That's all right, Bjorn,' replied the elderly man. 'Could happen to anyone.'

To his great surprise, Bjorn managed to say something. It sounded like 'Ggnnk.'

The General walked up and down the improvised line, inspecting his troops.

'Right,' he said. 'This is the big one. What is it?'

'The big one, chief,' said those few spectral warriors who were directly in his line of sight. The rest of them shuddered. Looking back, they were thinking, it hadn't been so bad being dragons' teeth. Hot, maybe, and smelly from time to time, and perhaps if you were really unlucky you'd get filled, but at least you knew where you were coming from.

'And you're utterly fearless spectral warriors, what are you?'

'Terrified.'

'WHO SAID THAT?'

There was a squeak from the end of the line; then a flash of blue light; then a tiny puff of smoke, and then there was an empty black robe lying on the ground. It was neatly folded, and had its canteen, mess tin and water bottle lying on top of it. Habits get deeply engrained when you're in the Army.

'Now then,' said the General. 'What are you?'

'Utterly fearless spectral warriors, chief,' quavered the line as one shit-scared spectral warrior.

The General paused and looked up and down the line slowly. 'Good,' he said. 'So let's get to it.'

'Long time no see, Bjorn,' the elderly man continued. 'How're you doing, anyway?'

'Yeah,' Bjorn mumbled. 'Hey . . .'

The old man frowned slightly, although it was hard to tell; his face seemed to have set rock hard, like araldite, as if it had been marinaded and case-hardened in boredom. He spoke in a relentless dead monotone, like somebody's cousin showing you holiday snaps. 'Aren't you going to introduce me to your friend?' he said.

Bjorn swallowed hard. 'Jane, this is Ulysses. Ulysses, Jane,' he said. 'Ulysses and me go way back,' he added, trying to avoid Jane's eyes. 'Haven't seen you since . . .'

Jane looked again. The sack-shaped thing the man was wearing, the droopy leather hat, the sandals . . . 'Excuse me,' she said, 'but are you . . .'

Ulysses nodded. 'You heard about me, then?' he said. 'Shocking, isn't it?'

Jane rewound her memory quickly; fairy-stories, a film with Kirk Douglas, something they'd made her read at school. In any case, shocking wasn't the word she'd have chosen herself. 'Oh yes?' she ventured.

'If it goes on much longer,' Ulysses droned on, 'I'm going to complain about it. It shouldn't be allowed, really it shouldn't.'

'Um.'

'I mean,' Ulysses said, scratching his nose with his little finger, 'there I was, Trojan War over, all set to go home, got my return ticket and everything. Only Penelope – that's my wife, Penelope – she said, "You be sure and bring me back some of that purple wool they got over there." Very keen on embroidery, my wife. With her, it's nothing but embroider, embroider, embroider, all the time. Anyway, I remembered to get the wool, and I packed it in my small suitcase, and then when I got off the plane I came down here to collect it . . .'

Jane tried to cover her ears, but found it impossible to do this without moving her hands, and her hands wouldn't move.

'The big suitcase came through all right, but God only knows where the little one's got to. I think they may have lost it, you know.'

'Two thousand years,' Bjorn hissed in her ear. She nodded and smiled brightly.

'Very possibly,' she said. 'Maybe it got sent on somewhere else.'

Ulysses nodded. 'Maybe,' he said. 'I think I'll just wait a little bit longer, though, just in case. She won't half play me up if I go home without that wool, you know.'

There was a long silence, during which Jane and Bjorn tried walking backwards, a few millimetres at a time. This silence was broken by a number of sounds.

There was a yell from Ulysses as he caught sight of a small, battered leather suitcase on the belt and threw himself on to it.

There was a similar shout of triumph as a man in a long raincoat pounced on a bundle wrapped in newspaper, which happened to contain the Maltese Falcon.

There was a deafening bang as the stun-grenades thrown by the spectral warriors (or, in one unfortunate case, not thrown by a spectral warrior) exploded.

There was a shrill scream from the hostage, who had

woken up and wanted his teddy.

There was a confused whooshing noise as Bjorn hurled Jane, his long-lost baggage and himself on to the conveyer, which whisked them round for a few feet before thrusting them both under the little rubber flaps that separate the world of light and life from the black void where the luggage comes from and, ultimately, goes back to.

And then there was silence.

It didn't last. When the smoke cleared, there was coughing and swearing and whimpering (from the spectral warriors) and shouting (from the General), while the tannoy announced the arrival of Flight TR8765 from Atlantis, and part of the ceiling collapsed on to the carousel.

When it came round for the second time, most of the debris had little stickers on it.

'Where *are* we?'

'Hey, this is great, you know? All these years I've been wishing I knew where this lot'd got to, and now...'

'It's okay,' Jane said. 'I think I know where we are.'

As if in answer, the lights came on.

Or at least the conveyer belt brought them out into the light. They looked up, and saw the baggage handlers.

It wasn't a pretty sight. Take a line through what ordinary baggage handlers are like (which is bad enough) and then imagine what they'd look like in industrial-grade heavy-duty distorting mirrors.

'It's okay,' Jane said, extending her legs and stepping lightly off the carousel. 'It's all okay. Relatively speaking, of course.'

'Is it?' Bjorn looked at her and so failed to notice the overhead derrick. 'Ouch,' he added.

'Stop fooling about and follow me,' Jane replied. She walked rapidly away, leaving Bjorn in the position inherited by all males at airports of running after a female while holding more luggage than he could cope with.

'Look,' he grunted, 'slow down a minute and explain.

What's come over you all of a ...? And you can shut up, an' all,' he added, as the hostage wailed at him and tried to poke its wee fist through his head.

'It's very simple,' Jane replied. 'Gosh, if I'd realised it before, we could have been out of here an hour ago. Come on. I never knew anyone who dawdled so much.'

She had marched up to the nearest wall, and now stood facing it. She put her hands on her hips, smiled, and said 'Open.'

It ignored her. She might as well have been talking to a brick wall.

'Oh,' she said. 'That's awkward.'

Bjorn arrived. The suitcases and the hostage's carrycot (which had materialised somewhere inside the works of the carousel, and had pink ponies on the sides) were only adhering to him through a misunderstanding of the basics of gravity. He sagged, and his burdens flumped to the ground.

'You see,' Jane went on, 'I'd thought, you know, we wanted to go somewhere, so suddenly there was an airport. We needed tickets, suddenly we had tickets. We needed luggage, we've got luggage. And then all that business with the Duty Free shop; I mean, it was as if someone was reading our minds for what, deep down, we really wanted in a Duty Free shop. So I thought, this is all basically wish fulfilment.' She frowned at the wall. 'Only it doesn't seem to work quite like that. Maybe it's got to be consistent with the illusion, or something.'

Bjorn looked over his shoulder. 'Look,' he said, 'I don't want to hassle you or anything, but there's ...'

Tentatively, Jane prodded the wall with her fingers. 'If it was wish fulfilment, you see,' she said, 'then it'd be easy to work out where we were, we'd still be somewhere inside our own heads. Or somebody's head. A sort of generalised head; you know, the collective subconscious or the race memory or something. Species memory, probably, only of course, you're not ... What are you pulling my arm for?'

'Because,' Bjorn replied urgently, 'there's a platoon of spectral warriors coming through the baggage machine and . . .'

He was wrong, at that. The baggage machine was spitting out empty black cowls, while the strips of black rubber over the gateway between the two halls were rising and falling in a manner suggestive of chewing teeth.

'Yuk,' said Jane. 'Come on, let's get out of here.'

'Pathetic,' the General observed.

There were still quite a few of the spectral warriors; only, like the British at New Orleans, there weren't quite so many as there had been a while ago. Had the General more experience in commanding spectral forces, he'd have known better than to try and bump them across dimensions. As it was, he was angry.

The remaining spectral warriors fell into line quickly. The General paced up and down, snarling.

'This time,' he said, 'no mistakes, right?'

'Right, chief.'

'No getting blown up. No getting sucked away. No forgetting to jump off the escalators and being dragged screaming down into the works. Got that?'

'Got it, chief.'

'Fine. Now then.'

There were two gateways.

One was green, one was red. That was all right. It was what was written over them that worried Jane.

The green one said SHEEP and the red one said GOATS. There was also a huge needle, with the hindquarters of a camel sticking out of its eye. Two men in Italian suits were standing behind it, pushing, while a third was making frantic efforts with a bar of soap.

Jane sat down on Bjorn's suitcase, took off her left shoe and examined a large hole in the sole of her stocking. It shouldn't be like this, she thought. In fact, if she had her way, pretty soon it wouldn't be. But they had to get out of here first.

They became aware of someone standing over them. At first he looked like a spectral warrior, but it was a superficial resemblance only. Same black baggy cowl, absence of face, unpleasant metallic-looking sidearms, but this one had a badge with his name on it.

His name was George.

'Having trouble, miss?' asked George.

Jane looked up. 'As a matter of fact I am,' she said. 'I wonder if you could help me?'

The black hole that was George's face flickered into the anti-matter equivalent of a smile. 'Do my best, miss. That's what we're here for, after all,' he said. 'Now, what seems to be the trouble?'

Jane took a deep breath. 'For starters,' she said, 'where are we, what happened to the dimensional shift, who is it chasing us, and how do we get back to the mainstream dimension without going through those gates over there? I take it you do have to be dead to go through there.'

'Quite right, miss,' George replied. 'Although dead is as dead does, as I always say. Still, that's by the by, isn't it?'

In the far depths of his hood, something twinkled cheerfully. Jane nodded and smiled encouragingly.

'Well,' George went on, 'where you are now, miss, you're in the main entrance hall of judgement control. That's where you have to show your credentials to Immigration, to see if you're going to go first class or economy, smoking or non-smoking. Your baggage will be weighed, and if it's tried in the balance and found wanting then you get charged excess. And like you said just now, miss, being dead is essential. No exceptions, you see. Rules is rules.'

Jane nodded. 'I quite understand,' she said. 'So we're quite a few dimensions away from normality, I take it.'

'Absolutely right, miss,' George replied. 'Well spotted, if I may say so. If I were to hazard a guess, I would say you left the mainstream by falling through an artificially created hole in the dimensional shift. I wouldn't be at all surprised if it happened while you were in a restaurant somewhere. Does that sound right to you?'

By this stage, Bjorn had given up listening. He was going through his kitbag. It was a thousand to one chance that the big jar of Greek olives was still in there, but it was worth a shot.

'I think I was kidnapped out of my own dimension by an official called Finance and General Purposes, to stop me finding out about why he's trying to sabotage the human race,' Jane said. 'Would that account for it, do you think?'

'Oh, I should say so, miss,' George replied. 'Happens more often than most people realise, that sort of thing. We get a lot of that down here.'

Jane nodded. 'And then,' she went on, 'I think he hid me away in the back of his mind – well, in his conscience, actually, which is the nastiest place he could think of. It's where all the horrible things which he knows deep down inside ought to happen to him are stored. I didn't like it much in there, to be honest with you.'

'Don't blame you, miss,' said George. 'Dodgy places, consciences. Then what happened?'

'Well,' Jane said, trying to remember, 'shortly after that ...'

'Got them!' Bjorn shouted. 'Hey, that's brilliant!'

'Shortly after that I was rescued, and I'm not quite sure where I was then, but I suppose it must have been in one of the Administration office blocks, because if I'd just escaped from inside this person's head, it would stand to reason that I'd end up pretty close to where he was, don't you think? Or am I way off beam?'

'Sound right to me, miss,' said George encouragingly. 'Go on.'

Jane thought for a moment. 'That's where I sort of lost track,' she said. 'You see, my... this man here, he sort of

265

pulled some dimensions apart and we just sort of fell through, and here we are in an airport sort of thing.'

'A very neat way of putting it, if I may say so, miss.'

'And at first I thought I must be inside my own head this time, or at least sort of, because everything I wanted to happen sort of happened, only not quite, if you see what I mean. And I thought, Yes, because all through my life people have been telling me that where I've been going wrong is not really knowing what I actually want.'

George nodded, or at least the gash in the side of reality which he represented wobbled a bit. 'Pretty close, miss,' he said. 'You're on the right lines, but not quite there. If I might explain?'

'Please do.'

'Hey, *and* my Proud To Be Weird T-shirt. I've really missed this, you know?'

'Bjorn,' Jane said, 'shut up.'

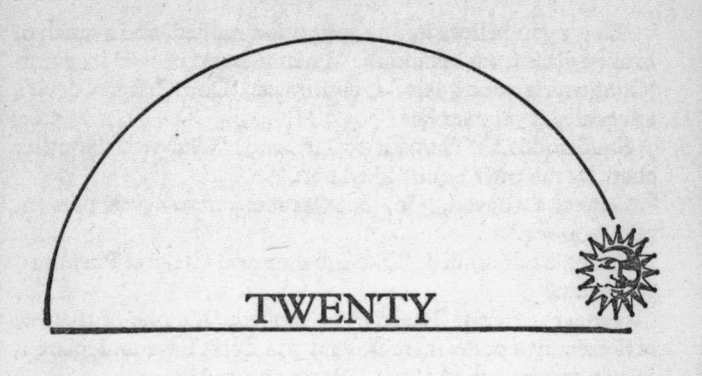

TWENTY

ALL RIGHT, said the wall, YOU WIN.

Staff nodded and opened his eyes. I'm listening, he thought. Can we do this the easy way, because I've had a hard day, and burning bushes or anything like that really wouldn't be a good idea.

... And then there was a flash, and a cloud of foul-smelling yellow smoke, and a buzzing sound, like all the flies in all the kitchens of all the transport cafes in the whole world ...

'Stubborn, aren't you?' said a voice from the chair opposite. 'I expect you're going to insist on visual interface as well?'

''Fraid so, yes.'

'More fool you, then.'

... And another flash, red this time, and the chair was full of a huge scarlet figure, with horns at one end, cloven hooves at the other, and a sour look somewhere in the middle.

'What a bloody pantomime the whole thing is,' it said. 'The dressing up, I mean. You've no idea how uncomfortable this get-up is, especially when it's hot. Do you think we could have the window open?'

'I don't think it does open, actually.'

'Don't you believe it,' the apparition replied, and a crash of broken glass from behind the Venetian blind proved its point. 'Confirming your guess,' it continued, 'Dop Ganger, devil's advocate, at your service.'

Staff nodded. 'Thought so,' he said. 'Who was the other chap, by the way? I quite liked him.'

Ganger shrugged. 'Oh, that was me. I have a dual personality, you see.'

'I see,' Staff replied. 'Like Finance and General Purposes, you mean?'

Ganger nodded. 'Exactly,' he replied. 'It's one of the few real executive perks there is. And you don't have to declare it on your tax return. At least, I don't,' he added.

Staff rubbed his chin thoughtfully. 'But of course,' he went on, 'the Ganger I've been running about with – oh I *see*, your *double*; oh, very clever – he's just a tiny part of you, like the tip of the iceberg or something?'

Ganger moved his head slightly in confirmation. 'It's a staff-saving exercise,' he said. 'We're really hot on that in our department. Instead of having lots of different members of staff, you see, we just have the one. But I'm flexible. I spread myself thinly, you know.'

'Lots of different hats, you mean?'

'Some with holes in them, some not,' Ganger replied smoothly. 'We call it going corporate, but that's just a term of convenience.'

'I see,' said Staff. 'So, why you?'

'Someone has to do the audit,' Ganger replied, 'and I suppose we're naturally type-cast for the role of auditors, aren't we?' Staff allowed himself a brief smile. 'We remain separate entities,' Ganger continued, 'even though we work for the same main boss. And if your lot are way off course, we have to give you a helping hand now and then. Unfortunately – from your point of view, that is – we can't help introducing a little . . .'

'Devilment?'

Ganger scowled. 'That's supposed to be a joke, I suppose,' he said. 'Do you want me to write it down, or do you trust me just to remember it?'

'So we're way off course,' Staff said quietly. 'I thought so. Is it all to do with him? You know, Finance and . . .?'

'Mainly,' Ganger said carefully. 'But your lot helped. Believe me, they really did. Some of them have a real natural talent for . . .'

'Yes,' Staff interrupted, 'I dare say they do. That's Administration for you.' He stopped briefly and his brow wrinkled. 'Hold on, though,' he said. 'I thought you told me you weren't a . . . or at least the bit of you I knew as Ganger wasn't a . . . that he was sort of co-opted. That's why I was so keen to try and introduce mortals, you see, because you said you'd tried it and it worked.'

'Oh, absolutely,' Ganger replied. 'We do. We subsume the part into the whole, that's all. The only problem we have with that is getting rid of the squishy bits afterwards.'

Staff shuddered slightly. Separate entities, he reminded himself. 'Okay,' he said, 'I'm all clear on that one. And you've done a thorough audit, and you've worked out that where it all went wrong is with Finance making a cock-up with the sun that time. And now you're in a position to nail him, once and for all. Is that it?'

The air was becoming thick with yellow smoke, and there was an offensive smell of brimstone. Ganger nodded.

'We shall make a full report,' he said, 'and we'll make it stick, because we've got a witness. We shall recommend that he be redeployed in our department.' And Ganger licked his lips noisily.

'That's fine,' Staff replied, looking away. 'The only thing is, you seem to have lost your witness.'

'Not quite,' Ganger said (and his voice wasn't a voice any more so much as the buzzing of a million flies). 'In fact, he's right where he should be.'

'Is that so?'

'*Indeed.*' Staff tried not to look as the shape which had been Ganger turned out to be the illusion of a solid body created by a huge swarm of flies in close formation. *Where better? Rather than go to all the trouble and expense of arresting him and arranging for him to be delivered to the Seat of Judgement under armed escort, why not just persuade him to go there himself? You learn little wrinkles like that when you're a . . .*

'And all that mucking about,' Staff said, leaning forward until his head was in the centre of the swarm. 'All that trying the poor girl out in various departments and so forth, that was just to lure him into the trap?'

Certainly not. That would have been pretty inefficient. We think she's ideal for the job, don't you?

'Which job?'

Buzz.

'Don't ask me,' Rosa said. 'Twenty years in catering and suddenly he decides he wants to be a monk. A monk,' she repeated. 'Can you beat it?'

The County Palatine exchanged glances with the Count of the Saxon Shore. 'It's a phase he's passing through,' said the County Palatine. 'And even in monasteries they've gotta eat, you know?'

Rosa stared for a moment. 'You know,' she said, 'I think you guys are as crazy as my crazy brother. I'll get you the check.'

She walked away. The Electors looked at each other.

'Pity,' the Lord High Cardinal said. 'That Rocco, maybe he makes a lousy Emperor, but give him a pound of mozzarella and a bucket of anchovies and you're in business.'

'And the profiteroles,' groaned the County Palatine. 'Don't forget the profiteroles.'

'I mean,' added the Count of the Saxon Shore, 'Charlemagne, yes. Charles the Fifth, yes. But could they do you tagliatelle verde that's absolutely *al dente* and still leave you change out of twenty bucks? Like hell.'

The Lord High Cardinal nodded sadly. 'Still,' he said, 'there it is.' He glanced down at his watch; and a strange-looking watch it was, at that. Where your watch has hands, it had eyes. 'Hey, we'd better shoot.' He picked up the bill and signed it. 'So long, Rosa,' he called out. 'Our best to Rocco, tell him to say one for us.'

He stood up, emptied the toothpick-glass into his pocket, and led the way.

'I see,' Jane said. 'We were brought here.'

'Yes, miss.'

'Just so as to bring him here?'

'That's right, miss.' George extended a largely non-existent arm and took firm hold of the carrycot. 'And your friend, of course. He's our star witness, you see, miss.'

'I see,' Jane repeated.

George hesitated, and bit the whirling expanse of nothingness that would have been his lip. 'I expect you're a bit upset, miss, what with the way you've been treated and everything. Only to be expected if you are, miss, if I may say so.'

Jane shrugged. 'You'd have thought so,' she said, 'but I'm not really. Or at least I am, but ... You see, all my life I've really wanted to know what was going on, and why it's all such a *mess*. And now I'm beginning to see. Or at least, I think I am.'

'That's the spirit, miss,' said George. 'Now, can I just see your passports a minute, please?'

Jane nodded, and produced them. After a moment's perusal, George handed them back to her. They were both open.

Jane's passport had her name, and her photograph, and the rather embarrassing bit where it says about any distinguishing marks, the bit she tended to keep her thumb over whenever possible. Bjorn's, however, had a name and a photograph, but ...

Bjorn took it from her and grinned sheepishly. 'When these

lads say under cover,' he explained, 'boy, do they mean *deep* cover.'

He reached up into his face and pulled. Jane gave a little scream, and then opened her eyes. Bjorn was holding a limp rubber mask in his hand and grinning.

Only his name wasn't Bjorn, of course.

'Just one question,' she asked. 'Why Bjorn?'

'Because,' Bjorn replied, and shrugged. 'I happened to see it on the back of a packet of cornflakes, if you must know, and . . .'

'Thank you,' Jane said, bitterly. 'Serves me right for asking, I suppose.'

(Because what Bjorn's passport gave as his name was, in fact, Gabriel; and what Jane really wanted most of all right now was somewhere where she could be sick in reasonable privacy.)

'It wasn't easy for the lad,' George was saying. 'Personality surgery, all that sort of thing. Very proud of him, we are, back in the department.'

Jane turned on him furiously. 'Oh yes?' she said. 'And what department would that be?'

There was a puff of yellow smoke.

'Right,' said the General, 'We go in, we zap everything that moves, we rescue the hostage, we come out again. All clear so far?'

The spectral warriors nodded uneasily. That wasn't what was worrying them.

'And afterwards,' continued the General, 'we have a full kit inspection for the survivors. If there are any survivors, that is. Do I make myself clear?'

There was a murmur of assent from the spectral warriors, and then they shuffled into battle formation, ready for the attack. Despite the mechanical precision of their combat drill, there was a certain amount of unseemly pushing and shoving for places in the front rank and other positions of maximum danger. Although spectral warriors naturally tend to think of survival as something that only happens to other people, there was no point in taking unnecessary risks.

'On the command Charge,' the General snarled, 'charge. Understood?'

'Understood, chief.'

'That's fine. Now then, boys. *Cha* . . . '

The word froze on his lips as a door, which hadn't been there a few seconds ago, opened and a figure in uniform came through it.

Spectral warriors are trained in destruction rather than mathematics, but they can count pips, and the newcomer had more pips on his shoulders than you'd expect to find in a fruit-juice factory.

He strolled along the line and stopped, about three yards away from the General, who for his part seemed to have frozen solid.

'Stand easy, men,' murmured the newcomer, and the overhead strip lighting gleamed on the gold lace of his epaulettes and the peak of his cap. The odd thing about his cap was the fact that it had two neat round holes in it just above his ears, for the horns to go through.

With a tremendous effort the General opened his mouth, but nothing came out except a few woodlice and a rather laid-back-looking spider.

'Arrest that man,' said the newcomer. 'Come on, look lively about it.'

Sixty-seven spectral warriors were suddenly very, very happy.

The world stopped.

It didn't come to an end, of course, it simply stopped. The sun jerked to a halt in mid-air and hung there, its engine idling. The earth seized on its axis, but without the juddering crash there should have been, as so much inertia suddenly found itself with nowhere to go. There was a general paralysis of clocks, water stood still in rivers, winds evaporated. Entropy's meter stopped running. Raindrops hung in the air like astronauts in zero gravity.

Except, of course, in New York, where they always have to be different. Anyone looking very closely indeed would have detected some movement there, but only a tiny amount. The majority of the citizens were caught in the general freeze-frame effect; but there was a small party of rather fat men strolling up Thirty-Sixth Street with their hands in their pockets. Three of them were smoking big cigars. They weren't in any obvious hurry.

At the corner of Thirty-Sixth and Broadway, they stopped and waved. A yellow cab without wheels floated noiselessly over the top of the motionless traffic and pulled in to the kerb. Metal steps extended themselves to sidewalk level, and the fat men climbed aboard. The cab pulled away, drifting at the speed of, say, a rather slow gondola, and slowly climbed up into the sky until it was lost among the clouds.

By an oversight of the sort which was only to be expected, given the overall level of efficiency of the Administration in general, there was another tiny cell of people left awake and functioning during the general shut-down. They were sitting in an office in Wall Street when it happened; two men and a girl. The girl was the first to speak.

'Darren,' she said quietly, 'I think it's the end of the world. What'll we do?'

The man called Darren thought for a moment. 'You sure about that?' he said.

'Jesus Christ, Darren,' the girl yelled back, 'just come to the window and look for yourself.'

Slowly, Darren put down his telephone, stood up and walked to the window. Years in Wall Street had trained him to analyse situations immediately.

'Yep,' he said, 'it's the end of the world all right.' He sighed; then he strode back to his desk again. 'Okay, guys,' he said. 'Let's get to it.'

'So,' the other man shouted, 'so what do we *do*?'
Darren smiled. 'Sell,' he said.

'Basically,' the Lord High Cardinal summed up, 'we find you
guilty as charged of – what was it? Tony, where are my
goddamn reading glasses, you know I'm as blind as a bat
without ... of gross negligence, failure to disclose material
information, mismanagement, misappropriation of funds
and – hey, what's that, I can't read your writing – yuh, being
guilty. You have heard the testimony of Mr, uh, Gabriel. Have
you anything to say?'

The accused, formerly head of the Finance and General
Purposes committee, mumbled inarticulately but said nothing. The six layers of insulating tape over his mouth may have
had something to do with it, of course.

'No? You're sure? Well, okay then, I guess that just leaves
the sentence. Any thoughts on the sentence, guys?'

There was a brief exchange of whispers on the podium;
then the Lord High Cardinal leaned back in his chair,
straightened the white bands at his neck (which looked very
like a napkin tucked into his collar if you looked closely) and
set his features in a judicial expression.

'Opinion,' he said, drumming his fingers on the desk in
front of him, 'is a bit divided here. Tony says rip your lungs
out with a plastic fork, Louie says no, that's too good for a
scumbag like you, you ought to be shoved down the toilet
along with the alligators until you've learned your lesson, and
my learned friend the Count of the Saxon Shore ... Yeah,
well, anyway, I disagree.'

There was absolute silence in court. Sixty-seven spectral
warriors stood as still as rock-hewn statues, their faces behind
their masks bathed in silly grins.

'Personally,' continued the Lord High Cardinal, 'I say, so
what, everybody makes mistakes now and then.' He frowned.
'The point is,' he added savagely, 'only losers get found out.
Hey, Tony, where's that stupid cap thing? No, not that,

dumbo, that's somebody's sock. Right, now then, where were we?'

The other accused wailed, and waved his hands and feet in the air. Nobody took any notice. When it comes to changing the nappies of the guiltiest creature on God's earth, there are no volunteers.

'This court,' said the Lord High Cardinal, 'sentences the two of you as follows. You first. Stand up.'

The erstwhile General was lifted to his feet. He made a mooing noise against the tape, but no-one heard.

'By the special request of the prosecuting advocate,' intoned the Lord High Cardinal, 'and in recognition of your special talents in the field of administration and public relations, you are to be assigned to the staff of the Prosecuting Department.' The Lord High Cardinal winced. 'Hey, you know, that's *inhuman*. Oh well, never mind. As for you — somebody lift the kid up so he can hear, all right? — as for you, since you have temporarily taken up residence in the body of a mortal, this court — say, who thought this one up? It's *wicked* — this court has no jurisdiction over you. You will therefore be deported back to the world to live as a mortal.' The Lord High Cardinal grinned. 'In Kansas City,' he added; then he turned to his closest colleague and winked. 'Okay, Tony?' he said. 'Does that beat the plastic fork idea, or what?'

There was a scuffle, and the two accused were taken away. The Lord High Cardinal settled himself more comfortably in his chair, and took off the black cap.

'Which brings us finally,' he said, 'to the last item on today's agenda.'

How, you may ask, does the Administration work?

It doesn't, of course; but supposing it does . . .

There are the Departments. Each separate department is manned by a permanent staff of officials, and is headed by an officer of Grade II or above. The heads of department form the Finance and General Purposes committee, which passes resolutions for the approval of the College of Electors. It is the job of the Electors to turn the recommendations of the committee into draft orders for ratification by the Main Boss.

The Main Boss. The Man Himself. Numero Uno. The Top Brass. The guy you'd eventually get to see if you absolutely *insisted* on seeing the manager. The Emperor.

All perfectly logical, yes? It would be quite wrong, after all, for the real power to lie in the hands of career civil servants who don't even belong to the same category of life-form as the people being governed. The main boss inevitably has to be a mortal. The trouble has always been finding the right mortal for the job.

Many centuries ago, the Electors hit on the clever idea of not actually telling the Emperor what his job consisted of.

They didn't lie to him, of course, perish the thought. But they were distinctly parsimonious with the truth. To begin with, they did at least tell him that he was the Emperor, without going into all the tedious details of what the job description actually entailed. But even that little snippet of information caused severe problems, so they got into the habit of making sure that when they told him, he wasn't actually listening.

In practical terms, it worked, up to a point. It was intended as a temporary measure only.

In the last hundred years or so, the Emperor has been encouraged to keep a low profile. Rocco VI, as already noted, made pizzas. His immediate predecessor, Wang XIV, ran a small bicycle repair workshop in the back streets of Hong Kong, right opposite the best Cantonese restaurant in the Colony. Neville III (better known to history as Neville the Magnificent) had a paper round outside Macclesfield, and did a little window-cleaning on the side, strictly cash in hand. Joseph XXXIX Ncoba carved little wooden elephants. Gupta IX moonlighted as a petrol pump attendant, and was one of the few Emperors ever to abdicate as a result of an irreconcileable conflict of interests. François XXIII spent his entire reign in a room nine feet by five, firmly convinced that he was a ratchet screwdriver. He was, everyone agrees, one of the better twentieth-century Emperors.

Rocco, Wang, Neville, Joseph, Gupta and François were the successes; the rest weren't quite so hot. The worst was probably Wayne XI, whose five-hour reign was the second shortest in Imperial history. It wasn't the Electors' fault, of course; the first they knew about his disastrous latent tendencies was when he put up the Greenpeace poster in the front window of his tiny flat in downtown Brisbane.

The shortest reign on record was that of Everton I, who was deemed to have abdicated when he missed an easy chance at slip off Courtney Walsh.

The great problem facing the Electors is that only the true Emperor is going to be any good at the job; and the one and only qualification for being Emperor is being the heir apparent, by right of birth. That was why Rocco VI was originally chosen – but further enquiries revealed him to be nothing but a distant cousin of the rightful heir. It was the discovery of the true identity of Charlemagne's closest living relative that set in train the whole sequence of events; because this time, things were going to have to be slightly different. Even temporary measures have to come to an end eventually.

It was obvious who Rocco's successor was going to be; but this time there would have to be a little vocational training beforehand, because the next reign was going to be the crucial one . . .

And you will by now have guessed what Jane looks like – straight nose, strong jaw, the distinctive high cheekbones familiar from a hundred Imperial portraits. And you won't need telling that her second name, the name that appears on her passport, is Hapsburg.

'Oh,' said Jane. 'Fancy that.'

★

The world, which had stopped, started again.

Starting implies a beginning. Maybe it's just a cheapskate verbal trick, but we'll repeat it to let the true significance sink in. The world started again.

Nobody noticed, of course, apart from a few market-makers in New York who suddenly realised that they'd sold everything three minutes before the most colossal upwards swing the markets have ever experienced. By the time the markets stopped rising, staggered helplessly and then quite simply ceased to exist, they'd all pinned letters of resignation to their chairs and gone off to Wisconsin to make new lives for themselves as raffia weavers, and so never knew how right they'd actually been.

Starting implies a beginning. Within ten minutes, things were already very different. The sun moved along its inevitable course. The grass grew. The rain fell. Time ticked, gravity pulled, history coagulated, the tides rose and fell, men and women tripped and blundered their way through the darkened china-shop of human existence. On the wall of Plato's cave, nobody noticed the brand-new notice asking the last person to leave to make sure that the lights were switched off; but that was because, somehow or other, it had been there all the time.

What was different was that it was doing it all by itself. There was nobody running it. It was just . . . happening.

('Hey,' said Ganger, in the back of Jane's mind, 'you can't do this. Stop it at once.'

Why not? I'm the Empress, aren't I? I can do what the hell I like.

Ganger howled, as his fingers started to lose their grip on the projecting shelf of subconscious he was desperately clinging to. 'But it won't *work*,' he shouted. 'There's got to be somebody to run things, or they won't work. They won't run themselves, you know.'

Won't they? We'll soon see about that.

What Ganger meant to say was, 'Maybe they'll work for a while, if you give the sun and the moon and the earth and rain

and wind and time and all that sort of thing some kind of
semi-sentience, but who's actually going to supervise it and
fix it and put it all back on course if it starts to go wrong? Now
I suppose you'll say you will, but you're mortal, you won't be
around for ever, and so you'll have to train a successor, and
that won't be easy, believe you me, oh no.' But since it's
impossible to say anything at all if you've suddenly just ceased
to be, he only got as far as 'Ma . . .'

What Staff, the Electors and the rest of them said is
unrecorded, which is probably just as well. It's unlikely to
have been anything nice.)

And then, with a sigh like the switching off of a hundred
million computer screens, the great army of celestial officers,
functionaries, administrators, schedule clerks, programmers
and timeservers faded away into the air from which they had
originally come; and after them their offices, their desks, their
files, their hardware, their software, the memory of their
existence – until all that was left was one bright, golden
paperclip, spinning and sparkling in the upper air, falling or
rising weightlessly into the sublime emptiness which is all that
remains when Order has finally been tidied away.

And Jane thought, Right then, got that sorted, it should
work fine now. I could murder a glass of orange juice.

And in her mind, something said, No, not orange juice,
you'll get indigestion, think what happened the last time you
had orange juice on an empty stomach, you'll . . . but never
got any further, because a moment later it too was sucked
away, to its great surprise, and Jane was left alone –
definitively alone – with her thoughts.

And finally, the Empress saw everything that she had sorted
out, and behold, it was no worse than she'd expected, all things
considered. And the evening and morning were the sixth day.

And on the seventh day she ended the work which she had
made, and she rested; or at least she tried to rest. But all the
milk in the fridge had gone off because of a power cut, and
none of the shops were open because it was a Sunday.

*

The sun rose.

Being nothing more than a dollop of burning gas, it had no way of knowing that it was bang on schedule, right on course and in exactly the right place at precisely the right time.

Because nobody was watching, the slight movement on the face of the waters as the first organism twitched into life went completely unnoticed. No reception committee, no ribbon to cut, no brass band, nothing.

Because nobody was taking notes or filing reports to the appropriate quarters, the flawlessness of the sun's landing and the seamless interface of day and night were completely wasted.

Because it was nobody's responsibility and nobody's fault, the very first living cell was completely alone as it jerked open the window of its consciousness and let out the primordial scream of birth. But it screamed nevertheless. And screamed again. And waited.

There was no reply. There were sounds: the lapping of the waves, the sighing of the wind, the soft grinding of tectonic plates, the distant echoes of the scream itself wrapping themselves doglead-like around the poles and drifting back, but there was nobody to hear them except for one lonely consciousness.

It waited. It screamed again. It listened. Splash, swish, sigh, grunge, hiss. Nothing.

Now, when you're feeling uncertain and apprehensive and you're not a hundred per cent sure you should be here anyway, there's nothing quite so beneficial to morale as a good old sing-song. There was a small, embarrassed cough and then a reedy, squeaky but grimly determined voice began to sing . . .

The sun has got his hat on,
Hip hip hip hip hooray . . .

It was a very small voice, a still, small voice, an infinitesimal voice alone in an infinite sea.

The sun has got his hat on . . .
it repeated firmly. Silence.

A few yards away, something stirred. The movement was so tiny that even if there had been anyone to see, they'd have missed it. But it stirred, and listened, and became alive; and sang:

The sun has got his hat on,
And he's coming out today.

And that was that. There was no going back from here. The continents braced themselves, contorting their rocky coastlines into sheepish grins. They were going to be needed after all.

So, when the next dawn came, not one but many voices – soprano, alto, contralto, tenor, baritone, bass, flat, thin, loud and soft – many millions of voices were raised to greet it, and they sang:

Here comes the sun, little darling,
Here comes the sun,
It's all right . . .

And the evening and the morning were the eighth day.